FOR *better,* FOR *worse*

BOOK FOUR IN **THE PASTOR MAGGIE SERIES**

ISBN: 978-1-68313-197-7
Library of Congress Control Number: 2019931492

First Edition
Printed and bound in the USA
Pen-L Publishing

Cover and interior design by Kelsey Rice

FOR *better,* FOR *worse*

BOOK FOUR IN **THE PASTOR MAGGIE SERIES**

BARBARA EDEMA

Pen-L Publishing
Fayetteville, Arkansas
Pen-L.com

Books by Barbara Edema:

THE PASTOR MAGGIE SERIES

To Love and To Cherish

To Have and To Hold

For Richer, For Poorer

For Better, For Worse

Dedication

This book is dedicated to my mother, Dr. Mimi Elzinga-Keller.
A woman who has lived through the best and the worst of days.
She chooses to remember the best.

In memory of

My brother, Todd Alan Hubbell
Born July 21, 1963 – Died August 12, 1989
There wasn't enough time.

List of Characters

RECENT AND NEW RESIDENTS OF CHERISH, MICHIGAN

Jim, Cecelia, Bobby, and Naomi Chance – A new family

Juan, Maria, Gabby, and Marcos Gutierrez – A new family

Ryleigh and Zoey Teater – Sisters and school friends in Cherish

Jacob and Deborah Stein – Jack's neighbors at his condo

Lydia Marsh – New hairstylist at We Work Miracles Beauty Salon

Sylvester Fejokwu – New CEO of Heal Thyself Community Hospital

Jasper and Myrna Barnes – Parents of Myla, Mika, Misha, Manny, and Milford

Myra – Myrna's mother

Sabeen, Mahdi, Amira, Iman, Jamal, Karam, and Samir Nasab – Refugees from Syria

Anya and Shrina – Workers from Ann Arbor Refugee Support Services

OUR OLD FAVORITES

Pastor Maggie Elliot – Pastor of Loving the Lord Community Church (LTLCC)

Dr. Jack Elliot – Family practice doctor, on the staff of Heal Thyself Community Hospital; husband of Maggie

Hank Arthur – Administrative assistant at LTLCC; married to Pamela

Pamela Arthur – Hospital volunteer

Doris Walters – Custodian at LTLCC; married to Chester Walters

Irena Dalca – Organist at LTLCC; fan of miniskirts and vodka

Marla Wiggins – Sunday school superintendent; married to Tom, owner of The Cherish Hardware Store; mother of Jason and Addie

Howard and Verna Baker – Recent newlyweds

Officer Charlotte Tuggle – Cherish Chief of Police; married to gravel pit owner Fred; mother of twins, Brock and Mason, and daughter, Liz

Officer Bernie Bumble – Charlotte's inexperienced deputy

Martha Babcock – Nosy police dispatcher

Cate Carlson – Maggie worshiper and a student at the University of Michigan, soon to be studying for a semester in Ghana

Cole Porter – Owner and proprietor of The Porter Funeral Home; husband of the lovely Lynn; father of Penny, Molly, and Samuel

Harold Brinkmeyer – Successful young lawyer; in love with Ellen Bright

Ellen Bright – Nurse at Heal Thyself, good friend of Pastor Maggie, Jack Elliot's cousin, and Harold's girlfriend

Sylvia Baxter – Owner of The Garden Shop; married to Bill Baxter

Bill Baxter – Handyman and master of construction

Mrs. Polly Popkin – Owner and proprietress of The Sugarplum Bakery

William and Mary Ellington – Owners of The Grange Bed and Breakfast

Carrie and Carl Moffet – Children adopted by William and Mary Ellington

Jennifer and Beth Becker – Sisters and owners of The Page Turner Book Shop

Max Solomon – Always sits in the last pew

Julia Benson – Reporter for the *Cherish Life and Times*; mother of Hannah

Lacey Campbell – Owner of We Work Miracles Beauty Salon

Dr. Dana Drake – Veterinarian at Cherish Your Pets Animal Hospital

Winston Chatsworth – Friend of Howard Baker; can't seem to comb his hair

Dr. Ethan Kessler – Teaches African Politics at the U of M; married to Charlene Kessler

Dr. Charlene Kessler – A family practice doctor and partner of Jack; mother of Kay and Shawn

Skylar Breese – Owner of the Pretty, Pretty Petals Flower Shop

Fitch Dervish – A building inspector in Cherish

Arly Spink – Cherish artist and owner of Cherished Works of Art Gallery
Darcy Keller – Owner of The Mill
Priscilla Keller Sloane – Darcy's sister, a widow

RESIDENT OF ANN ARBOR, MICHIGAN

Detective Keith Crunch

RESIDENTS OF BLISSFIELD AND DETROIT, MICHIGAN

Ken and Bonnie Elliot – Jack's parents
Anne and Peter Hubbell (Detroit) – Jack's older sister and brother-in-law; parents of Gretchen and Garrett
Andrew Elliot – Jack's younger brother
Brynn Thomas – Andrew's fiancée and Jack's soon-to-be sister-in-law
Richard, Nicolette, Randy, and Michael Thomas – Brynn's family
Leigh Elliott – Jack's younger sister and the owner and operator of the maternity shop Kanga and Roo
Nathan Elliott – Jack's youngest brother

RESIDENTS OF ZEELAND, MICHIGAN

Dirk and Mimi Elzinga – Maggie's parents

No one is born hating another person because of the color of his skin, or his background, or his religion. People learn to hate, and if they can learn to hate, they can be taught to love, for love comes more naturally to the human heart than its opposite.

– NELSON MANDELA

NEVER A BYSTANDER

Watching, waiting, praying for a world that's kind and just;
Where all are fed and nourished deep, with hope and peace and trust.
Arise brave bearers of the light and do not stand aside.
Boldly, bravely live for love and press against the tide.

Defend and help our neighbors, the forsaken, weak and lost;
Share clean water, bread and health, no matter what the cost.
Reclaim this world of broken lives with faith God's peace will reign.
Listen, trust, bring light and hope, and help to ease the pain.

Arise brave bearers of the light and never turn aside.
Boldly, bravely stand for love and press against the tide.

– MARSHA RINKE

Prologue

Maggie listened for the whispers.

So many other voices swirled in her mind. She listened intently when the howls around her subsided. There seemed to be fewer silences and more shrieks.

Pastor Elisha in Bawjiase, Ghana, had told her trials were headed her way. And pain.

God told her in a dream that difficulties would find her in Cherish. "There is work to be done. My voice must be heard. My people must know. I have met you in Bawjiase, Maggie, but this is not where I sent you. Don't lose hope! Don't waver in courage! Walk the path. Wash the feet. Speak the truth. My truth is good news. I give you hope in all things."

But Maggie felt hopeless. What happens when hope dies?

She spent the early mornings in her parsonage study, trying to hear God's voice. But it was all so fuzzy.

Since the "Big Fight" began, Maggie needed the whispers more than ever. It felt as if God had little to say. Where was the hope? Where was the good news?

She waited.

And waited.

Then she jumped. The Westminster chimes rang.

Again.

1

Maggie hated these visits. She began her drives to the Milan Penitentiary the day after Easter, in March. She tried to visit once a month. She drove down early in the morning, went through the large security gates, showed her ID, and then parked near the entrance. Now, the third week of August, marked her fourth visit. They were fruitless and frustrating. She looked up from the metal chair where she sat as the door opened and Redford Johnson was led inside. The guard stood back in the corner of the small, stifling room.

Redford sat in his chair with a contrived look of weariness on his face.

Maggie sat up a little straighter in her chair. "Good morning, Redford."

"Good morning," Redford said with a dramatic sigh. He looked down at his cuffed hands.

Maggie had learned in the prior visits there were no easy questions when visiting someone in jail. For instance, she couldn't ask:

"Did you have a nice weekend?"

"Hasn't the weather been gorgeous?"

"Do you have any plans this week?"

"What's new?"

She already knew that Redford spent the majority of his time in his cell. Some of that was by choice. He was outside for minimal hours each week. His daily plans consisted of being locked in his cell, eating in the cafeteria, and occasionally joining other inmates either outside or in the recreation room watching television. He didn't read books. He didn't cultivate relationships. But he had learned—the hard way— to keep his sarcasm in check after being badly beaten by another inmate he had insulted. Maggie had been shocked in April to see Redford's eyes swollen shut, stitches in his lower lip, and a gauze bandage around his head covering a large contusion. It had taken a couple of weeks for his injuries to heal, but his fragile ego and deep insecurity had not rebounded.

He was a slight man. Maggie guessed he was one of the kids who was bullied on playgrounds as a child. She knew he was an abusive husband to one of her new parishioners, Julia Benson. Julia had divorced him after having their baby, Hannah. She was afraid he would harm the baby. When he skipped town and resettled in Cherish, Julia was left penniless, with no child support money. She had finally tracked him down after years of searching. Hannah was a beautiful little girl, unscathed by her father's physical abusiveness, thanks to her mother.

"How are you feeling today?" Maggie asked. She unconsciously reached her hand to her throat and fingered the small gold cross hanging there.

"Well, I'm feeling kind of sad," Redford said with a slight catch in his voice. "I've been thinking about Hannah."

Maggie stopped and stared at him. She felt protective of Hannah, and he had never mentioned her name before. It was as if he had no idea he was a father.

"What about her?"

"I think . . . I think, at some point, I would like to know her. But by the time I get out of here, she'll be a teenager."

Maggie remained quiet.

"I'd like to know who she is as a person. I don't know anything about her, except she has red hair and she must be in school."

"She'll be in first grade this year. She's very excited," Maggie said, smiling. Then she checked herself. Maybe she shouldn't be sharing things about Hannah without asking Julia first. But Hannah was Redford's daughter too. Would this be a way to help him find his very lost heart? A child could do that.

"What does she like to do? What are her hobbies?"

Maggie thought for a second. As far as she knew, Redford was unaware that Julia had been given a home, free and clear. Julia had also landed a good job as a reporter for the local newspaper, the *Cherish Life and Times*. She was just going to share some recent news about Hannah and Julia when she felt little red flags go up. *When am I going to learn? He doesn't care about Hannah.*

"She's a normal six-year-old. She has friends and enjoys lots of activities," Maggie said quickly.

"She and her mom are living off other people. That's not good. No kid of mine should think that's okay." Redford was losing his sad and pathetic demeanor, and the edge in his voice returned. "How long are those dopes going to let them stay at their boarding house?"

"It's not a boarding house. It's a bed and breakfast. You might be thankful Julia and Hannah have a good place to live with kind people."

Maggie wanted to leave the room. She wasn't going to tell Redford anything else about Julia or Hannah. Especially not about their new home.

"What about money? What's Julia doing for money? Just taking handouts?" He sneered.

Maggie knew Redford was aware his bank accounts had been frozen when he was arrested. After a judge heard the fraud case against him, the money was dispersed to those he had stolen from. Julia received the child support money owed to her, along with the money due her for the coming years until Hannah was eighteen.

Maggie looked into his hard eyes. "What happened to you, Redford? Who damaged you so badly?"

"Shut up, you dumb bitch!"

The guard moved to the metal table in one swift motion. "Okay. That's it. Back to your cell."

3

As Redford was led away, he looked back at Maggie. Then he spit. She scooted back quickly as the spittle landed on the table. She wanted to vomit.

As she turned to leave through the opposite door, she could hear Redford laughing. It didn't sound human.

She drove back to Cherish with a heavy heart. She believed her visits were part of her pastoral duty, but she saw nothing, not one spark of goodness, in the man. What was she doing? It was like banging her head against a wall. She wouldn't go back. Redford was truly poison to everyone.

Once back at the parsonage, Maggie changed her clothes, threw her long blonde hair into a ponytail, locked the front door of the parsonage, and tied her running shoes into knotted bows. Then she ran. The house key thumped lightly on her right foot, where it had been laced. It was early in the day and she had a to-do list a mile long, but she had to get away. She needed to run. She shut out the harsh words from Redford. Then her mind switched gears as she let the memories of the summer drift back in. Different harsh words rang in her ears—the words of her parishioners, those painfully cruel things that were said at what was supposed to be an informational meeting. She felt hot tears well up as she ran down Middle Street toward the cemetery.

Instead of the usual run down her favorite and familiar dirt road, she stayed on Freer, ran past Cherish High School, then made a left at Trinkle. As the road changed from asphalt to dirt, Maggie's feet pounded out every step. The late August heat beat down on her as she picked up speed. She ran as though her life depended on it. It didn't. Her life was not threatened, but it certainly appeared her ministry was.

Maggie ran past Fletcher Road, then Lima Center, and all the way to Dancer Road. She turned around at the dead end and took off toward home and her suffocating to-do list.

She couldn't go to her church office, yet she didn't want to stay home because the parsonage didn't feel like a private, safe space. Even working from her parsonage study did not keep her from interruptions. When she attempted work in her church office, work simply did not get done. Parishioners ignored Hank as he tried to keep them out of Maggie's office without an appointment. As soon as they discovered Maggie was doing some of her work in the parsonage, they just changed course. People came over unannounced more than ever before. The Westminster chimes grated on her ears and rang all the live-long day.

So, Maggie ran. She ran ten miles in two hours.

As she made her way out of the cemetery and back down Middle Street, she could see someone standing on the front porch of the parsonage. Her heart sank. It was the Cherish building inspector, Fitch Dervish.

Maggie had met Fitch shortly after her arrival in Cherish two years earlier. Loving the Lord Community Church had been in the middle of updating a handicapped ramp, which gave access to the sanctuary for wheelchairs and walkers. The first ramp had been slapped together like something made in a kindergarten art class. Popsicle sticks and thick paste would have been sturdier. Fitch Dervish, the number-one building inspector in Cherish for what felt like the last one hundred years (more or less), unleashed his grand powers, knowing he had the final say in any building project. Fitch did everything by the book and took his time to double-check zoning regulations, local ordinances, and building codes, among other codes of construction practices. All residents of Cherish knew Fitch Dervish had an eye for any plan or structure out of compliance. His regular notices and fines to those foolish enough to try and put a deck on the back of their home without his permission, for example, were legendary.

Maggie's pace slowed. She knew why Fitch was on the parsonage porch. She also knew he was not going to leave until he had spoken to her directly. And she was pretty sure what he was going to tell her. She sighed. So much for the long run to recalibrate her heart, mind, and soul.

As she walked down the sidewalk toward home, she looked at Fitch, who saw her and waited right where he was for her to arrive. Maggie noticed his clipboard clenched to his chest and his man bag slung over his shoulder. She didn't know exactly what he carried in his man bag, but he was never without it. He never varied in his dress while doing his work about town. He wore a white button-down shirt, which always had some kind of stain on the front, either dirt or lunch. Khaki pants and large white tennis shoes finished off his attire. Fitch cinched in his pants with a brown leather belt, which left wrinkles and puckers around the waistband. He had an unbelievably large rear end, underbalanced by small, thin shoulders. His razor blade tended to miss patches of facial fur, and his gray, wispy hair blew any way the wind did. The whole look was topped off with glasses that changed from dark to light depending on where Fitch was, indoors or out.

Maggie took a deep breath and walked up the parsonage steps.

"Hello, Fitch," she said politely but without warmth. "How may I help you?"

Fitch cleared his throat and looked down at Maggie. His glasses couldn't decide if they should be dark or light due to the semi-shade on the porch. Maggie could barely see the outline of his dull-brown eyes.

"Pastor Maggie, may I come in, please?" he asked.

"Yes."

She retrieved her key from her shoelace and opened the front door. Fitch followed her inside. He followed her through the front hall, and his tennis shoes made a squeaking sound on the kitchen floor as she led him to her study. She pointed to one of the red-and-white-checked wingback chairs as she took a seat behind her desk. Fitch sat and placed his man bag on the floor and his clipboard on his lap.

"I'm afraid I've got some bad news for you and your church." Fitch never sounded as if sharing bad news bothered him. Maggie was sure he enjoyed his bit of power to build up or tear down. "I'm afraid there is no way Loving the Lord Church can meet the building codes to be used as a childcare center. I'm sorry about this bad news, but . . . " He continued with the list of inadequate exits, lack of space due to small rooms, no outdoor area, and several violations against the hope of caring for forty-plus children in Cherish.

Maggie tuned him out almost immediately. She had been expecting this, but to sit and listen to King Fitch hand down his decree was more than she could bear. She was also sweating from her long run in the heat and felt her legs sticking to her chair. She wanted a glass of water, a shower, and to punch Fitch in the face.

"Now I have compiled my list of ordinances for you and your council, but it would be easier to tear down the church and rebuild than to get a legal childcare center established." He shuffled some papers from his clipboard and handed them to Maggie. "I made duplicates for you. You know, I don't understand why you want to have a childcare center in your church anyway. There is a perfectly good center in Cherish already. It's completely up to code. People can use that one."

Maggie looked up into his now-clear glasses and bland eyes. "Do you know how much the center costs parents in Cherish, Fitch?"

"Does that matter?"

"Yes. It does."

Maggie sighed and looked at her desk. Her eyes landed on her graduation picture with her seminary professor, Ed James. Ed grinned back at her. She looked up at Fitch's blank expression.

"Thanks for the information, Fitch. I will pass this on to the council at our next meeting. I guess it's back to the drawing board."

Maggie stood up. Fitch seemed confused for a moment. Maggie suspected he had hoped for a longer opportunity to share each specific reason the church couldn't possibly be used for childcare—to impart his building-inspector wisdom to Maggie. Fitch was in a dither. He unwittingly dropped his clipboard as he tried to stand, papers falling around his feet. As he bent over, his large posterior bumped into a small table next to the red-and-white chair. The lamp on the table wobbled precariously, then crashed to the floor with the table quickly following.

"Oh, well now, hey . . . oops there, oh!"

Maggie wanted to scream.

Fitch began to pick up the broken glass of the lamp, along with his papers and clipboard. Predictably, one of the shards of glass sliced neatly into Fitch's right index finger. Blood began to smear on the papers and the clipboard. Fitch ran his hand through his hair, where some of his gray wisps turned a punk-rock pink.

Maggie moved quickly to the other side of the desk. She picked up the small table and set it by the bookcase to make room to get Fitch out of the office.

"Stop, Fitch!"

Fitch stopped. One small drop of blood dripped on the hardwood floor.

"Fitch, go into the kitchen and wash your hands." *Am I talking to a preschooler?* "I'll clean this up and get you a bandage."

As Fitch left the study, Maggie collected his items, left the shattered glass, and made her way to the kitchen. She opened a drawer and pulled out a package of Mickey Mouse Band-Aids she had bought as a joke for her husband, Jack. Fitch had managed to get blood not only in the sink but on the countertop and on one of Maggie's new autumn leaf dish towels. She took a piece of paper towel, wrapped it around Fitch's finger, and held it tightly to staunch the bleeding.

"Here, hold this," Maggie ordered.

As Fitch held the paper towel, Maggie unwrapped the bandage and peeled off the tabs.

"Okay, take off the paper towel."

Fitch did, and Maggie wrapped Mickey Mouse around the chubby finger.

"That should do it," she said as she threw the paper towel away. Now, I'll clean up the rest of this so you can get on to the remaining tasks of your day." In a flash of insight, Maggie realized she sounded exactly like her mother.

"I'm sorry about all this, Pastor Maggie," Fitch said, looking flustered. "I'll replace that lamp for you."

Maggie held out his things. He took his man bag, the clipboard, and clipped his copies of the bloodstained papers.

"Don't worry about it," she said as she moved him and his squeaking shoes through the kitchen and toward the front door.

The Westminster chimes rang.

Maggie pushed her way to the door, opened it, and saw a very pregnant Sylvia Baxter with two bags of vegetables in her arms.

Sylvia and Fitch didn't seem to know quite how to navigate the door blockage of each other. Maggie was positive she was going slightly insane. She gently pushed past Fitch to Sylvia out on the porch and took the bags from her. Then she looked at Fitch.

"Goodbye, Fitch, and thanks again."

Fitch tried to say something but gave up and walked out the door with a quick nod.

Finally, he was gone.

2

Maggie stood on the porch, holding the over-stuffed bags of veggies. Sylvia looked at her and began to giggle.

"Pastor Maggie, those bags are bigger than you are. Let me help you."

She took one of the bags and walked into the parsonage, straight to the kitchen. Maggie followed Sylvia with the second bag and noticed Sylvia staring at the blood on the counter.

"Fitch was here to tell me the not-surprising news that the church is not up to code, and can never be, for a childcare center. He dropped things, knocked over a table and broke a lamp in my study, then spilled his blood on my countertop. There you have it." Maggie grabbed her Clorox Clean-Up from under the counter, along with more paper towels, and began cleaning. "I wasn't surprised, of course. I think we all knew the church was too small and too old to make the center work."

Spray, spray, wipe, wipe.

The smell of bleach filled the air. She tossed the soiled hand towel into the laundry.

"But what are we supposed to do now? Cassandra wanted us to create a center for children free of charge. We don't have enough money to begin from scratch."

She moved into the study with a broom, dust pan, and Swiffer. Three furry beasts were sniffing around the broken glass.

"Hey! Scat, cats!"

Marmalade, Cheerio, and Fruit Loop stared with unblinking eyes at her rude voice tone, then ran for the door, where they almost tripped Sylvia as she entered.

"Whoa, felines!" Sylvia said as she held onto the doorframe of the study. "I think this house is possessed today."

Maggie swept up the glass, Swiffered the floor, and put the table back in place.

"Done and dusted," Maggie said. "Or done and Swiffered, as the case may be."

They both went back to the kitchen and sat at the table while the cats investigated the bags of vegetables.

"You've worked so hard to get the childcare center up and running," Sylvia said as she gave Fruit Loop a pet. "But maybe we will have to figure out another way to make Cassandra's wish come true."

Maggie stared out the kitchen window at the bell tower of the church. Cassandra Moffet had been a young mother diagnosed too late with ovarian cancer. Her two children, Carrie and Carl, lost their mother when they were seven and five, respectively. Before she died, Cassandra had the chance to orchestrate as much of her children's future as possible. A couple in the church, William and Mary Ellington, who owned The Grange Bed and Breakfast, decided to adopt Carrie and Carl. Cassandra's unknown fortune from the death of her husband was liberally shared with her children, William and Mary, Loving the Lord Church, and other special people in the dying woman's life. One of her specific wishes was that the church would open a childcare center with her donation, and she wanted it to be free of charge for all children of families without means and in need of care. Maggie had taken this gift and worked tirelessly to make it happen. The visit from Fitch was the final "no," and Maggie couldn't imagine a way beyond.

"I don't see how we can make it happen now," Maggie said, desolate.

"Pastor Maggie, no offense, but you have been trying to tackle a plethora of problems since we all got back from Ghana. It's been only, what, six or seven months?"

Maggie looked at Sylvia. "Oh my gosh! You are almost to your due date! You shouldn't be lifting bags of vegetables. I'm going to tell your husband." All thoughts of the childcare center dissipated for the moment.

"Go ahead. I don't care. I just want this baby to get here. I feel like a human Crock-Pot. And my due date was three days ago." Sylvia smiled ruefully.

At the age of thirty-nine, Sylvia's pregnancy had been watched by Dr. Jack with great care. She and her husband, Bill, who was three years older, knew this would probably be their one and only chance for a child. Maggie snapped out of her bad mood and stared at Sylvia's un-believably large tummy.

"You're huge. And this weather is so hot and sticky right now. You actually are a human Crock-Pot. May I get you something cold to drink, or would you like to just sit in the refrigerator for a while?" Maggie put ice into two glasses and filled them with water. "Drink up, madam. By the way, how long will my husband let you go past your due date? Do I need to have a word?"

"I have an appointment tomorrow morning. I think I might be sent to the hospital after that to help get labor started. That's why I wanted to make these last deliveries to folks."

Sylvia tried to find a comfortable position in her chair but gave up.

"Well, you sure are calm about all this. Sylvia, there's an excellent chance you're going to be a mother tomorrow."

"Maybe. Labor could take a while. But back to the subject at hand. Bill and I support all the great ideas going on around here. We think Darcy Keller's plan is fantastic, and we will do everything we can to help with the Syrian family. We also want the childcare center to be a reality. You don't have to solve this all by yourself. We're with you all the way." Sylvia smiled her sweet smile.

"I can't believe you are going to the hospital tomorrow." Maggie was overwhelmed with emotion for her friend and not refocusing as Sylvia suggested.

Sylvia was usually the one who was most emotional about any sub-ject. Tears flowed easily over the smallest joy or sorrow of someone else, but she seemed completely under control regarding this minor task of birthing a human into the world. Maggie felt the emotion for both of them.

"Back to the Syrian family," Sylvia redirected again.

"Well, yes. Thank you. I wish more of the congregation felt that way. For some reason, I thought everyone would want to act like Christians. Go figure."

Maggie took a large gulp of water. She realized how thirsty she was after her ten-mile run and drained her glass.

"We've been surprised, as well," Sylvia continued. "I've been afraid Dr. Dana, Skyler and Sylvester Fejokwu, along with the Gutierrez family, might leave if there are any more statements about people of color from certain members of our church. Why should any individual or family have to listen to that bigotry and hate? In church?!"

Loving the Lord Community Church wasn't known for being racially diverse. It was the same for the entire city of Cherish. Dr. Dana Drake was African American, the city's veterinarian, and an active member of LTLCC. She was one of the members of the church who went on the mission trip to Ghana earlier in the year. Juan, Maria, Gabby, and baby Marcos—a Latino family in Cherish—found their way to LTLCC after receiving Thanksgiving and Christmas baskets, then regular visits from Pastor Maggie and other members of the church. Skyler Breese, owner of Pretty, Pretty Petals Flower Shop, caused a stir in the congregation when she floated into the sanctuary one Sunday morning dressed in one of her typical scarf-like dresses, holding hands with the new CEO of Heal Thyself Community Hospital, Sylvester Fejokwu. Sylvester had moved to Cherish in late February. He and Skylar met at a hospital get-to-know-the-new-CEO function. Skylar took the purpose of the get-together seriously and asked Sylvester out for coffee the next day.

Maggie had watched with happy interest as "Sky and Sly" navigated their relationship throughout the summer. Sky's flaky and fairy-like affect was the perfect foil for Sly's sharp intellect and word-perfect communication skills. Sly was class and confidence personified. His accent had a British lilt, which seemed to make all the women melt. Maggie had asked Sly to be the liturgist on several Sunday mornings as the summer progressed. Listening to him read Scripture made the Bible come alive even more for Maggie. Interestingly, Sly was also Jack's new boss.

So, Loving the Lord Church had an interracial couple sitting in the pews. Maggie wanted the church to welcome everyone. No barriers. No judgment. She knew Jesus wasn't a bigot or a racist. Her church wouldn't tolerate such attitudes.

It was unnerving when Dr. Dana left before the service finished, two weeks prior, after Martha Babcock made a comment about "foreigners" during prayer request time. Maggie remembered the horrible moment. Martha seemed to hold firmly to beliefs opposite of anything Jesus ever said or did. She had left the church the previous November because of food baskets assembled and given to Cherish neighbors in need at the holidays (she was anti this "ridiculous" practice). But then she decided to come back with a vengeance. Martha defiantly decided to stay in the church to speak her mind *ad nauseam* and to stir up as many disagreements as possible against the "wasteful" practices she perceived. Maggie felt Martha was a cancer in the congregation.

When Maggie had asked for prayer requests two Sundays earlier, Martha stood up and said, "Pray for the safety of our country from foreigners and illegals who want to do terrorism." She then looked right at the Gutierrez family, along with a passing glance at Dana Drake and Sky and Sylvester. Maggie saw movement at the organ. Irena, the church organist, was fuming as she leapt down from her perch on the organ bench. Maggie wondered if Irena, who was brought to the United States from Romania as a child, would actually attack Martha with a right hook to the jaw. Fortunately, Irena's love interest, Detective Keith Crunch, who always sat in the pew in front of the organ, took her hand as she passed by and dragged her down next to him. Maggie ignored Martha and moved on to the next prayer request. It was an awkward moment added on to months of awkward moments.

Sylvia interrupted Maggie's thoughts. "I've brought vegetables out to Maria Gutierrez the last few weeks on my regular route and enjoyed visits with her. She's fun and bright and has a great sense of humor. Did you know she is taking a couple of classes at Washtenaw Community College?"

Maggie did not know this.

"Gabby and Marcos are adorable," Sylvia continued. "I know that a free childcare center would help them out, as well as so many other families in town. That's why we're going to make it happen, Pastor Maggie. We have people in our church and community with needs for food, childcare, healthcare, the basics. Now, thanks to Darcy, we have the opportunity to welcome a brand-new family into Cherish because they can't live in their own country anymore."

Sylvia took a sip of water and leaned forward in her chair with a small groan. Braxton-Hicks contractions.

Maggie nodded a bit wearily, not noticing Sylvia's discomfort.

"It's what we are called to do. Welcome the homeless, feed the hungry, care for the sick, love everyone. It's what we learned when we went to Ghana—no pity, just do the work of love." Maggie got another glass of water, secretly pined for a hot shower, and switched gears. "So, what delectable veggies do we have this week?"

"A mix of fruit and veg," Sylvia said, letting out a deep breath as she struggled to stand up and unpack the bags. She laid her offerings on the kitchen table, looking quite satisfied.

"This is wonderful," Maggie said as she filled the kitchen sink with water and put six ears of corn to soak. "I think I have some inspiration for dinner tonight. Thank you, Sylvia. You are so generous with your bounty."

"It's fun to share, but I think I'd better be on my way." She waddled toward the front door. "I can barely fit in the front seat of my car."

"May I come by the hospital tomorrow?" Maggie asked. "I won't stay long. I think you won't be in the mood to chat, but I'd love to hug you and Bill and say a prayer for that little one." She looked again at Sylvia's stomach. *What in the world does that feel like?*

"Yes, please. I'll need to see a friendly face. I think Bill will need me to keep him from fainting throughout the ordeal." Sylvia smiled and patted her stomach.

The Westminster chimes rang.

Maggie groaned. Her home felt like a board room. One meeting after another, even if it was with the people she loved the most.

Maggie opened the door.

Darcy Keller stood before the two women.

"Good afternoon, Pastor Maggie, Sylvia. May I come in?"

SYRIAN REFUGEE CAMP IN SURUÇ, TURKEY

Mahdi Nasab watched his children sleep. His two sons, Karam and Samir, were on blankets in one corner of the large tent. His daughters, Iman and Jamal, were curled together in another corner. Their lives had been violently interrupted the night the soldiers came to their city of Kobanî in Syria. Mahdi had been led outside with his brother and his father. The soldiers aimed their guns and shot. The bullet that removed Mahdi's left ear caused enough blood for the soldiers to believe he was dead on the ground. He was as still as he could be, holding in the screams of pain and fear until, finally, the soldiers got in their truck and moved their torture to another home. Mahdi cupped his hand over his ear, but there was no ear. Just blood. He'd sat up and looked at the bodies of his father and his brother. His two best friends. They were not pretending to be dead.

Inside his house, Mahdi had found his mother on the ground. She was unconscious, barely breathing. Her arm was bent in an unnatural angle. It had been broken and pulled from the socket. He looked around the house, then to the back garden.

"Amira?" he called. "Karam? Samir? Iman? Jamal?"

He'd watched as his wife and children slowly came from behind a small three-sided brick structure behind his olive trees. Mahdi had built the low wall when rumors of raids drifted into the villages. His wife, Amira, had her arms around her children.

"Mahdi! We heard gunshots!"

Mahdi knew that the next day they would leave their home and their olive trees. He would leave his shop. He would leave his father, his brother—his two best friends—in their graves. He had no choice but to get his family away from the war.

Now, after living in the refugee camp for two years, his pain came only from memories.

He and his family would be moving again. This time to America. For the first time in a long time, Mahdi had hope.

3

Before the mission trip to Ghana the past January, Maggie's mother, Mimi, had suggested Maggie keep a diary of the trip. Mimi had travelled the globe and always kept a diary. It made it easier to recall lost details of visits around the world. Maggie wasn't a regular diary keeper, but when her mother said that even writing one or two sentences per day would be enough, Maggie thought she could manage. Of course, once begun, Maggie wrote many sentences, even paragraphs per day, and she realized her recollections were memory gold mines. If details began to fade regarding the trip, she opened her diary to find each thought and experience.

Once the mission trip ended, Maggie had kept up with her daily jottings. It turned out to be a providential exercise as the church began to wrestle with issues like the childcare center. Maggie kept a perfect record of where the lines were drawn. In her diary, she listed who spoke and exactly what they said. The council minutes were appropriate but less detailed.

At the February council meeting, when childcare within the church came up on the agenda, Maggie was surprised at the backlash. She sat with a knot growing in her stomach at each negative comment.

"We don't want children in the church on a daily basis. It would be too much work," Doris griped.

"They might damage things," Harold said cautiously. "And we don't want to be libel for any accidents."

"What about all the traffic in front of the church, dropping off kids and picking them up?" Charlotte's leather holster creaked as she moved forward in her chair.

"This is a church. A sacred place. How would any church work get done?" Doris huffed. "And why should it be free? Everyone should pay their fair share."

Maggie audibly groaned. "The whole point is to help those who can't afford childcare."

"We've never done this before. Why change?" Beth Becker said. She was new to the council but had a long history with the church.

"There's already a childcare center in town. If people can't afford it, too bad," Fred Tuggle said.

Fred was also new to the council. Because of the small size of the congregation, several couples served on the council. Maggie and Jack, Marla and Tom, Charlotte and Fred, Bill and Sylvia, and a not-yet-legal Harold and Ellen. Verna and Beth rounded out the members. Redford Johnson had been a council member before he was arrested.

Maggie thought she was going to lose her mind.

"Do you even hear yourself, Fred? We are a church. We are not a business. Stop thinking you can run this place the way you run your rock quarry. We are here to take care of people who have needs. It's something Jesus used to do!" she yelled. Her face immediately flushed. She had never felt such pure anger, and it scared her.

"It is a business," Fred responded calmly, as if talking to a child. "Money goes in, money goes out. Property needs to be maintained. Don't try to talk about something you don't understand."

"That's enough, Fred," Verna said curtly. "You have crossed a line. You may know about business, but it is clear you do not know about church. You will respect our pastor, and you will respect this council." Verna did not suffer arrogance and condescension from fools. She glared at Fred.

He opened his mouth to retort, but his wife spoke first. "We have a variety of opinions here. The first thing that would have to be done, if we want to discuss this further, is to have Fitch Dervish come in and tell us if this old building would work in the first place. I don't think a childcare center is a good idea, but before we all go screaming and yelling, we better find out if it can even happen."

That moment of common sense shut Fred's mouth.

Maggie took a deep breath. Her prayer at the close of the meeting was flat and brief. When she and Jack had seen the members out, they went into the living room. Maggie burst into angry tears. The whole situation felt deeply personal.

"I hate being surprised by people when I think they are nice and normal but turn into condescending, ignorant blow-bags." She punched a once-white-now-gray pillow, then quickly smoothed it over with her hand, as if in apology.

"We are in a strange time," Jack said reflectively. "People who used to live in control of themselves seem to believe rudeness and condescension are okay. I was ready to throw Fred out tonight."

Maggie looked at him with tear-stained eyes. "You were?"

"Yes. I don't want to fight, I also don't want to lose sight of our goals. Fred is not going to keep us from making lives better, meeting basic needs for people in our community, or any other good intention brought to us. He doesn't get to have that kind of power."

"Who would have guessed a year ago our church would be in this kind of turmoil?"

"A year ago, Redford was running amuck, but that seems different. He had a personal vendetta. Now we have a faction of people who are part of a national movement of hatred. I think it will die down after the election in November." Jack thought about the hardness of Fred's face and the cruelty of his words. "Something ugly has been boiling beneath the surface of the country, and it has been unleashed with a vengeance."

"I don't know why I thought Cherish would be immune from the national conversation. I have to remember never to assume other people believe exactly as I do. What's so difficult is we're all wrapped up in the church together and I'm the leader. Have they never read their Bibles? Do they not know who they are following? Jesus began a revolution, but it was one of peace, acceptance, and love."

"You're preaching to the choir, preacher," Jack said. Then he kissed the top of her head. "We'll get through this."

Maggie continued to write down each comment on a notepad as the heated council meetings continued. The next month, not only did council members attend diligently, but church members began to attend as well. The meetings had to be moved from the parsonage dining room to the church sanctuary.

One night, after a particularly contentious meeting, Maggie put the newest comments in her diary. She also added the positive comments made by those who began to use their voices for a constructive perspective. These folks saw the church as being something beyond a beautiful old building and something beyond its past.

"Our church is practically empty during weekdays. Why not fill it with children? What a beautiful use for our building," Marla had said in her gentle voice. She knew that Cassandra Moffet's dying wish was to have free childcare in Cherish, and Marla was going to be the director of the potential center.

"I'll happily volunteer to help with lunches for the children." Everyone knew Ellen Bright worked long hours at the hospital. "I will purchase snacks and healthy produce and have it here before the children arrive. I would love to be part of this."

"This would bring relief to parents under stress. Why wouldn't we help?" Verna Baker's voice came across clear and precise.

Perhaps the Verna of two years ago would not have been so magnanimous, Maggie thought. She had once been Maggie's greatest foe, but being married to Howard Baker had softened the older woman's heart.

Maggie also took credit for depositing an orphaned kitten into Verna's life to begin the softening process.

"Not to sound utilitarian, but if children come here for daycare, perhaps they and their parents will come on Sundays too. That would be a positive outcome." Bill Baxter spoke with quiet strength.

"It would take more time to clean. Doris shouldn't have to be responsible for that. We can put a team together to clean different evenings of the week. Count me in!" Sylvia Baxter said. She had momentarily forgotten that she would have a newborn by the time it might all take place.

"For heaven's sake!" Polly Popkin, not a member of the council but a "guest" of the meeting, spoke with ferocity. "We sent a group of our own members to Bawjiase, Ghana, to help children at United Hearts Children Center this year. We can't even help the children in our own town? Something is wrong with this picture. Hokey Tooters!"

One person stood up and quietly said, "Let the little children come to me, and do not stop them; for it is to such as these that the kingdom of heaven belongs." It was Hank's wife, Pamela.

The "Big Fight" had begun in February. As spring and summer progressed, the meetings had become more combative. Maggie knew the news from Fitch Dervish would thrill some of her parishioners. They would feel vindicated. They would sleep better at night because their church wouldn't be defiled by children.

But the childcare center hadn't been the most divisive issue the congregation had to deal with. Darcy Keller had proposed that Loving the Lord Church "adopt" a Syrian refugee family. He had been doing his research with Refugee Support Services in Ann Arbor, and he was on a mission—a true mission of action, not just words.

Darcy was the owner of The Mill, producer of Quick Mix baking products. Darcy was used to getting his way because he was a powerful businessman, not to mention the richest man in town. The past summer, he'd suffered the embarrassment of his wife and his best friend trotting off into a sordid affair that turned more serious. His wife left him. Since Darcy and her father ran a lucrative business in New York, his soon-to-be-ex-father-in-law made a deal with Darcy, perhaps to get him out of town—or more likely to pay him guilt money to cover what his daughter had done. Either way, Darcy came home to Cherish in the fall with presumably more money than God. He licked his wounds of humiliation for a while, then got a kick in the butt from his sister, Priscilla. She dragged him to church against his will until December, when he shocked one and all by putting together Christmas baskets for families in need. That benevolent activity, along with a *Time* magazine article about the Syrian refugee crisis, did something crazy to Darcy's broken heart. Or, perhaps, he finally grew one.

With money never an issue, Darcy got the information he needed to adopt a family of six who had been living in a refugee camp for the past two years. Darcy wanted to share this great good news with the congregation of his church. He was surprised when some members greeted his proposition with disdain, fear, and even hatred.

Back at the February council meeting, still in the parsonage, Darcy had come as a guest and shared his plan.

"I have a packet for each of you describing the work that is done through Refugee Support Services. There are many needs for a new family, as you can imagine."

People began shuffling through the pages of their packets. There was excitement among most of the small group.

Darcy continued, "They will come with literally the clothes on their backs. They have been living in a tent at a refugee camp for two years, far from their home. The children, two boys and two girls, have not had decent health care or any education. The adults have also been without health care. They are all malnourished. Many of their family members were killed in their city of origin. But they have each other."

Darcy took a quick breath. "So, we begin from scratch. They will need a home, furniture, clothing, food, personal hygiene products, toys, dishes, and other kitchen items. They will need to be taken to doctor appointments, registered for school, and at some point, find jobs. They will need friends most of all. The only way I have begun to imagine their plight in the smallest way is to think of myself leaving America because it wasn't a safe place anymore and going to a country that is nothing like my own country. The language is different. The food is different. I would be homeless. I would be completely dependent on others. I wouldn't have any personal possessions. I wouldn't have my culture." Darcy paused. "I would need a friend or friends. That is the opportunity I offer you and the rest of the church. We can give this family a second chance at life. They have been through the worst. I would like to give them the best."

Maggie and Jack had known about Darcy's proposal ahead of time, having had several discussions privately.

The meeting tiptoed along gently until Police Chief Charlotte Tuggle said, "I'll be honest, I'm worried about who might show up here . . . you know . . . in this Syrian family. It seems like a dangerous idea. It's my job to protect this community."

"What sounds dangerous about it?" Darcy asked smoothly.

"Well, Syria is one of those countries," Charlotte stumbled.

"One of *those* countries?" Darcy's eyebrows arched slightly.

"Yes. It's full of . . . full of . . . you know . . . " Charlotte looked around the parsonage dining room table for reinforcements.

"Full of what, Charlotte?" Maggie asked.

"Terrorists!" Charlotte blurted.

Silence.

Maggie's mouth dropped open unattractively. She couldn't believe that was coming from Charlotte, one of the biggest supporters of caring for the neediest residents in her city.

"I suppose we should look at the legal ramifications," Harold said.

Maggie turned and looked at Harold with unbridled shock, which quickly turned to anger.

Charlotte took Harold's words as an affirmation of her position. "Yes, we should look at the legal ramifications. What are the laws for foreigners to live in our country?"

"I'd be happy to share the details of what it takes for people of other countries to move, live, and work here," Darcy said sharply, not used to being argued with. "I can also tell you about the path to citizenship they will have to navigate in order to stay. I have been doing a lot of work on this for the past two months. In fact, there is a three-month educational process we will go through with the Refugee Support Services in Ann Arbor. They will provide materials and informational meetings for those of us who are interested." These last words had an edge to them.

"I think we can all do with more education on the process of welcoming a homeless Syrian family into our community," Maggie said and then hurried on. "What if we let Darcy and the people he has been working with in Ann Arbor speak to the entire congregation? Then all of our questions might be answered."

The doomed congregational information meeting had taken place in March. Charlotte had spread her own fears quietly among those she thought would be sympathetic, and several parishioners supported her side of the issue. Maggie tried to explain that the Refugee Support Services group did a thorough screening of families they helped. There was nothing to fear from this family, who was in desperate need. But that didn't sway Charlotte or those on her side of things.

However, there were others who believed helping refugees was a very Christian and humanitarian thing to do. Pastor Maggie and Dr. Jack were two of those who saw the need to care for a family they didn't know, and the need for the church to act like the church.

Maggie had watched as her congregation began to take sides on the two issues: opening a childcare center and welcoming Syrian refugees. Her heart broke. Then her anger and frustration burned. The biggest problem was figuring out how to pastor this discordant flock. She knew she wasn't neutral on these issues, and her congregation knew it too.

What had begun as a hairline fracture in February on both issues was now a divide that had widened drastically. People were threatening to leave the church.

Loving the Lord Community Church was in crisis.

4

It was almost the end of August. For six months the council and the congregation had met and argued and gossiped and maligned one another.

Maggie was bereft after her conversation with Fitch Dervish. Now Darcy sat across from her in the parsonage study.

"I stopped by to let you know that I'm going ahead with the resettlement of the refugee family without the church," Darcy said matter-of-factly. "It's been six months of no progress. I'm thankful for the small group of parishioners who have gone through the training at Refugee Support Services, but I don't have time to listen to small-minded people. I have money. Frankly, that means I have the power to do what I wish. I'm sorry it has turned out this way." He sounded determined and a little arrogant. Then his tone changed.

"I actually have to move forward because about three months ago I told Refugee Support Services to begin the process of bringing the family here. Because they had worked with a group of us, I knew I could go forward, even if the church wasn't totally supportive. I didn't know how long it would take, but I found out today they will arrive in six weeks. October third, to be precise. I should have told you earlier, but I was hoping the church would eventually embrace the idea. I don't have a choice. I have to move on this."

"Six weeks? Oh dear." Maggie's head began to spin. A refugee family would be right in their midst in six weeks. "I'm so sorry, Darcy. This would have been a perfect chance for the church to live out our faith and beliefs. Is it possible for those of us who back this resettlement to still help? You will need to get so many things in order before they get here and once they've arrived. I want to help in any way possible. Oh! I'm so frustrated!"

There was just the slightest shake of his head. "I'll let you know, but I've set things in motion. I think I've found a home to purchase for the family. I've been working on it for a while." He began to stand, then actually looked at Maggie's face. He sat back down. "I'm sorry, Maggie. It was a good idea, but the church said no. I will let you know in the next few days what the needs are for anyone who went through the training and wants to help. How about that?"

"I'm not giving up on this yet, Darcy. I'm embarrassed by some of our members, but there are plenty who want to be part of the resettlement. I'll keep working on it from my end. I do understand why you need to get moving on this. Six weeks isn't very long, and a precious family is waiting."

Maggie stood with him, shook his hand, and walked him to the door. Then she went upstairs to finally shower and change after her run and her visits with Fitch, Sylvia, and Darcy.

She sorted laundry and began a load, went to her study and tried to organize her already perfectly organized bookshelf, and filed some magazine articles she had been saving for possible sermon illustrations in the future. Her thoughts just wouldn't settle. She looked out of the beautiful floor-to-ceiling window and saw birds enjoying the feeders she had filled that morning. She noticed kitty nose prints smudged at the bottom of the window and grabbed some Windex and paper towels, ferociously cleaning the entire window with the help of her handy step stool.

She knew she should be working on her sermon for Sunday but couldn't bring herself to do so. She had read Luke 14:12b-14, the Gospel passage from the lectionary, and felt like God was playing a joke on her.

When you give a luncheon or a dinner, do not invite your friends or your brothers or your relatives or rich neighbors, in case they may invite you in return, and you would be repaid. But when you give a banquet, invite the poor, the crippled, the lame, and the blind. And you will be blessed, because they cannot repay you, for you will be repaid at the resurrection of the righteous.

This passage described the divisions in her church perfectly.

With a congregation already at odds, this commendation to welcome "the least of these" didn't offer Maggie much hope for a good-news sermon. She washed the window over again.

Eventually, she went into the kitchen to the mountain of fresh vegetables. She washed and sliced tomatoes, an eggplant, carrots, cabbage, and zucchinis, while onions and garlic were snapping and popping in a wok. The ears of corn had soaked and would be ready for the grill. She sliced another tomato methodically, until a thought struck her and her knife clattered out of her hand.

She could barely follow her own rapid flight path. Her mind went from one idea to the next and the next. She absently reached up and fingered the small gold cross around her neck.

Darcy was just going right ahead with his plan to adopt a family. As a CEO, a successful businessman, and, well, a rich, white, male, he could do as he pleased. But it would be more beneficial if the church and community could be part of this welcoming committee. Darcy was generous but unable, or too impatient, to see beyond himself and his personal power.

Her mind flitted.

The church building would not work for the daycare center. The end. But was there another place that would work? There had to be somewhere in the city. Marla had been working on her certification to be the director of the childcare center. Certain members of the congregation were eager to help. Cassandra demanded it from her grave!

It was as if the finale of a firework show was going off in her head. Maggie saw the possibilities in one beautiful sparkly thought after another.

Then she smelled something burning. *Drat! The garlic.*

She turned down the temperature of the wok, spooned out the burnt garlic, and added fresh. She finished slicing Sylvia's vegetables and stirred them into the olive oil, onions, and garlic. Then she poured soy sauce and a spoonful of brown sugar over all.

The kitchen door opened, and Jack walked in. He was carrying a large bouquet of bright-red carnations.

"It smells good in here," he said as he gave Maggie a kiss.

"Hi, husband. Flowers! Thank you. You have no idea how much I need to see and smell carnations today. I'm so glad you're home. Have you had a good day?"

Jack smiled and said, "I had a busy, good, and frustrating day. Like most days."

Maggie immediately grabbed a red glass vase from the pantry and filled it with water. She cut the bottoms off the stems and put the bouquet in the vase with small adjustments. Then she put her nose in the middle of her flowers and breathed in deeply. Red carnations were her favorite.

Jack headed toward the stairs to go up and change his clothes. When he returned to the kitchen, he noticed the soaked ears of corn.

"Shall I light the grill?"

"That would be great. Sylvia brought us all these veggies today. You grill the corn, I'll boil the pasta, then yum. And get ready, I have some big news."

"What might that be?" Jack's eyebrows raised with curiosity.

"It's crazy. Just crazy. I'll tell you over dinner."

When the food was ready, they sat at the kitchen table with their feast.

Maggie prayed, then she dipped an ear of corn into the pitcher of butter-water and let the butter slide down the golden kernels.

The Westminster chimes rang.

"I think I hate those chimes," Maggie grumbled, putting her corn on her plate.

"I'll get it," Jack said. "I can get rid of people better than you can."

Maggie smiled. It was true.

Jack opened the door, and Maggie could hear voices but couldn't quite place them. They weren't parishioners. Jack returned with two people Maggie was absolutely delighted to see: Jack's brother Andrew and his girlfriend, Brynn.

Andrew looked like his older brother, and both looked like their father. Andrew worked with their father, Ken, on the family farm and was ready to take over the family business. Ken and Bonnie had loved farm life but were ready to let Andrew take the helm. It was fortunate that Andrew enjoyed farming as much as his father. The other siblings were completely uninterested.

Jack had two sisters. Anne was the oldest of the siblings and lived in Detroit with her husband, Peter, and their children, Gretchen and Garrett. Anne taught high school in Detroit and worked with emotionally impaired students. Maggie was in awe of her. Leigh, Jack's younger sister, lived at home and owned and ran a maternity shop in Blissfield called Kanga and Roo.

The youngest of the siblings was Nathan. He had graduated the past spring from the University of Michigan and was now planning to join Maggie's brother, Bryan, for three months in Ghana, working at United Hearts Children Center. Ken and Bonnie were only willing to let Nathan go after they heard about Jack and Maggie's trip to Ghana with a group from church the past January. Nathan would leave in September.

Brynn was five foot ten inches tall, wore her chestnut-brown hair curling at her shoulders, and her brown eyes twinkled, as if she always had a delicious secret to tell. Today, she did. It only took Maggie a few seconds to see Brynn might actually be more than Andrew's girlfriend. Brynn smiled as she watched Maggie's eyes travel to her ring finger. A diamond sparkled there. Maggie jumped up and threw her arms around the tall girl.

"Congratulations!"

She pulled Andrew in, and Jack joined to complete the familial group hug.

Andrew and Brynn sat down at the table as directed, and Jack set two more places while Maggie quickly made more bow tie pasta to go with the mountain of vegetables. She had bags of monster cookies in the freezer and grabbed one to thaw on the counter.

"How did you propose?" Maggie asked as they all settled in to eat.

Brynn looked at her ring in disbelief, then laughed as she looked at Andrew. The two had met at the Michigan State University College of Agriculture and Natural Resources. Both loved farming and agriculture, and it didn't take long to decide they also loved each other. But it had taken Andrew five more years after graduation to finally put a ring on it. Brynn was happy with her job at the 4-H program in Lenawee County. She didn't need a fairy tale. She knew she loved Andrew and could happily go about her days waiting for him to grow some courage.

"Well," Andrew began, obviously proud of his wild trickery, "I told her that we had purchased a new tractor for the fall planting."

Jack rolled his eyes. "You are truly the romantic of the family."

"Shut up. Anyway, we went into the barn, and I had a hay bale tied with a red ribbon and a dozen roses sitting on top."

Maggie stopped chewing. She hoped he wasn't going to say what she thought he was going to say.

There was a dramatic pause.

"Then I told her to open it." Andrew was about to burst with astonishment at himself.

"Open what?" Jack asked, looking at Brynn.

"What do you mean 'open what'? The hay bale!" Andrew grinned.

"Oh no!" Maggie looked at Brynn in disbelief.

"Oh yes," Brynn said. "I had to untie the bow and dig through the bale until I found a lovely silver ring box." She laughed. "It was the perfect proposal. I decided I could do it in under twenty minutes, and I did! I dug and dug and dug and finally found the box."

"By then," Andrew continued, "I was on my knee. I asked her to marry me and popped the ring right on her finger. Then we raked up the hay."

Andrew ran his fingers through his hair, and indeed, a piece of hay was handily removed.

"Were you both wearing overalls?" Jack asked, trying to hide a smirk.

"Of course. We had just finished work." Andrew thought his brother was a little thick. "How did you ever pull off a proposal to Maggie?"

"She proposed to me," Jack said.

Maggie rolled her eyes. "No, I didn't. He drugged me, and I said things I don't remember. But imagining Brynn digging through a bale of hay is too much. Andrew, you're a nut!"

After days of disappointment in her personal ministerial abilities, along with her fickle flock, Maggie felt a euphoric relief. She threw her blonde head back and laughed. She laughed hard and long and could hardly catch her breath. It felt so good to be happily out of control.

The other three joined in until finally all the laughter was exhausted. They wiped their eyes with their napkins.

"So, you proposed just this afternoon? On a Monday?" Jack asked, removing another piece of hay from his brother's hair.

"Yes. What's wrong with Monday?" Andrew snipped. "I knew she would never expect it. It was a real surprise, wasn't it?" He leaned over and gave Brynn a kiss as she nodded. "Mom and Dad knew I was going to propose. Brynn's folks did too. And Leigh was in on it from the beginning. So, after we showed them the ring, we cleaned up and decided to drive up here and show you."

Maggie watched Andrew as he talked and teased. His mannerisms were so much like Jack's. He had the same dark eyes, long, straight nose, and deep laugh. When he teased Brynn, his nose wrinkled. Just like Jack's. She realized she didn't know Jack's siblings well. It was fun to watch the two brothers so at ease and unaware of their casual connectedness.

"We're here for another reason," Brynn said.

Maggie and Jack looked at Brynn and Andrew.

"We want you to marry us, Maggie. You'll make it so special." Brynn smiled at Andrew.

"It will be more than an honor," Maggie said. "I'll try not to cry during the ceremony.

"You aren't going to make her stand on a hay bale to officiate, are you?" Jack asked.

"Only if she wants to," Andrew said. "We are thinking of having the wedding at the farm."

"Really? What do Mom and Dad think of that?"

"Well, they agreed that as Brynn and I will take over the farm, it would be a meaningful place to be married. Mom probably wanted the wedding to be in a church, but we talked about ways to make it a sacred and holy service."

Brynn jumped in. "The fact that you will officiate the service means a lot to all of us. You automatically make it sacred—you know, God says so."

Maggie laughed. "Did you hear that, Jack? My very presence is sacred. God says so."

"I'm not sure it's you. I think it's your cats," Jack said.

"I don't know, that sounds kind of blasphemous, Jackie." Andrew looked dramatically at the ceiling, as if waiting for a lightning bolt to strike Jack right on the head.

"Well, there are three of them for the Trinity," Jack said.

Maggie giggled. "Would you like Marmalade, Cheerio, and Fruit Loop to be your flower cats?"

They all laughed at the ridiculousness of herding three cats down the aisle.

"Seriously, though," Maggie continued, "have you thought of a date or any other details? Or are you just basking in the happiness?"

Brynn looked at Andrew and smiled. "We're actually thinking about a Christmas wedding. We know it's just four months away, but it will be small and intimate."

"We talked with Mom and Dad about it, and they seem to be ready to begin 2017 as retirees. They have already booked a trip to Hawaii in January."

Andrew reached for a monster cookie as Maggie set the bag on the table.

33

"Hawaii? That seems kind of exotic for them, doesn't it?" Jack asked.

"Let's not talk about it. Mom already ordered a bathing suit, and I heard Dad call her 'sexy mama' when she tried it on. Puke."

"Good for them!" Maggie said. She could say this easily about Ken and Bonnie. She knew full well *her own* parents would never engage in this kind of talk or action. Never, ever, ever!

Jack knew his parents were ready to be done with the farm. Ken had already had both knees replaced, and the threat of a hip replacement loomed. Bonnie had worked hard through the years. Running a farm was not done by one person. Jack was glad they could begin long years of relaxation that would not be dictated by seasons or weather.

"What about Leigh?" Jack asked about their youngest sister. "Is she going to live with you, or is she finally going to be booted out of the nest?"

"I wouldn't mind if she lived with us," Brynn said. "I love Leigh."

"Uh, nope," Andrew said. "Not a chance. Unless she lives in the barn."

"Actually," Brynn said, ignoring her fiancé, "she has already found an apartment downtown. She'll be a few blocks away from the shop. She moves in on October first."

"It's a good thing Mom will have the wedding to think about," Jack said, helping himself to a cookie, "so she won't have to go through mother withdrawal when Leigh moves out."

"Mom is excited," Andrew said. "And because my fiancée is so kind, she's inviting Mom to be part of everything for the wedding. I hear it doesn't always go that way. Please pass me another one of those cookies."

Jack slid the plastic bag to his brother.

"I'm happy to have all of Bonnie's ideas," Brynn said. "She knows everything about the farm and how to orchestrate a wedding. We're looking at Saturday, December seventeenth, for the ceremony. It's the week before Christmas. We know you will be terribly busy," she looked at Maggie, "so if it needs to be moved, we can still do that. We just thought it would be fun to wake up married on Christmas morning.

We think we'll use the third floor of the farmhouse for the ceremony."

"That's a great idea," Jack said. "It's so open, and the windows give a wonderful view of the orchard. Remember when we would all play up there?"

"I remember the times we locked Nathan in the room after we told him it was full of all the dead people who had ever lived on the farm." Andrew laughed. One of his teeth was covered in chocolate from an M&M in his cookie.

"That is so mean!" Maggie said. "How could you do that to a little boy?"

Jack and Andrew laughed.

"He deserved it," Andrew said. "He was a brat. Mom and Dad babied him, and he followed us everywhere." Andrew licked the chocolate off his tooth after Brynn discreetly pointed it out.

"Didn't you ever play tricks on Bryan?" Jack asked.

"Of course not. I'm decent. And I also thought he was my very own baby. I might have been a little overprotective." Maggie looked whimsical, remembering baby Bryan.

"Anyway," Andrew said, "we're getting married, and Mom and Dad can begin the retirement they deserve, and Maggie will officiate the wedding, and . . ."

Everyone stared at him.

". . . and you will be my best man." Andrew looked at Jack.

Jack smiled. "Yes, I will. Do I have to wear a tux?"

Andrew looked at Brynn.

"We'll get back to you on that one," he said. "We only got engaged this afternoon. We haven't figured everything out yet. But I do think we should be on our way. Thanks for dinner and for listening to our engagement story."

"It's an awesome story," Maggie said as she stood up and went to the freezer. She grabbed two bags of monster cookies and put them in Andrew's arms before he and her husband devolved into small boys fighting over what was left in the bag on the table.

"Off with you!" she said as she gave Brynn a huge hug.

Jack and Maggie walked the happy couple to the door.

"Thanks for driving up here and telling us the good news in person," Jack said as Andrew and Brynn walked down the porch steps. "Tell Mom and Dad congratulations on their new future. And don't eat all those cookies before you get home!"

5

After Andrew and Brynn left, Jack and Maggie cleaned up the kitchen and went out for a walk. The air was cool, and stars were beginning to twinkle.

"That was the absolute bright spot of the day," Maggie said, thinking of Brynn's face as she talked about the hay-bale proposal.

"What about right now?" Jack asked, squeezing her hand.

"You are always the brightest spot," she said. "After days like today, I think we should get in the car and drive right back to North Carolina and live at the Biltmore. We could sneak in there and hide for months. No one would ever find us." Maggie sighed.

Five months earlier, right after Easter, Jack and Maggie had gone on a get-a-moon. They had not had time to plan a real honeymoon after their surprise wedding, unless a mission trip to Ghana—while sleeping in separate rooms—counted, which it definitely did not. As a Christmas present for Jack, Maggie planned a get-a-moon for the spring. They'd taken their time driving down I-75, stopping to sightsee along the way. They had told the church, Jack's office staff, and their families that they would only check their phones once per day. No one called them.

Once south of Asheville, North Carolina, they'd wended their way through the Biltmore Estate and checked into the Inn on Biltmore. The four days that followed surprised them.

Amid long walks on the estate, leisurely bike rides, tours of the historical house and gardens, ice cream cones from the dairy, and picnics by the French Broad River, Jack and Maggie fell into a love they hadn't experienced before. Their life in Cherish was quick-paced and regularly interrupted. The fishbowl that was the parsonage meant visitors were at the door at all times, and often extra plates were set hurriedly at the dinner table for unexpected guests. They'd also been unaware of how their different schedules hindered their time together. They never had a weekend. Jack was winding down on Friday evenings (unless he was on call), while Maggie was gearing up for the Sunday worship service. This took its toll, but like most everyone, they kept going at their hectic pace because it was their "normal."

Far from home at the Biltmore, romantic dinners led to romantic nights. Without interruptions or alarm clocks, they could sleep, play, and finish every conversation. The only people they had to interact with were those who made their week so extraordinary around the estate.

One afternoon, while visiting the petting farm, Maggie looked up from the baby goat she was holding and said, "I think I want to stay here. I'm sure they need a doctor to look after people who overindulge on delicious food and wine, or children who tumble down hills or fall off a horse. And I can be a docent. I think I've already memorized the entire tour of the house. Or I could work here and take care of these darling animals. Or I could work at Antler Hill Village in one of the shops. Or the Christmas shop at the stables. Imagine, Christmas every day."

"You could. But what about the cats? They would be homeless. I worry about them, you know." He knelt down and tickled her neck.

"You do not. Anyway, we'll ship them down, and they can live here in the petting farm."

"They're too spoiled. And fat. They could never survive out here." Jack gave the baby goat a little scratch behind her ears.

"Okay. I guess we have to go back to Cherish." A little dark cloud crossed her face.

"There is a lot of work to do when we get back," Jack said, "but it's not work to do here. It will wait for us. Now, may I buy you an ice cream cone and then take you to a wine tasting and then have my way with you?"

"Well, okay. If you must." She gently put the goat down, stood up, and gave Jack a very romantic kiss. "I'm glad no one knows us here. It's fun to be as love-crazy as we want without concern of appearances. Ice cream, please."

Jack and Maggie's get-a-moon had happily continued until it was time to pack up and reluctantly meander through the winding roads. They pulled out of the gates of the estate and into Biltmore Village. Then they were back in reality. The fairy tale was in the rearview mirror.

"I was a visitor today," Maggie said with a sigh as she and Jack walked down Middle Street after dinner, "and then I had three visitors here. I went down to Milan."

Jack looked sideways at her face as they walked. "How was Redford this time?"

"Horrid, as usual. And I'm embarrassed. I feel gullible. I always think there might be a chance to help him, but he's just toxic with hate. I don't think I can go back."

"You don't have to go back. I know you feel commanded to 'visit the prisoner' along with all the other things you do for people around here, but every visit leaves you discouraged and unnecessarily embarrassed and stressed. You have nothing to be embarrassed about. Redford is sick, and it's a sickness that would take years of therapy to heal. You're not a therapist. You're a pastor. Some people can't be redeemed because they don't want to be."

She stopped and looked at him. "Is it because I'm a woman?"

"He looks down on women, but he looks down on everyone. Again, he's sick. And our prison system doesn't provide many services to help the inmates."

They crossed the street and began to walk back toward the parsonage.

"Then help has to come from the outside," Maggie said.

"But it might not be from you."

Maggie absently fingered the cross around her neck. Jack knew this familiar move, when his wife was either anxious or just lost in thought.

"I've lost you. Come back to me," he said. "Tell me who your three visitors were today. I hope they were more enjoyable than the prison."

Maggie looked at Jack and rolled her eyes. "Here we go: Fitch, Sylvia, and Darcy. Fitch said the church can't be used as a childcare center. Sylvia brought berries and veggies and looked as though she would have her baby right there in the kitchen. And Darcy said he's moving ahead on his own to resettle the Syrian family. Jack, he began the process three months ago. The family will be here in six weeks. Six weeks! They will arrive on October third—our first anniversary, by the way."

Jack took in this information then said, "I do know when our anniversary is, wife. Well, we knew there might be a chance that Darcy—"

"But wait!" Maggie interrupted. "I was definitely deflated after Darcy left, until I had a thought."

"Here we go." Jack smiled. He knew how Maggie's brain worked, and he liked it.

"Okay. There is nothing we can do with the church building regarding the childcare center, but we can continue to use it to make care baskets for people in our community. Why do we just make baskets at Thanksgiving, Christmas, and Easter? What if we add two or three other times during the year? I can check with Grace in Action about working with them to do this."

Her brain was whirring, and Jack's eyebrows were raised in anticipation.

"Then, the childcare center. What if . . ." They walked up the steps to the parsonage porch and sat down on a bench there. She looked around and gathered her words. "What if the parsonage could be used as the center? It has so much room, plenty of exits, a large backyard, a beautiful kitchen, enough bathrooms, all the things that are necessary to meet code. I think."

"So, we would be living in a childcare center? What about the cats? Have you thought about them? I worry about them, you know."

"No, you don't." She rolled her eyes. "We wouldn't live here, of course. We could get a little distance from the church next door and the Westminster chimes. What do you think?"

"Well, I guess we could move into my condo. It's just sitting full of my unused furniture."

"Nope. This is the best part." Maggie sat straight up and began to wiggle. "We will give your condo to the Syrian family! It's a beautiful condo, just like brand-new, full of furniture—as you just mentioned— and they wouldn't have to worry about keeping up a yard or shoveling snow. It's close to the elementary school and the park. What do you think? What do you think? What do you think? I want to call Darcy and tell him he doesn't have to buy a house or worry about that part at all." She was speaking in rapid-fire now and looked at Jack expectantly.

"I think we have a lot to think about," he said. "You just threw some big ideas at me. You've got to give me three seconds to catch up."

"One, two, three." She grinned.

"I'm still a little confused. So, are we going to erect a tent behind the church? Where are we going to live?"

"Somewhere. Over the rainbow. I don't know, actually, but I'm pretty sure we can do a little house hunting and find a new place big enough for the two of us and three cats. I feel like I'm suffocating in this parsonage. Ever since February, when chaos was unleashed, we, at least I, have had no respite from the Big Fight. Except for our get-a-moon, of course. Meetings at church take up enough of my time, but now meetings are drifting over here. It's too much."

Jack stood and helped her up. "Listen, short wife, I think these are great ideas. I also think there will be many steps to make them reality. But I agree, we could think about where else we might like to live." Jack had a little thought creep from the back of his mind to the front.

"Yes, we do have control over that part," Maggie said. "And maybe the condo too. If we tell Darcy it's available, he might be able to check that off his resettlement to-do list. He really is an amazing man. I can't wait to meet the family from Syria. Whoever they are." Maggie already had ideas of how to love these faceless, nameless strangers. "But tell me about your day. I've been babbling on when you've had a day full of your own stories. Spill."

"I had a good lunch with Sylvester Fejokwu," Jack said. "I finally decided to broach the subject of beginning some free clinic hours."

Jack and Maggie had talked with Jack's partner, Dr. Charlene Kessler, about free medical care for patients in and around Cherish who had health issues but didn't have the money or insurance to get help. Maggie knew that many administrators weren't interested in "giving away" care.

"What did he say?"

"He wants to keep the conversation going. He sees it as good for the hospital's reputation, but also understands the need. It will take a lot of logistical work, but he has vision. You can tell he says 'yes' more than he says 'no.'"

"Mmmm . . . I like people like that. I get cranky when people tell me 'no.' Let's get Sylvester on the church council tout de suite!"

"Slow down, Pastor. Let's not chase him away."

"He's not going anywhere. He has the exquisite Skylar to keep him right here at Loving the Lord. Thank goodness for her! Anyway, what's the next step with the possible clinic?"

"We'll keep meeting to talk about if and how it could work. It's a lot to consider." Jack knew what it would take and hoped the needed staff would have the appetite to step up.

"Well, speaking of doctors and patients, I hear Sylvia is going to the hospital right after she sees you in the morning." She wiggled again.

"Yes, I don't want her pregnancy to go any longer. That baby has been baked long enough."

"She said she feels like a human Crock-Pot. Poor thing. How long do you think it will take for the baby to be born? Just a guess."

"Only a fool would guess at that question. I am not one. Every labor is different."

"I won't plan on you for dinner tomorrow night. You'll most likely be taking good care of our friend and her shy, nervous husband." She gave Jack a kiss. "They are so lucky to have you."

"Thank you. May I have another one of those kisses, please?"

"If you must."

"I must."

∞

Sylvia looked at her phone. Four a.m. She was beginning to wonder if the Braxton Hicks were becoming something more than just "practice contractions." How would she know? People could describe what was going to happen to you in every stage of pregnancy, but every feeling from morning sickness to the first flutter of the "butterfly baby" around sixteen weeks to the actual birth experience was brand-new for every new mother. Sylvia had witnessed the birth of a baby in a small clinic in Bawjiase, Ghana. She had been admitted to the clinic with a leg infection. One of the beds in her room was needed for a laboring mother, leaving Sylvia just feet away from a woman bringing new life into the world. It was one of the scariest, and most miraculous, nights of Sylvia's life.

Fear and another hard contraction gripped her. She reached over and touched Bill's shoulder. He rolled over and sat up when he saw the light of her phone.

"Are you okay?"

"I think we might need to pay attention to our baby. He or she seems to be getting ready to be met."

6

It was five a.m. when Jack's phone rang. "Hello, Jack Elliot speaking." His voice was sleepy but calm.

"Dr. Jack, it's Bill. Sylvia is having contractions between four and five minutes apart. It's been an hour now. What do you think?"

"I think I'll meet you at the hospital. It's time."

Jack got out of bed, quickly pulled on his jeans and a casual short-sleeved shirt, grabbed his car keys, and was out the door.

Maggie watched him leave and prayed.

Jack drove with haste to the hospital. Without much traffic, he didn't wait for red lights to turn green. As he sailed past the police department, Officer Bernie Bumble, who'd just arrived for duty, looked at the hurried driver, saw it was Dr. Jack, and gave him an awkward salute. If Dr. Jack was speeding, he was in a hurry to do important doctor things.

Jack pulled into the parking lot, got out of his car, and raced toward the emergency department. Before he got to the door, he noticed Bill and Sylvia's car parked haphazardly across two parking spaces close to the entrance. He ran through the sliding doors and toward the emergency patient rooms. Stopping at a supply closet, he grabbed a gown and shoved his arms through the sleeves.

Jack lifted his head. He heard the smallest of cries. Stepping across the hall, he opened the door and saw a nurse holding a tiny wailing baby. Jack took in the rest of the room and saw Sylvia on a bed with tears streaming down her face. She couldn't take her eyes off the slimy little being in the nurse's arms. Bill, his red hair standing straight up due to fingers that had run themselves through it mercilessly, had tears in his eyes and on his cheeks as well.

Ellen Bright, a nurse and Jack's cousin, was checking the placenta, which was in a bowl. The gown she was wearing was soaked in the typical mess of childbirth.

Ellen looked at Jack and said, "Everything's fine here, doctor. But it's nice of you to drop by." She smiled. "If you want, you can tidy up our beautiful new mother with a few sutures."

"Ahh, thank you. Perhaps I'll scrub in." He looked back at Sylvia and Bill. "Congratulations, you two. This is one of the fastest deliveries I've seen—I mean, not seen." Jack felt slightly rattled.

"You know, doctor, it's a very natural process." Ellen gave Jack a wink.

Jack laughed and looked at his cousin with a smirk. "Then why do I even need to show up?"

He turned his attention to the new parents. "So, may I ask, who is this new member of your family?"

The other nurse had quickly wiped down the baby and returned the little one back to Sylvia. The moment had rendered both mother and father speechless. Jack and Ellen looked at each other. This was one of the most moving and miraculous aspects of what they did; they watched a family be born.

Then they heard Sylvia whisper, "Her name is Katharine Marie. She is named after our mothers."

The room rested. It was as if the walls themselves sighed deeply at the amazing work that had been done in their midst.

The only noise was little Katharine Marie, snuffling at her mother's breast.

In the parsonage kitchen, Maggie made a Keurig cup of coffee. Three felines began meowing in a minor-chord dirge, lamenting the lack of their own breakfast. Maggie set her cup down and grabbed three kitty bowls and cans of cat food. As they heard her making their breakfast preparations, the chorus reach a crescendo. Cheerio began turning in tight circles, and Fruit Loop stood on Maggie's toes. Once the bowls were on the floor, immediate and blissful silence commenced. Maggie took a sip of coffee and said another prayer for Jack, Sylvia, Bill, and baby Baxter.

After a bowl of oatmeal, she cleaned up her and the kitties' dishes, brewed another cup of coffee, and walked into the study. *Sermon, sermon, sermon . . .* She stood at the floor-to-ceiling window and stared out at the three beautiful pine trees. The little red wagon stood below them, loaded with orange and yellow marigolds. Birds fluttered down from the trees to the feeders, and four fat squirrels and a bunny sat underneath, waiting for the seed to fall. She and Jack had seen a skunk wander through two evenings before. He'd also stopped for a snack. The kitties had their noses glued to the window when the black-and-white "not-a-cat" crunched down some seed and then wandered away. The backyard was such a peaceful place. There was enough food for residents and visitors and even little skunky aliens. She sipped her coffee. Why couldn't people be more like animals? Perhaps human evolution was a regressive process, not progressive.

What am I going to say to a group of people so divided? The children of the church are more mature than the adults! A tiny lightbulb flashed in her head. *Oh my! Can I get away with it? What's the worst that can happen? I don't think I can be fired over one sermon.*

She quickly sat down at her desk, turned on her computer, and began to type. Her fingers flew until she noticed she was skipping words because her brain was on warp speed, her fingers tripping over each other to keep up.

Maggie heard a noise and looked up. She was surprised to see Jack come through the study door. She eyed the small clock on her desk: six thirty a.m.

"What are you doing back so soon? Was it too early for Sylvia to go to the hospital? Does she have a long way to go yet? Poor thing." She glanced down at her computer screen to add another forgotten word. Then she looked back at Jack.

"Well, in one way she does have a long way to go," Jack said. "She'll be a mother for the rest of her life. That's usually a long way."

"I don't understand."

"By the time I got there, the baby was already here. My dear cousin Ellen delivered her."

"What? The baby? It's a girl? Ellen did it? How?"

Jack grinned. "Sylvia did what most first-time mothers don't do. She had her baby very quickly. I didn't get there in time, but Ellen had everything under control. Sylvia and Bill have a little girl named Katharine Marie. They've been settled in a room on the second floor. All is well on the maternity ward at Heal Thyself Community Hospital."

Maggie was dumbfounded. "I should go visit. I can't believe it. I figured Sylvia would have her baby tonight or tomorrow. This is so exciting!" She got up from her desk and walked to Jack. "Do you need some breakfast? When are you going back to check on Sylvia and the baby? Oh, you probably need a shower. I'll call Pretty, Pretty Petals and have Sky make up a beautiful girlie bouquet. Katharine Marie . . . " Maggie quickly went to her bookshelf and grabbed *The Very Best Baby Name Book in the Whole Wide World*.

"Uh, yes, I'd love some oatmeal for breakfast. I'll check in on the new family around eight. Yes, I do need a shower. A girlie bouquet sounds . . . very girlie. What are you doing, wife?"

Maggie was quickly thumbing through the pages in her book. "I'm looking up the meanings of Katharine and Marie, but I think I remember them. Yes, yes. Mmmm . . . " She closed the book, then turned back to Jack. "Let's get you some oatmeal." She kissed him and went to the kitchen.

Jack smiled. He was again amused by her brain flits.

As she put the milk and oatmeal in a bowl, Maggie said, "We have a lot to celebrate. Andrew and Brynn are getting married, and Bill and Sylvia have a brand-new, perfect little girl. It makes some of our other struggles fade a bit. I was thinking of calling Darcy today. Can we meet with him together and offer your condo to the refugee family?"

She put the bowl in the microwave and tapped the buttons to get it started.

"If I can get ahold of Darcy," she continued, "and he has time, can you sneak away for a while this morning? It's just that we don't have the luxury of time. The Syrian family will be here so soon."

"I have a short break around ten o'clock. But it's short. Maybe you can get him up to speed if this all works. See if he can meet us at my office."

Maggie picked up her phone and sent a quick text.

She was rewarded with a small *ding* and read Darcy's response.

"Yes, Darcy and I will see you at ten. You know, I really think this is going to work!"

"We'll see. Darcy may have already taken care of things. He has been going forward with this plan without the rest of us knowing. Just be prepared that he has a house already lined up."

While Jack finished getting ready for his day, Maggie went for her morning run, grabbed a shower, and then called the church office.

"Good morning, Loving the Lord Community Church, Hank speaking. How may I help you?"

"Hi, Hank. It's Maggie."

"Well, howdy doody! What's up?"

"First of all, Sylvia had her baby this morning. Katharine Marie Baxter. Isn't that amazing?" Maggie got a little teary.

"Well, well, well, she did? Then today is a beautiful day, yessireebob, it is! I'll get that announcement emailed to the congregation and right into the bulletin for Sunday." Hank's voice grinned.

"Yes, perfect. Also, I'm going to run to the hospital and see the little darling, so I'll be in the office a little later. Any other phone calls this morning?" Maggie cringed. She hoped not.

"Just one from Lacey Campbell. She asked if you had time in your schedule today. I told her after lunch because I thought you'd be working on your sermon this morning."

"Thanks, that's great. Let her know one o'clock will work for me. And I do have a sermon title for you. I birthed my sermon this morning while Sylvia birthed Katharine. It's called 'Enough.'"

Hank was silent.

"Did you get that? 'Enough.'"

"Yes, Pastor Maggie, I got it. But what do you mean by 'enough'? You don't mean anything like you've had enough of us, do you? Not that I would blame you. But you aren't leaving, are you?"

Maggie was silent.

"Pastor Maggie?"

"Yes. I mean no. Hank, what would make you think that?"

Maggie was shocked. She had been so busy being mad and frustrated with her congregation, she hadn't realized there were some who were scared and sad and worried right along with her. Her focus had been too much on the troublemakers and not enough on the peacemakers.

"Well, it's been a little rough around here," Hank admitted. "Some of us feel when we come to church, it's like walking into a fight club. The uglier side of folks is on full display, yessireebob, it is. But we can't lose you."

"Hank, my sermon title has nothing to do with me leaving Loving the Lord. I admit, these last few months have been harder than I ever could have imagined, but we are all trying to follow Jesus the best we can. I won't stop doing that."

Maggie heard a door bang in the background.

"Hunk! Verreee ees Pastooor Maggie?"

Maggie said, "I'll be in later. Tell Irena to calm down."

She hung up the phone and grabbed her car keys.

Then she got into her car and drove to Pretty, Pretty Petals to pick up the "girlie" arrangement for little Miss Baxter.

She breathed into the peace of that new life. For a brief moment, she could hold a newborn and remember God was somehow in control.

Syrian Refugee Camp in Suruç, Turkey

Amira jumped. She'd heard the baby cry. She sat up on the floor next to her sleeping husband, Mahdi, and immediately wrapped her arms around her stomach. She felt the pain of emptiness. A baby was crying. But it wasn't her baby. Her little girl had died shortly after she was born. No one could tell Amira why. The baby didn't seem to be able to breathe easily. She didn't have enough energy to nurse. The little one struggled to catch her breath, but she just couldn't. Amira had held her baby close. She watched the little one struggle, and her mother-heart broke with every gasp. She kissed her little girl, trying to put breath into her. But she couldn't. She couldn't help her baby. No one could help. Then the struggle ended, and the baby lay still in her arms.

Amira didn't think she could survive this pain. She had lost so much already. But losing her baby was more than she could bear. They'd buried their daughter in a makeshift graveyard six months ago. They'd planted flowers on her grave.

There were many flowers now. Too many graves. Amira visited the grave every day. And still, she was startled awake.

Whenever she heard a baby cry.

7

Katharine Marie, wrapped in a cozy pink blanket, rested sleepily in Maggie's arms. Maggie couldn't take her eyes off the tiny face. The little rosebud mouth, exquisite eyelashes, and eyebrows that looked as if an angel had gently brushed them on with a feather.

"She's so perfect," Maggie whispered without looking up.

The visit was mostly silent. Miracles often elicit such a response.

When Maggie had finally relinquished the baby to her mother, she said a prayer of thanksgiving and felt her eyes well up as she remembered that God's goodness would always overcome the bad that swirled in human lives.

Darcy was already in one of Jack's leather chairs when Maggie arrived. She saw his fingers tapping impatiently.

"Hi, Darcy," Maggie said.

Before she'd gone to the hospital, she sent Darcy a text briefly stating that she and Jack would like to donate their condo for the Syrian family's use. They hoped it would expedite the housing issue and take the burden off Darcy's plate.

"Hi, Maggie," Darcy said, then stood and kissed her on the cheek. "I was surprised by your text. When do you think Jack—?"

Jack walked in wearing his white coat. Maggie grinned.

"Well, let's get down to business," Jack said, sliding into his chair behind the large oak desk. Maggie sat down next to Darcy. "What do you think of moving the family into our condo?"

Darcy was used to controlling any meeting he was part of, but Jack had taken control of this one.

"I think it's an interesting idea," Darcy said. "We will have six people. How big is the condo?"

"Eighteen hundred square feet. Three bedrooms—I used one for an office when I lived there—two and a half baths. Kitchen, dining room, living room, finished basement. Except for the office furniture, which we've already moved to the parsonage, everything else would stay. That would save some time and money getting furnishings. I suppose just a bed or two would be needed for what was the office space."

"I've been looking at a home out on Dexter-Cherish road," Darcy said. "It's a farmhouse situated on several acres of land. The house needs some work, but it's vacant and the owners want a quick sale. With our short time frame before the family arrives, your condo sounds like a better fit."

"Even if you go forward with the farmhouse," Maggie said, "the condo would certainly be a more comfortable place to bring the family first. I can't imagine the chronic exhaustion and physical and mental issues they have endured for so long. The condo will provide them with every physical relief. We'll help them with the rest in time." Maggie wondered if the family could ever completely heal after what they had survived and were surviving still.

"Will there be any problems with neighbors in the condo community?" Darcy asked.

"I don't know," Jack said. "There's an older couple next door. Very kind. I'll stop over this evening and let them know what we're thinking. The fact is, we own the condo. We can do what we want with it. I'm sure we will be navigating many things we can't imagine yet."

"What about the financials on all this?" Darcy continued.

"We'll keep the mortgage and take care of the costs."

Darcy's eyebrows raised. "That's very generous of you."

"It's the right thing to do, that's all."

Darcy hesitated. "I'm continually surprised when I see people willing to give so much without trying to get something back."

"But that's exactly what you are doing," Maggie said quickly. "Darcy, you are literally saving a family. Six human beings will have a new chance at life. You are quite remarkable."

"As a friend of mine said, 'It's the right thing to do, that's all.'" He looked at the floor.

"You know as well as we do how many people don't know how to, or don't want to, do the right thing," Maggie said quietly.

"We'll get everything cleaned up and ready for the family," Jack said. "We'll see who at church would like to help clean and bring in some groceries. Perhaps someone has a couple of beds to donate." He rose. "I've got to get back to work."

Darcy and Maggie stood also. The three filed out of the office, and Darcy thanked them again before heading on his way.

Maggie had planned to go home and give her sermon another read-through but decided to go to the church office instead. She wanted to see Hank and tell him about the family and the condo and see if he and Pamela would help with the preparations. She knew fights in the church could keep anyone from doing anything. Fighting took up all the air and time. It was so maddening when people who said "no" seemed to always win. She saw that in marriages, friendships, business deals, and just about anywhere in which two or more people had to make a decision. The word "no" won more often than "yes." But it wouldn't this time.

Irena sat sullenly in one of the cream-colored visitor chairs in Pastor Maggie's office. She had been waiting there for over an hour after practicing her Sunday selections on the organ. She tapped her small feet ensconced in five-inch heels. She shuffled through the stack of music piled on her thin lap. She huffed. She puffed. She noticed an apple on Maggie's desk, reached across her music, grabbed the apple, and began munching. Doris, the janitor, walked in with her large rolling trash can and yellow apron stuffed full of cleaning products.

"What are you doing?" Doris asked.

Irena's mouth was so full of apple, she spit small pieces as she spoke. "Vaiting forr Pastoorr Maggie."

Doris looked down at the apple bits on Maggie's floor. Irena followed her gaze, then took another large bite. Doris bit her tongue. She would clean up Irena's "applesauce" on the floor later.

"Irena, I want to tell you something," Doris said, trying not to look at the masticated apple in Irena's opened mouth.

"Vat?" (spit)

Doris couldn't help but watch the half-chewed fruit hurtle to the ground. "Ahem, well, I wanted to tell you that even though there are people in this church who are saying mean things about foreigners, Chester and I like you real well. Yes, we sure do. We'd never want to see you get sent back to Russia, or wherever you're from. We're not in favor of this Syrian family thing. That's just too risky. But we're glad you are part of us. Even though you talk a little funny."

Doris waited expectantly for Irena's response to this generous compliment and unsolicited acceptance.

Irena stopped chewing and swallowed too much apple with one gulp. Her eyes narrowed, and her green eyeshadow glistened. She stood up, clutching her music, and dropped the apple core on the floor.

"I'm frrom Romania. Not Russia. I can't vait to meet de Syrians. Dey hev nut one ting in de vorld. Eef you don't vant dem, you don't vant me."

Irena stalked out of the office, stabbing the apple core into the carpet with her very high heel.

Doris stood in the middle of Maggie's office with her mouth hanging open. "What in the world is wrong with her?" she said to thin air.

As Maggie walked through the beautiful oak doors into the sanctuary, she almost ran right into Irena, who was moving like a mini freight train.

"Oh! Irena. Sorry, I didn't see you." Maggie looked at Irena's reddened face. "Good grief. What's the matter?"

Irena dropped her stack of music on Maggie's feet.

"Ouch!" Maggie stepped back

"I qvit!" Irena spat. Some leftover apple made its way onto Maggie's cheek.

"Why?"

"Dis church ees full of shtupid peoples. Dey know noting about being lost, homeless, hungrry, hopeless. Dey tink rrefugees are vastepaper. Dey tink 'just trow dem in de trrash'! My muder was nut trrash! I am nut trrash!"

Maggie watched as Irena's face crumpled. The tears flooded down her cheeks bringing mascara, eyeliner, blush, and foundation along with them. It was ghastly. Irena let out a sob and then gulped in a breath. Her small shoulders heaved as she sobbed again.

Maggie put her arms around Irena and let her cry. She knew she was holding living pain.

Irena had existed in the uncertainty of life when her mother died. Irena had only been fifteen. She'd had to hide in the streets of Detroit, then sneak back home and run her mother's music business. She hid from police. She figured out how to pay bills and keep customers coming for lessons. There wasn't one day as a teenager that she hadn't felt at risk, scared, and lonely.

Maggie looked up and saw Hank standing in the doorway of his office. Doris was behind him. Maggie wondered what to do. Her first impulse was to take Irena over to the parsonage and let her cry without prying eyes. But then she realized that almost certainly Hank or Doris had said something that brought on this torrent of emotion.

"Irena," she whispered, "let's go back to my office. I want to completely understand what happened here."

Irena shook her head and then wiped her nose on Maggie's sleeve.

"Please?" Maggie gently turned Irena and led her to the offices. "Hank, Doris, will you join us?"

Hank pulled his chair into Maggie's office while Maggie led Irena to one of the visitor chairs and Doris sat in the other with her apron full of supplies bunched up around her. Maggie handed Irena a box of tissues.

"What happened here?" Maggie looked at Hank and Doris.

Irena blew her nose loudly just as Doris was going to speak. Then the brief story tumbled out, with both Irena and Doris cutting each other off to make their points.

"Okay, both of you, please be quiet now." Maggie tried to keep the frustration out of her voice. "I understand what happened. Do you?"

Both women stared at her.

"I thought I gave Irena a compliment," Doris said. "I wanted her to know that I like her. Chester does too. We don't want her sent back to anywhere. We hear things on the news as this national election heats up. Depending on who wins, there won't be any more of those refugees coming to our country. But I'm sure Irena will be allowed to stay."

"See!" Irena screeched and looked at Maggie. "Eet's like dey arrn't humans!"

Maggie took a deep breath. She knew this was a deeply divisive issue, not just in Cherish but throughout the country. She also knew she couldn't fix it. Doris, in the pageantry of her ignorance, had stirred up all of the fears of Irena's youth. But Irena wasn't feeling them only for herself. She felt them for an unknown family from Syria, who had been through far worse things than she had endured.

"Irena, you are not the only so-called refugee sitting in this office. We all are. My great-grandparents came over from the Netherlands. Doris and Hank also had relatives who came from some other country. Unless, of course, one of them is a Native American."

Doris looked slightly confused. Hank nodded his head. Then he piped up.

"My ancestors came from Wales. You're right, Pastor Maggie, we've all come from someplace else. And then when we got here, we treated the people who could truly call this land theirs in a despicable way. The Native Americans have suffered and still do because of us."

Maggie nodded her head, then continued. "Our country is made up of foreigners and refugees. We aren't better than, or above, any other nationality or race. We are all equal. Some people like to think they are more important because of their skin color, the size of their bank account, their religion, or their race. They are fools." She looked at Doris. "I know you thought you were being kind to Irena, but your words let her know that you think of her as 'foreign.'"

"Well, she is!" Doris said.

"And so are you. Where are your ancestors from?"

"Well, my mother's parents were from Hungary. My father's parents were from Greece and England. There's some Norwegian or Swedish in there somewhere." Doris looked thoughtful for a moment, as if this news was just sinking in for the first time.

"And what about Chester?"

"His real name is Charles. He's German on his father's side and Polish on his mother's side. His parents came over from Germany when his mother was pregnant with him."

"You know," said Hank thoughtfully, "my maternal grandma was Irish."

"Right. And Irena is Romanian," Maggie said decisively. "It doesn't matter how far back you go, a relative of yours came over here on a boat. What if you were told you had to go back? What if you couldn't go with your spouse? Or your children were taken from you, or you were locked up in a refugee camp? This is happening in our world. There are people who treat other people the way Irena described: like wastepaper. It is intolerable!" Maggie took a deep breath and got herself under control. She was getting preachy.

She said more quietly, "This church will follow the teachings of Jesus Christ. We will love those who are different from us in any way. We will recognize the humanity in all people. We will welcome the stranger. We will feed the hungry, house the homeless, care for the sick, love the unlovable, visit the prisoner."

There was a cough.

"Pastor Maggie."

The four people in the office turned and looked at the door.

"That's exactly what I would like to talk to you about."

8

Julia Benson stood in the doorway. Julia had lived in Cherish with her daughter, Hannah, for the past year. She'd come in search of Redford Johnson, her abusive ex-husband who owed her child support, but his sins turned out to be much larger than child support evasion. Julia marveled at the evil of which Redford was capable.

With Redford in jail, Julia finally breathed easily again. She'd embraced her new job at the local newspaper, the *Cherish Life and Times,* and the unimaginable gift of a free home from Cassandra Moffet. Julia had been able to let the heaviness of life ebb away and begin to find some comfort in her new community. Once surly and combative, she was now involved and finding joy in many corners of her life.

She did not look joyful standing in Maggie's doorway.

"Come in, Julia," Maggie said.

She looked at the others, and with a little nod, she excused them. They filed out of her office with plenty to think about. Julia waited for the others to leave and stepped into the office. Maggie closed the door and offered Julia one of the cream-colored visitor chairs. Maggie sat in the other.

"How are you, Julia?"

"Not great."

Maggie felt her hands begin to sweat. She sensed another battle coming straight for her.

"I'll get to the point. Since March, you have made visits to the prison. You visit a terrible person who has terrorized me and could harm my child. Why do you do it?"

Maggie was caught off guard. Only a small group of people knew she went to the prison, but a small group in a small town meant a large percentage of people knew about the visits. She believed she was a good pastor to painstakingly visit Redford in prison, practically a martyr. Now she wondered if she'd been blind to the fact that this action hurt another of her parishioners, one who had already been traumatized by Redford.

"Julia, I'm so sorry. I've been visiting Redford because I thought it was the right thing to do. I never thought about what it must feel like for you."

"In a word, betrayal." Julia's face was hard.

Maggie felt as if she'd been slapped.

"Listen," Julia said, "you, this church, and this town have been so good to me and to Hannah." Julia's nose crinkled, and Maggie saw tears in her eyes. "I'll never understand why Cassandra gave me a house or why all of you have loved and cared for us. We came here as total strangers." Maggie handed her the tissue box, and Julia blew her nose. "But Redford hurt me so badly. I know he would have hurt Hannah. She was the only reason I was able to leave him. When he went to jail, I felt like life had righted itself. Justice was finally served. But you go and visit him—pastor Goody Two-shoes. You don't get it! There are some people who are just evil. I'd like to know what you have told him about me. About Hannah. He has no right to know anything about us, do you understand that? You can't fix him. There aren't enough prayers or visits or second chances. He will destruct and destroy, but I refuse to live in the desperation I left behind. If we need to move, we will." Julia took another tissue, wiped her eyes, and blew her nose again. Then she looked straight into Maggie's eyes. "Either you are my pastor, or you are his. But you can't be both."

Maggie couldn't gather herself. She felt her breath quicken. She heard Julia's words but couldn't get her thoughts organized enough to respond.

Julia stood abruptly. "I've got to get to work. But you know my mind. Pastor Maggie." The last two words were like nails as Julia left the office.

"Pastor Maggie?" Hank's voice was quiet. "I'm sorry to disturb you, but you have a phone call. Should I take a message?"

Maggie turned and faced Hank. "No, I'll take it. Do you know who it is?"

"A Myrna Barnes." Hank hesitated. "It looks like our friend Julia is having a rough day." Hank didn't usually butt into Maggie's private meetings. "It's just that when she left, she seemed distressed. Is there anything we can do for her?"

"There's something *I* can do," Maggie said as she stood. Her face burned with humiliation at Julia's words. "I think I'm living in what could be called a 'teachable moment,' Hank. I don't like it much. I'll take that call." She moved around her desk and picked up the phone.

Hank left the office without his curiosity satisfied.

"Hello, this is Pastor Maggie."

"Myrna Barnes, well, almost Barnes. Do you do weddin's?"

"Well, yes." Maggie was surprised by the brevity of the woman on the other end of the line.

"Jasper Barnes and I wanna get hitched. No other pastor in town will do it because we live together. Not that it's any of their gosh darn business. I'm sick of bein' told I live in sin. Do you do weddin's for everybody, or do you pick and choose like the rest of the hypocrites?"

Maggie had to stifle a laugh. Something about this woman's direct-ness and irritability tickled her.

"I would be happy to meet with you and Jasper. When were you thinking of getting married?" Maggie opened her calendar and flipped through the months into the following year.

"Friday."

Maggie gasped and snorted at the same time and began to cough uncontrollably. She moved the phone away from her mouth, coughed hard to clear her throat, and took a deep breath.

"Excuse me. Do you mean *this* Friday?" she asked. Her throat tick-led, and her eyes were watering.

"Yes."

"That's in three days."

"Yes."

"Do you have a marriage license? It takes a minimum of three days to pick it up from the county clerk's office in Ann Arbor once you apply." Maggie was reeling.

"Well, blast it all. We didn't think of that. We also didn't think we'd have so much trouble findin' someone to do the deed. Lot of snobs out there in the so-called church. But we never once thought about a license. Just a sec, I better write this down." Maggie could hear a drawer being opened and Myrna rummaging around. "Okey dokey. I'll tell Jasper we have to get ourselves down to the courthouse, pronto! I guess we'll have to make it a week from Friday."

Maggie sighed. "I'm just curious, but why do you want a pastor? You could have a justice of the peace?"

"Nope. It won't seem proper without someone like yourself. God is God, after all."

Maggie had no idea what this had to do with it but soldiered on. "Well, okay. Did you want to be married in our sanctuary here at Loving the Lord?" Maggie imagined the frenzy the staff would be thrown into if there was a wedding a week from Friday.

"Nope. We wanna get married right here. In our barn. We hear barn weddin's are gettin' popular. Plus, it's free. Speakin' of which, what do you charge for your services?"

Maggie pondered this. The weddings she had officiated so far in her young ministry were for friends. She'd refused to take a dime for any of them, but this felt different. She knew some pastors charged between four and five hundred dollars for the weeks of premarital counseling, the rehearsal, and the ceremony.

"One hundred dollars," she said.

"We can certainly handle that. Can we meet you ahead of time?"

"Yes. Where is your farm? I could drive out and you can show me your . . . barn, and we'll make the plans right there." Maggie wondered what she was getting herself into.

"Yep. We live off Scio Church Road." She gave Maggie the address. "What day works for you? Jasper gets home at four thirty."

Maggie looked at her calendar. "Well, I could come out today, if that works for you."

"Today it is. We'll see you around four thirty. Goodbye." Myrna clicked off.

This was going to be interesting.

She walked out of her office and looked at Hank. "I'm doing a wedding a week from Friday in a barn off Scio Church Road."

"Okay," Hank said. He waited for more.

"It would have been this Friday, but they didn't know they needed a license."

"Yes. Having a license is a tricky part of a wedding."

Hank could tell Maggie was working up to something else entirely. He just had to wait. She reached up and fingered the cross around her neck.

"Hank, our family is coming." Her eyes began to fill. "Darcy has gone forward and arranged for our Syrian family to be here in six weeks. He's doing it all by himself because our church is behaving so badly. Jack and I are going to help. I thought maybe you and Pamela could too. We will bring them to Cherish, and they will live in our condo. We will clean it up and get it all ready, full of whatever they might need." The tears began to flow. "And I know there are people in this church who are going to keep fighting this because they are scared of a stereotype and unwilling to meet this family face-to-face. I'm so excited to meet them, and I'm so angry at the intolerant people around here who judge without knowledge and live without conscience or heart!" *Sob.* Maggie grabbed a tissue out of the box on Hank's desk.

Hank calmly looked at Maggie. "What should we do first?"

Maggie snorted. She wiped her nose and looked at Hank with her weepy eyes, then she smiled.

"Thank you."

"Of course."

Maggie pulled herself together. Hank's no-nonsense and practical response was exactly what she needed.

"Fortunately, the condo is furnished, except for a couple of beds where Jack's office used to be. We will need food, toys, and once they get here and we know their sizes, new clothes. We'll need help at some point registering the children for school, but I think that will take some time. They will need to adjust to being out of the refugee camp into a whole new world."

"Is there anything else we can do at the condo? I'm sure Dr. Jack kept things in good repair, but are there small things we could do to make it more comfortable?" Hank was ready for action.

"I'll ask him. What do we do about the people here who will fight this?"

"They are allowed to have their opinion. But if Darcy is going ahead with this, it is no longer a church issue. It's private."

"But isn't that depressing, Hank? We have this amazing opportunity to do something Jesus would be busy with, and it will get swept away because it's Darcy's private project. What is wrong with this church?"

"Pastor Maggie, I'm sorry, but you are going to have to stop. You are right, the church is not acting like the church. This issue is not going to be solved quickly or easily. People are afraid. We have a political climate in this nation which encourages the fear of anyone different. Who would have guessed we'd be living like this in 2016? Hopefully, that ugliness is not going to last once the election happens in November. But for now, we must carry on with our plans. Pamela and I are with you every step of the way. Just tell us what to do, and it will be done."

It was true. The political climate in the country had been building, with two campaigns fighting very ugly battles. But one was more insidious. It was giving rise to hatred—hatred of "the other." People were either appalled by the rhetoric or they seized upon it with a vengeance. People who wanted to hate now had license to do so. In two and a half months there would be an election and an answer. But whatever that would be, a displaced family coming from a Muslim country would certainly feel hatred from someone. Maggie couldn't change that.

"I'll talk with Jack and Darcy. We need a meeting to do some 'welcome home' planning. Thanks, Hank."

"You're welcome. Now if you don't mind, I need to finish this week's bulletin." He gave her a grin.

"I'm going home to clean up my sermon and grab some lunch before Lacey gets here. I need a cup of tea."

"You do that. I'll hold down the fort around here."

Hank turned to his computer and began typing.

At one o'clock, refreshed with tea and peanut butter on graham crackers, Maggie pushed through the sanctuary doors. She had worked her sermon around and was feeling both nervous and excited for Sunday.

"Did you get some lunch, Hank?" she asked, looking at his desk for evidence.

"I must confess, I went across the street to The Sugarplum and enjoyed a large piece of strawberry-rhubarb pie a la mode. I figure I got my servings of fruit, veg, and dairy." He grinned. Everyone knew Hank had a sweet tooth.

Maggie looked down and noticed a bright-red splotch on Hank's blue shirt. She didn't say anything.

"How was Mrs. Popkin today?" Maggie asked.

"Dandy. It was busy, so she was happy. Her new homemade soups smelled delicious, and her salads were going left and right. She has turned that bakery into quite a little restaurant."

Mrs. Popkin had been running The Sugarplum Bakery for as long as anyone could remember. Nothing made her happier than feeding people.

The door to Hank's office opened, and Lacey Campbell walked in.

"Well, hi there, Hankster and PM. What's shaking?" Lacey was dressed in her black work clothes with her signature red lips. Her delicate nose ring lay against her left nostril.

"Just waiting for you to show up," Maggie said, laughing.

"Hey, Hankster, you have a very red stain on your shirt. Did Irena stab you with one of her fingernails or did you spill something again?"

Hank looked down. "Darn." Then he looked at Lacey. "It was Irena. Please tell her detective boyfriend she's a menace to society."

"Speaking of Detective Crunch," Maggie said, "remind me to give him a call, will you, Hank?"

Hank wrote a note on his pad of paper while Lacey and Maggie went into her office.

Lacey owned the We Work Miracles Beauty Salon in town. She had also been on the mission trip to Ghana. Lacey was a lesbian. When she told her parents and her sister many years ago, her parents had told her she was going straight to hell. They hurled so much hatred at her, she left home and changed her name from Hannah to Lacey. She packed up her few belongings and moved from Bloomington, Indiana, to the big city of Chicago. She arrived with her new name to her new life. She put herself through cosmetology training, worked for a large salon in Chicago, and began to save money bit by bit. Eventually, she'd moved to Cherish and literally set up shop. She lived with her new name and her old shame, frosting her life (and people's hair) with a sense of humor she had discovered once she was in Chicago and far away from home.

She'd kept her secret, until it became too much to bear and the words of her parents haunted her continually. She'd met Pastor Maggie and gone on the church mission trip, hoping God might forgive her if she did. Then one night at the volunteer house in Bawjiase, Ghana, she sat in the dark and told Pastor Maggie her story—her identity. Expecting to be ridiculed or rejected, she only received grace and love from her pastor. Lacey then tried to reestablish a relationship with her parents. Not only were they shocked to see her at the door but they were disgusted by her name change and chosen profession. The fact that she claimed to "still be a lesbian" was the final straw.

Leaving home that second time felt more like freedom than exile. Lacey had tried her best to explain who she was and why she believed she was truly loved by God. She wanted to be loved by her family as well, but they could not let go of their rigid religious beliefs. It had been easier to cut her out of their lives than to have a conversation and perhaps a conversion of love themselves.

Now Lacey sat next to Maggie in the cream-colored visitor chairs. Maggie was aware of Lacey's visit home in March. Lacey had come back to Cherish and decided to move forward with some joy in her life, and Maggie supported her parishioner and friend completely.

"How's it going, Lacey?" Maggie asked.

"Well, PM, it's going pretty darn great. That's why I'm here. You know Lydia, right?"

In April, Lacey had hired Lydia Marsh to help at the beauty shop. Lacey was able to have the occasional weekend off, and Lydia enjoyed getting to know everyone in Cherish. But Maggie had never seen her in church, even after making several invitations.

"Of course, I know Lydia. She's trimmed my hair twice this summer. She's fantastic. I wish she'd come to church."

"She probably won't ever do that. It's not her bag. Anyway, she and I are dating."

Maggie was thrilled. She knew many of the people at church and in Cherish sat in Lydia's salon chair and appreciated her as much as they appreciated Lacey. She also knew this would be the third "fight" her church would undertake, along with the childcare center and re-settling the Syrian family. There were still a few people who thought homosexuality was a sin. Maggie had no patience for this attitude of ignorance.

"I'm so happy for you!"

"I feel unbelievably in love, and it's crazy because I have never felt this way before in my life."

Lacey smiled and then laughed. Maggie understood the giddiness. She and Jack had kept their relationship quiet at the beginning. The secret was part of the excitement. Clandestine evenings together were that much more fun.

"Well, how did it all start?" Maggie asked.

"I met Lydia in Chicago at cosmetology school. We liked each other right away, but she accepted a job in Minneapolis. I already knew I wanted to come to Cherish. I had an aunt who used to live here, and we visited every summer when I was little. After my aunt died, we stopped, but I have happy memories of this town. Anyway, Lydia called me from Minneapolis after my disastrous visit back home in March.

She wanted to work together and also be together. I was so happy. But now we are in idyllic Cherish and have to live in secret."

"Are you thinking of moving?" Maggie could understand if they were. "I hope not."

"We don't want to move. We want to live here and be a couple. But we haven't figured out how to do that. We do know there is a risk our whole business could be ruined."

"I think that's a little dramatic. We have some small-minded peo-ple around here, but I believe for the most part the people of Cherish are open-hearted and open-minded." Maggie wanted to believe that so badly it hurt. "Can the two of you come over for dinner some evening next week? Let's figure this out together. If you want to."

"What if someone sees us?" Lacey asked, losing her lightness.

"What if someone does? I mean, it's up to the two of you if you want to be public with your relationship. But you don't need to hide. Your love is something to celebrate."

"I'll talk to Lydia and let you know. Is that okay?"

"Of course, you nut."

Lacey looked at Maggie. "You will never know what you did for me in Ghana. You helped me find my life.

"I'm sorry you had lost it for a while. I'm so happy you and Lydia found each other. Call me later and let me know about next week."

The two women stood up and embraced.

"And by the way," Lacey said as she opened the office door to leave, "that whole Syrian family project, Lydia and I are in one hundred per-cent. Free haircuts and pedicures for all. If there's anything else we can do to help, just let one of us know. Love is going to win this one, PM."

9

Jack left his office and drove to the condo. Mr. and Mrs. Stein, his neighbors, were sitting on their front porch as he pulled into the driveway. He got out and walked across the lawn to the couple.

"Hi, Jacob and Deborah. How are you doing today?" he asked with a smile.

"Jack, we haven't seen you in such a while," Deborah said she stood and shook Jack's hand, followed by Jacob.

"I know. I guess married life is taking up all my spare time." He laughed.

They all sat at the small table on the porch.

"We've missed you in the neighborhood. How do like the parsonage?" Deborah asked as she poured Jack some lemonade.

"I like the person I'm living with a lot." He smiled. "The parsonage is fine, sometimes a bit like a fishbowl."

"I would imagine," Jacob said. "Right next to the church. People are nosy. It's human nature."

Jack looked over at his condo. "I've stopped by tonight to let you know my condo won't be so quiet in about six weeks."

"Are you moving back in?" Deborah asked hopefully.

"We aren't, but we are working with others to bring a refugee family from Syria to America. They need a place to live, and my condo is sitting here empty."

He waited to see if and how their faces changed, realizing he was feeling more anxious about their reaction than he had thought. Jacob and Deborah looked at him, interested.

"You see," he continued, "there are so many displaced families because of the war in Syria. Families are sometimes separated, or if they stay together, they end up in a refugee camp with nothing. This particular family has been in a camp for two years already." Jack could feel himself begin to sweat.

Jacob and Deborah remained speechless.

"They have children. Four children who haven't been in school this entire time."

Jack stopped and looked at his neighbors. They were in their seventies. They were Jewish. And he was talking to them about a large Syrian family moving in next door.

Holy cow!

After a quick phone call to Detective Keith Crunch, Maggie left her office and drove south of town toward Scio Church Road. She had Google Mapped the address to Myrna and Jasper's farm. The nice Google lady told her which way to turn and then announced when she arrived at her destination.

The August heat was relentless as Maggie walked up to the old farmhouse. It had wooden steps leading up to a long porch and the front door. Maggie noticed dog toys and a large water bowl, along with two pine rocking chairs badly in need of a coat of varnish. Maggie knocked on the door and was greeted by a small white-haired woman of about eighty.

Oh dear. Is this Myrna?

"Hello, Myrna? I'm Pastor Maggie."

"I'm not Myrna. I'm Myra, Myrna's mother. I just added an 'n' to my name and gave it to her when she was born so's people could tell us apart. So, you're the parson, heh?" Then she turned her head and shouted, "Myrna! The lady parson is at the door!"

Maggie heard several noises at once. Dogs barking in different keys, a loud crash and glass breaking, a high-pitched squeal, and many feet stomping downstairs—or upstairs. Who knew? Maggie saw Myra step away from the door and then, like a tsunami coming to shore, she was immediately knocked over by four large dogs, three young children, and a pig. She realized too late that her gauzy skirt had floated up as she fell to the porch. One of the children began to laugh.

"Look, you can see her undies!"

More laughter.

Maggie stood as quickly as she could and patted her skirt down. Her long blonde hair was hanging in her face, and her right shoulder blade ached. That was far more of a welcome than she had been prepared for.

The dogs took that moment to sniff her in every private and un-private place. As she pushed them away, she felt something wet on her foot. She was relieved to find it was just snot from the pig's snout as he, or she, investigated Maggie's toes.

Someone took her left hand. She felt something sticky. Maggie looked down and saw a little girl with beautiful brown eyes and happy gaps where her front teeth should have been. Maggie smiled back at the little girl then looked at both their hands. A partially eaten Tootsie Roll stuck them together.

At the front door, a large woman appeared.

"Well, hi there. I'm Myrna."

Maggie took in the entire vision.

Myrna was a good foot taller than her mother. She wore a flowing, voluminous sea-green sundress, and her thick brown hair was held up in a wayward bun with two painted chopsticks. She had bright-brown eyes and beautiful white teeth, which shown out from her tanned face. She also had a baby on each hip. Maggie was quite certain she was looking at Mother Earth.

A large SUV rumbled down the driveway and pulled into the open garage. Myrna's smile beamed. A lanky man got out of the vehicle just as dogs, kids, and pig whirled themselves down the steps and straight into the man's legs. With his arms outstretched, he bent down and seemed to embrace the entire menagerie. Myrna nudged past Maggie and walked with her babies down the steps.

Maggie watched the riot of happiness before her. It was a pure lovefest.

They slowly made their way back onto the porch. Myra had sidled up next to Maggie to watch her family.

"I'm sorry, Pastor Maggie, it's a busy time of the day, but it's the best time, right kids?" Myrna asked, looking at her brood.

A cacophony of children's voices and dog sounds, along with a few oinks, filled the air.

Myrna continued. "This is Jasper."

Maggie shook Jasper's hand. He had curly blond hair and small blue eyes that crinkled when he smiled. Maggie was surprised to see him wearing a suit and tie. Dust from the driveway and sticky handprints were on the pant leg of his trousers, but he didn't seem to mind. One of the babies reached out to him from Myrna's arms, and he took the little one easily.

"How do you do?" he asked Maggie.

Maggie was going to speak, but Myrna continued. She pointed to the three older children. "This is Myla, Mika, and Misha. The twins are Manny and Milford. And this," she said, slowly waving her long arm, "is our home."

Maggie waited to see if Myrna was done. It seemed she was.

"It's a real pleasure to meet all of you. What a beautiful family!"

One of the dogs licked Maggie's hand, just as she felt snout snot on the calf of her leg.

"Of course, we must introduce you to the pups and the piggy. We have Munchkin over there, Mable is by the rockin' chair, Magnus is lickin' your hand, and Melvin is in his bed down there." She pointed to the other end of the porch. "He is a good ole boy."

"So many 'M' names!" Maggie laughed. "Do you ever get them mixed up?"

"All the time."

"What about this little pig?" Maggie asked.

"Well now, that's Juliet. Jasper got to name her. Shall we go out to the barn?"

"I'll change my clothes and meet you over there," Jasper said, taking one of the "M" babies with him.

Maggie followed the crazy parade of animals and children out to a large gray barn. Hay was stacked to the roof on one side. Other bales were scattered around haphazardly. It made Maggie think of Andrew and Brynn and their engagement day.

Myrna walked to the back of the barn. "We thought we could get married back here, and our family and friends can just stand over there." She pointed toward the large doors. "They can sit on the hay bales, if they want."

The children began climbing on the bales and chasing each other with shouts of "You can't get me!" As expected, the dogs began to bark and chase the children around the barn. Juliet began to roll in the hay, making happy piggy noises. Myrna and Myra watched with amusement, and Maggie was just grateful the dogs had taken their invasive noses away from her for a bit.

Jasper, now dressed in jeans and a Harley-Davidson T-shirt, came in holding a baby.

"Pastor Maggie, it's nice of you to do this for us," Jasper said. "We've meant to do it for about ten years now, but somehow we kept forgetting."

Maggie looked around at the children. "I can see you have been somewhat distracted. I mentioned to Myrna that you two will need to go to Ann Arbor and get a marriage license. Now what would you like in the ceremony?" Maggie pulled out a pad of paper and a pen, ready to write.

They spent the next hour planning the ceremony, with many interruptions from kids and pets. Maggie was enchanted. Myrna had specific ideas of what she wanted for her special day, while Jasper and Myra chimed in with their ideas.

"So, can you come a little early next Friday for a walk-through?" Myrna asked.

"Of course. I'll be here around four o'clock, and we'll make sure we're all set and ready." Maggie bent down and scratched Juliet on her tummy. "I'm so happy to know you all. And I'm really looking forward to next week."

"I see you have a weddin' ring. Do you have a husband?"

"I do. His name is Jack."

"Well, you better bring him along. We all want to meet him."

"If it works for his schedule, he'll be here. Thank you for the invitation." Maggie impulsively hugged Myrna and Myra. She kissed the children and petted the dogs and shook Jasper's hand with enthusiasm. "I'll see you next week."

As she drove home, it was hard for her to believe that Katharine Marie had been born just that very morning. With all the happenings of the day, it felt like a very long week had been crammed into a Tuesday.

Jack sat patiently. Jacob and Deborah had stopped sipping their lemonade, but he couldn't read their expressions. A bird was singing in a nearby bush. Jack thought it was a cardinal.

"When will they be here?" Jacob asked.

"October third." Jack began to quickly think of where else they could put the family.

"Do you know when exactly they will arrive?" Deborah asked quietly.

"I don't know, but I can find out."

"We will prepare their first supper," Deborah said. Jacob nodded. "Just let us know ahead of time. After that, we will be available to help in any way. What an extraordinary thing you are doing."

Jack sighed in relief. "It's a few people from our church, one man in particular, who has made this happen."

"Are the family members Muslim?" Jacob asked.

"Yes." Jack waited.

"They will need to find a mosque. I will look into that and talk with our rabbi. She's very connected with the interfaith organization in Ann Arbor," Jacob said.

"Thank you," Jack replied. "Your kindness is, well, overwhelming."

"Why?" Deborah asked.

"We've had so many people, not just of our own faith, but from our own church fight this tooth and nail. Maggie and I seem to always be on the defensive. You have graciously and gracefully welcomed these strangers from another land and another faith. I can't wait to tell Maggie."

They sipped their lemonade and chatted about happenings in the neighborhood. When Jack left, he reflected during his short drive home that he had been with "angels unawares" and his soul was lifted.

10

It was Sunday morning. Maggie had worked all week on the craziest idea for a sermon she'd ever had. She hadn't told Jack. She hadn't told Hank. She'd sat with her computer and her imagination for part of every day that week. She'd tweaked, questioned, tossed, and finally completed her sermon.

Now it was time to preach it.

Before worship began, she went into the women's restroom and locked the door. She knew there would be no other place in the church where she could have a few quiet minutes alone. She was excited and curious about how it would go. It was too late to change anything now. She took a few deep breaths and prayed for God to take over and speak to the congregation through her.

When she opened the door, Irena was standing there, tapping her tiny angry foot.

"Vat you doing?" she barked.

"What do you mean?" Maggie asked, startled. Then she became irritated. "Irena, sometimes you are so rude."

"You veren't going to de bathroom. De toilet didn't flush. No water rrun in de sink," Irena said accusingly.

"No. No water ran, not that it's any of your business. This was the only place I could have a few seconds alone. I needed to collect my thoughts. But the restroom is all yours now." She wanted to add "you little weirdo," but she refrained.

She walked past Irena and found Marla sitting in one of the cream-colored visitor chairs in her office.

"Marla! Good. Thanks for your help this morning."

"My pleasure, but I'm still not sure what I'm doing," Marla said with a smile. "I've also enlisted Addie to help. She should be here in a second."

"Good morning!" Addie breezed into Maggie's office.

"Hi, Addie," Maggie and Marla said in unison.

Addie was Marla's daughter. Her long brown hair was pulled up in a wavy ponytail, which swung across her back as she looked at the two women in front of her. Addie had been the youngest member of the mission trip team that went to Ghana earlier in the year. She had graduated from Cherish High School in June and was ready to head to Hope College in Holland. Even though it was only three hours away, Marla felt as if she would never see her daughter again.

"What are we up to today?" Addie asked as she plopped down next to her mother.

"Thanks ahead of time for your help," Maggie began, then she went on to detail what she would need them to do when it came time for the sermon.

"This sounds like fun!" Addie enthused. Addie always had enough enthusiasm to fill a room.

After Maggie detailed the plan, she heard the first notes of the organ. Irena was at her post, no doubt shushing all parishioners who talked and greeted one another. Maggie grabbed her Bible and sermon, followed Marla and Addie out of her office, and slipped through the secret door, which was a little difficult to do that morning. She sat in the chair behind the pulpit.

When it was time for the sermon, she left the pulpit and opened the secret door. In the silence of the sanctuary, she pulled out one of the rocking chairs from the nursery. She had hidden it there earlier. She dragged the chair to the middle of the altar, then shut the secret door.

"I'd like to invite all the children to come forward, including the youth group," she said.

The congregation looked confused, but Marla and Addie stood up and began leading the children forward. The members of the youth group followed. Maggie was thrilled when Maria Gutierrez came forward with Marcos and Gabby. Lynn Porter brought Sammy, but he had other ideas—being two years old. He began to toddle around and got a little too close to the altar flowers before his mother grabbed him and cuddled him in her lap. The best surprise was Bill and Sylvia cradling Katharine Marie. They made their way to the front.

While everyone began to drape themselves on the altar and steps, Maggie took a seat in the rocking chair. She had placed her sermon in a notebook that was covered with pictures of baby wild animals. The smaller children looked at the pictures, pointed, and whispered the names of the animals to one another.

"Thank you for joining me," Maggie said. "For the sermon today, I have a story that I wrote for you this week."

She looked at the children first, then lifted her gaze to the adults in the sanctuary. She saw Jack, and he grinned at her.

She began.

"The title of this story is 'Enough.'"

> Once there was a backyard full of beautiful oak trees and pine trees, a lovely, soggy marsh, and a small pond. A tall man and a small woman owned the backyard. From their window, they loved to watch the many beautiful birds and animals that lived there. The tall man and the small woman set out bird feeders and suet cages. They filled them every day. They set out a bowl of cat chow under their deck for the stray cat who visited regularly. The food was an invitation for all the backyard guests. The man and the woman did this to honor their Great God by caring for creation.

"Are the tall man and the small woman you and Dr. Jack?" Carrie Moffet interrupted.

Maggie smiled. "Maybe."

Marla pulled Carrie onto her lap and whispered, "Let's just listen to Pastor Maggie."

Maggie continued,

> Mrs. Snuffles, a mama bunny, was sitting under the bird feeder for breakfast. She often brought her children with her, but this morning they were too sleepy to get out of their nice bunny-fur nest. "We'll come in a minute, Mama," Henri said with a yawn. The other bunnies sniffed in agreement. "That's fine, babies," Mrs. Snuffles said, "but don't miss breakfast, my dear ones." She covered them with fur from the nest and hopped off to the bird feeder.
>
> Mrs. Snuffles quietly ate the fallen birdseed while contemplating her world. Mrs. Snuffles was the oldest and wisest animal in the large backyard. Every morning Mrs. Snuffles said a long, loving prayer thanking her Great God for the backyard, for every bird and animal (almost all by name), and for the bird feeders that provided everyone with enough to eat. The bird feeders were where all the animals could eat while they talked.
>
> Mrs. Snuffles jumped as she felt the fast breeze of feathers coming too close to her large, soft bunny ears. She saw a flash of blue and knew immediately who it was: Young Screech, the blue jay. Young Screech was the son of Old Screech and his wife, Squawks. Young Screech had been told by his parents that the bird feeder was only for blue jays. It wasn't meant for bunnies, deer, raccoons, squirrels, ducks, cats, or any other animal or bird whatsoever! The other animals

and birds had to put up with the unfriendly screech-es and squawks from the blue jays, but everyone still came to the bird feeder to eat. And everyone always had enough.

Young Screech landed close to Mrs. Snuffles and fluffed out his bright-blue feathers. "What are you doing here, Mrs. Snuffles?" he said in an unfriendly, sneering voice. Mrs. Snuffles finished chewing the seed in her mouth, then said, "Young Screech, good morn-ing. What are you doing here?"

"This is my bird feeder! Squawk!"

"No, Young Screech, it isn't. And you know that. This bird feeder is for everyone who lives here." Mrs. Snuffles sighed deeply. Often, she was able to get to the feeder before any of the blue jays showed up. But occa-sionally, she had to share her breakfast time with one or more of them. It tired out her patience. And she was a very patient bunny.

Just then, Mrs. Snuffles heard a rustling through the tall marsh grasses in the backyard. She was happy to see a black nose come through the grasses followed by a small masked face.

"Hi, Bandit!" Mrs. Snuffles said to her dear friend Bandit the raccoon.

Bandit sniffed around the bird feeder for her favor-ite seed, her round black nose bobbing up and down.

"Hi, Snuffs. How's it going?" Bandit asked, taking a mouthful of seed. Then she looked around and saw Young Screech.

"Hey!" Bandit said with her mouth full of seeds. "What are you doing here? You aren't pretending this is your bird feeder again, are you?" Bandit didn't have any of the patience Mrs. Snuffles had.

Young Screech was just getting ready to be rude, when Mrs. Snuffles said, "Bandit, aren't you usually asleep by now? I don't often see you here until dusk."

"I thought I'd come for a little snack. The tall man and small woman always leave cat chow outside for that stray cat, Smudge, and I usually get to clean up the leftovers. Last night Smudge ate it all! So I needed a little snack before bed." Bandit was chomping merrily as she told her story. Her mother must not have taught her to chew with her mouthed closed.

Then there was more rustling in the marsh grasses. Mrs. Snuffles watched as Pockets, Pouches, and Bags, the chipmunk brothers, came scurrying up to the birdseed.

"Good morning, ladies," Pouches said as he began cramming sunflower seeds into the sides of his mouth. His brothers did the same. Soon their faces were three times their normal size.

"Good morning, boys," Mrs. Snuffles said. "Storing up, are you?"

"As always," Pockets said with a funny grin.

"You can never be too prepared!" Bags chimed in.

Mrs. Snuffles wiggled her nose at them. "But you always have enough, don't you? Even during the coldest winter." The chipmunks nodded lopsidedly.

Everyone watched as Mr. and Mrs. Scarlet gracefully swirled down to the ground. The cardinal couple were loved by all. They were polite, and they sang so beautifully. They were quickly followed by Robin and his wife, Robinette, who glided to a perfect landing near the cardinals.

"SCREECH!" Young Screech yelled. "None of you belong here! My parents said so! This bird feeder is only for the blue jays!"

Nuts and Honey came chasing down the tree, with several of their babies following at a quick speed. Mrs. Snuffles always marveled at the squirrels. They could actually hang upside down on the bird feeders and eat. How did the food get to their tummies when they were hanging upside down? It was a puzzle. Mrs. Snuffles had to admit that sometimes she mixed up the names of the baby squirrels, but there were so many of them. And they all looked alike. Oh dear!

"Hi, Nuts! Hi, Honey!" said Bandit with her mouth still full of seeds. "Hi, baby squirrels!"

"Hello, Mrs. Bandit, Mrs. Snuffles, the Scarlets, the Robins, Young Screech, Pockets, Pouches, and Bags . . . Let's see, is that everyone?" asked Nuts. All the baby squirrels began rolling around and swishing their tails at one another.

"Ahhhhhh! Screeeeeeech! Get away from my bird feeder!" hollered Young Screech.

"Then where shall the rest of us eat?" Mrs. Snuffles asked, as she did every time she was confronted with this ridiculousness.

"I don't know, and I don't care!" Young Screech sneered.

Mrs. Snuffles knew Young Screech was too young to really believe what he was saying. He'd heard this meanness from his parents and mimicked them. It was a shame. Mrs. Snuffles looked up and saw Gladys Number Seven coming through the marsh grasses from the pond. She was so elegant and delicate. Such a lovely deer. There were twelve Gladyses living in and near the backyard. Mrs. Snuffles loved them all.

"Good morning, Gladys Number Seven!" Mrs. Snuffles, Bandit, Pouches, Pockets, and Bags all said in unison.

"Well, good morning, dear friends!" Gladys Number Seven said as she blinked her large brown eyes at them.

"Where are the other Gladyses this morning?" Mrs. Snuffles asked.

"Some are drinking at the pond, and some are already sleeping. I heard you all talking, and I just had to come over. Have you heard the terrible things Old Screech and Squawks are saying? They are starting a petition to keep us all out of the backyard. They are saying we don't deserve to live here or eat here because we aren't blue jays." Then she caught sight of Young Screech.

"That's right," Young Screech said and began prancing around, stretching out his beautiful blue feathers. "We're going to get you all out of here. You don't belong. This is our food and our backyard!"

"Quack, quack, quack, quack," came up from the marsh grasses. It was Richard and Delores. They had waddled over from the pond behind Gladys Number Seven for breakfast at the bird feeders. The two ducks nodded their beaks to the other animals.

"Good morning, Richard and Delores!" the other animals exclaimed.

"How is the nest?" asked Bandit, who longed for a family of her own.

"Just dandy!" Richard said with pride.

"We've got six eggs," said Delores. "I hate to eat and run, but I must get back to sitting!" She gobbled up the seed around her.

Following right behind the tail feathers of Richard and Delores came Henri, Bernadette, Vivienne, and Nicolas. All four baby bunnies were yawning, and Vivienne's ears were flopping over to one side. She must not have had time to straighten them before leaving the nest.

Mr. and Mrs. Scarlet were now sitting up on the bird feeder, enjoying the sunflower seeds. They purposely spilled many seeds for Pockets, Pouches, and Bags to cram into their cheeks. They knew there was always enough. Mrs. Snuffles cleared her throat.

"I think it may be time for a backyard meeting. If the blue jays are working so hard to keep us out, then it's time to talk about this. Will everyone please come back at dusk?"

"We'll tell all the other birds today," said Mr. and Mrs. Scarlet.

"We'll help!" exclaimed Robin and Robinette.

Everyone nodded and finished their breakfasts. They would be back at dusk. Young Screech flew off quickly to tell his parents of the meeting. The blue jays had been working on their plan for many days. They believed anyone who wasn't a blue jay should NOT be allowed to eat any of the delicious seed from the bird feeders. Anyone who wasn't a blue jay should NOT be allowed to live in the backyard! The blue jays knew very well there was plenty of food. There were bags and bags of food the tall man and the small woman brought to the shed in the backyard. But the blue jays wanted to be the only ones in the backyard. No one who was different was welcome.

"That's so mean," piped in Kay. The smaller children nodded their heads.

Maggie continued:

Because Young Screech had informed the other blue jays of the backyard meeting, they were now prepared.

At dusk, the animals gathered under the bird feeders. Even Smudge came out for the meeting, keeping one eye on the cat chow bowl, in case Bandit tried to get there first. In the tops of the oak trees and the pine trees, sat the blue jays. They had gathered from the entire neighborhood. They had their mean plan ready.

Mrs. Snuffles, the wise bunny, began the meeting with a prayer, thanking their Great God for the backyard where there was always enough and where they could live peacefully together.

When she said "Amen," the blue jays began to squawk as loudly as they could. They were so loud no one could hear any more words from Mrs. Snuffles.

The other birds and animals became frightened as the blue jays began to swoop down. They pecked at all the Gladyses noses. They screeched in the ears of the baby bunnies and squirrels. They tore out chunks of fur from the furry animals, and they hit the other birds, along with Richard and Delores, with their strong blue wings. "You don't belong here!" they yelled. "You're not blue!" they screeched. "We will chase you out of here! You are different, and that means you are bad!" they hollered. "You are not as smart or beautiful as we are. You don't count!"

They were on the ground now trying to scare the small animals. Smudge ran to the cat chow bowl and tried to hide behind it. Pouches, Pockets, and Bags hid under a bush. They were so afraid. All the squirrel babies began to cry at once. They had never seen such meanness.

Maggie heard a little sob and looked up from the book. Molly and Penny were holding hands. Both little girls had tears falling down their cheeks. Addie quickly put her arms around them and hugged them close. The children were riveted.

Maggie continued:

Suddenly, one hungry, sleepy little animal came out from the marsh grasses. He hadn't been at breakfast that morning, but then again, he usually wasn't. He hadn't heard about the meeting at dusk. He just wanted something to eat. When the blue jays saw him come out of the marsh grasses, they all stopped their screeching. They all stopped their pecking. They immediately flew up to top of the oak trees and the pine trees, and they became silent.

Mrs. Snuffles looked up. Her ears were bleeding from the mean bites of the blue jays.

"Well, good evening, Tulip!" Mrs. Snuffles said. Henri, Bernadette, Vivienne, and Nicolas came out from under their mama's tummy, where she had protected them.

"Hi, Tulip!" they all said. All the animals chimed in with greetings to their little striped friend. Tulip the skunk smiled shyly. Then he yawned one more time. "Hi, everyone. What are you doing here?"

"We're having a backyard meeting. I'm sorry we forgot to tell you, Tulip," said Mrs. Snuffles. "The blue jays have been causing trouble again, but you scared them away. How did you do that?"

"Oh, gee. It was an accident. The other day when I was walking to the pond for a drink, Old Screech, Squawks, and Young Screech began to chase me. I was so afraid, my perfume . . . uh . . . went off. I'm afraid all three were covered." Tulip looked shyly at the ground, where he found a piece of corn and ate it.

The children began to giggle, as did some of the adults in the sanctuary.

Mrs. Snuffles hid a smile beneath her whiskers. Everyone knew about Tulip's "perfume," but only by accident. He was the sweetest, most gentle, timid little skunk any of them had ever met.

Mrs. Snuffles cleared her throat.

"Old Screech and all the blue jays, are you listening?"

"Yes! Yes! Screech! Squawk! Yes!" they said.

"We can't have any more of your cruelty. You cannot keep us from the backyard. We have been put here together. Your lack of tolerance and acceptance is, well, embarrassing. Can we all be friendly? Please?"

It took a little bit of time. There were many more meetings under the bird feeders. Some of the blue jays decided to leave the backyard for good, which was too bad. But Old Screech, Squawks, and Young Screech chose to stay. Young Screech learned to play with the Scarlet children, as well as Robin and Robinette's young ones. Old Screech never scared Tulip again but would holler from a distance, "Tulip! It's me, Old Screech. Do you have time for some breakfast and a chat?"

And the babies of the backyard grew. Bandit found a husband named Mask, and they had a family of their own. Three baby raccoons named Stripes, Wiggles, and Nosy enjoyed playing with all the other babies.

Richard and Delores had six beautiful ducklings, whom they paraded around the backyard each morning before their swimming lessons on the pond. All the Gladyses stayed protected in the backyard, where no one could harm them.

And the next winter—when it was very, very, very cold—the tall man and the small woman filled the bird feeders every day, sometimes twice. They filled the suet cages and put two bowls of cat chow under the deck instead of one. They did this because they loved the birds and animals. They wanted to honor their Great God by taking care of creation right in their own backyard. They wanted to make sure there was always enough.

As for Tulip—the sweet, gentle, timid skunk—he never shared his "perfume" unless he was very surprised or scared. Everyone understood.

And . . . shhhh . . . this is a secret: Tulip almost always made it to the bowl of cat chow before either Smudge the cat OR Bandit and the other raccoons. He just continued to let them think they were the only ones eating. He never ate the whole bowl. That would be rude. And there was enough food and enough backyard for all.

And the animals and birds and the tall man and the small woman lived peacefully together, just as their Great God intended it to be. Amen.

Maggie closed her notebook. The church was silent. Then she heard someone blow their nose. It was Darcy. He, Jennifer Becker, and his sister Priscilla sat together in the fourth pew. Darcy finished blowing, then rubbed his thumb across his eyes. *Is he crying?* As Maggie looked around, she saw others dabbing tissues against their eyes. She also saw some blank stares and glowering countenances. Apparently, her story had hit some chords, as she'd intended.

"Don't you mean, 'The End'?" asked Carrie.

Maggie looked down at Carrie and absorbed her question.

"No, Carrie, I mean 'Amen' because this story is my sermon today. I always say 'Amen' after a sermon. It means, 'So be it.'"

"Could you tell us a story every week?" Carrie persisted.

"Well, that's what I try to do, Carrie," Maggie said, chagrinned.

Maggie looked up and saw Darcy's hand in the air, as if he were in any classroom.

"Darcy?"

Everyone watched as Darcy stood up and walked to the front of the sanctuary.

Maggie held her breath as Darcy stood on the step below her in front of the congregation.

"I mean no disrespect, Pastor Maggie, and I'm not trying to hijack this worship service." He looked at Maggie. She nodded. "I'd just like to say that the sermon we just heard represents our beliefs if we want to call ourselves Christians or even just people of faith. I turned my back on this church, and all churches, early in my life. Religion seemed quaint and antiquated. It meant nothing in the midst of business, power, and prestige. But eight months ago, I was in the basement of this place packing food into Christmas baskets for people in our community. And then I delivered them and met folks face-to-face. Then my sister made me aware of another crisis happening across the world."

Priscilla didn't know if she wanted to take the credit for Darcy's newfound faith excursion. She'd never thought leaving a stack of magazines on Darcy's desk would cause such a change in her brother.

Darcy continued, "I would like to apologize. I made a decision and acted on it. When a group of people from this congregation went through the training at the Refugee Support Services, I thought we would be working together to help a family in dire need create a new life. When some of you seemed to put up a barrier to stop the family from entering our community, I decided to do it on my own. I judged you as intolerant and uninformed. I'm sorry. Pastor Maggie's sermon reminded me that I am part of a community. This community of Loving the Lord. I am part of you. I am thankful for that. We can all work together on this. This past week, I met with Pastor Maggie and Dr. Jack." Darcy looked at Maggie and then found Jack in the congregation. Darcy paused until they both gave him a nod. "They have made an incredibly generous donation to the cause to bring a Syrian family to Cherish. They have donated their condominium for the family to live in."

Little huffs and gasps fluttered around the congregation. Maggie stepped down to where Darcy was standing and spoke.

"Our church has an opportunity to do something that really matters," she said. "We can literally save the lives of a family who have lost everything. We are the ones who can welcome the strangers into our midst and care for them in basic and profound ways. They are not a threat. They are not terrorists. Muslims are not bad people. Let's break the lie-filled stereotypes we hear on television and live up to the standards of Jesus Christ. We are called to love our neighbor, not just the ones who look and think as we do."

She took a breath.

Before she could go on, she saw Martha Babcock stand and push her way out of the pew and down the aisle. Martha huffed loudly as she banged through the oak doors.

Maggie winced when she saw Chester and Doris stand and move past the people in their pew. They were both looking down at the carpet. When they got to the back of the sanctuary, Chester looked up.

"I'm sorry. We learned a lesson with the holiday baskets last year. We know there are needs in our community of Cherish, but this Syrian thing is going too far. Who knows what could happen once they are settled here? Doris and I cannot support this." They both turned and walked out.

A creak of leather brought all eyes to Charlotte. Dressed in her officer's uniform, the leather gun holster around her waist creaked as she stood up. Her husband, Fred, stood next to her. He looked down at their twins, Brock and Mason, and daughter Liz. The boys stayed seated until their father's gaze moved them to stand. They looked humiliated. Liz stayed seated, staring straight ahead.

"Danger is danger," Charlotte said. "I'll protect and guard this town my whole life long. With all the unrest in the world, and the terror attacks happening in so many countries now, I can't allow a Muslim family to live here."

Darcy stiffened. "You can't keep them out, Chief Tuggle. You don't have that much power."

Charlotte took the hit badly. "I certainly do. You will see just how much power I have. And it's not just me, Mr. Keller. There is an election soon, and you will see our country rise up and change the ways of this liberal government. The Republicans are ready to take back the country, and we will do so with a vengeance." She turned and left the church, followed by her family.

Charlotte was quite unaware of how her word choice was falling on the ears of the congregation of Loving the Lord. "Vengeance" was, perhaps, a poor but accurate choice.

Liz was last in the family pew. She turned and looked sadly at Addie before following her family out.

"Why are people leaving?" Carrie asked. "Are they blue jays?"

Maggie watched to see who might leave next.

Jim Chance, still in his wheelchair since a forklift accident at work, began to roll himself toward the back of the sanctuary. His wife, Cecelia, and two children, Bobby and Naomi, watched him from their pew.

"Cecelia! Kids! We're leaving."

Maggie was dismayed. They were a new family in the church and only because they had received holiday baskets when Jim was first out of work.

Cecelia's neck turned red, and the flush slowly moved up her face. Both Bobby and Naomi looked at the walls of the sanctuary. Cecelia had to decide if it was worth listening to Jim bellow again or just leave as quickly as possible. She stood up.

"Come on, kids," she whispered.

"I don't want to go," Naomi whispered back.

"Me either," said Bobby.

"We're leaving!" Jim yelled from the back of the church.

His family slowly left their pew and followed him through the bell tower and down the handicapped ramp.

Then Harold Brinkmeyer stood. "I want to say that I'm not against a group of people working on this resettlement project, but I can't be part of it. I think we could find ourselves in some legal trouble down the road. This is not going to be an easy process, and the election could make a difference in this whole plan. There's a chance the family won't even be able to stay."

Maggie winced again.

He looked down at his girlfriend, Ellen Bright. Ellen shook her head no. Harold shrugged and left the sanctuary.

Desperate to staunch her hemorrhaging congregation, Maggie said loudly, "Let us all turn to our closing hymn, 'Blest Be the Tie That Binds.'" She heard herself and caught the irony.

Irena had been waiting impatiently. She plunged into the hymn with a flourish. The organ rang out at full volume.

Maggie looked at her hymnal. She didn't want to see any more departures. Her "Enough" sermon hadn't made a difference. It was just a stupid children's story. Her face grew hot with embarrassment. Darcy was still standing next to her, sharing the hymnal and singing slightly off-key. She suspected he was more determined than ever.

Martha Babcock walked through her front door and slammed it shut. G. Gordon Liddy Kitty was startled awake.

"You'll never believe it, G!" Martha stormed. "It's bad enough they want to give food away to the riffraff in Cherish, but now they want to bring some of those Arabs here. The ones who terrorize the rest of the world!"

G. Gordon Liddy Kitty stared at his mistress with round eyes.

"I'll fight this one, G. You bet I will! And the police chief is with me. She told me so, Gordon. Charlotte doesn't want trouble around here. She's not going to let those terrorists loose in our town. I'm sick of that pastor and her doctor husband. They think they are king and queen around here. Well, they are not! The election is coming, and there will be a new day in this country. The Republicans will win it all! And that's the truth, Gordon!"

G. Gordon Liddy Kitty jumped down from his chair and stretched lazily. Then he walked over to his empty food dish. It would be nice to see something in there. He looked up at Martha. "Meow."

"I know, Gordo." Martha picked up the cat and scratched the top of his head. "The chief will keep them out."

SYRIAN REFUGEE CAMP IN SURUÇ, TURKEY

Iman was small for a nine-year-old, but she hoisted her little brother Samir, who was five, on her tiny hip. She walked back to the tent for the midday meal. Her sister, Jamal, eight, and brother Karam, seven, followed along. They had been playing on the west side of the camp with some of the other children. Sometimes they just sat and talked. Sometimes they ran around or kicked a ball if they found one. Iman tried to remember some of the things she had learned at school before they left when she was seven. When her mother had time, they practiced letters and numbers together. Then she would teach them to her sister and brothers. Iman was tired of the camp. She remembered a different life in Kobanî. She'd played in the yard and helped pick olives off the ground when her father shook the trees. Her mother was happy. Since the baby died, Iman would sometimes hear her mother crying softly in the night. All she wanted was for her mother to be happy again.

11

"I'm going to drive to Ann Arbor and see Keith Crunch this morning," Maggie told Jack. "I'll talk to him about Charlotte. I also must straighten things out with Julia this week. I've decided to call the prison and pass off Redford's care to the on-site chaplain."

"I think Julia will always have a tendency to feel betrayed. Redford perpetrated that. He's where he belongs." Jack picked up his briefcase. "And by the way, I'll say it again, your sermon yesterday was great. I know you are second-guessing yourself. So, stop it. We are going forward with the resettlement. We have good work ahead of us. Don't think about those who won't be part of it. Just remember all the people yesterday who sang 'Blest Be the Tie That Binds.' And always remember, I love you like crazy."

"I love you the most. How do you always know what's in my head?"

"I just do. I see it in your eyes and the crinkles in your forehead."

She gave him a smile and a kiss before he left.

Right in the middle of her second cup of coffee, Maggie heard the Westminster chimes. She cringed. With a deep sigh, she walked to the front door of the parsonage, knowing who would be on the other side. But she was wrong. Instead of Fitch Dervish, whom she was expecting, the handsome Detective Keith Crunch stood on her doorstep.

Maggie smiled immediately.

"Good morning, Keith. I thought I was going to meet you at your office later this morning. Come on in." She held the door open for him.

"Sorry about not calling first, but I spent the night at Irena's and figured it was a lot closer for me to come to the parsonage. I thought it would save you a trip. I hope it's okay."

"It's great. Would you like some coffee?" Maggie focused on her Keurig to avoid thinking of Keith with Irena all night. Sometimes she knew too many secrets.

"I'd love some. And by the way, your sermon yesterday was one of the best I've heard. And it's not because I'm a regular reader of children's books." He smiled at her.

Maggie felt her face turning red. "I appreciate that, but I don't think all of your fellow parishioners felt the same way. I tried something, but I don't think it will work again." She handed him a steaming cup.

"The sermon and the exodus of some of the members aren't cause and effect," Keith said. "Everyone could see the strong message in your story. It was when Darcy stood up and laid out the final plan for the Syrian family that people reacted. The sermon was a clear reminder of who we are as a community—inside and outside the church." He took a sip of coffee.

Maggie was somewhat relieved. Keith didn't just blow sunshine around. He said what he meant.

"Thanks. I've been reliving the exodus out of the church yesterday. I don't know if what Darcy did was good or not."

"He let the congregation know he is moving forward with the resettlement and you and Jack are part of the process. I have to say, you and Jack are generous to take care of the housing."

"The condo just sits empty. It's a good place for the family to land. We hope it helps as they heal from so much trauma. But, moving on, I wanted to meet with you to find out if there are any barriers we should be aware of. Charlotte is obviously against this, but are you worried at all about this family coming to Cherish?"

"I'm not worried about Cherish. I'm more worried about the family. It would be rough if they had to endure any more hardship from people here in what should be their safe place. But racism and bigotry are growing everywhere. People feel emboldened to show their hatred in many ways. Some are violent. It is Charlotte's duty to protect Cherish. But it is not her duty to censor a family because they are from a foreign country."

"So, what do we do? Can she really block the whole thing?"

"Charlotte is a good police officer. She will come around."

"Would you talk to her?"

"No. That would be disrespectful. I trust her, I really do, Maggie."

"Okay, then we have work to do. We're getting a group together this Saturday to do some indoor painting to spruce things up and move some bedroom furniture into Jack's old office. We're also going to plant flowers outside. The following weekends, we'll stock the kitchen and purchase some toys for the children."

"It's a wonderful thing you and Darcy are doing. It's a piece of good news for all of us. Even the ones who don't know it yet. I've got to get to work, but call if you need anything."

"Thanks, Keith. I will, don't you worry."

She walked him to the front door and as she opened it she saw Fitch standing there, poised to ring the bell.

"Well, howdy," Fitch said. His transition glasses were heavily shaded from being outside, so Maggie couldn't see his eyes. "Detective Crunch, is the little pastor here in some trouble?" Fitch chuckled to himself.

"No. Reverend Elliot is not in trouble." Then he looked at Maggie. "Thank you for your time and the update."

He walked past Fitch and down the steps.

"Come on in, Fitch," Maggie said with no enthusiasm.

She led him to the kitchen, hoping there was nothing he could smash into, break, or use to do any bodily harm to himself or to her. They sat at the kitchen table. She quickly put Keith's coffee cup in the sink along with her own.

"Now, Fitch, here is what I need." She decided to bypass the small talk and more Fitch condescension. "Because the church is unable to meet the guidelines for a childcare center, our next thought is the parsonage. It has a much different layout, enough entrances and exits, and plenty of bathrooms. This is all a little hush-hush for the moment until we get your assessment. How long do you think that will take?"

"About a second," Fitch said. "This house will never work as a child-care center."

"Why not?" Maggie almost shouted.

"It has many attributes the church doesn't have. That's true. But you still have one big problem."

"What?!" Maggie did scream, ready to throttle the big lug.

"It's not handicapped accessible. And stop yelling at me."

"I will yell, Fitch. Are you just making this up to put a halt to a childcare center? Because that's what it feels like!" Maggie began to spin slightly out of emotional control.

"Now, now, Pastor Maggie, let's talk about this sensibly. The doors are not wide enough, you don't have any kind of ramp from the front of the house, and the stairs are too narrow and too steep. This is an old house. That's just that."

Fitch sat back in his chair, and his man bag slid to the floor with a thud. As the bag rolled over, the contents spilled out around his feet. Pens, papers, his clipboard, packs of gum, several granola bars, a box of rubber bands, two tape measures, and some lint-covered jelly beans all made an appearance. The kitties, who had been napping in the sunshine of Maggie's study, came running when they heard the noise. Fruit Loop found a linty jelly bean and began batting it around. Marmalade tried to steal it from him, and a game of kitty soccer began. Cheerio daintily sniffed through the other strange objects scattered around Fitch's feet.

"Whoa . . . wait . . . What in the world?"

Fitch tried to stand up but saw the cat and sat back down, hard. The heft of his body slid the chair on the clean kitchen floor, and it flew backward and hit the wall below the window. Fitch's head went right through the glass and then down hard on the sill. The shattering of the pane sent the cats running back into the study as Maggie jumped to her feet.

"Fitch! Are you all right?"

Blood oozed from the back of his head and down his left ear. Glass was everywhere, inside the kitchen and on the bush outside the window.

"Oh . . . oww . . ."

Fitch reached up to his ear and felt the warm, sticky blood. He looked at his hand. Maggie watched as his eyes rolled back in his head and he fell like a lump onto the floor.

"Good grief!"

She grabbed two mostly red kitchen towels and put them under Fitch's head. Then she called for an ambulance. Fitch was out cold. It was an EMT truck that arrived outside the parsonage with screaming siren and flashing lights. Maggie let the one woman and one man into the house through the front door. They carried what looked like super-sized tackle boxes. Maggie directed them into the kitchen.

As the EMTs checked Fitch's vital signs, Maggie simultaneously began to explain what happened while she put his belongings back into his man bag—minus the jelly beans, which were gross, so she threw them away.

"He dropped his bag, stood up, but then sat down too hard, which pushed the chair backward into the window. When he saw the blood, he fainted." She didn't mention the cats. It wasn't their fault. She couldn't even tell the story with compassion. Fitch was a constant calamity. She looked at the man bag in her hands. *Why am I always cleaning up this man's messes?*

The Westminster chimes rang.

Maggie walked to the door to find Hank, Mrs. Popkin, Arly Spink, Irena, and Doris standing on the porch. They began to speak at once.

"Are you okay"

"Vat ees going on arround here??"

"We heard the siren and saw the EMT pull up right here!"

"What's happened?"

"Where is Dr. Jack?"

Maggie pushed them all to the end of the porch and shushed them.

"It's Fitch. He's had an accident."

"Again?" her friends said in unison.

Fitch was the most accident-prone adult any of them had ever met. It was unfortunate that he was always on building sites.

"Yes. Another one. He smashed his head through the kitchen window and then passed out after realizing blood was coming out of his head. I called for help, and the EMTs showed up. How about you folks go back to church and I'll meet you over there in a bit?" She tried to herd them off the porch. Then she looked at Arly. "Arly, what are you doing at church today?"

Arly Spink owned the Cherished Works of Art Gallery downtown. Maggie had tried to get her to attend church for months and it was finally working. Arly was in a pew on more Sundays than not. Maggie thought about Sunday. *Arly was in church yesterday. She didn't leave. She stayed for the whole service.*

"Well," Arly looked around at the others, uncertain if she should speak in front of them. She answered hesitantly. "I came to church today to ask if I could host an art auction to raise money for the Syrian family." She looked away from the others.

Maggie saw Doris's head give a slight shake, as if to say "no."

"What a fabulous idea!" Maggie over-enthused. *Why is it a person like Arly, who is new to the faith, is offering to do such a generous thing, while Doris, a long-time member who knows a whole lot more about Jesus, is fighting it?* "I would love to talk about it with you, Arly! I just don't know how long this Fitch accident is going to take. Can I call you later?"

"Of course. I'll be at the gallery all day. Call or drop by." Arly smiled.

She turned to go, and Maggie gave Doris a light shove in the same direction. "Thanks for stopping over," she said, giving Hank and Irena little shoves too. "Let's just allow the EMTs to do their work. I'll be at church soon, I hope."

They slowly left the porch, trying to look through the open front door as they passed. Maggie quickly went inside and shut the door. *Good grief!*

She walked into the kitchen and saw Fitch still lying on the floor. His eyes were fluttering, and he was moaning. One of the EMTs went out to the truck to get a gurney. When he returned, he said to his partner, "The door isn't wide enough. I brought these blankets. The gurney is on the porch."

Maggie sighed. Fitch had been right. If the front door wasn't wide enough for a gurney, there was no way it could accommodate a wheelchair. The parsonage could not be turned into a childcare center. She watched as the EMTs neatly made a sling out of the blankets. They rolled Fitch onto the sling, and he groaned. They used one of the blankets to make sure he was secure, then hoisted him up, carried him out of the kitchen, through the front door, and placed him on the gurney. They still had the porch steps to manage, but finally Fitch was ensconced in the vehicle, his man bag at his side, and on his way to Heal Thyself Community Hospital.

Maggie went back into the kitchen to survey the wondrous mess of Fitch. Broken glass and blood were everywhere. The window was almost completely gone, with shards of glass dangling here and there. Of course, the whole window would have to be replaced. She found the three cats under the chairs in her office. She gave them pets and apologies, then shut the door to keep them away from the shattered glass.

She grabbed the broom and dustpan and began to sweep the kitchen floor. Bloody glass was swept into the dustpan and dumped in the trash. She grabbed a bucket from the closet, filled it halfway with bleach and stuck the bloody broom in to soak. Then she began to clean the blood off the floor. More bleach, a scrub brush, and finally the Swiffer.

Maggie made a cup of Lady Grey tea and called Tom Wiggins at the Cherish Hardware store.

"Hello, Cherish Hardware, Tom speaking."

Maggie swallowed the tea in her mouth and choked. She began coughing as she tried to answer. "Hi" *cough, cough, cough* "Tom" *cough, cough* "it's" *BIG cough* "Pastor Maggie. Ahem."

"Hi, Pastor Maggie! Are you all right?"

"Yes. A gulp of tea decided to go down my windpipe instead of my esophagus. Sorry about that. I'm calling because I need a new kitchen window at the parsonage. Do you have any time this week?"

"I would guess you need it sooner than that. What happened?"

Maggie quickly filled him in on the Fitch disaster.

"You certainly don't want an open window for long. I'll tell you what, Jason is here today helping me with the shop. I'll come over and measure and get you taken care of quick as a wink."

"Thanks, Tom. That would be great. See you soon."

Maggie hung up and carefully took another sip of tea.

The Westminster Chimes rang.

Good grief! What now? I don't want any more people in my house!

She opened the door to Fred Tuggle. His bright-red pickup truck was parked in front of the parsonage. Fred was Chief Charlotte's husband and the owner of the rock quarry just north of town. He was also the fire chief of the Cherish Volunteer Fire Department. Before he had joined the council, Maggie had heard Fred speak fewer than twenty words. Now there he was on her doorstep.

"Hi, Fred. This is a surprise."

"Hello, Pastor Maggie. I stopped by the church and Hank said you were here. I need to talk with you for a minute. If you've got time."

"Sure. Come into the living room."

Maggie led the way with a feeling of dread. She sat in the blue chintz chair while Fred sat on the once-white-now-gray couch. Maggie could smell bleach from the kitchen pervading the house.

"Pastor Maggie, I'll get to the point. Charlotte and I are strongly opposed to the resettlement of this Syrian family. You must know that by now. Charlotte has made herself clear at the church council. We don't want trouble here in Cherish. Things are fine the way they are. To bring in a foreign family, especially Muslims, is just asking for trouble. I wanted to make it very clear to you that Charlotte and I are united in this. She's been the chief of police for over a decade now. She does her job well. Inviting this kind of trouble won't work in our town. You need to know that if you don't halt this resettlement, the Tuggle family will be leaving Loving the Lord Community Church. And we will take our resources with us. We have told our children of the decision. Brock, Mason, and Liz all know the consequences if you go forward with this scheme. We won't have the possibility of terrorists in our town. Now, we like you, Pastor Maggie, but you have pushed things too far this time."

Maybe it was the fact that Maggie was getting tired of hearing and seeing all the negative words and actions regarding the Syrian family. Maybe she was tired due to lack of sleep over the past few months. Maybe she had just finished cleaning up another man's mess and was sick of it. Maybe she had finally had it with men telling her "no" about childcare centers and resettlement projects. Whatever it was, as Fred stood to leave, she calmly looked at him.

"Sit down, Fred."

Surprisingly, he did sit back down.

"I see you have you finished your monologue," Maggie said. "You certainly didn't come here to have a dialogue." Maggie was surprised to hear her mother's voice coming out of her own mouth. "My guess is you are used to making important decisions at your quarry. You shout out an order and someone does what you demand, or heads roll. Your wife has one of the most important positions in our town. She is well respected and good at what she does. But you're still the one in charge. Charlotte has made her position clear about the resettlement. She's against it. I saw your entire family walk out of church yesterday. It's obvious what you believe. But to come here and threaten to leave the church is kind of dramatic, don't you think?"

"It's not a threat. We'll leave."

"You will be missed. The youth group will miss your kids. But more than that, Brock, Mason, and Liz will miss out on a chance to help people in need. They'll miss out on an opportunity to learn about another culture and learn how to respect that culture. But I would guess those aren't the kind of discussions you have around your dinner table. Whatever you are afraid of, you are passing that highly contagious disease right down to your children so they can learn to be skeptical, judgmental, and perhaps even hateful. That's an ugly little gift you are giving them."

"I'm keeping my family safe!"

"From what? An image? A tactic of fear? A stereotype? What is threatening your safety?"

"They're animals. They strap on suicide bombs and blow up villages. They torture and kill anyone who is different. They plot and plan how to kill Americans. They are terrorists! I'm not talking about this anymore. I have made myself clear. You are a simple-minded girl living in a Pollyanna land. You are unwise and foolish. I'll wait to hear that this plan has been halted. Why don't you ask your husband about this? I'm sure he could explain things and help you understand world issues."

With that parting swipe, Fred rose to his feet and stalked out of the parsonage.

SYRIAN REFUGEE CAMP IN SURUÇ, TURKEY

Mahdi made his way to the food distribution center. The earlier he got there, the better chance he would have to get the best food for his family. He passed by tents and some other structures made of corrugated metal.

He and his family had been in their tent the entire time they had been in Turkey. There had been hope of education for the children, but it had taken up until the last month for the school to be staffed and organized. His children had spent the better part of two years making up quiet games, helping with other people's younger children, and sitting in the numbness of their stagnate reality.

Mahdi wanted to hear his children laugh again. He wanted to see them run and play. He wanted to listen to them read from books—the simplest children's story would be the sweetest gift. Their lives were being wasted. They needed to be in America. They needed to be out of this camp. He took his bags of food and walked slowly back to his tent.

Soon. They would be leaving soon. The paperwork was being processed. He just had to be patient.

12

The sting of Fred's patronizing words left Maggie reeling. She never would have guessed that quiet Fred was so fearful. *How does Charlotte stand his condescension? Does he talk that way to Liz?*

The Westminster chimes rang.

Maggie slowly made her way to the door. It was Tom Wiggins.

"Hi, Pastor Maggie. I'm here to measure the window."

"Hi, Tom. Thank you. Come on in."

Maggie led the way to the kitchen.

"Well, that is quite a broken window, isn't it?" Tom pulled out his tape measure and a small notebook. He measured and jotted. "This is a standard-sized window. I'll be back."

"Thanks again. I'll be here."

Maggie made a fresh cup of Lady Grey tea. Then she picked up her phone and dialed.

"Hello, this is Mimi."

"Hi, Mom."

"Maggie, what's the matter? You don't sound like yourself."

"I'm not. I'm having a hard week. But I want to talk about something else."

"Okay."

"Bonnie and I are planning a shower for Brynn. We both agreed it would be fun to have you be part of the planning. What do you think?"

"I'd be happy to help. I don't know Brynn well. Her name reminds me of Bryan."

"How is that brother of mine? I haven't heard from him in a while."

"He's leaving Kenya tomorrow for Ghana. He'll be there for a month. But the best news is, he will be home for Christmas. We will all be together. By the way, have you seen Cate?"

"Actually, yes. Bryan's beautiful girlfriend left for Ghana two weeks ago. She is taking classes in Accra for half the semester, then working in Bawjiase at the orphanage for the second half. She will fly home with Bryan for Christmas too."

Bryan and Cate would be home for a long holiday break. Maggie smiled with a sneaky suspicion Bryan might want to cement his deal with the lovely Cate. She pulled herself back to her mother and their conversation. Jack's youngest brother, Nathan, was excited to get to Ghana like Bryan.

"I know Nathan is excited to fly to Ghana," Maggie said. "The two little brothers together. Ha! I'll WhatsApp Bryan later."

"About the shower, when is it?"

"October eighth in Blissfield at the Elliot farm. The thing is, they will have a fully stocked house when they get married. Jack's parents have updated everything. What kind of gifts do you get a couple who have absolutely everything already?"

"Ask her."

"Who?"

"Brynn. Ask Brynn what she would like. She might have some ideas of her own. What did Bonnie say?"

"The only thing we thought of was a family cookbook, with all the ingredients wrapped up for each dish. It was my idea."

"That's good. But still check with Brynn."

"I'll call her. Maybe there's something she and Andrew can think of."

"Now, why are you so blue?"

Maggie unloaded everything that had been going on the past two weeks.

"I'm sorry for the attitudes of some of your parishioners," Mimi said. "Small-minded and closed-hearted behaviors are difficult to deal with. I affirm what you and most of your parishioners are doing. Affordable childcare and welcoming immigrants are two lofty and generous goals. I have never known you to give up without a fight."

"Thanks, Mom. I'm tired."

"I'm sure you are, but now is not the time to rest. Stand up straight, shoulders back, and march right into the fray! Think of Queen Elizabeth. She became ruler of an empire when she was younger than you are."

"Not helpful, but thanks."

"We are living in strange times right now. The church is not immune to cruelty, as you know from your Redford experience. But I realize the hatred has spread far and wide. You are right where you are supposed to be. I believe that."

"That is helpful. Thanks a lot, Mom. I'll keep you up to date on all this stuff. And I'll talk to Brynn soon. Love you!"

"Love you too!"

Wednesday morning, two days after the Fitch incident and the Fred confrontation, Maggie drove over to Julia Benson's home. She had called first to make an appointment. Once they were settled in Julia's cozy living room, Maggie began.

"Julia, I'm here to apologize. You are right, I didn't consider how you would feel when I visited Redford."

Julia nodded.

"I thought, as his pastor, I should visit him. But I know I never was his pastor. Church was a place for him to do damage and take advantage of good people. You know that better than anyone."

"Thank you for saying that," Julia said quietly. "I know I was harsh the other day, but it didn't make any sense to me. I can't believe he enjoys your visits to prison."

Maggie thought about the last visit and how Redford had spit at her as she left. It was revolting.

"No. My visits didn't make a difference. I kept going because I thought they could. You gave me a wake-up call. I talked with the prison chaplain. He will visit Redford as he has time, but I think the chaplain will receive the same treatment I have. You and Hannah are gifts to this community and to our church. I am truly sorry for hurting you."

Julia, who had spent so many years carrying a mountain-sized chip on her shoulder, visibly softened.

"I appreciate that. Hannah and I love it here. In fact, last night she asked me if we could buy some stuffed animals for the Syrian children. She and Carrie and Carl are hatching little plans for play dates and visits to the park. We want to help any way we can."

Maggie was relieved. Julia had moved on from her pain to her wish to help with the new family.

"That would be amazing. The children will be . . . well, I don't know how they'll be. I'd guess confused and exhausted and scared once they get here to Cherish. Other children can be the bridge to a new normalcy. Tell Hannah to keep planning. We'll need all the help we can get."

"I would like to write a piece for the paper. I think the more positive publicity we have, the better. Who should I talk with to get some details about the family members?"

"Darcy. He is in close contact with the organization who does all the resettlements in Southeast Michigan. What if I send you both an email about this? Then you can contact each other and set up an interview."

"That would be perfect. Thank you, Pastor Maggie."

That evening, Maggie was in the parsonage kitchen, where she spooned a mixture of cooked chicken and vegetables into squares of puff pastry. She folded them into triangles and glued the edges together with an egg wash. Lacey and Lydia were coming for dinner. A fresh green salad and a pan of corn pudding would round out the meal. Michigan blueberry pie and ice cream would be eaten on the porch of the parsonage, where Maggie and Jack had added a porch swing and two rocking chairs.

Maggie was certain this evening would be a respite from the days upon days of what she called "Christian Chaos." She wanted to create a safe place for Lacey and Lydia, where their love and relationship were accepted and affirmed.

The week had also held some balm for Maggie's soul. Besides her new kitchen window and a pleasant visit with Tom Wiggins on Monday, she had called Brynn to talk about plans for the wedding shower.

"Brynn, how are you doing? It's been one whole week since your engagement. Do you have the whole wedding planned yet?"

Brynn laughed. "Oh, of course. We're going to get married in our overalls out in the pasture with the cows. We're going to have a potluck reception. What can I put you down for?"

"I'll bring a bag of potato chips."

"Great. Yum!"

"What I really want to know," Maggie said, "is what you would like for your shower. We all want to celebrate you, but you're moving into a beautiful, completely stocked home. What are we supposed to buy you?"

"Bonnie mentioned that to me too. She and Ken have the farm house updated, and they aren't taking much with them to the new condo. Bonnie has already picked out furniture and kitchen things. But for me, it's hard. Andrew and I don't need anything." Brynn stopped.

Maggie waited.

"I just had a thought," Brynn said slowly. "We don't need anything, but other people need so much. What about this? I want my wedding shower to be a shower for a person or people who really need things. What about your immigrant family? Or I can find something here in Blissfield? Or both?"

Maggie had felt her arms and face tingle. "What a great idea. You choose whatever sounds good to you, and I will put it on the invitations."

"I'll get back to you by the end of the week. This will be so much fun!"

"I'm so glad we're going to be sisters," Maggie said.

Adding to the balm of the week, Arly Spink had solidified her plans to host an auction in her gallery to raise money for the Syrian family. The auction would be in two weeks. Maggie and Arly were both getting the word out. Arly had called Julia Benson and had a full-page ad put in the *Cherish Life and Times* newspaper. They had no idea how the auction would go once it became common knowledge the money would help the Syrian family. So they planned and prayed and trusted.

Jasper and Myrna were getting married Friday night. Maggie felt more warmth and tingles when she thought of being on their farm in two days' time, officiating their nuptials.

Lastly, Saturday would be the first work day at the condo. Mrs. Popkin was already planning the food, and several people had volunteered to paint outdoor trim and plant flowers.

Maggie tried to focus on all these good things as the sting of Fred Tuggle's words slowly faded. She brushed beaten egg over the tops of the chicken pies and put them in the oven, along with the pan of corn pudding. Then she pulled vegetables out of the refrigerator and began to tear lettuce and slice cucumbers, tomatoes, red peppers, and green onions. She mixed the vegetables, then whisked a vinaigrette together, dressed the salad, and thought about how to make Brynn's homemade cookbook of family favorite recipes along with ingredients creatively wrapped for each recipe. She would call Bonnie tomorrow and get her input.

The Westminster chimes rang.

Jack opened the front door to Lacey and Lydia.

"Hello, ladies. Come on in." Jack held the door open as they walked through.

Maggie came from the kitchen, wiping her hands on a towel with images of black cats all over it.

"Lacey, Lydia, we're so glad you're here. I hope you both like cats. We have three, and they are experts at forcing affection out of any human."

"Thank you," Lacey said as Maggie gave her a hug and then did the same to Lydia.

"We love animals," Lydia said. "We're actually thinking about getting a cat or a puppy from the humane society."

"What a great gift to give a homeless animal," Maggie said. "I found ours in abandoned places. Come on into the kitchen. We have a dining room, but it seats hundreds, more or less. The kitchen is cozier."

Jack opened two bottles of wine. "Would either of you like a glass of red or white?"

"White, please," Lacey and Lydia said in tandem.

Jack poured two glasses of white and handed them to his guests. Then he poured two glasses of red and gave one to Maggie as they all sat at the table. There was a wedge of stilton cheese covered with honey and slivered almonds, wheat cracker discs surrounded the cheese. Small plates and napkins were on top of each dinner plate. The appetizer munching began.

"Okay," Maggie said, dripping honey on her chin as she lifted a cracker to her mouth. "Spill. Besides the dream of rescuing an animal, how are you two doing?"

This abruptness didn't seem to faze the two women. Lacey spoke first.

"We are doing great. But isn't life always great when you're in love? Nothing seems quite so bad when there is someone to share it with."

"We both feel lucky to be able to work together and live together," Lydia said. "I moved into Lacey's apartment when I first arrived here. Lacey is my best friend. Maybe 'lucky' isn't the right word to use around a pastor, I am not a churchy person. But whatever it is, it's good."

"True love is always good," Jack said. He looked at Maggie and winked. "We are both happy for you."

"Thank you," Lacey said quietly. "We appreciate your support. But we aren't sure about others. We're worried we should keep our relationship a secret. We work together, and Lydia moved in with me, but people assume we're just roommates. Our clients come to the shop for haircuts and manicures and fake hair color, and do you know how many secrets we hear every day? So many secrets! People tell us everything. For some reason they trust us with their work frustrations, their family problems. I regularly hear a long-running story about an affair going on right under this town's very nose. Lydia and I keep everyone's secrets, but we are living the biggest secret of all. We don't want to hide anymore. This is a small town. There are some pretty backward opinions and some catty people around here. No offense to cats. We don't know how our relationship will be accepted."

"It is a small town," Maggie said, "and there are some small minds. I would expect a few bumps, but you will have much more support than anything else. Jack and I will certainly be open with our views. It's easy for us to completely support you."

"Thank you. Why do you believe the way you do?"

Jack spoke. "We don't put love in a box. And we don't put limits on where it can go or how it can be experienced. The two of you are in a committed, loving relationship. That's what matters."

"We don't want to mitigate the concerns you're feeling," Maggie said. "We know Lacey hasn't had a lot of acceptance from her family."

Lydia looked up with her beautiful Scarlett Johansson eyes and said, "Lacey and I have had two different experiences. She was raised in a strict home and a scary, judgmental church. That's *my* description." She looked at Lacey, then continued. "It's a crappy way to be raised. Conditional love and debilitating guilt. Woohoo. I was raised in a loving home, no church, and my parents and two brothers have accepted me from the time I figured out who I was right up to this day. They love Lacey too."

"They are awesome!" Lacey jumped in. "I've never experienced such love and acceptance, except from you two. I felt legitimate. I felt like I could live in my own skin." She got quiet. "I didn't realize how afraid I was of being 'caught.' Who would catch me first, and how far would I have to run to get away from the judgment? Lydia's family treated us like human beings and allowed us to be us."

"That's the way it should be," Maggie said. "It's unfortunate when certain people believe they know all 'the rules' about how we should live."

She stood up and pulled the corn pudding and chicken pot pies out of the oven. Jack put the salad on the table.

Maggie prayed.

They passed the food to one another and filled their plates.

"Tell us what we can do to help the Syrian family." Lacey cut into the flaky crust of her pie and smiled as the chicken, peas, carrots, and gravy spread out like delicious creamy lava on her plate. "This looks amazing. The Syrian family should definitely eat things like this when they get here."

"I'm grateful for my neighbors at the condo, Deborah and Jacob Stein," Jack said. "They are ready to help in every way. They offered to have dinner ready for the family on the day they arrive. They are also asking their rabbi about mosques in the area. Since our refugee family is Muslim, they will need their own house of worship."

"So, your Jewish friends are finding a mosque for their Muslim soon-to-be neighbors? That is awesome. And we Christians get to be part of all this as well. Who would have thought little Cherish could hold the secrets to world peace right here?" Lacey shoveled a forkful of corn pudding into her mouth.

"It probably won't be all smooth sailing." Maggie sighed, thinking of Fred Tuggle.

The meal continued with chatter about all the things the Syrians might need, how fun it would be to show them Lake Michigan, how to make school easier for the children, and many other dreams and hopes for the precious family.

By the time blueberry pie and coffee had been served on the porch, the sun was thinking about setting. Fireflies appeared like twinkle lights in the front yard of the parsonage.

Jack and Maggie each took one of the rocking chairs, while Lacey and Lydia sat on the porch swing. Jack had planted roses in the spring along the east side of the porch. Now, on the last day of August, they spilled their fragrance into the air.

"This is a beautiful old home," Lydia said. "I grew up in a house like this in Elgin, Illinois. Lots of big rooms and an attic where we played. It was a fun place to live."

Maggie smiled at Lydia. "This is a lovely house. But I've come to realize living next door to my work is more difficult than when I first moved in two years ago. We were hoping this parsonage could be used as a childcare center but found out this week it won't meet code for handicapped accessibility. A huge disappointment for us."

"We feel the lack of privacy at times," Jack said diplomatically.

"It would be hard if people expect that you *must* have time for them and their opinions," Lacey said, "especially now that there are pockets of discontent in our little church." She sipped her coffee and watched the fireflies. "I'd want to tell them exactly where to go if they came over and gave me sh— . . . uh, sass. But it's your job to be nice. Sorry about that, PM."

"I just hope things settle down," Maggie said. "A childcare center isn't something to fight about. Anything to help children and families should be easy to make happen. And helping refugees is a mandate from God, the way I see it anyway." Maggie sighed.

"None of this sounds particular to the church," Lydia chimed in. "It's a human thing. Who wouldn't help kids, whether they are from here or halfway around the world? It's a no-brainer." She ate her last bite of blueberries and ice cream. "This pie is amazing."

"I wonder how it will all turn out," Maggie mused.

The evening came to an end, and with hugs all around, Lacey and Lydia left the parsonage. Both felt a little lighter in spirit after an evening with the pastor and her husband.

Maggie's spirit was lighter too. She didn't know how the congregation would react to a lesbian couple, but she felt like the church would become even more of what it was meant to be with Lacey and Lydia there. She hadn't given up the hope of getting Lydia in the doors of Loving the Lord.

As Maggie loaded the dishwasher, she smiled, remembering how Lydia and Lacey, sitting on the porch swing, had intertwined their pinky fingers as they rocked back and forth.

13

Maggie drove up the long driveway of Myrna and Jasper's farm. It was their wedding day. Jack would be there for the ceremony, but Maggie was early to prepare and practice for the event. As she reached the farmhouse, she laughed out loud. There was a huge banner hanging from the porch roof. It said:

HAVE NO FEAR! THE WEDDING'S HERE!
COME TO THE BARN AND HAVE A BEER!

Maggie parked in the driveway, grabbed her wedding notebook, and walked up the porch steps. As she knocked on the door, she steeled herself for a wave of children and pets, but there was only silence. She knocked again, louder this time. Nothing.

Well, I guess I better take advice from the banner.

She walked down the porch steps, around the house, and out to the barn. She heard squeals and barks as she got closer. The kids ran around the inside of the barn, followed by the dogs and pig. Myrna and Jasper were each holding an "M" baby while talking with members of a band. A steel guitar and drum set were on a platform on one side of the barn. Guitars were set up in stands, and brass instruments were in their cases.

"Hi, everyone," Maggie said as she walked into the barn.

The wave came immediately. The children and dogs all looked at her and ran headlong straight at her. Already dressed in her cream-colored wedding suit, she saw many dirty little hands and slobbery tongues. She braced herself.

"STOP!" Myrna yelled.

The wave stopped. They all stood perfectly still.

"Look how pretty Pastor Maggie is in that suit. Don't you dare put a finger on her."

Myrna walked over to Maggie. The kids and dogs behaved, but Juliet waddled over to sniff Maggie's shoes. She left a nice trickle of snout snot dripping off the toe.

"We're so glad to see you!" Myrna was dressed in a pair of overalls. She had a yellow T-shirt on underneath and a pair of brown cowboy boots. "We're just talkin' to the band right now. They'll play durin' the ceremony and for the reception."

Maggie smiled at the band members. She felt overdressed and very small next to Myrna, who seemed larger than a week ago.

"Great. When would you like to run through the ceremony?"

Jasper walked over and stood by his soon-to-be bride. He hugged her and rested his hand on her stomach. Maggie didn't know where to look.

"Did you tell her yet?" Jasper asked Myrna.

"No, she just got here." Myrna looked at Maggie and smiled.

Jasper jumped in. "We have another fun-bun in the oven!"

It took Maggie a moment. "Oh! Another baby. Well, isn't that exciting?" Maggie felt dizzy. *Six children.* "When is the baby due?"

"We think maybe April," Myrna said. "Gotta get to the doctor and find out for sure." She turned toward her children and said, "Okay, you line up the way I told you to do. It's time to practice the weddin'."

Jasper hitched two of their dogs, Munchkin and Magnus, to a large red wagon decorated with Queen Anne's lace and tiger lilies. He set Manny in the wagon, and Myrna put Milford right beside his twin. Myla stood by Jasper and took the leashes for the dogs. She would be leading them down the sort-of aisle. Mika and Misha stood behind the wagon. With some hay bales askew, the way from the door of the barn to the back was a little twisty. All of the children were covered in dirt and hay, but their smiles blazed at Maggie.

"We've been practicin' and the kids have this part down. Don't ya, kids?"

"Yes, Mama," they answered.

"Where's Myra?" Maggie asked.

"She's pickin' corn for the dinner later on," Myrna said as she led the other two dogs, Mable and Melvin, to another red wagon just like the first. She hitched them up and then set a squealing Juliet on a pile of hay in the middle of the wagon.

Maggie stifled a laugh. She walked over to the band leader and jotted the names of the songs for the ceremony in her notebook.

After going through the ceremony three times, Maggie took a few minutes to speak with Myrna and Jasper individually. Then the happy couple and the "M" children went to the house to get cleaned up and dressed. Maggie took some time to adjust a few things in the ceremony, now that she knew all the participants, human and animal. A beer tent had been erected next to the barn under some shady trees. Kegs of beer were ready to service thirsty wedding guests. The band had their amplifiers full blast. Maggie felt a headache coming on. She walked out of the barn and saw Myra, in her overalls and wearing a large straw hat, pushing a wheelbarrow full of corn.

"Myra, let me help you." Maggie walked toward the elderly woman, but her high-heeled shoes made it difficult to walk in the dirt.

Myra turned and lifted the brow of her straw hat. "Oh, it's you, Parson. Glad to see you again." She set down the wheelbarrow and used an orange bandana to wipe her sweating face. "I'm just bringing this corn in for dinner. I think I have enough time to shuck it before all the folks show up."

Maggie didn't think so. The wedding would begin in just about an hour.

"May I help you?"

Maggie edged Myra over and took the handles of the wheelbarrow. She tottered along on her heels, trying not to spill the contents. Myra watched her and giggled. She followed Maggie, who almost spilled the corn twice, up to the porch.

"How do you get this wheelbarrow up the steps?" Maggie asked.

"I don't. I get my corn basket and fill it full and haul that up. It takes a while, but it works."

Myra went up the steps and grabbed a basket Maggie had seen one of the dogs sleeping in the week before. The two women filled the basket with corn. Dog hair stuck to the husks.

"Sit in that chair," Myra said, "and I'll sit here, and we'll have this done in a jiffy."

Maggie set the basket between the two rocking chairs and sat down. Myra handed her a square laundry basket and had a similar basket next to her chair. Myra sat and began to shuck. She threw the husks into a tin bucket. Each ear of corn went into her laundry basket. Maggie followed suit and tried to keep up with the wiry old lady, but she had only half as many ears shucked as Myra. The "dog basket" was filled again, and the two women worked away. The third dog basket filling emptied the wheelbarrow. More shucking until the last ear was ready to be cooked.

Maggie stood and picked up one of the laundry baskets. "Where do these go?"

"Oh dear," Myra said, clucking her tongue.

"What?" Maggie asked.

"Now what in the world was on that chair?" Myra looked over at Maggie's rocking chair.

Maggie looked down and cringed. She reached around and felt the back of her skirt. Something smushy. She brought her hand around and saw it was covered in something brown. *Oh no!* She didn't want to, but she sniffed her hand.

"What is it?" Myra asked, sounding perturbed. "Those dogs don't have any bathroom manners. Did you just sit in doo-doo?"

"No. I'm pretty sure it's Tootsie Rolls," Maggie said, chagrinned.

One of the little "M" darlings had left some partially eaten candies on the seat of the rocking chair. Maggie turned and looked at as much of her backside as she could see. It looked as though she'd had a very embarrassing accident.

"Well, it looks like you pooped your drawers," Myra confirmed. "What a shame. That's a pretty outfit you got on there. At least it was." Myra smashed down the corn husks in the bucket. "Do you want to borrow a dress? You're short, like me. You can wear one of mine."

Maggie didn't know what to do. She looked at her watch. There wasn't enough time to go home, change her clothes, and get back for the ceremony.

"Just a minute."

Maggie went to her car and grabbed her phone. She called Jack's number. No answer. She tried again. She let it ring. Finally, an answer. It was Jack's voice mail message. She hung up. She looked up and saw a line of cars and trucks snaking down the driveway then turning toward the barn. The band was welcoming the guests by blasting instruments and vocals as loudly as they could. She walked back to the porch.

"Myra, may I borrow some soap or detergent and try to get this stain out?"

Myra picked up one of the laundry baskets of corn and went inside. "Come with me."

She led Maggie into the house, then into a large open kitchen. She set her laundry basket on the island in the middle of the kitchen. There were four stainless-steel pots full of water on the stove.

Myra went into a large pantry and grabbed vinegar and baking soda. She then led Maggie into a laundry room where clothes were piled according to color. Myra took a small scrub brush from a sagging shelf. Maggie then followed her up two flights of steep, narrow stairs.

"I sleep on the top floor," Myra said. "It's quieter."

Maggie could hear children and dogs making their respective noises somewhere else in the house.

Myra had a room in the attic. Two dormer windows were open, letting in a warm breeze. She had a twin bed with a white afghan covered in yellow daisies spread over white sheets. There was a small rocking chair, and next to that, a basket of yarn and several pairs of knitting needles. On her bedside table was an old-fashioned lamp and a worn Bible. She had a dresser with lotions, face creams, and a bottle of perfume on top. A door led to a small bathroom.

Myra looked at Maggie and said, "Well, take it off."

Maggie looked at Myra. "What?"

"Take off your skirt so I can clean it."

"I can clean it, you don't have to do it."

"Of course I do. It was one of my grandkiddies that left that mess on the chair. Now give me your skirt."

Maggie slowly took off her skirt, handed it to Myra, and sat down in the rocking chair in her underwear, thoroughly embarrassed. She was the officiating pastor, after all, and here she sat in an old attic in her underwear while a wizened old lady tried to clean her dry-clean-only skirt.

Myra hummed "Standing on the Promises" as she mixed vinegar and baking soda into a paste and brushed it on the skirt in her small bathroom sink. Maggie smiled. She hadn't heard that old gospel hymn in years. It had been one of her grandma's favorites.

Ten minutes later, Myra came out and showed Maggie the back of the skirt. The stain was gone.

"I don't believe it!" Maggie exclaimed. "It looks brand-new."

"I know. Do you think I've never cleaned a piece of dirty clothing in my lifetime? I've cleaned more clothes than you'll ever wear. That's a fact."

Maggie shimmied into her clean skirt. The back was slightly damp.

"You need to change too, don't you?" Maggie wondered if Myra was going to wear her overalls to the barn.

"Of course I do. I don't want to miss my daughter's wedding."

Myra stripped off her overalls and checkered blouse and went back into the bathroom. Maggie heard water splashing and more humming from the older woman. The bathroom door opened, and Myra came out stark naked.

"Well, that felt good. I like a nice sink bath."

Maggie considered Myra's eighty-year-old body. Her skin looked like crepe paper that had been re-wrinkled several times. Lots of things sagged, but Maggie could see muscles in her arms and legs that showed Myra to be a tiny tower of strength. Myra walked over and opened a dresser drawer and pulled out clean underwear, a bra, and some nylons. She got herself dressed in a pale-blue polyester dress with a soft tied belt. Then she looked at Maggie for approval.

"You look beautiful, Myra."

Myra nodded. She powdered her face at the mirror above the dresser, then slipped on thick-soled brown shoes.

"Well, I'm ready. We've got us a wedding to attend." She grinned up at Maggie.

Maggie wanted to hug Myra. So she did.

"Myra, I want to be like you."

"I don't see why. I'm way past my sell-by date. The world seems to find folks like me useless."

That stung Maggie's heart. "You don't have a sell-by date, Myra. You are the backbone of this family. You are the keeper of the history. You are the keeper of your grandchildren's stories and heritage. You are the keeper of wisdom. You just become more priceless every day."

Myra looked at Maggie. "Well, I've never heard words like that before."

"Mama! Mama?" Myrna shouted up the stairs.

"We're coming! Quiet down!" Myra hollered back.

Myra looked back at Maggie. "Thank you for those nice words. I guess I got to go get another story to keep. My baby's wedding day."

Myra's eyes glistened.

By a quarter past six, the bridal party was still getting organized outside the house. Maggie smiled at the happy mix of children and animals. She and Jasper were getting ready to walk down the crooked aisle of the barn with the "M" children, dogs, and Juliet right behind. Juliet was sitting on the hay in her wagon. She had a pink net tutu around her piggy tummy and a bow taped between her piggy ears and was oinking happily. The male dogs were wearing bow ties around their necks, while Munchkin and Mable had bows on the tops of their heads that matched Juliet's.

The children were clean and dressed in what must have been their very best clothes. The girls wore colorful dresses, their hair curled into soft swirls around their shoulders. The twin boys were in white short-sleeved baby rompers. They looked ready for a baptism.

Jasper was in a perfectly tailored navy-blue suit. Maggie was struck by how professional he looked and remembered she had forgotten to find out what kind of work he did. It obviously wasn't farming. Jasper grinned at Maggie as they set off down the aisle.

Maggie gave a nod to the band leader, and they began to play Randy Travis's "Forever and Ever, Amen." She and Jasper wound their way to the makeshift altar. White tulle was twisted into a pretty arch for the bride and groom to stand beneath, and bunches of bright sunflowers were in large vases set haphazardly around the barn.

Maggie saw Jack sitting near the back and gave him a smile.

The "M" children, dogs, and wagons followed Maggie and Jasper. There were chuckles from the crowd sitting in chairs and on hay bales in the barn. Almost everyone was holding a plastic cup full of beer.

As Juliet's wagon stopped in front of the crowd, she squealed and jumped out and tried to run back down the aisle, her tutu bobbing around her. But she was too small to see where she was going and ran into a hay bale. Her squeals and oinks could be heard by everyone because the band had stopped playing to switch songs for Myrna's bridal walk.

Myla, the oldest daughter, ran down the aisle and grabbed Juliet. She carried the squealing pig back to the wagon and plopped her on the hay again.

The band began to play "I Will Always Love You." Myrna was dressed in a voluminous white gown and looked like a giant-sized cream puff. Smiling at her guests, she walked down the aisle with a bouquet of colorful wildflowers.

The congregation of people all stood and held their cups of beer in a kind of prenuptial toast. Some videoed the much-overdue walk with their cell phones. When Myrna reached the front of the crowd, Jasper stepped toward her and gave her a kiss. Everyone began to slap their thighs, while still holding their beers, with whoops and hollers.

The noise scared both children and animals. The twins began to cry and reached toward their mother. Myla, Mika, and Misha looked startled, but Maggie knelt down and told them people were happy their mom and dad were getting married. Myra bounced out of the front row of chairs and tried to calm the barking dogs and noisy pig.

Maggie motioned for everyone to sit down. She didn't have a microphone, so she yelled a greeting over the cacophony of noise.

Myrna handed her flowers to Misha and picked up Manny and Milford, who immediately calmed down once in their mother's arms. Maggie tried to pray but quickly abbreviated it. People were talking and laughing near the beer tent, which carried easily into the barn. *So much noise!*

Maggie moved on to the vows. Jasper and Myrna wanted the traditional vows, but when Maggie said, "Myrna, please repeat after me. Jasper, I take you to be my husband," Myrna began to cry. She repeated what Maggie said, but no one could understand her. Her tears confused the twins, who also began to cry, which turned into wails.

Maggie didn't know what to do. She looked at Jasper, who took one of the twins and tried to comfort him. The other twin howled while Myrna wiped her nose on her own shoulder. Maggie snatched a tissue out of the pocket of her notebook. She gave Myrna the tissue and took the other twin. She handed him one of the sunflowers in a nearby vase. That made him very happy. He cheerfully plucked at the pedals while Maggie finished the vows and Myrna sobbed along after each phrase. Maggie quickly repeated the vows for Jasper, who spoke clearly that he would take Myrna to be his wife:

> . . . to have and to hold from this day forward,
> for better, for worse,
> for richer, for poorer,
> in sickness and in health,

to love and to cherish,
as long as we both shall live.
To this covenant I pledge myself, truly, with all my
heart.

Myrna cried through this as well. She blew her nose and looked lovingly at Jasper.

The twin Maggie was holding began to hit her on top of her head with the sunflower. She swayed back and forth to calm him, but finally she dropped her notebook down on the floor after removing two index cards.

"Myrna and Jasper had some loving things to say about one another before this ceremony," she began. "Jasper, this is what Myrna had to say about you: 'Jasper is—'"

Myrna took the card out of Maggie's hand. She turned and looked at Jasper.

"Jasper Barnes, you are the most honorable man I've ever known. You are good and kind, which are both overused words, but I know what they really mean. You are the only person who has ever made me laugh so hard I peed my pants. You are a good daddy. Havin' babies with you is a whole lot of fun." She put her hand on her stomach. "This one's just another bundle of happiness."

Maggie heard small gasps from the guests in the barn.

Apparently, this wedding was also a baby announcement.

Myrna spoke before there could be another ruckus. "I can't imagine bein' married to a more magnificent specimen than yourself. Thank you for allowin' me to be a joyful woman. I can't wait to see what the future brings us."

Myrna took the baby from Jasper as the twin Maggie held waved his beleaguered flower and giggled to himself.

Jasper also took his card from Maggie. It was obvious this wedding was completely out of her control. She took a step back and listened to the love story in front of her.

"Myrna Mills, you are the sun in my sky. You bring the fun to my days. You love our babies the way no other mother has ever loved before, except maybe your own." Jasper gave Myra a wink. She was happily sitting in one of the wagons with Juliet on her lap. "I miss you when I leave for work in the morning and can't wait to get home to you at the end of the day. You are pretty, smart, tough as nails, and a really good cook. I'm going to love you forever and ever. Forever and ever, amen."

Jasper wrapped his arms around Myrna and the twin. He kissed them both, then he took the other twin out of Maggie's arms and pulled all his daughters in close. He and Myrna both got down on their knees, arms entwined. They whispered sweet words to their children. Someone said something funny, because they all started to laugh. Maggie watched as Myrna reached out and took her mother's hand.

"You get in this circle too, Mama," she said quietly.

Myra and Juliet were enveloped in the love.

Maggie felt herself choking up. She coughed and said as loudly and clearly as she could, "Myrna and Jasper have made vows and pledged their love to each other in front of God and all of us present. It is my honor to declare them husband and wife. I think they have the kissing thing handled."

Everyone laughed until Myrna yelled, "The rings! We forgot the rings."

She picked up Juliet and pulled the bow off her little pink head. Two sparkly rings were at the center of the bow. Myrna slid them off and gave Jasper her ring. She took his ring finger and as she pushed on his ring she said, "With this ring, I thee wed." Jasper repeated the gesture. Then the entire family stood together and faced the crowd of friends and loved ones. Applause and whistles filled the barn. The whole family began to weave their way out through the hay bales, followed by the four dogs and wagons, while the band played, "Anyone Who Isn't Me Tonight."

Maggie waited until they were near the beer tent, then picked up her notebook and walked out. Jack was waiting for her by the door.

"I don't think I've ever had so much fun at a wedding," he said. "It was even better than ours."

Maggie got on her tiptoes and gave him a kiss. "You're right. This takes the cake. Wait till you hear what happened beforehand. Hold on . . . I'll be right back."

She grabbed Myrna and Jasper and had them sign the marriage license before the festivities really got started. Two of their friends signed as witnesses. With that done, she found Jack in the crowd of well-wishers.

"I think I've done all I need to do to make this wedding legal." She laughed. Then her eye caught Myra heading quickly toward the house. "Oh, I've got to see if I can help her. You get a beer, and I'll be back."

Maggie quickly followed the older woman.

It was eleven p.m. before Jack and Maggie left the "Barn Wedding," as it would be known forever after. Maggie spent most of the evening in the kitchen with Myra. They boiled corn on the cob, organized huge bowls of fruit salads, pasta salads, potato salads, and squares of cornbread. Jack found himself standing next to Jasper and his friends as they grilled chicken and steaks. The beer flowed, the food was eagerly consumed, and after everyone had a piece of Myra's homemade wedding cake, the dancing began.

Maggie asked Myrna if she could help with the twins, who'd had enough of the wedding celebration. When Myrna thanked her, Maggie and Myra took the little boys upstairs and filled a large claw-foot bathtub with warm water and bubbles. The babies played and splashed soapy water on Maggie's suit. She didn't care.

After drying them off and putting them in diapers and pajamas, Maggie sat in the rocking chair and read bedtime stories until finally she could put them in their cribs and watch their eyelids flutter down into contented sleep.

I think I would like this.

She found Jack, and they shared one slow dance under the stars.

"You said you would be right back," Jack said. "That was many an hour ago."

"I played in the kitchen for a while with Myra, then I got to cuddle babies. What could be better?" She rested her tired head against his chest. She had taken her shoes off somewhere in the house. She didn't want to go find them. "I think I like babies."

"That's good to know." He kissed the top of her head.

Eventually, Maggie's shoes were found. Jack and Maggie thanked Jasper and Myrna for the wonderful evening.

Jasper reached into his pocket and pulled out an envelope. He handed it to Maggie.

"Thank you. You have given us the best gift. We would like to get together with you again. You both are new friends."

"I'll never forget your wedding." Maggie laughed as she took the envelope. "We'd love to see you again. And I really want to know who joins your family in April."

Myrna patted her stomach happily.

"Who knows, we may even show up in your church one of these days. It sure would make my mama happy. And the kids could use some Sunday school."

"We'd love to have you."

Maggie followed Jack home in a car loaded with Tupperware full of salads and cake. Once home, she put the salads in the refrigerator then sat with Jack at the kitchen table.

"Did you get a chance to visit with a lot of people?" she asked.

"I grilled the meat with Jasper. He's a smart man."

"Did you happen to find out what he does for a living? He comes home from work in a suit. At least he did last week."

She popped open one of the Tupperware containers that held the wedding cake and put a thick slice on a plate. She grabbed two forks and gave one to Jack.

"He works for Ford."

"The Ford Motor Company? Oh, he must be a salesman." She put a large bite of cake in her mouth. "That makes sense. He'd need a suit to sell cars," she mumbled through cake.

"No. He's a physicist. He works in Detroit at the Ford headquarters and works on a fuel cell for future automobiles."

Maggie stopped eating mid-bite. "What?"

"I was as surprised as you. But it's true. The guy's a genius. We had a lot of fun, and I met some of his coworkers and other friends."

Maggie quietly chastised herself. She had made a very wrong assumption about Jasper.

After finishing the cake, she sat down on the kitchen floor to pet the sorely neglected felines. She opened the envelope Jasper had given her at the end of the evening.

On the homemade card, a picture of Jasper and Myrna's barn was glued onto the front. Inside were the scrawls of the children, a loving thank-you note from Myrna and Jasper, followed by Myra's small, cramped signature.

But Maggie gasped when she saw what was with the card.

It was a check for five hundred dollars.

14

It took Jack and Maggie quite a while to fall asleep after the wedding celebration. Maggie read her G. M. Malliet mystery, *Death of a Cozy Writer*, until it hit her in the face. She turned out her light at one thirty a.m.

Jack's phone rang at four a.m. He reached over to his nightstand and grabbed the phone. "Jack Elliot speaking."

"Jack, this is Jacob Stein. I'm sorry for the early call."

Jack cleared his throat. "Jacob, what's going on?"

"We've just called the police. We heard breaking glass at your condo. Several windows are broken."

"We'll be right there."

Jack and Maggie pulled up to the condo behind Charlotte's flashing police car. She and Bernie were talking with Jacob and Deborah.

"Hi, Dr. Jack, Pastor Maggie," Charlotte said when they joined the small group.

Both Maggie and Jack looked at the front of the condo. Every window had been smashed, and ragged glass hung precariously. Two flower pots on the front porch had also been broken. On the front door, black spray paint left a message: "NO MUSLIMS ALLOWED!"

"I'm afraid there's more damage at the back of your condo," Charlotte said, subdued. "We don't see this kind of vandalism much, hardly ever. Right, Bernie?"

Bernie nodded. "That's correct, Chief."

Maggie and Jack walked together to the back of the condo.

Black spray paint on the grass spelled out the word "ISLAM" with a large X over the word. More spray paint on the deck spelled out hateful and vulgar words. Every window was broken, and the sliding back door was standing wide open.

"Oh no!" Maggie couldn't believe what she was looking at.

Bags of garbage were strewn in the kitchen and living room of the condo. She couldn't see how far back it went.

"Please don't go inside," Charlotte said, walking toward them. "Forensics are on their way. Whoever did this broke in first, then did this outside damage."

Jacob, Deborah, and Bernie joined the other three.

"I'm sorry, Jack. I wish I would have heard something earlier to stop so much damage. It wasn't until we heard the windows smash that we knew something was happening."

"It's not your fault," Jack said. "Who knows what more they would have done if you hadn't called Chief Tuggle?"

More police showed up, including Detective Keith Crunch. There had been a time when Charlotte was jealous, even threatened by the Ann Arbor Detective. But she'd learned that his expertise complimented hers.

Maggie watched as forensic technicians entered the condo wearing gloves and masks. They would gather the evidence of hatred.

The sun was barely touching the eastern horizon.

Maggie knocked on the door of The Sugarplum Bakery. The doors were locked, but she knew Mrs. Popkin was inside. The elderly woman came from the back and opened the door.

"Well, hokey tooters! Pastor Maggie, what are you doing up at the cracked-egg of dawn?"

"Hi, Mrs. Popkin. I wanted to let you know we won't be having the cleanup day at the condo. I'm sorry for the late notice."

"Come in. Come in and tell me what happened."

Mrs. Popkin's cheery face became serious. She poured two cups of coffee and put two cranberry bran bars on a plate. Maggie sat at a booth near the window and took in the smells of baking bread, fresh-brewed coffee, cinnamon, vanilla, and chocolate. She closed her eyes. It was aromatherapy. Mrs. Popkin squeezed her round self into the other side of the booth and looked at Maggie.

"The condo has been vandalized," Maggie said simply. "Thoroughly and totally vandalized, inside and out."

"My stars! Who would be so cruel?"

"I'm guessing quite a few people. We made it clear the Syrian family would be living there. Plenty of people were unhappy about that news. We don't know exactly what we'll do now, but it will take a lot to repair the condo. Jack is calling the insurance company this morning to make a claim. It's bad. I've sent out an email to the church to let everyone know the cleanup day is cancelled."

"I wonder what's happening in this world. It seems like hate and vulgarity are the new national languages."

"If you don't mind, I better get back to the parsonage. I just wanted to let you know. I'm sorry if you prepared all the baked goods already."

Mrs. Popkin squeezed herself out of the booth. "I suspect the police might enjoy some coffee and fresh donuts. I think I'll pack some up and head over to your condo." She put some goodies in a pink bag and handed it to Maggie. "For you and Jack, later." She stood still and looked at Maggie. "I don't understand all this, Pastor Maggie, but I do believe God is still in control. Yes, I do. Depravity will not define this country, this town, or our church. Goodness will carry the day."

She wrapped her short, thick arms around Maggie's shoulders and hugged her.

Pastor Maggie, however, was not certain in the least that God was still in control. God seemed to be MIA.

Detective Keith Crunch walked over to Jack after listening to the forensics team. "It's worse than expected. The destruction inside is extensive. The good news is, we have some fingerprints. There are also some hair samples and clothes fibers. They're going through the trash bags now. We'll find whoever did this."

"You sound like a television show," Jack said, slightly annoyed. "With the extent of the damage, I'm sure we can't have it ready for the Syrian family in time. Which, of course, was the intent."

"It's an act of cowardice." Keith looked at one of his officers, who was waving him over. "Excuse me."

As he walked away, Jack felt the full force of the hatred and fear bubbling up in Cherish. Until now, he had been able to rationalize what was going on with the changes in the country and even the behavior of some of the people in his town. The destruction of the condo was directly connected to the Syrian family and Islam as a whole. He wondered what would be next. Someone was emboldened now.

Jack walked onto the deck and through the slider door. What he saw took his breath away. Trash spilling out of bags everywhere. Rotten food, soiled diapers, and used cat litter. The odor made him gag. He saw that the carpet had been ripped off the floor. Spray painted words similar to the ones on the deck were on every wall. The refrigerator in the kitchen had been pulled out of the wall and was lying on its side. The couches had been slashed with something sharp.

Jack felt overwhelmed. He had to get outside. The wave of someone else's hatred pulled him under. All he could think was, *this was so unnecessary.*

A pickup truck headed north, away from Cherish. The driver's hands gripped the steering wheel. Glances in the rearview mirror showed no signs of being followed. *Maybe I got away with it.* The driver stayed just under the speed limit, no need to be noticed by some old granny up at dawn, staring out her window. The sun was just coming up. *They'll learn their lesson now. We won't allow terrorists in our town.* The truck pulled up to a locked gate. The driver got out and opened the gate with a key. Once the truck was through, the gate was relocked. *I made it.*

∽

Maggie went back to the condo to pick up Jack. She also suspected some people might not see her all-church email and come over for the work day anyway. Jack took her in the through the back door of the condo. The smell itself made Maggie sick to her stomach.

"Oh! The stench. It's horrible." Maggie gagged and held her breath.

But when she saw the destruction of furniture, floors, walls, appliances, she began to openly weep.

"Why?" She turned her tear-filled eyes to Jack.

"Fear. Someone is scared and cowardly." His voice was tense.

"There's no way we can have this cleaned and repaired in time for the family to move in. We've got to come up with another plan." Maggie wiped her eyes and took one more look at the main level. She tried breathing through her mouth instead of her nose.

"May we go upstairs?" Jack asked Keith.

"Yes. Be careful. There is a lot of debris on the steps."

Maggie felt her stomach churn. She picked her way up the stairs littered with broken pieces of furniture, lamps, and more strewn garbage.

"Whoever did this was so angry."

Jack looked around at his first home. The violation was astounding.

"Fear and anger are a lethal combination," he said, "but this is too much. This is pure hatred."

Keith stepped up behind Jack and put a hand on his shoulder. "You're right. This is a hate crime. It's obvious the person or persons involved did this specifically because they knew a family from Syria would be living here. I'm sorry about the destruction."

"When can we begin the cleanup?" Maggie asked.

"My team is almost done. I'll let you know when they are leaving. Charlotte and I will look over the evidence together and keep you informed."

Jack and Maggie walked out of the condo and sat in Jack's car. He made a call to the local insurance company and left a message for the agent he worked with. They would have to file a claim. Finally, Jack started the engine and drove away from the crime scene, but he didn't go back to the parsonage.

"Where are we going?" Maggie asked.

"I planned a surprise for you after the cleanup day today. I just want to show you now. We'll go back for a scheduled appointment this evening if you like what you see."

"You don't seem happy about this surprise." Maggie noticed his clenched jaw. Jack wasn't one to get angry or emotional. She loved that about him because she was unabashedly emotional about everything. She tried not to apologize for feeling things, but often did.

"Actually, I think it's a necessity, not a surprise. I'm tired of living in the parsonage. People have given up on being appropriate with your time. There are no boundaries. I listen to how many people you meet within a day, and how even if you're in the parsonage working on a sermon, or drinking a cup of tea, or staring at the cats, they think you have all the time in the world for them. I'm sick of it." He didn't raise his voice, but his intensity grew.

"I'm tired of it too. What are you thinking?" Maggie could tell how much the break-in at the condo was affecting him.

"You'll see."

Jack drove down Dexter-Cherish Road. He hadn't gone far when he pulled into a long driveway flanked by huge oak trees all the way down to a large two-story brick home. They drove past a field to the left of the driveway and right up to the house. There was a barn behind the field. Jack pulled onto a parking pad that could easily hold four or five cars. The large gray barn was newly painted, with gates and fencing around the pastures in front and behind. Maggie had noticed a "For Sale" sign as they turned into the driveway.

"I thought I would show you this property," Jack said, "and maybe look at other places. I'd thought we could consider moving sometime in the next six months or so. Maybe a year. But now I don't want to wait. This farmhouse is empty, and the owners are ready to sell. I'm pretty sure it's the house Darcy was looking at for the Syrian family, but there is one other large house for sale about a mile east of here. It's ready for a quick sale, as well. I prefer this one because of the land. But, but . . ."

"You are really upset. Look at your hands."

Maggie took one of his hands in hers. Both his hands were shaking.

He looked at her. "This doesn't make sense to me. I understand what happened, but I don't understand the amount of hatred it would take to be so destructive."

"It's your condo. It was your home for years. This is personal, Jack. It's an attack on you, on us, as much as an attack on a structure. It is *so* very personal."

Maggie carefully kissed each of his hands. Then held them for a few minutes.

"I agree with you," she continued. "The parsonage is worse than a fishbowl. We are part of a bigger issue now. The Syrian family is a community issue. Along with Darcy, we have been the strongest supporters. We won't stop. We'll keep doing what's right."

Jack's hands stopped shaking.

"This farm is beautiful," she said. "How handy that it happens to be for sale."

He said quietly, "I hope you like it."

They got out of the car and walked to the front porch of the house. The large front door was made of stained glass. The porch itself wrapped around the front and sides of the house.

"We can hang our porch swing here," Maggie said, standing at the east end of the porch. "And the rocking chairs will fit perfectly."

They walked to the back of the house, where there was a stand of pine trees near a small pond. Beyond that was another field.

"This seems too good to be true," Maggie whispered. "So much space."

"I think we would have a little more peace and quiet here," Jack said absently.

Maggie laughed. "The driveway is enough of a deterrent. People would be intimidated to drive all the way down. It must be a quarter of a mile. Let's look in the barn. Is it open?" Maggie felt her excitement rise.

"It was open yesterday when I was here with the realtor."

"You just saw this yesterday?"

"Yes. In fact, I thought I would be late for Myrna and Jasper's wedding. There was so much to see here. The house needs some work and a new roof, but it's manageable."

They opened the large doors to the barn. It was dark except for a shaft of light coming through an eastern opening near the top. Maggie could hear something scurrying.

"There must be a barn mouse in here." She laughed and took a deep breath, smelling years of hay and animals and machinery. "I love this place." She turned and put her arms around her husband. "When can we move?"

Jack's phone rang. "Hello, Jack Elliot speaking."

"Jack, it's Keith. People from the church have arrived at your condo for the cleanup day."

"We'll be right there." Jack told Maggie what was going on.

"Don't people check their emails in the morning?" Maggie asked, perturbed. "We will come back here tonight for our appointment, and we will buy this place, Jack."

Jack nodded and smiled. He loved how her mind worked, and knew the farm was one positive thing in all this mess.

They drove back to the condo to find members of the congregation standing in the front yard, staring at the destruction. Charlotte was speaking to them, and Jack and Maggie heard the end of her remarks.

"You can all go home now. There has been a break-in here. There won't be a cleanup day."

Keith stood to the side, watching.

"It seems like a cleanup day is more of a necessity now, doesn't it?" Ellen Bright asked.

"I agree," said Arly Spink. "This is terrible."

Howard Baker—standing with Verna and Winston—saw Jack and Maggie. "Dr. Elliot, Pastor Maggie, we're all so sorry this happened. Shall we get to work?"

Maggie took Jack's hand. It was shaking again. She held it tightly, and Jack cleared his throat.

"Thank you all so much."

He saw William and Mary with Carrie and Carl by one of the smashed flower pots. Darcy and Jennifer, along with Max and Beth, were dressed in jeans and T-shirts with buckets of supplies.

Another car pulled up. Jack recognized his insurance agent along with another person.

"It must be the insurance adjuster," Jack said quietly. Then he looked at the crowd. "You are all so kind. If you could give us a little time. We'll have an updated announcement in church tomorrow about the clean-up. We would appreciate the help."

The gathering of friends surrounded Jack and Maggie with hugs and words of encouragement.

"I'm sowy, Pasto Maggie," Carl whispered in her ear as she knelt down in front of him.

"Thank you, Carl. It's a sad day, but we will make it better. It is so nice of you to come and help." She kissed his cheek.

"Cawy and I will plant new flowas in the pots."

"That will make things so much better, Carl." She hugged him.

"I know. It will be all betteh, Pasto Maggie." Carl looked at her with his serious little eyes.

If only that were true. "We will tell all of you tomorrow when the cleanup day will be. I mean the flower-planting day. Thank you for helping us."

Darcy waited until the rest were gone. "Jack, I'm sorry about this. I had no idea the vitriol was so severe. I would be happy to pay for all the repairs of your condo."

"Thanks, Darcy. Money isn't the object. I am struggling with how this all happened. I don't seem to recognize our town. The main thing is, I don't think things will be repaired for the family by October third. You mentioned a house you had been looking at. Where is it?"

Jack desperately hoped it wasn't the farm he had just showed Maggie.

"It's east down Dexter-Cherish road. It's a large house on about an acre of land. I can call my realtor this morning and find out if it has sold already."

Jack took a relieved inward sigh. *It's not our farmhouse.* "Good luck. Let me know what you find out."

"Sure." Darcy and Jennifer went off to his car.

Jack took Maggie's hand. They walked in silence.

∞

SYRIAN REFUGEE CAMP IN SURUÇ, TURKEY

Amira wondered about America. She stirred the stew over a small one-burner cookstove. This had been her kitchen for two years. She and her family had eaten on the floor for every meal. She cooked on her knees.

Without context or concept, she was being sent to a new country: America. She and her family would be in a foreign land again. They were going on an airplane. She stirred the stew. In less than a month they would be taken to Istanbul and they would fly away.

She felt a tear slide down her cheek. Would she ever be in Kobanî again? Would she ever see her home and her garden? Those thoughts made her throat clench and her eyes sting. She had already lost so much. Her sisters were dead. Her parents were dead. Her baby was dead. Death hung on her like a shroud. She just wanted to go home. She wanted to hug her mother. Never again.

But what broke her heart more than anything else was the thought of leaving her infant daughter underneath the bright flowers in the graveyard, here in this camp of the lost, the displaced, and the desolate.

136

15

Jack and Maggie sat in the office of Detective Keith Crunch in downtown Ann Arbor the Monday afternoon following the break-in.

"The perpetrator took trash bags from several different addresses in Cherish. That was immediately obvious by the junk mail found in the bags. The amount of used cat litter also points to several residences. We have fingerprints but haven't made a match yet. We also have an eyewitness, an elderly gentleman two doors down, who saw a pickup truck leaving the scene after the windows of the condo were broken."

Maggie shuddered.

"We're still waiting for the clothing fibers to be returned from the lab."

"We'll begin cleaning tonight," Jack said. "It sounds like some of our cat litter may be there."

"You, Ellen Bright, Howard and Verna Baker, William and Mary Ellington, and Martha Babcock are the people from church who have cats that we know of. Of course, there are many more cat owners in Cherish. It looks like a random gathering. The person most likely stole trash bags at different times when trash cans were on the street for pick up. I don't know where they would have been kept until the break-in. You smelled it yourselves. It would be difficult to hide. I'll let you know when we find out more."

Maggie had made it through the previous Sunday worship service by preaching on love and acceptance, even though she was angry over what had happened to the condo. Someone in this town tried to destroy it and thought that would keep the refugee family out.

The days after the break-in were fraught with shock and grief from most of the congregation. No one seemed to know what to do with themselves. Everyone in church stumbled over themselves to hug, apologize, and share their own fears with Maggie and Jack. It was an emotional drain to care for the dear people who were traumatized by the Elliot's personal trauma.

Before visiting Detective Keith Crunch for the updated information, Maggie had spent the morning in her church office. She was looking over the passages for the next Sunday's sermon when she heard a knock at her office door. Normally, Hank would tell her who was waiting to see her.

"Come in," she said.

Chester and Doris both stepped into the office. Doris closed the door behind them.

"Hi, Chester. Hi, Doris. What are you two doing here?"

The couple sat in the two cream-colored visitor chairs across from Maggie. Silence hung in the air.

Finally, Doris spoke. "We are here to apologize, Pastor Maggie."

More silence.

"Oh, did you two break into the condo?" Maggie lamely tried to lighten the mood, but it couldn't be lightened. It was too horrible.

"We've been talking," Chester said, "and wondering why we made such a fuss about the Syrian family settling here in Cherish. It began with fear. We watch the news, and it is everywhere that they need to be kept out of our country. They are terrorists. But we realized we know better. We have been rude and judgmental toward people we have never met. People from a country we don't know anything about, except they are in a civil war. We decided to do some reading, and we found out details we wish we didn't know. The people of Syria are caught in a war that their leader has begun against them." Chester choked. "I feel like a stupid old man."

Maggie felt a pang. Her nose crinkled, but she bit her lip and didn't cry.

"You are two very dear people," she said. "This whole situation has been a learning experience for everyone."

"But we walked out of church for no good reason," Doris said. "Your story about the animals and 'enough for everyone' made perfect sense. We were filled with stubborn pride, plain and simple. We are sorry, Pastor Maggie. We would like to be forgiven."

Doris looked Maggie straight in the eyes.

Maggie wanted to say they didn't need forgiveness, but then she thought about it and realized they did. They had beaten themselves up over their words and actions.

"You are forgiven. You are pillars of this church, and I don't know what we would do without you."

"Thank you. What can we do to help with the cleanup of your condo?"

"The insurance company is almost done with its report. Jack and I have permission to go and at least do the preliminary cleaning. Some things will have to be done by professionals. We'll be over there this evening."

"We will be there too," Doris said.

Maggie could just imagine Doris wheeling around her big trash can with her yellow apron filled with cleaning supplies while she barked out orders in the condo.

"Thank you. You know I love you both, right?" Maggie smiled.

She gave them each a hug before they left. Then Maggie took a deep breath.

One little healing step.

With all the emotion flying around, there was a different kind of excitement and pain at the Detroit Metropolitan Airport. Jack and Maggie met Ken, Bonnie, Andrew, Brynn, Leigh, Anne, Peter, and their children Gretchen and Garrett. Jack's entire family came together to say goodbye to Jack's brother Nathan.

Nathan would fly to New York, then on to Accra, Ghana. Maggie's brother, Bryan, would be waiting for Nathan and a three-month adventure together. Bryan and Nathan had met through their older siblings. Two years earlier, when Bryan and Cate spoke at the Elliot's church in Blissfield about the orphanage in Bawjiase, Ghana, Nathan caught the excitement and began planning a trip to meet up with Bryan and work at the orphanage. Today, he was off.

"Please give my brother a punch in the arm," Maggie said as she gave Nathan a hug. "I'm jealous of you, Nate. I wish we were going back with you. I know you will give everyone our greetings."

"I sure will. I can't wait to meet all the people you've told me about. And thanks for the gifts." Nathan nodded at the carry-on bag Jack and Maggie had brought him.

"We know what some of their favorite things are," Maggie said. "We also suspect there are some things you might miss from home. Enjoy."

Maggie stepped back so the rest of the family could get and give their hugs and well-wishes. Bonnie and Ken, both with tears in their eyes, sandwiched their youngest child. Jack bear-hugged his little brother, while Anne reminded him to take his anti-malarial medicine and vitamin pills every day and on time.

"I'm not ten, Anne," Nathan said with a little annoyance.

"Well, you'll always be ten to me. So just do as I say."

Andrew and Brynn had spent the day with Nathan as he packed last-minute things and dreamed of his new surroundings. Now they also hugged him goodbye.

"We're so glad you and Bryan will be back for the wedding," Brynn said. "You will have so many stories to tell us. December will be a month of celebrations all around."

"Just don't lose too much weight, Nate," Andrew chimed in. "Your tux won't have time to be altered before the wedding."

Leigh lightly pushed Andrew aside. She got on tiptoes and whispered in Nathan's ear, "I'm going to miss you. I put a surprise in your suitcase. You know, so you won't forget us now that you're beginning your exciting new life." She kissed his cheek.

Once he made it through airport security, the family left the airport and went out for a late supper. Jack and Maggie were the only two at the table who could truly imagine all the smells, tastes, sights, and sounds that awaited Nathan. It gave Maggie comfort and joy to think of their two brothers living in the volunteer house and working at the orphanage with the children who lived in her heart.

The evening after Nathan's departure, Arly Spink had the auction at her Cherished Works of Art Gallery. People came from the church and the community to bid on the local paintings. Once it got around that Dr. Jack Elliot's condo had been badly damaged, his patients and colleagues quickly aligned to do whatever they could to help. Arly sold every painting she had hung on the walls. The day after the auction, she gave Darcy a check for seven thousand dollars.

"Thank you, Arly," Darcy said. "This will help purchase a van for the family to use. Once they get assimilated, we will help them get driver's licenses. That's a way down the road, though."

"I hadn't thought of that," Arly said. "But with such a large family, a car wouldn't be enough. I'm glad this money can help. I think the break-in has finally knocked some sense into people around here. Of course, this family is welcome in Cherish. We will love and protect them as our own."

Each evening more and more people joined Maggie and Jack at the condo for cleanup work. Jacob and Deborah Stein, along with some of the other neighbors, helped too.

Maggie could hardly breathe the first time they went to clean. The stench of rotten food, soiled diapers, and cat litter permeated every room. The August heat hadn't helped.

"I've got extra trash bags," Doris said. She had her yellow apron tied around her middle and a matching bandana around her head. "My word, it smells like Satan has been camping here. Well, onwards and forwards!"

Maggie looked at Doris in her apron and laughed. She appreciated the sense of normalcy. Doris being Doris.

"Are we removing the carpet?" Tom Wiggins asked Jack.

"Yes. We'll need to put in new carpet and repaint. Furniture will be ordered. But it will take a while to get it ready for those things. Almost every window has been broken, and we need a new back door."

"I'd like you and Pastor Maggie to pick new appliances when you have a chance. They will be my gift to this project."

Maggie's heart warmed at Tom's generosity. Two years earlier, preparing the house for her arrival in Cherish, Tom had installed all new appliances for the parsonage kitchen.

"Thanks, Tom. It means a lot," Jack said.

Jack and Tom went upstairs with extra-large trash bags and gloves. Marla, Addie, and Jason Wiggins were all wearing gloves and picking up random trash that had been strewn around the living room and the downstairs bedroom.

"Well, hokey tooters! Look at this little disaster." Polly Popkin waddled into the kitchen with three large bakery boxes. "I've got more in the car. I thought the troops might need sandwiches and cookies to keep up their strength. Whoo! It sure does stink in here." She waddled back out and brought in thermoses of lemonade.

Mrs. Popkin was there each night with Sugarplum bakery goods. More normalcy.

Irena came, ate treats out of the boxes, then loudly pointed out what people were missing as they cleaned. Being in her typical glued-on dress and very high heels, she was useless as a helper. But then again, Irena never helped with these kinds of things. More normalcy. Keith Crunch would pick Irena up after he was done in Ann Arbor. Maggie assumed they went back to Irena's apartment, but she didn't want to think about that.

Each evening, Maggie noticed there were a few more folks joining in the cleanup. The Gutierrez family came with Gabby and Marcos.

Julia and Hannah came on the same day. William and Mary brought Carrie and Carl. The Porter's arrived with Molly, Penny, and Sammy. Two sisters, Ryleigh and Zoey Teater, who lived in the neighborhood, came over to see what was going on. They were school friends of the other children.

Since the smaller children couldn't help much, Deborah Stein took them to the play equipment at the nearby park so the adults could work.

"Someone really mean made a mess of Dr. Jack's and Pastor Maggie's other house," Carrie said as she climbed the ladder of the slide.

"Who was it?" Gabby asked. "Did they get in trouble?"

"I think whoever did it will go to jail for a thousand years," Molly said in her know-it-all voice.

"And whoever did it will get a spanking," Penny said somberly. Penny herself had never received a spanking, but she was sure it was a horrible punishment.

"I think whoeveh did it should pay Dr. Jack lots and lots of dollehs and say I'm sowy." Carl added his two cents' worth.

"Our mommy told us about it. She said it was not nice to throw trash on the floor," Ryleigh said, following Carrie up the ladder. "But I already knew about it."

"You did?" Zoey looked at her sister as if she had been betrayed.

"How did you know?" Hannah asked.

"I was awake," Ryleigh said, sitting down on top of the slide.

"Does your mommy know?" Carrie asked.

"No. I forgot to tell her." Ryleigh landed on her bottom at the end of the slide and laughed at the bump.

"Did you see the mean person with the trash?" Hannah asked.

"Yes, I saw. It was a man. He moved very fast. He put all the bags in the condo. It was lots of bags. I didn't count them." Ryleigh ran over to the sandbox.

"What else did he do?" Gabby asked, following her.

"He made a big mess. He had bricks and threw them at all the windows. Then all the windows crackled into pieces and it was really loud.

I didn't like that sound." Ryleigh squeezed her eyes shut. "Then he left in a big red truck."

Ryleigh was done. She'd finished her tale. So she ran off to the swings.

SYRIAN REFUGEE CAMP IN SURUÇ, TURKEY

Sabeen walked slowly toward her tent. She carried a gnarled stick to help her walk. Eighty years of life had taken its toll on her body. She thought she might be the oldest person in the camp. At least she hadn't met anyone over seventy to date. The pain in her joints was excruciating. Her fingers were bent into hooks. Her toes made shoes impossible to wear. Even her sandals had been bent out of shape by her arthritic feet.

She stopped for a moment to catch her breath. She looked at the rows of tents surrounding her. Children ran past and accidentally bumped her as they chased one another. Sabeen winced as they jarred her hip.

The same thoughts ran through her head as she looked at the monotonous sight around her every day. Tents. Families displaced. Children trapped. Every freedom stripped away.

How did I get here? What happened to my life? Why have we been punished? I will surely die here. Does my life even matter?

She tried to grasp her stick a little harder, but couldn't. She pushed it forward with her bent hand and took another step toward her tent.

16

It didn't take long for the members of the congregation and the community to speak up about the destruction of the condo, but also about having a Syrian refugee family living in Cherish. Articles, editorials, and letters to the editor filled the *Cherish Life and Times* paper each day. Maggie had another unending stream of people in her church office and in the parsonage study.

"The problem is, we all feel helpless," Hank said one morning. "Redford was a bad man, that's for sure. But we all knew he had problems. Someone else allowed hate to consume them and then destroyed your condo. Many of us are a mix of fierce anger and sick to our stomachs."

"I know, Hank. Jack and I go from shock to acceptance to outrage. But the fact is, a family will be here soon, and we have promised them a place to live. The condo won't be ready, not even close. So we, I mean Darcy, have come up with plan B. He's purchasing a house on Dexter-Cherish road. It's about a mile from the house Jack and I are buying."

Hank was the only person at church who knew Pastor Maggie and Dr. Jack were moving out of the parsonage.

"It's going a little more slowly for Darcy, but he's hopeful by October third it will be ready for the family."

"I guess we will all need to get ourselves over there at some point to get it ready," Hank said. He actually felt a little weary from all the cleaning and fixing.

"It is exhausting, isn't it?" Maggie said, as if reading his mind. "The condo still has such a long way to go. Jack and I will easily be able to move our things to the farm, but the house for the family will need to be readied. Darcy will get us a list as soon as he knows the sale is complete."

"We will soldier on. Yessireebob, we will! And as Doris would say, 'onwards and forwards'!"

Conversations spread as people dealt with their feelings about the recent happenings. So much talk transformed into many discussions and then one large impromptu gathering for dinner on a Friday evening.

Tables and chairs were dragged out of the church and parsonage basements and set up on the large lawn between the church and the house. Food was bought and brought to the gathering. Maggie watched as Harold and Ellen set up chairs around the long tables. Naomi and Bobby Chance helped Addie and Jason Wiggins, who were taping tablecloths on the tables. Cecelia brought two huge bowls of orzo and roasted vegetable salads.

Maggie overheard some bits of conversations. The repeated question from everyone was "Who did it?"

"Who would have done something like that to their condo?" Cecelia asked Marla.

"It's terrible, just terrible," Howard Baker said to Winston Chatsworth. They had gone to look at the damage earlier in the week. "They must have to replace everything. They'll get insurance money, but the work of it all." Both elderly men shook their heads.

"Who could have done this?" Harold Brinkmeyer was talking to Verna Baker. "Someone in this town has crossed the line. I'm embarrassed. I've been wrong about this whole refugee family idea. I'll do whatever I can to make this resettlement happen and give them the best possible start. Their legal issues will be handled for free."

Irena ran around in her five-inch heels, taking food off different plates and cramming bites into her mouth.

When everyone was seated and Maggie had prayed, plates were filled, and a true communion supper began. As desserts were passed around, Jack stood up and spoke.

"Thank you for coming together for this unplanned but needed meal. Thanks also goes to everyone who has helped with the clean-up at the condo. I think we have all witnessed some brutal behavior. It did not come from foreigners, but from our own town. The police are getting closer to finding the perpetrator. Maggie and I have been moved by your concern. It's hard to get our heads around why this would happen."

Everyone nodded in agreement.

"We can't thank you enough for being a true church family. You have given up a lot of your own time to help us clean and repair the condo. We appreciate each one of you."

There was polite applause.

"Darcy Keller has begun the process of purchasing another home for the family. As soon as we have updates on that, we may need a little more help. Take a deep breath. We will plan the work, then work the plan." This was one of Jack's personal mottos. He was trying to keep spirits up. His false enthusiasm was sensed only by Maggie.

With the meal and pep talk finished, people began to gather their leftovers and help put chairs and tables away. Maggie found each member of the council and asked if they would be willing to stay for a brief meeting. Charlotte and Fred were the only two council members not at the dinner or the meeting.

Once the other council members were settled in the parsonage dining room, Maggie said, "Jack and I have some other news we would like to share with you." She took a very deep breath, then looked at the familiar faces around the table. "We are in the process of buying a house on Dexter-Cherish road. We will be moving."

Gasps.

"Wow. I don't think anyone saw this coming," said Ellen, glancing at her cousin.

Jack gave her a slight smile.

"We are looking forward to having some space," Maggie said, "and no offense, a little privacy. We began the process before everything happened at the condo and have decided to continue with the move. We will be out of the parsonage on September thirtieth." Maggie paused.

"This is a bit of a shock," Verna said, sounding like the old Verna.

"Yes, we didn't mean to shock you. The pressure has been building since we began the discussions of a childcare center and a home for the Syrian family. I have personally felt like I had nowhere to go to just be still. I love this parsonage. It's a beautiful home, and I fell in love with Loving the Lord Community Church, Cherish, and my husband while living here. We will be less than a mile away from church. I plan to walk to work whenever I can. I will still be available as your pastor. I promise." She smiled and saw a few smiles back.

"Good for you two!" Ellen said, grasping the significance. "We don't want to wear out our welcome with either one of you. And now you have the stress of the condo situation. It will be good for you to have a place to just be the two of you, I mean the five of you." She winked at Maggie. The kitties were family.

"We'll miss having you so close," Marla said sadly, "but I guess that's the point."

"I think we will need to do some triple duty," Tom chimed in. "There's still work at the condo and the new house for the Syrian family, but I think we can get your things moved out of here too."

"That's not a worry," Jack said. "Maggie moved in here with some books and kitchen things. Oh, and only one cat. I have a few pieces of office furniture, but most of the furniture here belongs to the parsonage. Don't bother about our move. I'll try my best to get all three cats to the new place. We can clean the parsonage once we're out. You have all done so much already. We feel like we should let the congregation know soon but wanted you to know first."

"Thank you, Jack," Verna said, gathering her wits and manners. "And congratulations to you both. But what will we do with the parsonage?"

Everyone looked at each other.

Verna continued, "I've never known a pastor of our church who didn't live in the parsonage." She sniffed airily. "Times are certainly changing."

"We hadn't given that a lot of thought," Maggie said. "I did ask Fitch to look and see if it could be a childcare center."

Many eyebrows raised.

"That's when I thought Jack and I would move to the condo. Fitch saw immediately it wasn't workable. Like the church, it's not handi-capped accessible."

Eyebrows lowered.

"Figuring out what to do with the parsonage can be done at a later date," Bill Baxter said.

"I suppose we could sell it," Beth Becker said quietly. Beth and her sister Jennifer owned and ran The Page Turner Book Shop. Both wom-en were savvy in business. "We could use the money for a childcare center somewhere else in town."

Maggie felt a little frisson of excitement, then annoyance. *How did my brain miss that idea?*

"That might be the way to go," Harold said, perking up. "Hopefully, Pastor Maggie will be here for the next hundred years or so, but I'm guessing our next pastor will want her or his own property too. A par-sonage doesn't help a parson build any home equity." He chuckled at himself.

"I think we'd be in for another big fight if we tried to sell," Jack in-terjected. "But the matter at hand is that Pastor Maggie and I will move out of the parsonage on September thirtieth. We will leave it clean for whatever the future holds."

"I'd like to thank you all," Maggie said. She looked at Harold. Her sense of relief that he'd come back on board with the refugee family surprised her. God was mending some of the brokenness in the con-gregation. "It's been quite a summer, and nothing seems to be slowing down. Within seventeen days, Jack and I will be moved, and we all will be moving the new family into their new home. Then the work really begins. I know Charlotte is not here tonight, and that makes me sad. I believe we might lose the Tuggle family in all the difficulty we've had. I would like to end this meeting with a prayer."

Maggie prayed.

∞

The next morning, cleanup continued at the condo. The furniture that hadn't been damaged was moved out, and now the carpet was being removed in long, smelly rolls.

"I'm glad you ordered this dumpster, Jack," Tom said. "Hauling everything to the dump one truckload at a time would have taken us forever."

"It's just about filled," Jack said as he took an end of the carpet and pulled. "It will be picked up on Monday."

Maggie waited with the others outside. As soon as the carpet was in the dumpster, the paint crew would begin their part of the job. Once the painting was done, new carpet and furniture would be ordered. Even Mrs. Popkin's donuts, sandwiches, and beverages couldn't lessen the exhaustion in Maggie's body and soul. She knew everyone was feeling the same. Besides restoring the condo, each of them had personal daily jobs and responsibilities. They'd all given up their evenings and weekends to help.

But then the work at the house Darcy was buying for the Syrian family would need all the energy the congregation could muster. Maggie hoped they could get into the Syrian family's house the coming weekend. She felt a tap on her shoulder.

"Darcy. I was just thinking about the new house." She smiled at the unsmiling Darcy.

"I need to speak with you and Jack."

"He's ripping out carpet. Can you wait a few minutes?"

There was an awkward silence as Maggie and Darcy watched carpet rolls being carried out of the condo in a long succession. Finally, it was done. The rest of the helpers applauded and cheered for one more big job finished. Maggie waved Jack over.

"We've got a problem," Darcy said. "The house didn't pass the inspection. That Fitch Dervish is an idiot." Darcy looked like he might spit at Fitch's name.

Maggie sighed. Fitch had recovered from his head injury and was back on the job with gusto.

"I didn't know he did inspections for sales," Jack said. Someone else had done the inspection for Jack and Maggie's new farmhouse. It just needed a new roof.

"Well, he does. I guess I can't blame him completely."

I bet you can, Maggie thought.

"The house has more problems than anyone expected. Dry rot in the floors. Lead paint. A family of raccoons destroyed the attic. The basement has been flooded more than once. If I buy it, there will be no possible way to have it up to code in two weeks. How long will it take to finish the condo?"

"We're expecting the new carpet at the end of next week. The appliances have been ordered by Tom, but we don't have a delivery date. Maggie and I will order furniture next week, if we have two seconds." Jack watched as the painters entered the condo. "I don't think we can have this all done by October third."

"But, I suppose we could put the family in our new house," Maggie said slowly. The thought of staying in the parsonage made her head ache.

"We don't have furniture ready yet," said practical Jack. "All we've ordered is a bedroom suite and a kitchen table and chairs. We're ordering the rest after we take care of what's needed here."

"All I can think is to bring the family to my own home," Darcy said. "It's just that I wanted them to get here and be settled. They have been moved around too much already. Damn it!"

Some of the children playing nearby looked up at Darcy.

"He meant 'darn it,'" Maggie said, smiling.

"There's one other thing," Darcy said as he absently ran his fingers through his hair. "I got a call from Anya at Refugee Family Services. It looks like we have a family of seven, not six. The mother of the father of the family was processed separately when they arrived at the camp. She went in seriously ill and was taken to the hospital immediately. She wasn't on the family information papers at first. But she is now. I don't know any more than that. We need to be prepared for one more person."

Maggie's head was spinning. "Of course, of course. We will make sure there is plenty of room for her. Poor woman." Maggie felt her eyes fill. *What has this family really been through? It's unimaginable.*

"Let's talk about this after church tomorrow," Jack said. "Maggie and I will see what we can do tonight to order more furniture for the condo and have it rushed. It doesn't sound like the house you were going to buy is worth it."

"No, it would have been a huge mistake. But we're coming down to the wire now." Darcy turned and walked away.

"I don't think he's used to not making things happen in his own time and his own way. It must be a hard lesson to learn at his age and perceived status," Maggie said thoughtfully.

Maggie woke up at three a.m. *Of course! How stupid of me. Everything is going to be fine.* She tried to sleep for another couple of hours, but once she realized she was fully awake for the day, she went down to her study and began to pack the books from her bookshelves into boxes. She loved this old study. She loved the floor-to-ceiling window. She always had a view of the bird feeders and the little red wagon full of happy flowers underneath the pine trees. Her sermons had taken shape in this room. Ed had blessed it by his presence.

Ed, we're moving. But you already know that. You also know I have a new idea for our Syrian family. I need you and God to work it out, okay? I miss you and love you so much.

∞

It was time for worship. Maggie felt the wind at her back—the Holy Spirit wind. Her confidence radiated from her eyes as she looked at the faces that filled the sanctuary.

Church began with Irena pounding out "Guide Me, O Thou Great Jehovah." Her recently dyed hair matched her orange spandex dress. A pink lacy bra worked hard to contain her breasts, both of which seemed to be looking for an escape route. She shushed and barked at anyone talking over her prelude.

There were plenty of people to shush because the church was full. People filed in smiling at one another, some even dared to speak the occasional word of greeting in spite of Irena. The only people Maggie did not see were Martha Babcock, the entire Tuggle family, and Jim Chance. But Cecelia, Naomi, and Bobby Chance were there. William and Mary Ellington had two little girls sitting with them and Carrie and Carl. They were the two neighbors at Jack's condo, Ryleigh and Zoey Teater. Maggie laughed out loud when she saw Jasper, Myrna, Myra, and all the "M" children file in and cram themselves into a pew. She half expected to see Juliet the pig in a basket on someone's lap. Maggie smiled at Myrna, then she looked up at the sanctuary doors as they swung open.

Fred, not-in-uniform Charlotte, Brock, Mason, and Liz Tuggle walked into the sanctuary. Their regular pew was filled with other parishioners, so they walked down the aisle, looking for a place to sit. Maggie wondered if they were there to disrupt the worship service, particularly Fred, but it was a small voice that got everyone's attention.

"That's him! That's the one!" Ryleigh Teater was jumping up and down, clinging to Mary's arm. Her other arm was pointing at the Tuggles. "The man with the trash and the bricks! He made the big mess!"

17

Ryleigh kept jumping. Everyone stared at the Tuggle family, who had stopped in the aisle. Maggie felt fury bubbling inside her as she rose to face them. *Fred devastated the condo. That arrogant, ignorant, idiot of a man.*

"Who do you mean?" Detective Keith Crunch stood and walked to the child. After Hannah told the adults what Ryleigh had seen, Keith had talked to her, but he didn't realize she had seen a face.

The Tuggles were frozen in place. Keith took Ryleigh's hand and walked her to the family.

"Ryleigh, who did you see with the trash and bricks at the condo?"

Ryleigh stopped and stared up at the family. She looked confused.

Silence filled the sanctuary.

Keith knelt down. "Ryleigh?"

"Why are there two of them?" Ryleigh asked.

Keith looked up. He'd believed Fred was the guilty party. Then he looked at Brock and Mason. Twins.

"Ryleigh, can you point to who you think had the trash bags?"

Ryleigh stood still and looked up from Brock to Mason and back again. "But there are two of them," she repeated.

Brock suddenly stepped forward and shoved Keith in the chest with all his strength. Keith fell on Myra in the pew. Brock pushed Ryleigh to the ground and ran toward the sanctuary doors.

Maggie gasped while chaos erupted.

Ryleigh began to cry.

Myra squawked and pushed Keith back up and into the aisle.

Mary got to Ryleigh, picked her up, and brought her back to the pew to comfort her.

Irena flew from her perch on the organ bench and wrapped her body around Brock's legs. He fell face-first to the floor. Keith was there immediately, followed by Charlotte, who grabbed her son and stood him up.

"Brock Tuggle, did you do what this child said you did?" Charlotte asked. "Did you destroy Dr. Jack's and Pastor Maggie's condominium?"

Irena stood up, repositioned her breasts, and pulled her skirt down just a tad. She looked at Brock.

"Vell, deed you?"

"Yes."

Gasps and groans filled the sanctuary.

Fred Tuggle walked up to his son. "What the . . . What did you do that for?" He raised his hand, but Keith caught it before he could strike the boy.

"Because I thought that's what you wanted." Brock tried not to cry, but fear overtook him. He began to sob. "You (sob) said you didn't (sob) want those damn (sob) Muslims in Cherish. You (gasp) said they were filth and scum." He took a deep breath and regained some control. "You said if you saw one of them, you'd shoot them dead. I thought I would keep them from coming here."

Maggie couldn't believe the poison in those words. *Shoot them dead? Who would say that in front of their children? Who would say that at all?*

Fred was fighting Keith's grip, so Bernie Bumble came to the rescue. He was on duty and in his uniform. He pulled out his handcuffs and cuffed Fred.

"Don't touch me!" Fred turned red. "Brock, don't say anything more!"

"We have fingerprints, Fred," Keith said as he pulled out his cell phone and dialed.

Brock and Fred were moved outside by Keith and Bernie. Charlotte stood next to Brock on the church lawn. Brock wasn't handcuffed—he wasn't going anywhere now. They could hear a siren in the distance.

Inside the church, Mary had calmed the crying Ryleigh while Zoey held her sister's hand. Maggie flew into action and put her arms around Mason and Liz.

"Let's go to my office, shall we?" She led them through the secret door as the congregation murmured behind her.

Once in her office, the two siblings sat in the visitor chairs.

"Are you all right?" Maggie asked.

"Why would he do that?" Liz asked.

Her eyes were red from crying. Maggie handed her a tissue.

"I just don't know *how* he did it," Mason said. "He would have had to sneak out of the house in the middle of the night a bunch of times. I would have heard him. Where did he get all the trash? Mom said there was so much trash and smelly diapers and cat litter. We don't have a cat or a baby at our house."

"I think he took trash from different bins around town," Maggie said.

"Is he going to go to jail?" Liz asked.

"I don't know." Maggie didn't want to instill any more fear, but she knew Brock was in trouble.

"Dad's been talking about Muslims and stuff for months now," Mason said. "He's never been like this before, but he's been watching more TV and listening to people scream and yell about people from other countries and how awful they all are. It's like anyone who isn't white is the enemy. I guess Brock proved them wrong. He's white, and he destroyed your house." Mason couldn't look Maggie in the face.

"I don't think Mom knew what to do when Dad wouldn't turn off the news," Liz said softly. "But then she started believing it too. I don't get it. Who judges people by the color of their skin? Or if they're a different religion? You don't believe that, Pastor Maggie."

"No. I don't. We're all created by God. We are all equal in God's sight. I've seen more cruelty from white people in the last year than I ever could have imagined." Maggie caught herself and stopped. There was no need to continue.

"I just don't get it," Mason said absently.

"Would you like me to bring you home?" Maggie asked. "Or would you like to go to the parsonage?"

Liz and Mason looked at each other.

"We should probably go home," Mason said. "We can wait for everyone there."

The three of them quietly walked out of the sanctuary doors. Some people noticed, but no one said anything. They were all still in their pews, stunned and shocked. Maggie drove Liz and Mason home.

Taking charge of the situation, Irena trip-trapped up the aisle of the sanctuary, then turned to face the congregation.

"Vell, dees ees eet forr today. Obviously, ve got beeg trroubles herre. Cookies and coffee, I tink." With a flourish of her small hand, she pointed to the basement.

Doris stood up. "Irena, what's that on your hand?"

Irena smiled coyly. "I vas vaiting for prrayer rrequests today. My Captain Crunch asked me to marrry heem. I decided to say yesss."

The congregation applauded, and Irena basked in the glory of her engagement by taking several bows and holding up her hand so they could see the sparkling diamond.

Myra turned to Myrna and Jasper. "Well, by golly! I guess church has changed since the last time I went. It's a lot more exciting now. Let's make sure to come back next week and see who else gets arrested and engaged."

"Dun't vorry," Irena said, "you vill all be invited to de vedding." She looked at Jasper and Myrna and their pew full of children. "I dun't know you peoples, but you can come to de vedding too."

The congregation finally stood up and made their way down to the basement. The odd mix of horror at the Tuggle boy and the hilarity of their beloved Irena left most of them emotionally off balance. They got cookies and coffee and sat quietly at tables with one another.

Maggie returned from dropping off Mason and Liz at the Tuggle home. She heard murmuring in the basement and felt relief. The congregation was still there. She would go forward with her middle-of-the-night plan.

When Maggie entered the basement, everyone looked up. She searched for Jack's face, found it, and carried on with her idea.

"May I say a prayer?"

People nodded, and heads were bowed.

"God, there is a family in turmoil this morning. They are part of us, and we care for them deeply. We ask you to protect them and prepare them for whatever is to come. May we love them the way you love them—completely, with all our hearts. Amen."

"Amens" rose from around the tables.

"I have something else I would like to say. I think we have had enough division, not just in our country, but within our own church. Today we witnessed something terribly sad, a young person who thought he had to 'keep out' people from another country who look, live, and worship differently than we do. As Christians, we won't tolerate this bigotry and racism. We won't tolerate intolerance. At least I won't. If I know you, and I think I do, your hearts are breaking along with mine for Brock Tuggle and his family. So, I have a proposition for you, the congregation of Loving the Lord Community Church. Our homeless Syrian family is still homeless. There is no place for them, and they will be here two weeks from tomorrow. On top of that, we have found out there is a family member who had not been processed at the beginning of their time in the refugee camp. She's a grandma. The mother of the father of the family. She has been very ill but will be joining her family here in Cherish.

"Now, Jack and I are moving out of the parsonage to a small farm near here at the end of the month. Don't gasp. We are not leaving you, we are just leaving the parsonage. I propose our new family move into the parsonage. It's full of furniture. It has plenty of room. We can care for them easily. I'm sick and tired of hate. We are a community of Christ. Let's be kind."

It was a crazy mix of emotions to cram into the first few minutes of the worship-service-that-wasn't. Maggie looked around the room. She saw her people. Coffee cups and cookies lay on the tables. The children could be heard upstairs, playing in the nursery. Their laughter was music. She turned her head as a hand went up in the air. It was Doris.

"Do you have a question, Doris?"

"No, Pastor Maggie, I don't. I vote 'yes.' Bring them here. Bring the Syrian family to Middle Street right here in Cherish. Our new family will live next door."

Maggie's eyes stung as she watched her congregation and council members. One by one, every hand was raised. It was unanimous.

"Thank you," she said softly.

Myra's crackly voice broke the silence. "Well, I sure don't know what is going on around here, but by golly, I want that family to live next door too. Whoever they are!"

After the coffee-time vote, Jack and Maggie spent a while in her office to debrief on the morning.

"I thought Fred might have done the vandalism," Maggie admitted, "after his belligerent visit to the parsonage. But it seemed like too much effort for him. He's just a bully and a coward."

"I didn't know if it was him or someone in Cherish who heard about the family and retaliated. The fact that it's Brock makes me sick." Jack's jaw clenched.

"From what Mason and Liz said, Fred has been sucked into the hate rhetoric. It must have seeped into Brock. Hate is such a cancer."

"If Brock goes to jail, he'll struggle . . ." Jack didn't finish his thought.

"I know. I don't want him locked up with criminals, people like Redford."

"The thing is, he is a criminal. What he did to our condo is a hate crime." Jack shook his head.

"Should we go to the police station?" Maggie asked.

Jack and Maggie drove to the Cherish Police Department. Maggie was surprised to see Fred sitting in the back of a patrol car in front of the station. He was looking down and didn't see them enter the building.

Maggie took in the scene in the small station and found Keith sitting in a plastic chair next to Brock.

"I decided not to bring Brock to Ann Arbor. At least not yet," Keith said, looking at the couple.

"Why is Fred in the patrol car?" Maggie asked.

"This station is too small. He'll stay there until I'm done questioning Brock."

Maggie saw Martha Babcock behind the counter, working the phone and police radio, pretending to ignore everyone. Charlotte stood stone-faced by the door to the jail cell. Maggie saw the symbolism; Charlotte barred the way to protect her child. Bernie was writing something on a pad of paper behind the counter next to Martha.

"As you heard at church," Keith said, "Brock admitted to the vandalism of your condo."

Everyone heard Charlotte's deep sigh.

Keith continued. "He won't be eighteen until next month. But in Michigan, he'll be charged as an adult. It is a hate crime. Brock spoke directly against Muslims, verbally and in the spray paint at the scene, and made it clear he committed this crime in order to keep them out of Cherish. I'll proceed with the prosecution based on those facts."

Jack nodded.

Maggie squeezed Jack's hand. *A hate crime. Charged as an adult.* She could feel goose bumps up and down her arms. Then she looked over at Charlotte and saw her staring at Brock. The woman was in agony.

"I'm ready with the paperwork, Detective. We can charge him," Bernie said, looking sideways at Charlotte.

"What if we don't press charges?" Jack asked.

"What?" Keith looked at Jack.

"Do we have to press charges? It's our personal home. It's not the same as when Redford damaged the church, you know, public property. If we don't press charges, can Brock have a second chance?"

"What he did was bad," Keith understated. "Jack, I think I know what you are trying to do, but someone doesn't do what Brock did without having a more serious problem going on."

"The problem is his father," Charlotte choked out. "Fred has been spewing—"

"You have too, Mom." Brock looked at his mother. "I thought you both wanted the foreigners to stay away from here. Dad said he would shoot them dead."

The door to the police station opened and Irena walked in. She looked at Keith.

"Vat about lunch?"

"Irena, I'm working. I'll call you later."

"Irena! What's on your finger?" Maggie hadn't talked with Irena after coffee time at church.

"Oh, dat's rright. You meesed eet. I'm engaged to Captain Crrunch. It's supposed to be happy lunch to celebrrate. Den ve drive to Detrroit and show my mama." She stared unblinkingly at Keith.

Maggie knew that Keith had spent a great deal of time finding the grave of Irena's mother, Catrina, who had died when Irena was only fifteen. Irena had not known where her mother was until Keith brought her to a cemetery in Detroit.

"Well, congratulations," Maggie impulsively hugged Irena and was immediately rebuffed.

Charlotte coughed.

"Irena, we'll celebrate later," Keith said. "You can't be in here right now."

"Vy nut? I'm de one to capturre heem."

Jack interrupted. "Keith, we don't want to press charges. We don't think Brock is a bad kid. We do think he was influenced by his father. To prosecute Brock would just be spreading more ugliness."

Brock looked up at Jack and Maggie, then put his head in his hands. Maggie watched as his back silently shook. Charlotte went to him and knelt down, putting her arms around him. Maggie bit her lip.

"Vell, der ve hev eet. Eet's done!"

Maggie reached over and pinched Irena. "Shut it, Irena," she hissed.

Irena's mouth opened to object, but the look in Maggie's eyes helped her close it again.

"Jack, Maggie, and Irena, would you please step out of the station?" Keith said. "I'd like to speak with Brock, Officer Bumble, and the chief."

He then looked at Martha and gave her a curt nod.

"We will keep an ear on the radio, Martha," Keith said.

She slowly came from around the counter and followed the other three as they left the building. Fred was still in the patrol car, his face ashen. He looked up at the four people on the steps of the station. In unknown imitation of his son, he held his head in his cuffed hands and silently began to shake.

It was over an hour before Keith asked Maggie and Jack to come back into the station. Irena had stayed for a while, then toddled off to O'Leary's Pub for a drink.

"Tell heem to meet me at de pub," Irena barked before she left.

At one point, Bernie came out of the station and brought Fred back in with him.

Martha had fidgeted and fussed, wanting to get back inside and overhear what was happening with Brock. She finally ended up going behind the police station and sitting in her car. Maggie knew Martha couldn't stand being near her and Jack.

What a waste of energy. When does hate wear itself out? Ever?

Finally, Keith opened the doors and asked them to come in.

The station reeked of stress and perspiration. Maggie tried not to gag. The confined space and the strain of the situation was suffocating.

"I have told Fred, Charlotte, and Brock that Brock should be charged with a hate crime," Keith said in detective mode. "What he did to your property was obviously more than teen mischief. He would serve a prison sentence for a minimum of ten years."

Maggie saw Fred, now out of handcuffs, and Charlotte both stiffen as Keith repeated words they had already heard and rejected.

"The truth is, it's kind of you both," Keith looked at Maggie and Jack, "to offer not to press charges. I understand it's because you know

Brock personally, and you also know what prison can do to a young man. Our country's prison system is broken. But I know the law. I know how white males often get lighter sentences or no sentence at all compared to men of color. As a detective and an officer, I see this discrepancy every day. It's wrong. It's unfair. Brock deserves to pay for what he did." Keith finished his statement like a judge's gavel slamming down. He took a breath, then continued.

"Fred and Charlotte are aware how their own words and actions influenced their son. They didn't commit the crime, but they may as well have. They can't be charged. But," he turned and stared at the two parents, "you should be."

It seemed as if no one but Keith was breathing.

Maggie felt the oppression of all the anger and fear. *This is what bigotry does. A heavy cloud hangs over those who hate, and there's no way out from under its weight.*

Jack cleared his throat. "Keith, I understand everything you are saying. It all makes sense. But I wonder if there are other options. Something for the family and not just punishment for Brock."

"What are you thinking?" Maggie asked, puzzled.

"I don't know exactly. Is there some kind of psychotherapy for the family? Anger management treatment? Parole for Brock, and help for everyone?"

Fred and Charlotte stared at Jack. Maggie watched their desperation flow straight from their eyes to him.

"There are options. But Brock is guilty of a serious crime," Keith said slowly. "I don't want that downplayed. I know of inpatient facilities for youths who have anger issues and need psychotherapy."

"Inpatient?" Charlotte said. "What about outpatient?"

"What about prison?" Keith was laser-focused. "I'm not fooling around, Charlotte. You know the law as well as I do. If this was any other young man than your own son, you'd throw the book at him. Why should your son get a break?"

Maggie watched Charlotte open her mouth and then close it again.

How easy it is for people to judge and condemn others, but if it comes to themselves or someone they love, there's almost always an excuse to pardon the sin.

"This is what I suggest," Jack said thoughtfully. "I think an inpatient program for Brock with regular family sessions of therapy would be a good place to start. I imagine the programs are thirty days or longer. That's much less than ten years in a penitentiary. But I would also like to add that Brock will pay restitution for the damage he inflicted. Our insurance company will pay us for the damage, so Brock will earn the same amount of money and give it to the Syrian family. They will need a lot of help adjusting to life here in Cherish."

Fred stiffened again. Maggie suspected that racism and bigotry still stuck like cement to his mind and heart. It would take Fred quite some time, and a sincere wish to change his beliefs, to transform his hate into decency or any kind of goodness.

Keith looked at Jack. "What about parole?"

"I'm willing to see how Brock does with treatment, therapy, and a lot of hard work. If things don't go well, we'll revisit the other options."

Jack looked at Maggie. She knew he believed Brock was capable of change.

"Brock, you will enter a treatment facility within a week." Keith took control. "I will assist in finding an opening for you. Fred and Charlotte, you will begin therapy as a couple and have weekly meetings with your children. Charlotte, I'm tempted to speak to your direct supervisor and have you step down from your role as police chief until this is sorted out completely." He paused. "Do you feel you are able to carry out your duties while working through these personal issues?"

"I will take a leave of absence," Charlotte said quietly.

"Officer Bumble, you will take over the chief's duties, starting today. I will have another officer join you from the Ann Arbor squad."

"Yes, sir," Bernie said.

Maggie thought he looked a little shell-shocked.

The group of six left Bernie alone in the station.

The heaviness of the day bore down on each one. No one would ever forget the day Brock Tuggle was arrested for destroying Pastor Maggie and Dr. Jack's condominium. And the voice of a little girl in church who made the truth known.

18

Maggie used a screwdriver to pop open a paint can. Her long hair was wrapped on the top of her head in a messy bun. She carefully poured the pale-yellow paint into the plastic tray, then dipped her roller in, rolled it around, and lifted it to the wall. The first stripe went up the wall in her new farmhouse kitchen. She listened to the voices in other rooms.

Andrew, Brynn, Harold, and Ellen had joined Maggie and Jack for a painting party at the farm on Friday night. Brynn walked into the kitchen, her long brown hair wrapped in a braid around her head.

"Oooh! That is so pretty!"

"I really like it too," Maggie said. "It will make the kitchen so cozy. I can hardly wait to move here next week."

"It's nice you and Jack had permission to come in early and paint."

"Those three are crazy!" Harold said, walking into the kitchen. "I never would have guessed Jack to be such a practical jokester. Did you know he and Andrew once locked Ellen in an old trunk in their barn? It had saddle blankets in it and a family of mice. They were not nice cousins."

"I like watching Jack with his family," Maggie said, methodically rolling the paint. "More stories come out, whether he likes it or not."

"I know," Brynn said. "I love listening to Andrew and Leigh go at it whenever we're together at Ken and Bonnie's. Having five kids running around that farm must have been a riot."

Brynn grabbed a clean roller and rolled it into the yellow paint. She began to paint the wall next to Maggie.

"I don't know what kind of family I'm getting into," Harold said as he grabbed a slice of pizza from the box on the island in the middle of the kitchen.

"Are you getting into this family?" Brynn asked.

"Well, I think so. If Ellen will have me."

Maggie almost dropped her paint roller. "Harold! Are you and Ellen going to get married?"

"Probably," he said nonchalantly, then took another large bite of his pizza.

"Ellen!" Maggie yelled. "Ellen!"

Ellen hurried into the kitchen. "What?"

"Are you and Harold getting married?" Maggie asked.

Ellen looked at Harold. "Well, I don't know." She gave an airy little sniff. "No one has asked me about it."

Jack and Andrew walked into the kitchen just as Harold went down on one knee, right into a splotch of paint on the plastic covering. He reached into his pants pocket and pulled out a small velvet box. Ellen, who had been teasing about not being asked, stared in disbelief.

"What are you doing?" she whispered.

"Ellen Bright, you have certainly brought brightness and happiness and goodness into my life. I would like nothing better than to be your husband, if you will have me. What do you say?"

He opened the small box and held it toward Ellen. A diamond encircled by small sapphires sparkled in the kitchen light.

Maggie watched as Ellen helped Harold get to his feet.

"I would love for you to be my husband, Harold Brinkmeyer. So, yes. That's what I have to say."

Then she jumped up, threw her arms and legs around Harold, and kissed him. As she slid down to the floor, her pant leg was smeared with yellow paint from Harold's knee, but she didn't care.

Maggie clapped her hands, and the others joined in.

"Congratulations!"

They each took a slice of pizza and raised them in a floppy toast.

"This is so exciting," Maggie said with her mouth full. She swallowed. "First, Andrew and Brynn. Then Irena and Keith, which still boggles my mind a little bit, and now you two. When do you want to get married?"

"It will have to be sometime in 2017. I think your 2016 is busy enough," Ellen said, looking at Harold.

"Can we get back to you on this, or do you need an answer right now?" Harold asked.

"Let me know by Sunday. Two days should be enough time," Maggie teased. "Ellen, don't you want to wear that beautiful ring?"

Harold jammed the remainder of his pizza into his mouth, took the ring out of the box, and slipped it onto Ellen's extended finger.

"There! You're stuck with me now."

Ellen admired it for a moment and then slipped it off. "There's no way I'm going to risk getting paint on this beautiful ring. Put it back in the box until we're done here."

Harold did as he was ordered. The ring would have to wait a little longer to sparkle on Ellen's finger.

The painting/engagement party continued.

Maggie had just finished her kitchen wall when Harold said, "I wonder when Lacey and Lydia will decide to get married."

Maggie's arm went limp, and this time her roller dropped to the floor. Yellow paint splattered on her shoes and jeans.

"Harold, why would you ask that?"

"Well, Maggie, because they are in love, and sometimes people who are in love get married." Harold sounded like he was explaining this to a toddler.

"How did you know about Lacey and Lydia?" Maggie asked.

"It's obvious. Well, maybe not *obvious*. They are trying to hide their relationship. But the other day I opened the door that connects my office to the salon, and they were in the stairwell kissing. I apologized when they seemed to expect I was going to scream in horror. I just said, 'Good for you two. You make a great couple.' Then I went back to my office. Later, Lacey came in and told me all about it. She said you and Jack knew too. She seemed scared."

"I think she is scared," Maggie said. "I'm so glad you know. They deserve our support and love the same way you and Ellen do. I've wondered if the next huge battle in our church would be a same-sex wedding. It's hard to believe it would be. But then I didn't think a childcare center or resettling a refugee family would cause such animosity. We've got to get better at inviting people in, instead of shutting them out."

"Then let's invite them in," Ellen said. "Everyone loves Lacey and Lydia, but we can begin with something small for them. Like one of these evening painting parties."

"Who in your church could possibly be anti-LGBTQ?" Brynn asked, pouring more paint in the pan. "It's so . . . archaic."

"I don't know. I've been surprised by who was against the other two issues we've been fighting about all summer, but I do believe true feelings come pouring out when people are afraid. Fear is a great motivator of hatred and judgment. I'll ask Lacey and Lydia if they would like to come here on Sunday night. What do you think?" Maggie asked.

Jack and Andrew joined the others in the kitchen.

"Can we come back on Sunday, Andrew?" Brynn asked.

"Anything you want. I am your humble servant, even though it is a bit of a drive."

"I'll tell you what," Maggie said, "you come back on Sunday night, and I'll drive to Blissfield two weeks from tomorrow."

"You *have* to drive to Blissfield two weeks from tomorrow," Brynn said with a grin. "It's my wedding shower."

"I can't wait for your shower!" Ellen said. "I have some of the best memories in the farmhouse, minus being locked in the horse-blanket-mouse trunk and a few other unpleasant places. Are you sure you want to marry Andrew?"

"Pretty sure. But if he ever locks me in a trunk with mice, it's over."

"Okay," Maggie said, "back to the matter at hand. You engaged couples are difficult to keep focused. We'll all meet back here with the lovely Ls on Sunday. Harold and Ellen will have chosen a wedding date. We will finish all the painting. There will be food and drinks provided, including champagne to toast the newly engaged couples." Maggie rubbed her hands together like a happy sorceress. "It's so nice to have things to celebrate in other people's lives."

The painting continued until Andrew and Brynn decided it was time to make their drive back to Blissfield.

"We'll be back Sunday night for the big party," Andrew said. He had a lovely stripe of pale-yellow paint across his dark hair. He looked like a skunk.

"We should probably head out too," Harold said. "That is, *my fiancée* and I should be going. We have some of our own celebrating to do."

"We can finish up on Sunday," Jack said.

Everybody helped close up paint cans and clean rollers and brushes. Harold stuffed the last piece of cold pizza in his mouth and put the box in the recycle bin in the kitchen. Then Maggie and Jack saw their guests to their soon-to-be new front door.

Once they were alone, they sat down together on the front steps. The evening was cool. It was the first full day of fall, and the skies seemed to understand. Maggie snuggled under Jack's arm.

"This was a fun night," she said. "It looks we are going to have a wedding extravaganza around here. That will bring a lot of joy to the couples and to the congregation. Any good news is welcome, that's for sure."

"It's strange how the break-in at the condo, along with all the destruction Brock was able to render, changed so many people's opinions. It was as if they had to be confronted with how violent things could get if hatred and fear went unchecked."

"The change was immediate. I'm so glad we didn't press charges. Keith still could have charged him with a hate crime. It was surreal in that police station. Keith in charge. Brock in shock. And Charlotte . . ." Maggie trailed off.

Brock had gone to Jackson for inpatient treatment the day after their afternoon in the police station. He had been there almost a week. The rest of the family would begin their counseling sessions the following week with Brock.

"It was easy to not press charges," Jack said. "Brock is a kid. He needed to know we forgave him. I think paying the restitution money to the Syrian family is a more positive way to teach a lesson instead of sending him to jail. And the inpatient program will help him get some handle on his anger and actions. Charlotte was the one who got to me. She wasn't the police chief that afternoon. She was a mother. She knew what could happen to her son. I've never seen such anguish. I wonder what kind of conversations have been going on in that house this past week."

"I don't know, but Fred, Brock, and even Charlotte understood, at least for a moment, what being the 'hated one' feels like. The fact that it all happened in front of the congregation must have been humiliating. Fred and Charlotte were helpless. I don't wish that on them or anyone. Only," Maggie looked thoughtfully at the sky, "it's how so many people feel every day who are of a different race or religion. No one should be made to feel that way." Maggie sighed. "When I stopped by their house on Wednesday, Charlotte was polite, but she didn't invite me in. I told her we were praying for them and that we had no hard feelings. She couldn't even look me in the eye. How do we let them know they aren't hated?"

"Do you think they will be in church on Sunday?" Jack asked.

"I have no idea." Maggie switched gears. "We have a busy weekend, no matter what. Tonight's painting party, work at the condo on Saturday, church on Sunday, then more painting here at the farmhouse Sunday night with all our engaged friends. It will be nice to move in next week and maybe have a little peace and quiet."

Sunday morning was abuzz in the sanctuary of Loving the Lord. It had been one week since Ryleigh identified Brock. Irena tried to shush the talkers, but even she gave up and just played her prelude that much louder. Maggie peeked through the secret door and saw pew after pew filled with people. She was happy to see Myrna and Jasper and their crowd. Sylvia, Bill, and Katharine Marie slid into their pew. People oohed and ahhed over Katherine's baby pink princess ensemble. William and Mary Ellington came in with Carrie, Carl, Ryleigh, and Zoey. Maggie wondered if Ryleigh and Zoey's parents would ever be interested in coming to church. She hadn't met the Teaters yet but had heard about them from Mary. Maybe if the children did a Christmas pageant their mom and dad would attend. Maggie knew they would.

As she daydreamed about this, Irena finished her prelude and everyone sat in silence, waiting for Maggie. She was jarred awake from her faraway thoughts by the silence. She quickly opened the secret door and stepped out onto the altar. As she did so, the large oak sanctuary doors opened.

Everyone turned to see Charlotte, Fred, Mason, and Liz.

It was as if the whole sanctuary took a deep breath.

Maggie set her Bible and bulletin on the chair behind the pulpit. Then she walked down the altar steps toward the Tuggle family. As she got closer, she opened her arms and hugged Charlotte. Maggie had to stand on her tiptoes to get to Charlotte's shoulders. Next, she hugged Fred, then Mason and Liz. The absence of Brock was stark. Everyone knew where he was. It hurt to look at the rest of the family without one of their own.

Maggie felt someone behind her and turned her head to look. It was Jack. He squeezed past her and shook Charlotte's hand and then Fred's. He said something to Mason and Liz.

"Vell! Derre you hev eet!" Irena bellowed from her perch on the organ bench. "Eet ees all verry goot, and ve arre dun vit all de shenanigans, and now ve hev de love fest."

She hopped down and trotted over in high heels. Instead of beginning worship, the congregation of Loving the Lord had an impromptu receiving line for the Tuggle family. Row by row the congregation made their way to the back of the church. Maggie watched as Addie went to Liz and slipped her arm through Liz's. Charlotte and Fred both looked embarrassed, but as their church family surrounded them with acceptance, their embarrassment turned to gratitude. Finally, after people were seated back in their pews, Charlotte went forward and faced the congregation. Maggie stood next to her for moral support.

"Fred and I would like to thank you for your kindness to our family. We owe this congregation an apology for our words and actions. We are thankful to the Elliots for not . . ." She stopped for a moment, then took a deep breath and continued. "For not pressing charges against Brock." She stopped again. Her lips tightened, and her whole body stiffened. The congregation ached with her. "I'd like you to know, Brock has been in treatment this past week and will stay for another three weeks. He cannot have visitors besides immediate family, but if you would like to send him a card . . ." Charlotte used every ounce of energy she had to remain composed, "I can give you his address and room number. Thank you." She stalked down the aisle and sank into the pew next to Fred.

"Thank you, Charlotte," Maggie said. "I'm sure we would all like to show our love and support to Brock. You are all very dear to us here at Loving the Lord."

Someone began to clap their hands. Others joined in. Soon the sanctuary was filled with the sound of loud applause.

That's when Charlotte began to cry.

Sunday after church, Jack and Maggie drove to the farmhouse. They'd decided to spend the afternoon alone, painting and fixing a few needed repairs before they hosted their houseful of friends. They wanted to thank those who had helped so much already.

"I just want to tiptoe around each room and dream," Maggie said.

"You dream, I'll paint." Jack kissed the top of her head. "We got more done Friday night than I expected."

"Do you think we can finish it today?" Maggie asked.

"We can try."

They both walked into the dining room. It was already prepped. Jack popped open the can of dark-gray paint for the trim around the walls.

"I'm glad we could slow down on the condo," Maggie said as her paintbrush carefully applied the trim paint. "It felt overwhelming after the break-in. I hope the parsonage will be just the right place for our Syrian family."

She dipped her brush into the paint.

A few hours later, Jack and Maggie were ready. Jack had made shredded barbecue chicken sliders. There were also plates piled with hot dogs. Maggie had made trays of tortilla swirls with different fillings, opened bags of chips, and set out a fruit bowl on the kitchen counter. She had also baked a double batch of monster cookies the week before and set plates of them all over the house. Champagne was chilling in the ice-filled sink. The "engagement party" at the Elliot farmhouse was ready to commence. They had brought some folding chairs from the basement of the parsonage and a set of TV trays they found. Maggie had music playing in the living room from her phone and a speaker. If it wasn't exactly comfortable, it was festive.

Though they came from the farthest distance, Andrew and Brynn arrived first—dressed in jeans and T-shirts, ready to paint.

"Hey," Andrew said as he and Brynn noticed the paint supplies had been put away and that all the rooms on the main floor were finished. "Do you need us to paint upstairs?"

"We've changed plans a little," Jack said. "We aren't going to paint. Maggie and I finished almost all of it this afternoon. There wasn't much after Friday. Plus, we wanted to make this more of a party for all you lovebirds."

"You mean we drove all the way up here on a Sunday night for nothing?" Andrew said, sounding slightly perturbed. "Do you know how early we get up on the farm? Not like you lazy bums in the city."

"Poor baby," Jack replied.

Lacey and Lydia were on the porch when Maggie opened the stained-glass door after hearing a very normal *ding-dong* from the very normal doorbell.

"Hi, PM," Lacey said. "We're here and ready to paint!"

Both she and Lydia were casually dressed and had their heads wrapped in colorful bandanas.

"Come in, you two! I hope you're not disappointed if you don't get to paint tonight."

The two women looked confused.

"What *are* we doing?" Lacey sounded tentative.

Maggie looked at her and said, "We're having a party. We've only invited people who are in love. So, of course you two had to be here. Please don't worry. It's a small gathering of good people."

She pointed them toward the kitchen and held the door open for Harold and Ellen, who had just arrived.

Jack invited their guests to help themselves to food from the kitchen. "We've got plenty. It's just on paper plates. May I offer you a paper cup of champagne?"

Ellen stood next to Lacey and Lydia and said softly, "I'm so glad you two are here. Who would have thought we would get out of painting tonight?"

The normal doorbell rang.

Maggie opened the door to an odd sight—Keith Crunch, looking as handsome as always, blue eyes blazing out of his chiseled face had his arm around Irena, who was dressed in leopard-print spandex pants and a black, low-cut T-shirt which read: I JUST WANT TO DRINK VODKA AND SMASH THE PATRIARCHY. Her five-inch black heels finished the outfit.

Next to them stood Skyler Breese and Sylvester Fejokwu. Although dressed casually, they looked ready to walk a red carpet. Sky had on red jeans, which highlighted her beautiful long legs perfectly, along with a white shirt knot-tied at her waist, showing her perfectly flat stomach. Sly wore black jeans and Nike T-shirt.

Maggie took a deep breath and pulled herself together.

"Welcome! Please come in."

She stepped aside as the foursome walked through, Irena leading the way.

Once in the living room, introductions were made to Lydia. Then Jack ushered the new guests into the kitchen for food and champagne.

Irena hawk-eyed the different plates of food. Then she rubbed her little hands together, as if casting a spell. She picked up a plate and piled it high with two chicken sliders, two hot dogs, several tortilla rolls, and a mountain of potato chips piled on top. Next she commandeered an entire plate of monster cookies. Then she eagerly took a cup of champagne from Jack, stood by the island, and began to feast.

Jack felt a tap in his shoulder. It was Sylvester.

"Do you have a second?"

Jack set the champagne on the counter, just within reach of Irena, who gladly refilled her paper cup to the brim. Jack and Sly moved off into the laundry room.

"I'm sorry to bring up work issues here," Sly said, "but I thought you would be interested to know the board has given the green light for the clinic. We'll be able to give free or low-cost healthcare to those who are uninsured in our surrounding area."

Jack's eyes lit up. With everything else going on with the condo, farmhouse, and parsonage, the free clinic had easily slipped into the tiniest corner of his brain.

"That's great! What's the next step?"

"We have some options. The fastest way to begin the process would be to offer evening and weekend hours of free healthcare in the hospital and your offices. We can begin to search for land or property for a separate clinic somewhere between here and Manchester."

"I'd like to see the details. We've got to get Charlene in on this." Jack knew his partner was one of the biggest proponents of the free health clinic.

"I'll call you tomorrow, and we'll set up a meeting."

When they went back into the kitchen, Jack found Maggie and whispered the update in her ear.

She whispered back, "I'm glad it's moving forward. Sylvester must be a wizard with the board. They don't seem to ever move on *anything*. At least not this quickly. Would they like to help us set up a childcare center?" She smiled.

Maggie began to dream of all the good things a free health clinic could do in the surrounding communities. Until she was startled out of her happy thoughts by an all-too-familiar voice.

"So, you two," Irena said, munching on a cookie and staring at Lydia and Lacey. "Arre you two a couple?" Maggie closed her eyes and sighed. *Why did we invite that crazy little idiot?*

The awkward silence hung in the room while everyone tried to figure out where their eyes should be.

"I hope so," Irena continued as she took a sip of her champagne, "becuz you look heppy togetherr. Like you needed to find each otherr all yourr lives. I see dis. I underrstand dis. I thought forr de longest time in my head, no love for Irrena. I not hev anybody. But look, my Captain Crrunch! He says to me, 'Irrena, I meesed you and deed nut even know eet.'"

Keith smiled. "That's the truth."

"Beautiful . . . so beautiful." Sky looked at Keith and Irena, then at Lacey and Lydia. "Congratulations to, well . . . to all of you. When are your . . . hmmm . . . weddings?"

Maggie wanted to run straight out the back door and never return, determined the evening was a mistake she would regret forever. She imagined Lacey and Lydia packing up and moving far, far away.

Then she heard a laugh. A boisterous laugh. It was Lydia. Maggie stared as Lydia spoke.

"Lacey, you look white as a ghost. If you would have told me people in your church were this woke, I'd have shown up for church a long time ago."

Lacey looked around at the friendly, encouraging faces. Then she looked at Lydia.

"I love you, Lydia. I really do."

"Good," Lydia said, still laughing. "Ditto."

"Dis calls for de notherr drrink!" Irena made for another champagne bottle.

Lydia gave Lacey a kiss and whispered in her ear, "We're going to be okay. We really are."

19

The last week of September was a whirlwind for Maggie and Jack. Each morning when they awoke, they pulled on their old clothes and got ready for another day of moving, cleaning, and lots and lots of people. They were cleaning out the parsonage and preparing the farmhouse for their moving day on Friday. Thankfully, the drive back and forth from home to home was short. There was also work still going on at the condo, so there was no end to the tasks that needed accomplishing.

They had each taken the week off work, even though Maggie knew she would have to somehow write a sermon for Sunday morning. She kept putting that nagging thought out of her mind as the days flew by.

The owners of the farm had been more than generous to allow not just the painting and cleaning to begin before the actual close of the sale, but they also let Jack and Maggie move in boxes of their possessions and have new furniture delivered. It was one of the many blessings of living in a small town and community. On Wednesday, the paperwork was signed and the delightful farmhouse was officially theirs.

It was Thursday morning of their busy week when Maggie and Jack opened the front door and stared. Fred Tuggle stood on the porch of the parsonage. His bright-red truck was parked on the street.

"Hi, Fred," Jack said, reaching out his hand.

Fred shook Jack's hand out of politeness but couldn't make eye contact.

"Hi, Fred," Maggie chimed in a little too loudly. "Come on in." She and Jack stepped back.

"No, no, that's okay. I'm here to, uh, help. I know the foreign family is moving in here, and I thought I could help in some way. I have the next two days off, along with the weekend."

Maggie and Jack inhaled this information, as if breathing it in would make it sensible.

Fred continued. "I noticed the chimney is in need of repair. I'm a skilled mason and would be willing to fix it for you, if you would like." He stared hard at his work boots.

"That would be great, Fred," Jack said. "We knew the church would have to fix it but didn't want to try and roll that all in before the family arrives. We're all scrambling enough these days."

Maggie cringed inwardly. Part of the scrambling was due to Fred and his son Brock's bigotry.

The phone rang.

"Excuse me," Maggie said and quickly walked into the kitchen.

"Hello, Maggie speaking."

"Hello, Pastor Maggie. This is Reverend Hill from the chaplain's office at the Milan State Penitentiary. We've spoken once before when you asked me to connect with Mr. Redford Johnson."

Maggie felt her heart begin to race. "How can I help you?"

"You are listed on his personal contact form. There has been an accident."

"What kind of accident?" Maggie didn't really want to know. She wanted to slam down the phone and run.

"He was outdoors yesterday for recreation time. Three other prisoners dragged him out of sight of the guards and beat him. It was less than five minutes before they were found, but that was long enough to do their damage."

"Where is Redford now?" Maggie asked without emotion.

"He's at St. Joseph Mercy in Ypsilanti. He is in a coma with severe, traumatic head injuries, kidney failure, and broken and fractured bones, particularly in his neck, shoulders, and back. He may not live."

Maggie heard each word clearly, yet she felt nothing.

After a long pause, Reverend Hill spoke. "I wanted to let you know. I will keep you informed of his situation. Of course, you can visit, if you wish. He is being guarded, but your name is on the list to see him. You have security clearance."

"Thank you," Maggie finally said. She stopped herself from saying anything else.

"Have a blessed day," Reverend Hill said, then hung up.

Maggie picked up her coffee mug, took a Keurig pod, and made herself another cup. The first gulp burned her tongue and the roof of her mouth. She took a second gulp anyway.

She could hear Jack and Fred talking in the entryway. Fred must have come in after all. She listened as they discussed the brickwork on the chimney. She forced herself to walk to the two men. Fred seemed to be a little more animated. He explained how he could have it done in a few days.

"Fitch Dervish is on his way to check the chimney before I begin."

That woke Maggie up immediately.

"Fitch?" she asked.

"Yes. I knew I couldn't begin until Fitch okayed the whole thing, as usual, but I can handle him. He likes to bully people, but I can bully him right back."

It took a few seconds for Fred to hear himself. When he did, he turned red.

"I didn't mean that. I just meant I know how to deal with Fitch." He looked sheepish again.

Maggie walked out on the porch. She wanted to go to her farmhouse and never leave. No parsonage. No church. No prison. No Fred. No Redford. No Fitch. She was sick of it all.

"Yoo-hoo! Pastor Maggie!" Polly Popkin was bustling across the street with two of her just-out-of-high-school girls following behind. They were carrying pink bakery boxes and thermoses of beverages. "Hokey tooters! We were planning to be here an hour ago, but we got behind, didn't we, gals?"

The girls nodded.

"Come inside," Maggie said. She also said a silent prayer of thanksgiving to God for people like Mrs. Popkin, who cheered everyone they encountered.

Jack and Fred were shoved out of the way.

"We'll set these things in the kitchen, unless you'd like them somewhere else," Mrs. Popkin said, even as she was setting her boxes down and taking the other items from the girls.

"That's great," Maggie said. "Thank you for doing this. I don't know who all might show up today, but you always come through for any occasion and keep our spirits up with sugar and caffeine."

"My pleasure. We can't have folks fainting dead away due to lack of sustenance." She waddled around the kitchen, opened the boxes, and set up paper plates and cups from a large pink bag. "This ought to do it."

Maggie impulsively threw her arms around the baker. "I just love you!"

"And the feeling is mutual times ten," Mrs. Popkin said, patting Maggie on the back and then extricating herself from the embrace. "We'll check back in with you later. Come along, gals!"

Maggie watched out the living room window as Mrs. Popkin and her girls walked across the street, back to The Sugarplum Bakery. Her eyes were then drawn to a truck pulling up behind Fred's bright-red pickup.

Fitch.

Maggie quickly went to her study. Jack could handle Fitch today.

The cats were curled up in their beds, so she sat down and began to pet them. Purrs erupted, and Maggie smiled.

"We're moving, babies," she said softly. "You will have a new house to sniff and investigate. There are lots of windows, and I might even take you into the barn. And we will play and play and have so much fun!"

She heard a cough. She turned and saw Jack.

"What are you doing?" he asked.

She continued to pet the cats. "Oh, bits and bobs, odds and ends, this and that. What are you doing?"

"Looking for my wife. When did you show up, Snow White?"

"I wanted to find the cats. And I did. Look, here they are. I thought I would move them upstairs while we clean. Plus, I can't handle Fitch today. Plus, Redford may be dying."

Jack's eyes widened. "What?"

The Westminster chimes rang.

Both Maggie and Jack jumped. The cats darted from the room, off to somewhere safe, and Jack went to the door to handle Fitch and Fred.

Out of the beautiful floor-to-ceiling window, Maggie watched the birds fly to and from the bird feeder.

Friday began with moving the last few things to the farmhouse. The parsonage was ready for final touch-up cleaning and stocking with food and toys for the Syrian family. Maggie realized the move to the farmhouse was anticlimactic compared to the excitement of welcoming their new family.

Jack and Maggie sent the helpers from church who had followed them to the farmhouse away by early afternoon and took care of arranging their new home together, along with the three felines, who couldn't take in all the new smells fast enough.

Jack and Maggie cleaned what was left to clean in the farmhouse, arranged their new furniture, and made the new beds with freshly washed sheets. They unpacked, washed, and put away new dishes. They made a midnight run to the Meijer store in Ann Arbor for groceries, cat food, light bulbs, two lamps, and a bathmat for their new bathroom. Then they drove back to the parsonage for their last night in their first home. It was two thirty when they finally fell asleep.

At six a.m., the alarm went off in the parsonage, and they woke with a start.

"Good morning," Maggie mumbled as she kissed Jack's shoulder. "It's the last leg of this move of ours."

Jack kissed her back. "It's too bad we couldn't make more of our last night in the parsonage." He threw his arm around her and pulled her close.

"We're still here for a little while." She snuggled into Jack's arms.

When they came downstairs, coffee and oatmeal fueled them for the morning.

The Westminster chimes rang.

On the front porch were Bill and Sylvia, with little Katharine Marie cuddled in a sling around her mother's chest. Behind them were Marla, Tom, and Addie. Hank and Pamela Arthur were riding up on bicycles. Doris and Chester Walters were walking up the street. Mrs. Popkin was bustling over with the requisite goodies.

Maggie's heart leapt when she saw the Gutierrez family park across the street. Juan and Maria removed Gabby and Marcos from their car seats.

"Hi, there," Maggie said with a smile at Gabby and Marcos. "Come on in!"

Jack and Maggie stepped aside as their friends poured in the parsonage front door.

They had come to make final preparations at the parsonage for the Syrian family, but Maggie also knew that the members of the congregation wanted to be part of this day, whether there was anything for them to do or not.

Pastor Maggie and Dr. Jack were leaving the parsonage. And finally, the Syrian family would move into their new life. It was a big day for Loving the Lord Community Church.

"Hi, Gabby and Marcos," Addie said, immediately kneeling. "Shall we work together?"

Maria smiled at the older girl while the children squealed. Addie was a favorite with all the little ones at Loving the Lord.

"I have the perfect job for you," Maggie said. "I think the kitties have hidden their cat toys everywhere in this big house. Can you find them for me and put them in this basket?"

Maggie handed a wicker basket to Gabby. Addie led her little followers upstairs to begin the hunt.

"Thank you for coming, Juan and Maria. It is so nice of you to spend your Saturday with us." Maggie gave them each a hug.

"We are happy to be here. Tell us what to do," Maria said.

"Juan, how do you feel about trimming bushes?" Jack asked.

"I can do that. I was hoping you wouldn't ask me to fix the roof or anything like that. I don't like heights." Juan smiled.

"That's next. We thought you could help repair the brickwork on the chimney," Jack said, deadpan.

"No. We didn't," Maggie said quickly. "We're sending Jack up alone to do that job."

Everyone greeted one another, grabbed donuts and turnovers, and began to make plans for the day.

"Thank you all for coming," Jack said. "With three houses to clean and renovate all at the same time, we've been busy."

Everyone turned and stared as Fred Tuggle walked in the front door. Maggie could see he hadn't expected a crowd.

"Hi, Fred!" Maggie said, walking over to him.

Fred cleared his throat and looked down. "Fitch Dervish is checking out the chimney," he said. "Again." He paused and cleared his throat one more time. "As soon as he's done, I can get back to work."

"Would you like a donut, Fred?" Marla asked kindly.

She picked up one of the boxes and brought it over to Fred, who looked anguished. Maggie knew how hard it could be to receive kindness when someone was certain they didn't deserve it. It was a bit of a torment of the soul.

"Fred," Maggie said, "we are your friends. Consider this a 'donut of grace.' We are glad you are here and that you know how to do brickwork. It will be a huge gift to the church, the parsonage, and to our new family."

Fred took his donut-of-grace and looked around the room. "Thank you."

The Westminster chimes rang.

Jack went to the door.

Mason stood there, shifting anxiously.

"Hi, Mason. Come on in. We're having a party," Jack said easily.

"I told Mason he needed to be here to help," Fred said in a scratchy voice.

Maggie sighed. "Okay, listen. We're going to move forward now. We are a church family. We have work to do. Mason, have a donut."

The day commenced with outdoor and indoor cleanup projects. There were also several people sitting on the porch talking and helping themselves to treats. When she saw Fitch stalking around the chimney, Maggie expected him to fall straight off the roof and land on his head, but he was able to make it down the ladder without incident in the end. She was relieved when his truck drove away from the parsonage.

Fred worked tirelessly on the chimney, and it was beautifully refurbished. He also repaired loose roof tiles. He noticed a broken window frame hidden behind an overgrown bush and fixed that as well. Mason and Jason Wiggins put a fresh coat of paint on the garage. Maggie made a point to go out and talk with the boys.

"Thanks for painting," she said. "I think it's been a long time since this was done."

"Yeah, it took a while to sand it all down," Mason said.

"It's nice to have everything fixed up for our new arrivals," Maggie said. "I know they are a family with a mom, a dad, four children, and a grandma. The parsonage should be a good fit for them with all the bedrooms and bathrooms."

"How old are the kids?" Mason asked as he painted.

"They are elementary school age and younger. It will be nice to bring them here." Maggie thought for a moment. "So, Mason, how are things going with Brock?"

"We saw him this week for the first time. He's halfway done with his treatment. I think he's feeling okay, but he said he really wants to come home. Our whole family has to go, and we talk with a counselor all together."

"What will you and Brock do when he gets back home?"

"What do you mean?" Mason asked.

"I know you're taking a gap year before you head off to college. These first few months will be difficult in a lot of ways for the Syrian family. Darcy has a list of tasks that need to be done. Things like driver's training, enrolling the children in school, jobs for the adults, and all the legal things that must happen to make them US citizens. The list goes on and on."

"I'll help, and I think Brock will too. We both are working with my dad at the quarry to earn some money for school, but we'll have extra time."

"Perfect," she said. "Thank you for painting today and for being available in the days to come. We'll get this done together."

"When will they be here?" Mason asked.

"Monday. Their flight will arrive in Detroit at eleven thirty in the morning. The day after tomorrow. I can hardly believe it!"

"Who's picking them up?" Mason asked.

"Some of us are going to the airport to fetch them, and others will be here at the parsonage waiting to welcome them. We want to support them, but not overwhelm them with too many new faces."

Saturday continued with a thorough scrubbing of the parsonage, under Doris's command. New sheets and towels had been purchased, so all the beds were freshly made. Stuffed animals were on the children's beds, along with colorful blankets.

Howard and Verna Baker arrived with pots of zinnias for the porch.

"I know they won't last long now that fall is on the way," Verna said, "but they are hearty and will look nice for a while."

She commenced setting the pots on the porch and around the pine trees in the backyard. Then she and Howard collected several grocery bags from their car trunk and brought them into the kitchen. Marla, Sylvia, and Maria were washing boxes of new dishes and putting them in cupboards. The church's china had been packed and stored in the church basement. Groceries were sitting in bags everywhere.

"It appears we all thought the same thing," Verna said as she surveyed the food. "Well, good for us, and good for them. I'll begin in the pantry."

Fred Tuggle steered around on his riding lawn mower to give the grass one last cut before Monday.

Addie and the children had made a "Welcome Home" sign on a cloth banner with bright paint. The children had put their hands in the paint and left a print (or two) on the banner.

Maggie stood in the living room of the parsonage. She listened to the laughter in the kitchen. She saw Fred riding back and forth across the front lawn. She heard the children squeal when Addie said they could hang streamers and balloons on the porch. She could hear Doris's vacuum upstairs, and whiffs of Lemon Pledge and Pine-Sol pleasantly filled her nose.

Tonight, she and Jack would sleep in their new farmhouse. She would not live in the parsonage again. She wouldn't cross the lawn from church for a quick bite of lunch and a cup of tea. She would have to find a new room in which to write her sermons. Her beautiful study would be for the Syrians now.

Maggie closed her eyes.

Thank you, God, for this day. Thank you for the privilege of welcoming strangers to this land, this town, and this home. In this place, may they be healed from all their pain. May we be blessed as a congregation to know them and learn from them. And may you receive all the glory for putting this whole scheme together. Oh! And thank you for Fred and all the good that has come out of all the bad. You are awesome. Amen.

ISTANBUL, TURKEY

At the airport, Mahdi and Amira herded their children to the waiting area and patiently supported Mahdi's mother, Sabeen. Everything was new: a mix of exciting and frightening. The whole family huddled together and jumped every time the loud speaker blared an announcement. They would have two stops before they landed in a place called Michigan.

The night before, once everyone was asleep, Amira had slipped out of their tent and walked in the bright moonlight to the graveyard. She knew exactly where to go to be near her baby. She sat on the grave and wept.

> Goodbye, little one. We are leaving soon, and you must stay here alone. I am so sorry you are gone and that I couldn't care for you. You are in my heart. Please watch over us. I love you, my little child.

Amira sat for a time. She felt the breeze on her face. Then she fixed her eyes on the swaying flowers—the beautiful flowers that gently danced on the graves of the dead.

20

After church on Sunday, a small group of people met in Maggie's office: Darcy, Jennifer, Hank, Pamela, Irena, Keith, Ellen, Harold, Fred, and Charlotte, along with Maggie and Jack.

"I have purchased a ten-passenger van for the family," Darcy said. "I realize it will take time for them to get their driver's licenses, but I will drive it to the airport tomorrow and then leave it at the parsonage. Whenever they need to be taken places, there will be plenty of room for one or two of us to drive and go with them on errands and necessary appointments."

"That's great," Maggie said. "The rest of us can carpool to the airport. I can't imagine how exhausted they will be, but I know there will be another group of folks here waiting to greet them. Then we'll let them be for a while."

Darcy continued, "Anya and Shrina from Refugee Support Services will meet us at the airport. They will follow us back here to do their intake work, and then they will tell us the next steps."

"Ve vill velcome de family just fine. I know how dis goes. Dey vill be upside down in all de vays. Tirrred, hungrry, sad, confused. Dun't say too many vords to dem. Just be quiet!" said Irena, who was never short on verbiage.

"We'll meet here at nine thirty in the morning and caravan to Detroit." Darcy took control again. "Then—"

There was a knock on the office door.

Maggie opened it and saw Myrna and Jasper, each holding a twin.

"Hi, you two, I mean four."

"We don't mean to interrupt, even though that's exactly what we're doin'," Myrna said, adjusting the baby onto her other hip. "We would like to be at the parsonage tomorrow to greet the new family. We realize we are also a new family at Lovin' the Lord, but so what? We've got kids, and they've got kids. It's all the same in the parental world."

"Sure," Maggie said, and she heard Darcy sigh. "That's a great idea. It would be nice for the children to meet other children."

"And once they're all settled and we know how old they are, we'll get them out to the farm for some playdates and pumpkin pickin'."

Maggie smiled. She had already received an invitation from William and Mary to bring the children to The Grange for playdates with Carrie and Carl.

"Myrna, Jasper, Manny, Milford, thank you. A month ago, I never thought our church would pull together enough to welcome this family. I hadn't even met you yet. And now things have totally changed!" She realized Fred and Charlotte were standing right behind her, and the reason a lot of things changed was because of what their son had done to the condo. But they were all living in the truth of the situation and the grace of the outcome. They just had to keep moving forward. "We'll plan on seeing you here when we return from Detroit. It should be around two in the afternoon, depending on how quickly things go at the airport."

"We'll be here!" Myrna said.

Maggie closed the door and heard Darcy's intake of breath, preparing to protest, no doubt.

"Before you say anything, Darcy, everything will be fine. No one is going to stay here for hours with the new family. We'll let them decompress and catch their breath, but they will know they have a community surrounding them. So, don't say too many people are going to be here. There's never too much love."

Darcy closed his mouth.

After the meeting, Maggie left the church and drove over to Julia Benson's house. With all the other happy drama, she had set this uncomfortable visit aside. Fortunately, Hannah was at The Grange with Carrie and Carl.

Maggie dove right in.

"Julia, I've stopped by with some difficult news. I received a call from the chaplain at the prison this past Thursday. Redford was beaten by some other inmates. He's in a coma with some severe injuries. I have not gone to the hospital, but he's at St. Joe's. I'm staying in touch with the chaplain. I thought you should know. It's pretty bad." Maggie was curious how Julia would respond.

"Thanks for telling me," she said.

Silence.

"Is there anything you want me to do, or anything you want to do?" Maggie asked quietly.

"No."

"Would you like me to keep you updated? Should Hannah know?"

"No."

"What if he . . . you know . . . what if he . . . ?"

"Dies? I hope he does. He has wasted enough space being alive on this earth. He's added nothing but hate and despair to humanity."

"What about Hannah?" Maggie asked.

"Hannah was born from an abused mother. Her father was the abuser. One sperm was what he contributed to the world. Hannah is my daughter. *Mine.* There is nothing of him in her. He beat me through the entire pregnancy. Of course, I was pregnant before we got married. Six months after the wedding, I knew I was going into labor. I went to the hospital alone in the middle of the afternoon. I had Hannah the next day. He must have been out drinking all night because he never tracked me down at the hospital. The moment I saw Hannah's beautiful little face, I knew I would never go back to him. Eventually, he would have killed us both. I left the hospital with her, took all our savings out of the bank, which was only a few thousand, and I drove away with my baby. Hannah thinks he left us. He basically did. Let me know if he dies. That will be the second best day of my life."

Maggie winced. "I'm sorry he has caused you so much pain, Julia. I'll let you know what happens."

Maggie stood to leave, but she hesitated when she noticed Julia was shaking.

"Pastor Maggie, I know you are trying to help, but you must realize there are some people who are not redeemable. It's because they don't want to be. God has nothing to do with it."

Maggie didn't know what to say. She nodded her head and left.

Monday morning, October third, a small welcoming committee was at the Detroit Metropolitan Airport. Maggie held a bouquet of flowers. She would give them to the mother of the family. Ellen clutched four soft teddy bears. Pamela had a colorful assortment of Mylar balloons. Irena was a gift in and of herself. Dressed in a purple leather miniskirt, sheer white blouse, hot-pink push-up bra, and the requisite stilettos, she clung to Keith's hand and stared through sparkly purple eye make-up at the door the family would come through. Her breasts were precariously slipping over the top of her bra, as usual.

There had been one additional person who came along in the caravan. Earlier that morning, Myrna, Myra, and all the "M" children had rung the Westminster chimes at the parsonage. Maggie and Jack were there taking one last look around. They'd bought an exquisite bouquet of flowers for the kitchen table from Pretty, Pretty Petals. Sky had outdone herself. They both heard the chimes, and Maggie remembered how glad she was to have a normal doorbell at the farmhouse.

Myrna and Myra stood on the porch with the twins. The other children were running around the front yard playing tag.

"Well, hi!" Maggie said, surprised.

"We're not here for the family," Myrna said. "We're here because of Mama." She looked down at her mother.

"Pastor Maggie, I wonder if I could ride along to the airport. I know I'm not part of the group who did the training and all that, but I sure would like to welcome the family with you. I have shed a few tears thinking about those children. I made some cookies this morning. I thought maybe they would like one on the way home from the airport."

Maggie smiled. "What a nice thought. Yes, you can ride with Jack and me."

Myra smiled and went to get the cookies out of their van.

"We'll see you later." Myrna loaded up her brood and headed back to their farm.

Once at the airport, the whole group was led to a small holding area, where they waited for Shrina and Anya to bring the family to them. Charlotte had worn street clothes instead of her uniform. She was on leave from the police department anyway, and she didn't want to frighten the new family. Without knowing how they had been treated by the police in the past, she decided it would be better not to be waiting with a gun on her hip.

The door opened.

Shrina and Anya came through followed by a man, a woman, two little boys, and two little girls. A very old woman with a bent stick limped through the door as well. They all froze and stared at the strangers waiting for them.

Maggie could not control her emotions. She felt tears immediately and quickly wiped them with her sleeve. Jack took her hand and squeezed a little too hard. She knew he was as shocked as she was. She heard Jennifer sniffing. Darcy cleared his throat. Even Irena seemed to wobble on her high heels. Everyone stared and became silent.

Shrina spoke. "Members of Loving the Lord, this is the Nasab family."

She pointed to the man. "This is Mahdi." Maggie noticed he was missing his left ear. There was an ugly scar in its place. He nodded at the church group.

"This is Amira," Anya said. "She and Mahdi are the parents of these beautiful children."

Maggie stared at Amira and tried to smile without crying.

Shrina said, "Daughter Iman is nine years old. Daughter Jamal is eight."

Maggie thought the two girls looked younger than their ages.

"Son Karam is seven, and son Samir is five." Anya gave each child a gentle pat on the shoulder as she said their names.

"And this is Mahdi's mother, Sabeen. We only found out she was coming recently. We don't usually have confusion like this, but occasionally we do. Her paperwork is all in order, so we will do the catch-up on this end of things."

Maggie looked at each face and tried to remember their names, but she couldn't.

Maggie was staring at ghosts. People who had been emptied of everything. People transparent through loss.

Maggie felt the bouquet of flowers being taken out of her hands.

It was Myra. She took the flowers, handed Maggie the bag of cookies, and slowly walked toward Sabeen. The two elderly women looked into each other's eyes. Myra handed the flowers to Sabeen, then leaned in and kissed the weathered cheek of the other woman.

Myra whispered, "Welcome home. It will all be okay now."

Sabeen didn't understand the words, but she certainly understood the sentiment. She held the flowers and stared at the kindly woman who knew something about living through decades of life. Myra patted Sabeen on the hand, then looked at Maggie.

"Pastor Maggie, I think these dear folks ought to be sitting in their new living room. What do you think?"

Maggie walked toward the family and reached out her hand. She shook Amira's hand, then Mahdi's and Sabeen's. Then she knelt down and gently hugged each child.

She looked at Shrina. "May I offer them a cookie?"

"Sure, that would be nice."

Maggie opened the large Ziploc bag and held it toward the children. The smell of oatmeal, butterscotch, and chocolate wafted up. The children looked in the bag, then at their mother. Amira nodded. Little hands reached into the bag and pulled out the cookies. As they ate, they looked at Maggie and the rest of the group around them for the first time. A little spark of life came into their eyes. Maggie stood and offered cookies to the adults, who took them as well.

Myra began to move the little crowd toward the door while Shrina and Anya explained some of the first things that would take place once the family had rested and acclimated.

"The most important thing is to let them recover from what they have lived through the past two years. Helping them with some meals and short visits will begin their process of stepping into a new life."

Irena had toddled over to Amira. Amira stared at the spectacle that was Irena.

"I know you dun't understand de English. Okey. But, I em Irena. I em frum Romania. Romania, you heard of dis?"

"Romania." Amira nodded.

"Okey, yes. So, I em de immigrant too. You see? Eet ees very good. You vill be very good." Irena slipped her bony little arm through Amira's. "Ve vill be friendly, yes!"

Slowly, everyone introduced themselves. Maggie watched as Fred and Charlotte waited their turn to greet the family. Timidly, Fred reached out his hand to shake Mahdi's rough, brown hand. Fred continued to silently greet the rest of the family with a nod to each. Charlotte, her huge frame dwarfing them all, welcomed them one by one. Maggie was surprised when Charlotte put her hand on Amira's shoulder, then hugged the small woman.

It was apparent the exhaustion the Nasab family had carried for so many months was at its limit. Darcy and Jennifer helped the family into the van. Everyone else got into their cars and followed Darcy. The Nasab family watched silently out the windows of the van as views of Michigan whipped past them.

The caravan of cars headed toward Cherish.

When they arrived at the parsonage, the family was led inside and shown each room. It was obvious they could not take in the enormity of what was being given to them. The parsonage had more than enough space for a family of seven.

This is what this home was built for, Maggie thought to herself as she silently thanked God. She watched the children as they discovered the stuffed animals on their beds. The church members had also bought some new clothes. Maggie knew more would be coming. It was a true delight to see smiles on the faces of the Nasab children as the "M" kids played a simple game of hide-and-seek with them in the backyard.

The afternoon was exhilarating, until exhaustion took control of everyone. Maggie and Jack began to "invite" church members to leave the family to rest. All the final paperwork was done by Anya and Shrina, and after many hugs they headed back to Ann Arbor. The Nasabs watched the last visitors leave, including Maggie and Jack, and then they sat down at their kitchen table and tasted their first Midwestern casserole, thanks to Myrna.

Neither Maggie nor Jack remembered it was their one-year anniversary when they crawled into bed in their lovely farmhouse that night.

21

The first few days of the Nasab family's life in Cherish was a blur for them and full of excitement for the congregation. Each day someone else showed up with brand-new clothes, shoes, and even winter coats for when it got colder. Amira and Sabeen were awed when Verna came to them with a bag of clothing.

"These are dresses for you," Verna said, realizing the two women could not understand one word.

Verna had gone to Ann Arbor and bought the most modest dresses she could find, even for Verna. She suspected Syrian Muslim women would choose to be covered from head to toe. It was stereotypical. And it was wrong. Fortunately, the dresses Verna bought were not only acceptable but pretty. The recipients were thrilled.

The day after the family arrived, Maggie walked over to church from the farmhouse. She stopped at the parsonage and rang the Westminster chimes from the porch. The sound didn't make her cringe. She invited Mahdi and Amira into the garage. A chest freezer had been stuffed with casseroles, packages of meat, and desserts. Maggie wondered what the Nasab family would think of American foods and wondered what they ate in Syria.

"These are foods for you. We can help you cook them." Maggie made hand gestures, hoping she was communicating her message. "What do you eat in Syria?" Maggie made more eating motions, then swung her arm pointing far away.

Amira said a few things, and Maggie wrote them down, excited because she understood some of what Amira described. There were several Middle Eastern foods that Maggie had eaten when she lived in Israel: hummus, Syrian manoushi bread, falafel, tabbouleh, lamb, rice, chicken, baklava, and other nut pastries. Maggie knew she could never buy lamb at the store (Maggie was violently opposed to eating baby animals), so she bought everything else, including the ingredients for the manoushi bread. On Thursday afternoon, she watched as Amira made the bread into small rounds and fried them in a large pan on her new stove. They were delicious. The children came running when they smelled their familiar bread in the parsonage.

Jacob and Deborah Stein, Jack's neighbors at the condo, called Jack that evening.

"Our rabbi gave us the name of a mosque that the Nasab family might like to be part of," Deborah said. "It's in Ann Arbor." She gave Jack the address. "We are trying to think of what the family might need that they don't have already. They must be inundated with food and clothes. Is there something else we can help with?"

"Yes," Jack said. "School supplies. Maggie and I were just talking about it at dinner. The children have been registered and will have a few visitation days in a couple of weeks before beginning in earnest, but they will need school supplies. I can bring a list to you. I'm going to check on the condo this weekend."

"Wonderful. And if you need any help driving them to the mosque, we would be happy to help out."

"Thank you. We will tell them about it and make a list of drivers to bring them to worship."

And so, the first hours and days unfolded in Cherish for the Nasab family. Little pieces of life were given back to them through food, visits—where communicating happened more through sign language and gestures than words—and gentle kindnesses shared.

On Friday of their first week in the parsonage, Maggie looked out of her church office window and saw Fred's big red truck pull up to the curb. He got out, unloaded his lawn mower, and proceeded to mow the parsonage lawn. When he was finished, Mahdi came out on the front porch and walked to Fred's truck. He silently shook Fred's hand and then pointed to the lawn. Fred made some gestures and patted Mahdi on the shoulder.

"It feels like the Nasab family has been here forever," Maggie said that night to Jack. They were eating chili and corn pudding while the cats stared out one of the windows facing a large field. The deer were coming out to eat.

"They all had checkups today," Jack said, "but you didn't hear that from me. Charlene examined Sabeen, Amira, Jamal, and Iman. I examined Mahdi, Karam, and Samir. They are all malnourished and have parasites. All four children have upper respiratory infections and some skin issues. Sabeen's blood work showed signs of something going on. I'm pretty sure it's some underlying infection that we need to get to the bottom of, but we are on the right path. I agree, it seems like we've known them forever."

"I'm trying to switch gears for Brynn's shower tomorrow," Maggie said. "I don't want to be away. I might miss something at the parsonage. I'm glad Mom will drive down to Blissfield with me. That will be fun. And, of course, I can't wait to see your mom."

"I'll go to the condo with your dad while you're in Blissfield. I'm glad he's coming along with 'The Queen Mother.'" Jack had bestowed this title on his mother-in-law as a joke, but it had turned into a loving moniker. "The carpet should be laid tomorrow first thing in the morning, and the new appliances will be delivered by Tom Wiggins in the afternoon. It's nice that the condo is being put back together again, but we'll have to decide what to do with it once it is." Jack poured a little chili on top of his corn pudding and spooned it into his mouth. "This is a perfect fall dinner. There isn't any pie around, is there?"

"There is at the parsonage. I made a Dutch apple pie this morning and brought it over to the Nasabs."

Jack frowned, disappointed.

"Luckily, I had enough apples and cinnamon to make a second pie. It's in the pantry."

Jack's frown turned into a smile.

"Pie is the only reason I married you. Remember that first night I tasted one of your pies? We had just been at Mrs. Abernathy's, I mean Verna's, and she had ripped open the stitches on her back."

"I remember it vividly," Maggie said with a shiver.

"Then I came to the parsonage and you fed me pie. Then I decided I would marry you."

"You did not."

"Well, eventually."

"And then we got married and lived crazily ever after . . . WAIT! Jack, we missed our anniversary! Our first anniversary! Oh, how could we?"

Jack looked at his dramatic wife and began to laugh. "We sure did. I guess welcoming a refugee family takes precedence over a measly first anniversary."

"But we have to celebrate! Oh, good grief! I can't believe we forgot."

She sat pondering for a moment while Jack got up to find the pie.

"But you know what else?" Maggie lamented. "*Everyone* forgot our anniversary! We didn't get any cards or phone calls or anything. Not even from family! No one cares that we made it through a whole year of marriage."

"Do you think they were worried we wouldn't?" Jack asked as he brought the pie and two small plates to the table. "Maybe we did receive cards. They're still at the post office. Remember, we didn't do the change of address card until the last minute."

"You think you know everything." Maggie pouted. "They don't love us."

"Here, cry into your pie. I'm going to eat mine."

∞

The next morning, Mimi and Dirk stood on the front porch of the new farmhouse. They rang the normal doorbell that sang *ding-dong*.

"Well, I don't know. I think I miss the Westminster chimes," Mimi said.

She was dressed in a chic, tailored tan suit, white silk blouse, and a rust-colored scarf. Her practical pumps and perfect hair gave her the professional air she carried everywhere.

Maggie opened the door in her bathrobe.

"Hi, Mom, Dad." She gave them each a kiss. "Come on in and see our new home. Jack will get you coffee. I have to get dressed."

She quickly went up the stairs while Jack took over the niceties.

By the time Maggie descended, Jack had given Dirk and Mimi a tour of the barn and house and served them each coffee and a slice of Dutch apple pie, which was perfect at ten a.m. on a cool autumn morning.

Maggie looked at her parents. "Did you forget that Jack and I had our first anniversary this past Monday?"

"No. Did you?" Mimi asked, taking a sip of her coffee.

"Well, yes, as a matter of fact, we did."

"We sent you a card. My guess is it's trying to figure out where you live." Mimi smiled.

"You'll have to get over this tantrum, my love," Jack said, kissing Maggie on the head. "We settled a refugee family from Syria this week. It was a little busy. We will celebrate, I promise."

"We are looking forward to meeting the family tomorrow," Dirk said. He and Mimi would spend the night in the farmhouse and join Jack and Maggie in church the next morning. Jack's family would also be making the drive to meet the family and celebrate with the church. "What an experience they have had. Something we could never understand."

Maggie knew her crankiness wasn't totally due to missing her first anniversary. Her problem was she hadn't had time to write a sermon. All week she'd had the nagging thought of preparing a sermon for Sunday. She knew her family, and Jack's, would be there to celebrate and meet the Nasabs. Yet she hadn't spent one minute preparing anything. When Hank asked her for a title for the bulletin, she'd said, "Just put 'Welcome.' I don't have anything else right now."

After loading her little black Caliber with gifts, decorations, and several dozen monster cookies, Maggie and Mimi set off for Blissfield. The hour-long drive from Maggie's farm to Jack's childhood home was beautiful, with the trees just beginning to wear their autumn dresses.

But when they drove past the Milan exit, Maggie shuddered. She had been able to put Redford and his accident out of her mind for the entire week, but seeing the exit for the prison brought it all back. She would have to figure out what to do about his situation. She did not want to go to the hospital, and she knew a visit like that would infuriate Julia.

"You're quiet," Mimi said.

Maggie filled her mother in on the Redford state of affairs, along with Julia's response.

"Redford took his broken life and broke as many others as he could," Mimi said practically. "It will be difficult for Julia, no matter what happens, whether he lives or he dies. He is part of her life in a tragic way. Hannah might be the only one who has a chance to be free of fear and hate. Let's hope Julia is able to allow that for her daughter."

Maggie decided to put Redford out of her mind and drove on, chattering about the Nasab family and Andrew and Brynn's wedding.

"Settling the family and the wedding are the two biggest events before Christmas. I will also baptize little Katharine Marie Baxter tomorrow. There is so much to celebrate now, especially since Fred and Charlotte seem to have had an awakening about 'foreigners.' We have grown as a church family and chased out most of the negativity."

"There will always be some, but that's in every church. It's in every family. They are the people who live in fear instead of hope. It's just a shame they call themselves Christians when they act nothing like Jesus."

"Speaking of that," Maggie said, "the election is basically one month from today. You don't think he will win, do you? He won't be our president?"

"There is *no way* he will win. He has let his true colors show with his misogynist statements, his bigotry, his racism, and his xenophobia. The die is cast. I know there are people who aren't thrilled about the Democratic candidate, but she will win the day and take our country in the same forward direction it has been going for the last eight years."

Mimi spoke with certainty.

Maggie felt comforted. Even though the ugliness the Republican candidate and party had spread throughout the country had spilled into her town and church, she saw how healing could happen. How could the country survive if it lived on a diet of hatred and turmoil for four years?

Maggie pulled into the driveway of the Elliot farm. She loved the way chickens wandered at will. She and Mimi unloaded the car as Bonnie and Ken came out to help. They brought everything inside, and then there were hugs all around. Maggie loved Jack's parents. Andrew and Leigh were eating donuts in the kitchen. More hugs.

"Maggie," Bonnie said as she put monster cookies on a large platter, "did you have a nice anniversary?"

Maggie looked at Mimi and laughed. "Nope. But we will at some point."

Bonnie stopped and looked confused. "Did you get our card?"

Maggie explained the whole situation, which led into a conversation about the Nasab family and the stories of their arrival and new life beginning in Cherish.

They all looked up when Brynn, Leigh, and Ellen came down the stairs. Ellen had driven down the night before to have a "cousins night." Brynn looked radiant.

After all the hugs she said to Maggie, "It's beginning to feel real. Andrew as my husband and the wedding and this house."

"It is real," Bonnie said with a catch in her throat. "The farm will be loved through another generation."

Maggie didn't think she could handle any more emotion. She'd hit her limit during the past month. She smiled and said, "Let's celebrate! When will the others be here?"

Within a half hour, Anne, Jack's oldest sister, had arrived, as well as several of Brynn's friends and family members. Maggie made sure to connect with Brynn's mother, Nicolette. The mother of the bride was always a good one to make friends with. It was easy to see where Brynn got her beauty and her heart and especially her sense of humor.

"Pastor Maggie," Nicolette said, "I'm glad to see you are representing God in her true gender!"

Maggie laughed, as did everyone in the room.

"I have a feeling she is much taller than I am," Maggie replied. Nicolette Thomas herself was a tiny woman. Maggie continued, "Congratulations to you! Your beautiful daughter is marrying my husband's brother. It's a great match."

The party moved into the large living room. The windows looked over a pasture with a picturesque red barn plunked right in the middle. Bonnie had taken on the responsibility of making the family cookbook with recipes from both family and friends, and Maggie had greatly appreciated letting go of the project. All the non-perishable items for the many recipes were in baskets according to the section in the cookbook, but Brynn was most excited by the check for four thousand dollars that had been donated as a part of her shower gifts to go to the Nasab family.

"They need and deserve every penny of that check," Brynn said. "I can't wait to be in church tomorrow and meet each one of them. Thank you for your generosity."

Brynn wasn't an overly emotional woman, but Maggie could see the amount of the check had taken her by surprise.

The women filled their plates and chatted about the recipes they had contributed to the cookbook. The afternoon slipped away pleasantly. When most of the guests had gone, Anne went out to her car and came in with a box Maggie recognized.

It was a wedding dress. It was *the* wedding dress.

Anne had worn it. Maggie had worn it. And now it was Brynn's turn. After the engagement, Anne had asked Brynn if she would like to wear the dress, but made it clear there was no pressure to do so. Brynn was thrilled. Being a good five inches taller than her own mother, she knew Anne's dress would fit her perfectly. Maggie had worn high heels with the dress for her own wedding, but Brynn wouldn't need that kind of help.

While the younger women fussed over the dress in the living room, Mimi, Bonnie, and Nicolette were in the kitchen, where Bonnie had put a large taco casserole in the oven for the family.

"What did you think of Jack and Maggie's new farmhouse?" Bonnie asked.

"It's beautiful, and I think it's just what they needed. It seems they were being suffocated by love and intrusion at the parsonage. We have to pray that the good people of Loving the Lord will not treat the Nasab family with the same disregard of privacy." Mimi spooned sour cream into a bowl.

"We're happy there is another Elliot farm in the family," Bonnie said, "even though we know Jack and Maggie won't be doing much farming."

"They will all be fun to watch, won't they?" Mimi said and gave Bonnie and Nicolette a wink. Bonnie had two grandchildren, but all three women looked to the future with hope and expectation.

In the living room, Maggie, Brynn, Anne, Leigh, and Ellen chatted about the wedding plans.

"It will be simple," Brynn said. "We want a special day, but we want a special *marriage* most of all. We have already had a taste of how the wedding business takes over. The cost of a wedding is outrageous, and it seems every person we talk to begins with their 'cheapest package' and tries to move us along to the next package and the next. No thanks."

"Don't let them take the fun or happiness out of it," Anne said. "I mean, look at Jack and Maggie. They didn't even know they were getting married in Cherish until we all showed up and married them."

Maggie smiled, remembering how shocked she had been and how perfect and delightful her unexpected wedding had been.

Brynn and Anne went upstairs so Brynn could try on the wedding dress. When she came down the staircase, as she would on her wedding day, the others gazed at her loveliness. The dress fit her perfectly. The train flowed down the curved stairs in a stream of satin. The veil was set in her dark hair and gave her a sweet bridal air. Bonnie seemed to be the most choked up, besides Nicolette, whose eyes were brimming over.

"I love this dress," Brynn said quietly. "I didn't expect it to feel this way. So . . . so . . . like royalty." Then she giggled. "That sounds dumb."

Maggie remembered when Anne had helped her into the dress on the morning of her wedding. She had felt the same way.

"I think it's the weight of the dress itself," Maggie said wistfully, "along with the weight of the day. Every bride should feel royal on her wedding day. Remember that, Brynn, and order us all around all day long. We will be your humble servants and handmaids." Maggie gave a solemn bow of her head and then smiled.

"You look beautiful," Nicolette said quietly. She walked to her daughter and kissed her on her cheek.

After much oohing and ahhing, Brynn went back upstairs to take off the dress and get ready for the family dinner and celebration.

The men arrived by five. Jack and Dirk drove down from Cherish. Andrew came in from working in the fields, quickly cleaned up, and joined the family. Brynn's father, Richard, and her two brothers, Randy and Michael, also arrived. Bonnie's festive taco dinner filled everyone at the large farmhouse table.

"Well, we'll be making the trip up to your new farm tomorrow," Ken said, filling another tortilla with steaming taco casserole. "What a great thing you have done to bring that new family here and live and learn with them. I have a feeling they will have a lot to teach all of us."

Jack considered this. "They have already taught us that hope might be all you have, when you have lost everything else. But hope is the one thing that keeps your heart burning steadily until your hope is realized in one manifestation or another."

"There you go being philosophical again," Andrew said. "What if hope burns out after life has handed a person too much? I can hardly believe what they had to live through, and I bet we will never know the half of it. What happens when hope dies?"

"I think," Maggie said thoughtfully, "you find someone who hasn't lost theirs and hang on to them until yours burns softly again."

"On this somewhat somber note," Jack said, "we should be heading up north. My wife has to preach tomorrow, and she gets cranky when she doesn't get enough sleep on Saturday nights."

But Maggie did not sleep that night. She sat in the farmhouse living room wrapped in a quilt with her computer on her lap and three cats curled around her.

At five a.m. she typed the word "Amen."

Then she made herself a cup of coffee and ate a large piece of Dutch apple pie.

22

Maggie peeked through the secret door and caught her breath. The sanctuary of Loving the Lord was packed once again. Parishioners were crammed in every pew, and she could see Harold, Jack, and Hank quickly setting up folding chairs in the back. Jack's entire family was crowded together, laughing and talking with the parishioners they knew. Irena was pounding out "A Mighty Fortress is Our God." She had given up shushing and chose again to raise the volume in order to drown out people's chatter. It didn't work.

The Nasab family was sitting quietly in Maggie's office. The front pew had a "reserved" sign for the family. Maggie should have been exhausted but felt the excitement of the service to come. With absolutely no sleep, she was still ready for worship.

She brought the family from her office and led them through the secret door. They had been in Cherish for only six days. In that time, they had begun the process for the children's school enrollment, had preliminary medical care with treatments and medication prescribed and administered, and had made a trip to the grocery store, which seemed to render the new family spellbound by the amount of food all in one place.

On Friday, Maggie had brought them to the local mosque so they could worship. She had gone in with them and knelt on one of the prayer mats. She had a litany of prayers, which she lifted to God as the Nasab family worshiped and felt a bit of normalcy return to their spiritual lives. They were eating well and sleeping whenever they were tired. Most of all, the constant anxiety and stress of living in the refugee camp was dissipating. Many members of the church, as well as the Refugee Support Services staff, worked tirelessly with "their" new family.

Maggie began the worship service.

"This is the day the Lord hath made. Let us rejoice and be glad in it! We can rejoice because our help is in the name of the Lord who made heaven and earth."

The familiar words, recited each Sunday, carried a different meaning that morning.

"I would like to formally introduce to our Loving the Lord congregation the Nasab family from Kobanî, Syria." She stood next to each member of the family as she said their names.

"Sabeen is the matriarch of the family. Her name means 'morning breeze.'" Maggie moved down. "Mahdi, her son. His name means 'guided.' His wife, Amira. Her name means 'princess.'" Maggie stood behind the children. "Iman is the oldest. She is nine. Her name means 'faith.' Jamal is eight, and her name means 'beauty.' Karam is seven, and his name means 'generosity.' And Samir is five. His name means 'pleasant companion.' These are our new neighbors and friends. Thank you to everyone who helped out during this first hectic week.

"Darcy Keller has been the driving force behind getting the Nasab family to Cherish. Darcy, you have worked tirelessly, and today we thank God for the joy of this family."

Maggie looked around the sanctuary.

"I also see Shrina and Anya here today. We thank you, especially, for your work with so many families coming to America. The work of Refugee Family Services is truly a miracle." Shrina and Anya nodded back to Maggie. "I praise God most of all for trusting us with this significant task of welcoming and caring for these brave people. They will teach us much, and we will learn more about Syria, the traditions of their lives, and Islamic worship. They are a gift to us."

The congregation applauded, which startled all four of the children standing near Maggie. No one in the family knew English, so Maggie had asked Shrina and Anya to help explain ahead of time what church would be like that day. She put her arms around the children and gave each one a kiss on their cheek. She received smiles in return. Then she guided the family down to the front pew.

Worship continued with hymns and prayers and finally the sermon.

As she had done two months prior, Maggie had called Marla and Addie early that morning and asked if they could help during the sermon. It was time.

"I realize in your bulletin it says that the title of this sermon is 'Welcome.' That is what I told Hank before I had written it. I have changed the name. Today's sermon is titled, 'The House Next Door.'"

Maggie invited the children to come forward. Marla and Addie, who grabbed Liz Tuggle, helped all the children, including the Syrian children, to form a circle and settle in. Then she pulled out what she had written through the night and began to read.

> Let love be genuine; hate what is evil, hold fast to what is good; love one another with mutual affection, outdo one another in showing honor . . . Contribute to the needs of the saints; extend hospitality to strangers. Romans 12:9-10 and 13.

> "The House Next Door." There once was a church full of diverse and interesting people who loved God. That's what makes a church a church. They were people who did not always agree on everything, but they knew what being the community of God was all about. They knew that God wanted them to love each other the way God loved them. God wanted them to act like Jesus. He wanted them to use all their Holy Spirit gifts.
>
> Now this church owned a house right next door to the church building. The diverse and interesting

people had a disagreement about what to do with the house. Should the people of the church keep the house or, as someone suggested, should they sell it?

"That's just like our church!" Carrie Moffet said.
Maggie smiled at her and nodded.

At the same time, in a faraway land, there was a terrible war. People were forced to leave their homes. They were hurt very badly, and many were killed. Moms and dads and boys and girls lost everything. The very old, and the very young, and many in-between walked for miles in search of peace—in search of a home.
And God cried.
"This was not my plan," God said. "My plan was for my creation to live together, love each other, and love me the way I love them."
When the church full of interesting and diverse people heard about the war in the faraway land and saw terrible things on their television sets, their hearts broke, and they cried too. "This is not God's plan," they said. "All this war and killing is very bad."

Self-consciously, the children sitting around Maggie looked at Iman, Jamal, Karam, and Samir.
"This was your land, wasn't it?" Molly Porter whispered to the children.
But they had no idea what anyone was saying, so they just smiled and nodded.

The people from the faraway land began searching for new lands and new homes. Many of them felt they no longer had a country. Many churches, like the church full of diverse and interesting people, heard God's voice.

They remembered how God said, "Love your neighbor and love me, the way I love you." Many churches decided to follow God's plan. They created places where the people from the faraway and war-torn land could live without fear. Where they could rest and mend.

And so, the very old, and the very young, and all the others in-between began to come to the new land.

And God smiled.

A man from the church of diverse and interesting people listened to God and heard God, and he said to others at church, "I wonder if we could do something for the people of the faraway and war-torn land?" The man said, "I will find out what we can do."

The church gathered together to discuss the issue. It was suggested that the house next door should be used for a family from far away. Some people liked this idea. Some people did not. There was a man, an angry man, who said, "We should not share the house next door!"

There was shuffling and uncomfortable coughs in the sanctuary. Maggie knew there would be a reaction. She also knew they needed to hear the rest of the story. So she continued.

However, the people of the church made a decision to go ahead and share the house. They decided to invite a family from the war-torn land to live in the house. Some of the people of the church thought this would be the kind and loving thing to do. They thought it would be acting like Jesus. They thought it would please God.

And God smiled and said, "My people are glorifying me because they love one another. They are even loving people they don't know."

Once the decision was made not to sell the house next door, there was work to be done! Many people in the church began to prepare the house next door for a new family. There were walls to be painted with pretty, fresh paint. There were floors and cupboards to be cleaned. There was good food to be gathered. There were flowers to be planted and trees to be trimmed. There were toys to be bought because children were coming. There were so many things to be collected for the new family coming to a new land.

The angry man did not come to the house next door. He did not paint. He did not buy toys. He was not happy.

More coughs.

The other people of the church knew their work was important, and they began to realize there were many prayers that needed to be prayed. So, the people prayed.

In the church of diverse and interesting people there were some very old people who could not scrub floors or plant flowers anymore, so they gave money for food and clothes. And they prayed.

There were the very young ones of the church who could not trim trees, but they could choose toys and books for the children from the war-torn land. They prayed too.

"That's us!" Hannah Benson shouted.

Fortunately, that brought laughter from the congregation.

There were many people in-between, who were gifted in a variety of ways. The Holy Spirit had given them their grand gifts. They worked, and they prayed.

All the people decided to use their Holy Spirit gifts to act like Jesus and to glorify God.

And God smiled.

One day, the angry man came to the house next door. He drove a red truck, and in the back of his red truck he had a ladder. He put the ladder against the side of the house and fixed the chimney because it was broken. The next day the angry man drove his red truck to the house next door and did more work. But he didn't look angry. Then he brought a lawn mower and mowed the whole lawn around the house. Even though it was not his plan to share the house, he chose to glorify God, to act like Jesus, and to use his Holy Spirit gifts. He did not *stay* angry. He did not say bad things. He didn't even sound gruff or grumpy anymore. The angry man decided to be a kind man.

He fixed the chimney, he fixed a window, mowed grass, and loved God.

The man saw the big picture. Many members in the diverse and interesting church saw the big picture.

And the people smiled.

God had plans for the house next door.

The people of the church worked at their regular jobs during the day, then spent many evening hours in the house next door. They did this not for personal notice, not to have their name printed in the church newsletter, and not to say, "Look what I've accomplished!" They did it to say, "Look what *God* has accomplished!"

The house next door was complete and ready for a new family.

And God smiled.

One day, a family from a faraway and war-torn land came to a brand-new land. There was one who was very old, one who was very young, and five in-between. There was a grandma, a mom, a dad, two little boys, and two little girls. They were tired, hungry, and spiritually weary. They had lost their dignity. They had cried many tears. They were so very sad. They did not know the language of the new land. They did not know where they were going once they stepped off the airplane.

Carrie, Carl, Molly, Penny, and Hannah scooted over and put their arms around the Nasab children.

Many members from the church of diverse and interesting people were waiting at the airport for the new family. When they saw the faces of the family from the war-torn land, they cried. Then they changed their faces and said, "We've been waiting for you. You are our neighbors. Welcome home."

The family from the faraway and war-torn land were taken to the house next door. They walked through the front door of their new home. Because they had been living in a tent for quite some time, they were surprised when they saw the house next door. "This is your house!" the members of the church said. "It is all yours! It is a gift to you because you are our brothers and sisters."

At first, the family did not understand, but eventually they realized they were home.

The family smiled.

They had not expected so much. They had not expected anything. A small trickle of their human dignity began to flow back to them.

The kind man, who had been angry at first, came to the house next door to meet the family from the war-torn land. He smiled at the family. "You are my neighbors too," he said.

And the church full of diverse and interesting people loved their new neighbors and called them brothers and sisters. They played with the children, they brought food over unexpectedly, and they even learned how to talk with people who did not speak the same language. They glorified God. They acted like Jesus. They used all of their Holy Spirit gifts.

The family from the faraway land began to live without fear. They rested. They mended, inside and out.

And the day came when the church full of diverse and interesting people couldn't imagine a time without the dear family from far away.

The family who lived in the house next door.

And God smiled. Amen.

"How do you know everything is going to be fine?" Hannah asked. "They haven't been here very long. What if they don't like it here or they get sick or they can't read?"

Maggie sighed. Her night's work was for naught. Her sermon was ruined. *Why do children need to ask questions?*

"I vill tell you!" Irena squawked, quickly wiping tears from her overly made-up face.

She hopped off the organ bench and trip-trapped down the middle aisle of the sanctuary. Unfortunately, when she sat down on the lowest step, which led up to the altar, everyone got a look at her gold underpants shining through her fishnet stockings.

Sabeen, sitting in the front pew, made a strangled sound at such indecency. Irena glanced at her, noticed where she was looking, and put her legs together.

"Listen! Dis family is going to be goot, okey? Dey arre going to learrn tings and be heppy. Dere vill be harrd days, yes. Dat's vy ve arre herre. Ve arre going to help all de days it teks to mek dem family. Dis church made me family. It vorrks!"

Keith Crunch began the applause for his Romanian fiancée and was joined by the rest of the congregation. Irena carefully pulled herself up to standing and took a bow.

Maggie watched the whole spectacle and then began to laugh at her crazy little church and the way love and joy exploded out of Irena at the most unexpected times.

Maggie told the children to remain where they were and called Bill and Sylvia Baxter to the front of the church with small Katharine Marie. The baptismal font had been filled with warm water. Maggie believed surprising a small child by putting cold water on their face during baptism was cruel and unusual.

She invited the children to watch and listen as she took Katharine Marie in her arms and said the baptism liturgy. The beautiful words filled the sanctuary and sanctified it once again.

Katharine, wearing Sylvia's own baptismal gown, looked at Maggie with huge blue eyes.

Finally, Maggie dipped her fingers in the font and made three little water crosses on the baby's forehead.

"In the name of the Father, and of the Son, and of the Holy Spirit. Amen."

Then she invited the children to carefully dip their fingers in the water and remember that once, when they were babies, they had little water crosses on their foreheads too.

Maggie walked up and down the aisles in the church and told the congregation their new duties for the smallest member of the covenant. And she told them the meaning of Katharine Marie's name.

"Katharine means 'pure and clear.' 'Blessed are the pure in heart, for they shall see God.' Marie, the French form of Mary, means 'sea of bitterness.' Mary, the mother of Jesus, tasted bitterness. We pray that Katharine Marie will live a life touched only lightly by bitterness, but that happiness will surround her for all her days."

Maggie had been stumped when she'd looked up the meanings of the names. It took a little creativity to adjust things sometimes.

More hymns and another prayer and the service was complete. The Nasab family was ushered into the gathering area and offered some of Mrs. Popkin's most delicious treats.

Bill and Sylvia Baxter also were in a place of prominence at coffee time. Amira timidly walked to Sylvia to look at Katharine. Sylvia watched Amira, then she handed her the baby. Amira gently took Katharine in her arms. She closed her eyes and felt the soft little body. Amira's thoughts went back to the refugee camp, where her little baby was asleep forever. She opened her eyes, glistening with tears, and smiled shyly at Sylvia. Sylvia put her arm around the other mother. They both stared at Katharine as she stretched and yawned and slowly closed her blue eyes.

The children of the church surrounded Imam, Jamal, Karam, and Samir. Soon, with sticky mouths and fingers, the children ran outside and began to play on the lawn connecting the church and parsonage. The "M" children began a game of tag that caught on quickly. Soon the Syrian children were shouting, "Tag! You're it!" Those were their first English words. The laughter could be heard through the open oak doors, and the sun shone down on the laughing, happy children at play.

23

It had been three weeks since the Nasab family arrived in Cherish. Predictably, the children were learning English at breakneck speed. They had met their new teachers, spent one week going to school for half days, and then full days began.

Mary Ellington kept an eye on them now that she was a volunteer for both Carrie and Carl's classrooms. She was able to peek in on the Nasab children each day when she dropped Carrie and Carl off or picked them up. She'd also had Iman, Jamal, Karam, and Samir out to The Grange, where William showed them the barn and the farm animals and took them for hayrides behind the tractor.

Iman and Jamal enjoyed playing with Carrie in the large house. Thankfully, Carrie was a chatterbox, and the girls learned words and phrases easily from their new friend. Carl was six now, right in-between Samir and Karam. The three boys climbed over hay bales, ran in the field behind the barn, and filled their little souls full of crisp fall air, sunshine, and friendship.

Despite his joyful demeanor, Carl missed his mother terribly. Often at night Carrie would hear him crying in their "circle room," the turret of The Grange that they shared. She would crawl into bed with him and try to soothe him, but Carl felt the loss of his mother keenly.

Now he had a focus. His two new friends still had their mother, but they had lost their home and were living in a strange place. Carl's heart recognized the pain that Karam and Samir carried in theirs. It was an invisible bond that drew the three boys together.

"What about Halloween?" Carrie asked Mary one morning at breakfast.

"What about Halloween?" Mary asked back.

"I don't think Iman and Jamal have any costumes."

"Then maybe we can get them some. What do you think?"

Carl spoke up. "Can they come twick-or-tweating with us?" Carl had always had trouble saying "R" but was receiving help through speech therapy at school. He still slipped to a "W" sound now and then, which made Mary smile.

"I think there a lot of things we need to think about," Mary said. "I wonder if they have ever carved a pumpkin. Or have they tasted apple crisp and spiced cider? Shall we invite them to spend the night and try on costumes?"

"Yes!!"

Carrie and Carl thought this was the best idea they had ever heard.

With the help of Shrina and Anya, communication was shared, and Amira agreed that her children could spend the last weekend in October at The Grange for a slumber party. Mary also invited Hannah Benson.

Gingersnaps were baked, along with pumpkin pie and apple crisp. Spiced cider warmed in the Crock-Pot. William had pulled several large pumpkins out of their small pumpkin patch and let each child draw a face on their pumpkin. Then he carved out their design. Homemade tomato soup and grilled cheese sandwiches filled all small tummies.

"Now let's try on costumes," Carrie ordered her guests. "We have lots to choose from."

They all tried on some of Mary's creations until each child was ready for Halloween. The Nasab children were enthralled by this strange tradition. The fun of dressing up—along with several cookies, pie, and cups of cider—made the evening festive.

Sunday morning, William and Mary brought all seven children to church. The children were obviously better rested than the adults, but the weekend had been a turning point for the entire Nasab family. Mahdi and Amira had trusted William and Mary to care for their children overnight. To trust anything or anyone was a sign of healing. Iman, Jamal, Karam, and Samir found part of their lost childhoods. Mary and William had loved to hear them laughing when they tried on costumes and had a small parade around the kitchen, at Carrie's direction.

Maggie heard the whole story from Mary at coffee time after worship.

"You've done so much for them this first month," Maggie said.

"It's been easy. Anyone who would take the time to notice the Nasab children would see their different personalities. They are like every child on this earth. They want to be safe. They want to be loved. They deserve to be children and not thrust into adulthood at the age of nine or younger."

Mary thought of how Iman had gotten down on the floor when Samir spilled his soup Friday night. She'd tried to wipe up the spill with the hem of her dress. Mary had gently stopped her and said they would take care of the spill. She shared the story with Maggie.

"I hope she can still learn to be a little girl," Mary said, "but who knows what her life was like at the refugee camp?"

"Thank you, and William too. I do believe it will take our village to raise all the children around here. We certainly have a bunch now with the Porter children and Jasper and Myrna's clan. I've got to get their names straight."

"I've noticed," Mary said quietly, "that Amira loves to hold baby Katharine."

She nodded to the other side of the room. Sylvia and Amira were standing together as Amira held and swayed with the baby.

"Darcy told us Amira lost a baby at the refugee camp. Sylvia knows all about it and realized Amira was drawn to Katharine. She purposefully gets her baby in Amira's arms as often as she can."

"All in all, I think things are going better than any of us imagined," Mary said.

"Fred Tuggle has offered Mahdi a job at the quarry. The paperwork is almost finished, and Mahdi will be employed."

"It's all good news," Mary said. "We are planning to bring the children to your farm tomorrow night. We are excited to see your new place. But now I see Carrie is ordering everyone around, so I think I will relieve her of her duties and get our two little ones home."

Maggie had about five seconds to be amazed at how God had stitched so many broken lives back together. The Ellingtons and the Moffets, and now the Nasab family beginning to heal and trust.

But the quietest good news was Brock's return home. There had been no fanfare, no gathering of church friends. Fred and Charlotte, along with Mason and Liz, had driven to Jackson and had their last family therapy session with Brock. He had packed his few items ahead of time and was relieved to get into the car and go home.

That morning in church, Brock had entered the sanctuary with his parents and siblings. He was greeted like a long-lost son. No one listened to Irena's prelude. They were too busy shaking Brock's hand, giving him hugs, and welcoming him home. Maggie watched as Myra made her way to Brock. Maggie was sure he didn't even know who Myra was.

Myra peered up at Brock with her wrinkled face and wizened eyes. "It's a hard lesson to learn," she said.

Brock, who was already bright red with embarrassment, just nodded his head miserably.

Myra gently touched his chin. "The lesson of being forgiven with no strings attached. I don't even know you. I just know what I saw here in church weeks ago with you and the police. Today, it's obvious to me that, whatever you did, this whole dang church doesn't give a donkey's tail about it. They just love you to pieces." She gently laid her old hand on his young cheek. "Don't waste a lot of time doubting. Just believe them."

∞

Halloween on Monday night brought all the church children and a few neighbors to Jack and Maggie's new home. Candy was liberally shared, costumes were praised, and the three cats didn't come out from under the guest room bed for several hours.

The next day was All Saints' Day, November first. Maggie found that ironic as she pulled into the parking lot of St. Joseph Mercy Health System. She took the elevator up and went to the assigned room. There were two armed guards outside of Redford Johnson's room. She gave them her name and was allowed to go through.

She opened the door and stared. Redford was handcuffed to a hospital bed. She gagged, took hold of the door frame, as the hair on her neck stood on end. Redford was unconscious, and handcuffed, yet she felt threatened. She realized she was holding her breath and quickly exhaled. After another deep breath, she walked over to the bed.

Earlier that morning, she had received a call from Reverend Hill at the prison.

"Reverend Elliot, I'm calling about Redford Johnson. He is still in a coma, but the prison won't spend any more money for his medical care. He can breathe on his own, so he will be transferred to the Federal Prison Medical Facility in Rochester, Minnesota. It's the only facility in the Midwest. I wanted to let you know."

"When will he be transferred?" Maggie asked, trying to take in this news and what she should do about it.

"He'll be moved on Thursday."

"How does that work with his prison sentence?"

"He has to serve out his sentence, whether he's in the medical facility or a prison. He won't get the best medical care. He'll be monitored. If he recovers before his sentence is served, he'll go back to prison."

"Thank you for letting me know. You have a hard job." Maggie couldn't imagine doing what this man did. "Is there ever any *good news* in your job?"

"Yes. There are times when someone really turns around or when a mistake has been made in an investigation and someone is given back their freedom. But our country doesn't care about prisoners. They are treated worse than animals in a shelter. I work for the small miracles."

"God bless you," Maggie said softly. "Thank you for calling. I will go to St. Joe's today."

Then she'd dialed Julia Benson's cell phone.

"Julia speaking."

"Julia, it's Pastor Maggie. I just had a call from the prison chaplain. Redford is being transferred to Minnesota."

Silence.

Maggie continued. "He's still in a coma, but can't stay in the hospital, and the Milan prison doesn't have a medical facility to care for him. I am going to Ypsilanti to St. Joe's before he leaves to visit or . . . I don't know what since he's unconscious. I just wanted to let you know."

Maggie waited.

"I don't know what to say," Julia said. "Thank you for the update. I would hate to have your job."

"Most days are good." Maggie felt the lie roll off her tongue. Most of her days in the last few months had been hard. "I hope you have a good rest of your day, Julia. Goodbye."

Maggie didn't like the protective shell she wrapped around herself whenever she encountered Julia. She wanted to like and be liked by her parishioners. It didn't always work that way. Maybe Julia would be able to dismantle her own barriers once Redford was out of the state. Maggie wondered if it was possible.

And now, there she stood. At the bedside of a man who had tried to break and destroy so many lives. With a body unable to function, Redford would be put in a ward with the sick and the dying. Would he survive?

"Redford, it's Pastor Maggie. I know you are going to be transferred from the hospital this week. I will not be able to see you, but I will pray for you." Maggie felt tears in her eyes. "I am sorry you have had such a difficult life. And I'm sorry for the people you hurt along the way. I wish you no harm. I hope for your redemption."

She wiped her eyes and walked out the door. As it closed, she felt nothing but relief. She walked to her car and drove home to Cherish.

One week later, November eighth, it was the morning of the election. Maggie walked the short journey from farmhouse to church. She decided to stop at The Sugarplum for something sweet. She also wanted to purchase some treats for Hank, Doris, and Irena. With all the craziness in the past weeks, she felt like she had not been attentive to her small staff.

As she walked, she felt a wave of excitement for the outcome of the election. The hateful campaign that had raged for over a year would come to an end. Hate and bigotry were not going to win. She and Jack planned to drive to the old high school at lunchtime and vote together. The polls showed the Democrats would win the presidential election quite handily. Maggie felt like skipping down Middle Street but controlled herself.

She knew there were still some in her congregation who would vote for the candidate who had given license to bully and reject "the other." She had preached love and acceptance relentlessly all fall. If they didn't like her religion and politics, it was their choice to stay or go. Maggie saw "caring for the least of these" as a mandate for life—not just an occasional Sunday sermon.

The fairy bells tinkled as she opened the door. Mrs. Popkin was behind the counter with her white baker's hat floating like a meringue on her head. She was filling pink bakery boxes with scones, donuts, and fruit bars. Darcy Keller was waiting for the stack of boxes.

"Darcy, what are you doing here?" Maggie asked.

"Hi, Maggie. I thought I'd bring some of Mrs. Popkin's baked goods to the polls. I voted first thing, and it's a busy place. The workers will have a long day."

Maggie stared at Darcy and blinked. *I must be hallucinating.* "What?"

"Hokey tooters!" Mrs. Popkin laughed. "Rich man Darcy Keller has come down off his perch and is acting like a normal kind of human. Aren't you, Darcy?"

"Yes, Mrs. Popkin. I've come down to earth. I have this young woman to thank for it," he said, turning to Maggie. "My sister gave me a good kick in the pants, and Maggie gave me the practical work to do. Speaking of which, is there a day this week that you might have an hour to spare? I'd like to talk with you."

Maggie said, "I'm free later on Friday afternoon."

"Great. Where should I pick you up?"

"Pick me up? Are we going somewhere?"

"Yes."

"I'll be home. Does three o'clock work for you?"

"I'll see you then."

Darcy paid Mrs. Popkin and took his boxes.

"Well, it's nice to see a proud man step back into humanity again," Mrs. Popkin said as she wiped her hands on her apron. "Darcy used to act like he was too good to breathe our air. Now look! He's resettling refugees and feeding volunteers at the polls. What's he going to do next, I wonder?"

"I have no idea, but you're right. He's changed. You must see a bigger change because you have known him longer. But I have a question." Maggie's voice slipped into a conspiratorial tone. "What about Jennifer Becker? Do you think they will ever get married? They sit together in church every Sunday, and I've seen them together at the Cherish Café."

Mrs. Popkin leaned in and lowered her very loud voice. "I wonder if that's what he wants to talk to you about on Friday? I've heard that Jennifer spends as many nights at his mansion as she does in her own home. I think there's some hanky-panky going on there. Not that I judge either one of them, but they might as well make it legal."

Maggie's eyes widened. *Good grief! There are some things I just don't want to know about my parishioners.*

"Well now," Maggie said. "Isn't that interesting? I guess I'll have to wait until Friday."

Maggie left with her own box of treats and walked across the street. The parsonage looked quiet. She would stop over there after she voted.

After they cast their ballots at lunchtime, Jack dropped her off at the parsonage. They both felt the excitement of victory in the air. They had planned a small party at the farm to watch the election returns. Andrew and Brynn were driving up from Blissfield. Lacey and Lydia, Ellen and Harold, and Sylvester and Skylar were all invited. It would be a small but lively gathering.

Maggie walked up the porch steps of the parsonage, rang the bell, and heard the Westminster chimes inside the house. Moments later, Amira answered the door holding Katharine Marie.

"Amira," Maggie said, "how are you?" English for Mahdi, Amira, and Sabeen was coming much more slowly than for the children. "You have baby Katharine." Maggie smiled.

"Welcome." Amira stepped aside, and Maggie walked into her old home—"old" by only five weeks. When Maggie got to the kitchen, she saw Sylvia unpacking squash and potatoes from a bag.

"Hi, Sylvia," Maggie said and then laughed. "I see the Nasabs are new beneficiaries of your bounty."

"Yes! Anything to help. How are you, Pastor Maggie?" Sylvia kept unpacking.

"I'm very well indeed. I just exercised my civic duty at the old high school."

"Good work. I don't think we have anything to worry about. Truth will win."

"I agree." Maggie looked at the other woman. "Amira, are you well?" Maggie talked a little louder than needed and exaggerated her hands.

Amira smiled and nodded. "Well." Then she looked back at Katharine.

"I don't come just to bring vegetables," Sylvia said quietly. "I noticed from the start that Amira was drawn to Katharine. And we all know how she lost her own little baby in Turkey. I come over as often as I can, so she can hold Katharine. It seems to bring her some comfort."

"You are intuitive and kind," Maggie said. "You are good for my soul, Sylvia."

"Ditto. Now I wonder where I should put these vegetables. Amira?"

Sylvia pointed at the pile of vegetables and pointed to the pantry and the refrigerator, then shrugged her shoulders in a question.

Amira pointed at the pantry with one finger from underneath the baby.

Sylvia carefully placed all the vegetables on two lower shelves in the pantry.

Maggie looked up as Sabeen walked into the room. She smiled at Maggie, then went to a tray covered with a dishtowel on the counter. She removed the towel and revealed eight smooth balls of dough. She flattened each one on the counter and then pressed them flatter with her hands. Then she heated up a frying pan on the stove and added a little oil. She cooked each round until it puffed up and then flipped it over. After they were cooked, she laid each round on the counter. They smelled delicious. Maggie's mouth watered as she watched the process of Syrian bread making.

Sabeen took two of the rounds and gave one each to Maggie and Sylvia. They ate the hot bread like starving birds. Sabeen smiled.

"This is delicious," Maggie said with a mouthful. "I could eat this all day long." It was light and airy—crispy on the outside and softer in the middle.

"I could too," Sylvia agreed as she put the last bit of bread in her mouth.

Sabeen offered each woman another round, and they greedily took them. Then Sabeen began to mix up more dough.

Maggie had an idea. *What if we used Syrian bread for communion? What a beautiful way to remember the whole community of God's world. We could pay Sabeen to make the bread.* Maggie kept her thoughts to herself for the moment, but she couldn't help thinking she'd had a stroke of brilliance.

She was brought out of her reverie by the small wails of Katharine. The baby was twisting in Amira's arms, and her face was scrunched. Amira made soft noises to the baby, but Katharine wanted her mama. Reluctantly, Amira handed the baby back to Sylvia.

"Thank you for holding her," Sylvia said, smiling at Amira. "She is sleepy."

Sylvia plopped her head to one side and closed her eyes. Amira smiled and nodded.

Maggie and Sylvia left the parsonage full of Syrian bread and gentle thoughts.

Later that evening, the farmhouse was alive with family, friends, food, and television. Andrew and Brynn had arrived early to meet with Maggie and begin planning their wedding service. They'd spent an hour and a half looking at Bible passages, poems, options for handfasting, and other unity ideas, as well as musical pieces. Maggie enjoyed laying out the possibilities for a creative, personal service. She was almost as excited as the happy couple.

"Take time to look through these ideas," she said, handing them a large folder. "We don't have to finalize anything until we're closer to the wedding day. Think about whether you want to write your own or use traditional vows."

Andrew looked slightly startled. "Do you mean the 'for richer, for poorer; in sickness and in health' stuff?"

"Yes, that stuff." Maggie laughed. "I'm sure you could write all the promises you want to make to your bride while sitting on a hay bale in the barn."

"As a matter of fact, I could. I'm a romantic guy, as you will remember by my proposal."

Brynn had looked at the ring on her finger and smiled.

Everyone had brought something for the "election celebration" feast. Brynn brought a large platter of soft German pretzels. She and

Bonnie had baked them fresh that day. Some were sprinkled with salt and had honey mustard to dip them in. Some were covered in cinnamon sugar. Lacey and Lydia brought a large wooden bowl full of hot spinach artichoke parmesan dip. They had a tray of cut vegetables and a basket with chunks of pumpernickel bread to go with it.

"Here you go, PM," Lacey said, setting her offerings on the large kitchen table. "Lydia and I put this together for the party. It's going to be fun to watch the returns tonight. Another four years, at least, of rights for all people. These last eight years have changed so many people's lives for the good."

Maggie knew Lacey was talking about LGBTQ rights. She also knew how important the new laws and protections were in order to change lives from invisible and shunned to visible and affirmed. The country would not go backward tonight.

Sylvester and Skylar surprised Maggie with a tray of sweet peppers filled with spicy rice and vegetables.

"These are beautiful," Maggie said, setting them on the oven to keep them warm.

"Mmm . . . yes they are," Sky said. "Sylvester made the filling, and I scooped it into the peppers. I had the easiest part of the job." She smiled and looked at Sly. He was talking to Jack about something that seemed important. "But be prepared. He added some Nigerian spices . . . mmm."

Sky drifted over to Sly like a fairy princess and slipped her arm through his. He smiled.

Ellen and Harold arrived with a fancy platter of smoked salmon, shrimp, herbed cream cheese, and a variety of crackers.

"Well, you two have classed up this party," Jack said, taking the platter while stealing a shrimp.

"That's what we're here for," Harold said. "This is going to be a great night."

Along with Maggie's huge pot of white chicken chili and bowl of fruit salad, the feast was complete.

Jack grabbed Maggie and led her into the laundry room.

"What are you doing? We don't have time to make out right now," she said and laughed.

"Sly told me a piece of property has been found south of Cherish for the clinic. The board approved the purchase. The only thing is the time it will take to put a building on the land, but we are moving forward. The clinic is going to happen!"

He picked her up and swung her around, totally giddy.

"Sylvester is a miracle worker," Maggie said as Jack set her back down. "Won't if be fun to help design the clinic with the latest equipment and everything brand-new?" Maggie let out a squeal.

"Now, for making out," Jack said and leaned down for a kiss.

"Hey! Knock that off! You guys are gross." Ellen stood in the doorway. "We need more napkins. My dear fiancé spilled his wine all over the stack you have on the counter."

Jack gave Maggie a quick kiss and then whispered, "There will be more of this later."

"Good. I'm counting on it."

Then she went to deal with the great napkin crisis in the kitchen.

Jack filled up wine glasses, everyone heaped food onto plates, and they went to the family room and settled in for the evening. They all agreed Sylvester's Nigerian peppers were the hit of the evening. Excited chatter accompanied the good food and high hopes for the country.

Before midnight, it was all but over. The Republican candidate won the state of Florida, along with other key states. The road for the Democrat looked impossible. The happy gathering of friends had grown quieter and quieter until it was completely silenced. As each new state was handed to the Republican, heads shook in disbelief. Maggie saw Lacey quickly wipe away tears as Lydia held her hand. Sylvester leaned forward, elbows on his knees, his hands holding his head. Skylar stared unblinkingly at the television, as if hoping to change its mind. Harold and Ellen looked shell-shocked. Finally, Andrew stood up. He cleared his throat, but his voice was still scratchy.

"I think Brynn and I should be on our way. We have a long drive home."

Jack went to the front hall closet to get their coats. Harold followed him.

"Ellen and I will be on our way too. This is a nightmare."

The friends gathered their leftovers and various dishes. Then, with haunted looks on their faces, they said their quiet goodbyes.

Maggie looked at Jack when they were back in the kitchen and alone.

"This can't be. There will be so much suffering in the country if he wins."

"He *has* won," Jack said, putting his arms around her. "And he's unleashed hate and bigotry among the fearful. They will carry his message forward."

Maggie couldn't bear the words or the vision.

"Who can fix this? He isn't qualified in any way to be president. Congress? Who?"

"He'll have Congress in his pocket. It will be the people. It will have to be the people who don't want to live in darkness."

24

The following morning, Maggie opened her Bible and read the lectionary passage for the Sunday after the election: Luke 21:5-19. *Well, that sounds about right!* Not one stone will be left upon another, and the temple will be torn down. Maggie sighed and traced the lines with her finger.

> When some were speaking about the temple, how it was adorned with beautiful stones and gifts dedicated to God, he said, "As for these things that you see, the days will come when not one stone will be left upon another; all will be thrown down."
>
> They asked him, "Teacher, when will this be, and what will be the sign that this is about to take place?" And he said, "Beware that you are not led astray; for many will come in my name and say, 'I am he!' and, 'The time is near!' Do not go after them.
>
> "When you hear of wars and insurrections, do not be terrified; for these things must take place first, but the end will not follow immediately." Then he said to them, "Nation will rise against nation, and kingdom against kingdom; there will be great earthquakes, and

in various places famines and plagues; and there will be dreadful portents and great signs from heaven.

"But before all this occurs, they will arrest you and persecute you; they will hand you over to synagogues and prisons, and you will be brought before kings and governors because of my name. This will give you an opportunity to testify. So make up your minds not to prepare your defense in advance; for I will give you words and a wisdom that none of your opponents will be able to withstand or contradict. You will be betrayed even by parents and brothers, by relatives and friends; and they will put some of you to death. You will be hated by all because of my name. But not a hair of your head will perish. By your endurance you will gain your souls."

She and Jack had not slept the night before. They had lain awake talking while three cats curled around their feet in blissful ignorance. The felines had received their treats. All was right with their world.

Maggie called her parents as soon as she thought they were awake. Like Jack and Maggie, Dirk and Mimi had also not slept. Mimi put Maggie on speaker phone.

"I don't think anyone in the country saw this coming," Mimi said briskly, "especially the person who won." She wouldn't say his name. "We will have to see how this all plays out, but it's no use wringing our hands. We will have a lot of work to do if this is our new reality. I know you will have some Good News for your parishioners this Sunday."

"I'm glad you know that." Maggie sulked.

"In other matters," Mimi moved on, "we're looking forward to being in Blissfield for Thanksgiving."

"How in the world can any of us celebrate Thanksgiving?" Maggie yelped.

"Maggie," Dirk said calmly, "your parishioners will be looking to you, beginning today. They will need hope and reasons to believe they are going to be okay. People are not taking this election as a global happening. Yet. They are taking it personally. And remember, there are some who are *rejoicing* over this news."

After they hung up, Maggie thought about her father's words as she read through the dread-filled Bible passage once again. Then she went upstairs, got dressed, patted the kitties, and made the walk to church.

She was met with the hollowed stares of Hank and Marla. Irena was not at the organ, or anywhere visible. Doris was missing as well.

"Good morning," Maggie said, trying to smile like she meant it.

Marla looked at Maggie. "Pastor Maggie, we have a serious problem."

"Yes, I know. I watched the election results."

"No, not that. I got a call from Sylvia this morning. Maria Gutierrez called her. The Gutierrez family has been evicted from their home. Apparently, their landlord came over this morning and said the lease was done and then told them to go back to Mexico."

Maggie felt the rage begin in her stomach. "Where are they now?"

"They are packing. They have until Friday to leave their house."

"There has to be some kind of rental agreement. They can't be evicted because of the color of their skin or where they come from."

"Sylvia doesn't know what kind of agreement they signed. She said Maria is scared. They don't know where to go and are frustrated."

Maggie rubbed her fingers over her eyes. *So it begins. All the hate and racism has been released.*

"I'll get over there right away."

Martha Babcock awoke after a contented night's sleep. She and G. Gordon Liddy Kitty had watched the election results until her shock and surprise had turned into glee.

He won! By golly, he won!

Then she slept like the dead until her alarm went off. Once she remembered the shocking news of the night before, she looked at the cat and said, "Good things are going to happen, Gordon! We'll get this country straightened out yet. We'll have borders to keep the trash out, G. And you can bet that Syrian family will be deported. A new day has dawned, and the liberals are done! Their hands are tied."

She clapped her own hands together and laughed. G. Gordon Liddy Kitty jumped at the loud sounds and ran under the living room chair. This crazy behavior could not be tolerated.

Maggie quickly walked home, got in her car, and drove first to Jack's office to tell him the news. Then she drove out to Old US 12. As she pulled into Juan and Maria's driveway, her heart sank. She hadn't been to visit for several weeks. The little house looked desolate. Broken shutters hung askew and looked like they would drop any second, and the porch sagged dreadfully. Maggie hurried up the rickety steps and knocked on the door.

Maria opened it. She was holding Marcos. He looked at Maggie with his huge brown eyes, and Maggie felt her throat tighten.

"Maria, I hear there's a little trouble around here."

"Pastor Maggie, come in."

Maria stepped aside, and Maggie walked into the living room of the little house. There was a pile of clothes on the couch and several toys on the coffee table. Maria put Marcos down, and he toddled over to the toys and happily pushed them all on the floor. Then he giggled. The tragedy of his innocence in this new circumstance burned in Maggie. She was past tears. She was enraged.

"Maria, what are you planning to do? Marla said you have been evicted."

"Yes, we have. We have until Friday. Two days."

"Do you have a lease agreement?"

"We signed something, but we never received a copy. Our landlord said we could be evicted at will. We don't know where to go, but Juan has a sister in Iowa. He talked with her twice this morning. She said we could move in with them until Juan found a job."

"Do you *want* to move to Iowa?" Maggie asked.

"No. Not really. We like it here, and I'm . . . well, I'm taking classes at Washtenaw. I'd have to quit school."

"I heard about that." Maggie was mad at herself for not following up on this information when Sylvia first told her about Maria's education. "What if we can find a way for you to stay in Cherish and in school?"

Maria looked surprised. "How?"

As soon as Charlie and Naomi left for school, Jim and Cecelia Chance resumed the fight they had begun the night before.

"You will not spout that language in front of the kids again!" Cecelia said. "I've had it with you talking like a fool. How do you think Naomi feels when you laugh at that horrid man saying he grabs women by their genitals? You laugh at that! What message are you sending her?"

"She doesn't listen to it."

"She sure does! Every time you laugh or say that the women suing him for sexual harassment are a bunch of bitches or scream at the TV about Latino people or Middle Eastern people and how they are all scum, the kids hear you! I WILL NOT ALLOW YOU TO TEACH THEM TO HATE AND BE BIGOTS!" She took a breath. "I swear, I will leave you and take them with me."

"You're not going anywhere," Jim said with a dismissive wave of his hand. "Our country is going to get rid of the terrorists, and yes, they are scum! They take all our jobs, and they want to destroy our country. He'll get rid of all of them. And he's bringing jobs back from other countries. As soon as I can get back to work, my job will be better and I'll get more pay. There won't be any more competition from the Mexicans."

"I don't know what's happened to you, but you are not my husband. You have been sucked into this insanity. Listening to you parrot the ugliness and fifth over the past few months makes me sick. What are you so afraid of?"

"Well, you better get used to it because our new president is going to get some things done, finally."

After Maggie left the Gutierrez home with somewhat of a plan in place, she went back to church to discover Howard and Verna Baker waiting in her office. Even though Hank told them Maggie was gone, they'd said they would wait for her return.

"Hi, you two," Maggie said. She felt a surprising wave of relief to find the two older people sitting quietly in the cream-colored visitor chairs.

"Pastor Maggie," Verna said, "we are here to lend our support. We know you have everything under control, but sometimes it helps to know you have reinforcements."

Maggie sat down behind her desk and took a deep breath.

"Yes," Howard continued his wife's thought. "This is a sad day for our country, but we will all get through it. We've been through worse things."

"I can't imagine worse things," Maggie said dolefully.

"Of course you can," Verna said. "We don't need to recount American history for you. Our country has survived wars, depression, civil rights movements, and even Republican governments!"

"But anything like this?" Maggie wasn't giving up her grievance.

"Stop for a moment and think of countries like Syria and think of families like the Nasab family," said practical Verna.

"I have been thinking of them! What if they are deported and they have to leave and go back to Syria with those darling children and poor old Sabeen?" Maggie was gripped by this fear.

"They will be processed into US citizenship, and my guess is it will be expedited before the government changes," Howard said, although he did not know anything about the process.

"The point is," said Verna, "we will band together and continue to live as God intended—loving our neighbors and doing unto others, et cetera."

Maggie had to smile at this. *Just think of crabby old Verna Abernathy saying that two years ago!*

"Thank you. Both of you. I needed this gentle shove back into hope. We will continue to live out our mandate as Christians and decent human beings."

They all cocked their heads at a very loud bang.

Irena threw open Maggie's door, after slamming Hank's. She stood in the doorway in all of her tiny glory. She looked as if a giant bottle of glitter had spilled on her head and trickled down the rest of her small frame. Her eyes were blazing out of one blue and one green shadowed eye.

"Vell! Dat's eet! Ve now hev a verry bad man at de top of ourr countrry. Vat ve do vit de Syrians? Ve hide dem? Do dey leeve herre in de basement of churrch? Dey must be prrotected!"

"Hi, Irena," Maggie said. "You are so . . . sparkly."

"I hev sparrkles forr my hair. I spilt eet too much today. I vas tinking about de election."

Howard and Verna both stood, and Irena quickly scooted around and sat in Verna's chair, a bit of glitter shimmered in a trail behind her.

"I think we are all safe with Irena at the helm," Howard said with a wink.

"Ov courrse. You can go now." Irena tapped her foot impatiently. She wanted Pastor Maggie's full attention.

Maggie followed the Bakers into Hank's office to thank them again, then she returned to Irena. Before Irena could begin her tirade, Maggie spoke.

"Irena, this is going to take time. We have a breathing period before everything switches over in January. Let's do what we can to promote unity and comfort to our people. I will need your full support on this."

Irena warmed to this idea. She and Pastor Maggie would save the world—or at least the church.

"Now," Maggie said, knowing exactly what would distract and cheer Irena, "let's talk about Christmas. What do you have in mind for the music?"

∞

That evening, Jack and Maggie slowly ate leftover chili in the early darkness of November.

"I think it would be good if we drove down to Blissfield on Friday night," Jack said. "Is that okay? Mom invited us for dinner, but I think she needs some reassurance about the election. It has really thrown her."

"That's fine. I have some more wedding ideas for Andrew and Brynn." Maggie took a bite of cornbread dipped in chili. "I have a meeting with Darcy Friday afternoon. He wants to take me somewhere for something. I don't know what. But I should be back before you get home from the office."

"Good. Now tell me about the Gutierrez family. What did they say?"

"Maria was in shock. Juan wasn't home. He was getting some boxes from the gas station. I told her to talk with him and let me know. When she called back this afternoon, she was relieved and excited."

"Is there anyone who can help them move in on Friday?"

"What do you think? Yes! Hank, Pamela, Marla, Tom, and Bill Baxter. Sylvia and Katharine will go along to watch Gabby and Marcos. This is the perfect idea for everyone. Who would have guessed when the condo was broken into it would have such a good ending?"

"I'm glad there's a use for it. Do you have any idea who their landlord is?"

"I didn't ask. Some horrible racist. Who throws babies out of their homes! As if Juan and Maria don't have enough stress. They are good people, and they work hard to pay their bills and care for their family. Maria is going to school for an education degree. She's smart and motivated. Juan is managing the gas station now, and Maria said the owners have another station down toward Manchester and want him to oversee that one too. Then today happened. But . . ." Maggie took a breath and a bite of chili, "things are looking up. I called Arly, Priscilla, and Jennifer and Beth Becker to ask them for groceries and some homemade meals for Juan and Maria as they transition to the condo. Of course, those wonderful ladies jumped all over the idea. Myrna Barnes said she would talk to Maria about watching Gabby and Marcos while Maria goes to school—no charge! That way, Maria will be able to take more classes next semester."

Jack looked thoughtful. "When you think of all the people from our congregation who have pulled together in the last two months to help the two of us, the Nasab family, and now the Gutierrez family, it's pretty remarkable. We aren't a huge church, but we're doing huge things."

"I don't want to overtax anyone," Maggie said. "What could we do to thank the congregation?"

"What if we have a New Year's Eve open house here?"

"I love that idea! Maybe we could have some kind of small service. Prayers or candle lighting, wishes for the new year?"

"I think that would give everyone hope."

Friday at three o'clock, Darcy picked up Maggie and headed east of town down Old US 12. Before they reached the on-ramp for I-94, Darcy pulled off into a parking lot south of the road. There was a large building that looked like a barn, but more modern. There was a "For Sale" sign on the double doors.

"Maggie, I hope this will do. Welcome to the free Cherish Childcare Center."

Maggie looked at Darcy and looked back at the building. She had spent the morning helping move the Gutierrez family into the refurbished condo. Jacob and Deborah Stein had provided breakfast and friendship to their new neighbors. Juan and Maria seemed dazed by all the goodwill and help that surrounded them. By two p.m., their possessions had been moved. They had no furniture of their own to move and were surprised by the beautiful furniture all ready and waiting in the condo. Jack and Maggie (via the insurance company) had replaced everything after the break-in. The money they received weekly from Brock went into a savings account for the Nasab family.

Now, sitting in Darcy's car, the emotion of the past four days caught up to Maggie's eyes. She sat and wept. She wept for the hope and despair of Tuesday, for the shock of Wednesday and the Gutierrez family's plight, for the kindnesses of her parishioners as they cared for another family in need, and now this. The childcare center. Another gift from another kind and generous person in her life.

Darcy sat still as she cried out all her tears of sorrow and joy. When she finally wiped the last tear he said, "Would you like a tour, Pastor Maggie?"

"Yes. I would like that very much, Mr. Keller."

That evening, Jack and Maggie sat around the kitchen table at Ken and Bonnie's. Andrew, Brynn, and Leigh were there, but there was no spark of laughter or fun. Everyone was still reeling from the election. Jack and Maggie began to share the abundance of good news they had witnessed in the few days since their despair over the future.

"The childcare center looks like a barn, but it's completely modern inside." Maggie took a bite of steaming mashed potatoes drowning in butter. "It used to be a large insurance company, but they moved the business to Main Street. This building has four large bathrooms, a kitchen, and three areas divided for infants, toddlers, and fours and fives."

"And Darcy just gave it to you?" Brynn asked, her eyes wide and showing a hint of a tear or two.

"Yes! He found out about the sale of the building and made a deal with the owner of the insurance company. Fresh paint and new carpet will be done by the end of November. He's also having little toilets installed in the bathrooms for the children. I wouldn't have thought of that." She giggled. "Pint-sized tables and chairs will be delivered in December, hopefully before Christmas. The last piece of this project is to have the ever-annoying Fitch Dervish sign off on the renovations. Hopefully he can do it without shedding his blood all over the new carpet."

"How will you staff it?" Ken asked.

"Our Sunday school superintendent, Marla Wiggins, will be the director. We will have to hire more staff, but that's not a problem. I love that the best news is Maria Gutierrez can work there and get some school credit. It means she can also quit her job cleaning the Catholic church at night and bring her children to the center for free."

"And how will it be financed if there is no charge for the care?" Ken followed up.

"Cassandra Moffet left money and a mandate for this in her will. The interest from the investment should cover the costs. If not, we'll seek private donations."

Ken nodded. "I forgot about Cassandra's money. Let us know if you need anything. We'd be more than happy to help."

Bonnie looked happy for the first time that evening. "I think the childcare center might be the nicest story I've ever heard. Besides the stories of the Nasab family, your wedding, and Brynn and Andrew's engagement, of course."

"What about Anne and Peter's wedding?" Andrew asked.

"Oh, yes! And Anne and Peter's wedding. That seems like a long time ago. Besides, Gretchen and Garrett are the best part of that whole family. Grandchildren beat weddings, hands down." Bonnie smiled hopefully at Maggie and Brynn.

"So, our wedding only matters so you can get some grandkids out of it?" Andrew asked.

"Yes," said Ken. "You won't count much at all once Brynn has six or seven babies."

"C'mon, Dad! Gross!" Leigh couldn't imagine her own parents creating children and she certainly didn't want to think about her brothers "creating."

Brynn's eyes grew quite large at the idea of six babies, even in jest.

"What about you, Maggie?" Andrew turned and stared at his sister-in-law.

"I'm not having six or seven babies. I don't want a litter, I want a family."

"And no more questions from you," Jack cut off his brother before he got too annoying. "The next big event is your wedding. We can all talk about babies after that."

"Let us enjoy our honeymoon first," Andrew said.

"That's how it all starts." Ken laughed. Then his face grew serious. "Next year certainly has its fears, but maybe there will be a couple of little cousins around to chase away the gloom."

Ken gave Maggie a wink.

25

The Cherish Childcare Center was the hot news around town. Julia Benson did a large spread in the *Cherish Life and Times* with pictures and interviews. Maggie felt the same "thaw" in Julia's demeanor as she'd witnessed when Redford was arrested and imprisoned. Now that Redford was in another state and in a physical condition which kept him from any possibility of harming her, Julia was breathing and smiling and laughing again.

A January fifteenth start date was set for the opening of what was being called CCC. The news helped refocus many of the parishioners at Loving the Lord from the daily remembrance of the political situation in the country. Good things were happening in Cherish.

Marla sat in Maggie's office with a list of applicants for childcare workers. She had a separate list of families requesting care for their children.

"We have nine excellent candidates for working with the children. That doesn't include Maria, who is already hired. Addie has also asked if she can work during her summer break."

"What did you tell her?" Maggie teased.

Marla smiled. "I told her she had to have a background check and asked for three references."

"How are you doing with her in Holland?"

"I'm doing *terribly*. She's doing great. She has settled into college life and loves her friends, her classes, her exams . . . every phone call is full of sunshine and butterflies."

"When does she come home for Thanksgiving?"

"We'll pick her up the Tuesday night before."

Maggie saw Marla look down at the applications. Marla and Addie were such good friends, Maggie could see the pain on the older woman's face. *Mothering definitely has its downside. What does it feel like to watch your child become the person you always hoped she would be—independent and confident and loving her life—but not needing you so much anymore?*

Marla changed the subject back. "As of now, we have forty-two families applying for care."

She handed the applications to Maggie, who looked through the stack. Maggie smiled at Marla.

"Cassandra is so happy right now," Maggie said. "It took us almost a year, but we have honored her, and we will help many families."

"I'll never forget the day Harold had us all in his office and read her will. I had no idea why I had been asked to be there."

"Now you do! You are the director of a free childcare center. And you helped Cassandra by taking care of Carrie and Carl while she was ill. Marla, you are good for my soul."

There was a knock at Maggie's door. "Come in."

Sylvia came in with little Katharine in the sling around her chest. "Hi, friends!"

"Hi, Sylvia. Hi, Katharine," Marla and Maggie said in tandem.

"Doesn't this just feel like the good old days when we crammed in here to plan 'death curriculum' and pile veggies on Pastor Maggie's desk?" Sylvia laughed.

"Yes," Marla said, "the good old days. Except we need Irena to stomp in here and kick us out so she can tell Pastor Maggie how to do things and plan a Christmas cantata with four choir members."

Maggie remembered those first few months of life at Loving the Lord. She'd learned more that first year than all her years in seminary.

The "people" work. Her education continued with new personalities, struggles, and joys. She looked at the baby.

"Can you let Katharine out of her kangaroo pouch sling thing so I may hold her?"

"Of course, Auntie Maggie."

Sylvia unwound the wrap and placed Katharine in Maggie's arms. Katharine kicked and cooed. Maggie snuggled her close and then kissed the top of her head.

"Mmmm . . . she smells delicious."

"I've actually come for a more serious reason," Sylvia said, sitting in the visitor chair next to Marla. "I was just at the condo checking in with Juan and Maria. They are doing great and love their beautiful new space. Anyway, I decided to ask a few more question about their landlord. First of all, it wasn't a man, which surprised me. But I was more surprised when the person they described to me was the one and only . . . Martha Babcock."

Both Maggie and Marla reacted as Sylvia expected. "What?!"

"Are you sure?" Maggie asked, once again feeling anger rise up from her gut.

"I am. They were able to physically describe her, but Juan said he's seen her go into the police station in the mornings when he was going to work at the gas station.

"You know, I've wondered how she can live on the pay of running the police radio," Marla said bitterly. "Maybe it's enough for one person to live on, but it sure doesn't seem like enough. It makes sense if she has property to rent. Although, it sounds like she's much more of a *slumlord* than a landlord."

Marla had been horrified when she'd seen the living conditions of the Gutierrez family on moving day. Windows that didn't close properly, furniture with holes in the cushions, duct tape on the kitchen table legs, and other pieces of broken furniture. Not to mention the outside of the house with the sagging porch and need for a new roof and window shutters. To think, Martha was responsible for all of that decay.

Maggie looked down at Katharine, who was happily sucking her thumb and falling into a contented sleep.

"I will never understand people who take advantage of others just because they can. The Gutierrez family had no recourse. They needed a house, and that was one they could afford, and it was a dump."

Sylvia said, "I thought we could find out if Martha owed them any money because of the way she treated them and didn't take care of the house while they lived there."

"Harold Brinkmeyer would know," Marla said. "Maybe he could help them regain some rent money."

"I'll call him and find out," Maggie said. "It would be nice to see a little justice for a good family."

Later that afternoon, Maggie called Harold and poured out the whole story of the Gutierrez family and Martha Babcock.

"I can help with this," Harold said, feeling the injustice too. "It's not too complicated. We will have someone check out the house, find out how much the family paid in rent, and get our hands on the signed rental agreement, a copy of which Martha didn't see fit to give them. This won't take long. I'll get back to you."

"Thanks, Harold." Maggie hung up and went to Hank's desk. "I'm going next door to see Amira and Sabeen for a few minutes. I'll be back."

"I'll hold down the fort, yesireebob!" Hank turned back to his computer.

Maggie rang the doorbell of the parsonage. Once again, she heard the Westminster chimes ring out. Amira answered the door. She smiled when she saw Maggie and opened the door wide. Maggie went through toward the kitchen and could hear noises coming from her old study—older male voices along with the children.

When she peeked into the study, she discovered the room was being used as a playroom. Brock and Mason Tuggle were there, playing with the Nasab children. She took a moment to ponder the sight. A few months ago, she would have never believed the scene was possible.

Maggie's old desk and bookshelves were up against the wall. The red-and-white checked wingback chairs had been moved to somewhere else. She looked out the window and saw the three pine trees and the little red wagon beneath them. The wagon was empty, except for a few pine needles, but the bird feeders were full. She had shown Amira how to fill them and left a trash can full of seed in the garage.

"Hi, Pastor Maggie," Brock said.

He had both Karam and Samir on his back. He was crawling around the room on his hands and knees, and every few steps he would try to buck off the little boys. They screamed and laughed as they grabbed his shirt and hung on. Mason had Iman and Jamal on his back, doing the same thing.

"Horseback rides I see," Maggie said, giggling. "Do you do this often?"

"Two or three times a week. It's the time of day our mom calls the 'witching hour,'" Mason explained as he bucked. The girls screamed and held on.

"Mahdi gets home kind of late," Brock said. "Not until Dad is ready to leave and bring him home. Mom told us Amira needed a little help with these four while she prepares dinner. Apparently, we drove mom crazy when we were little. I think she's exaggerating."

Brock bucked, and Samir fell off and landed on his bottom. He scrambled back up again and crawled onto Brock's back, squealing.

"Thanks for doing this. I'm sure it helps Amira during the 'witching hour.'" Maggie said a little prayer of thanksgiving for the miracle of Brock. His life could have gone a drastically different direction. "When do you two work at the quarry, or did that change?"

"We go in at six a.m., and we're done at two p.m.," Brock explained. "The mornings are a little rough, but we have most of the day left after work."

Mason bucked, and the girls both tumbled off. Then he said, "Let's take a soccer ball out front. My knees hurt."

As that group cleaned up the playroom, Maggie went to the kitchen. Amira was stirring something that smelled of spices Maggie didn't recognize. They warmed her nose. Sabeen was preparing small rounds of Syrian bread.

"Amira," Maggie said.

Amira looked up. Maggie pointed at the bread in Sabeen's hands. "Bread."

Amira nodded.

Maggie pointed out the kitchen window to the church. "Church."

Once again, Amira nodded.

"Bread at church." Maggie again pointed to the bread, then to the church. She mimed eating the bread. She couldn't help giggling at these simplistic communications.

Maggie held up ten fingers, desperately hoping Amira would understand she meant ten rounds of bread.

Amira considered this for a moment.

"Bread." Amira held up ten fingers. "Church." She pointed out the window. Then she looked at Maggie and said uncertainly, "Now? Today?" She looked embarrassed, as if she had used the wrong words.

"No, not today." Maggie shook her head. She held up six fingers. "Six days."

There was a calendar hanging on the wall where Maggie had left it. She didn't know if Amira used it or not. She stepped over to it and pointed. "Today." Then she pointed to Sunday. "Bread. Church."

It clicked. Amira smiled and nodded. "Yes. Bread. Church. Six days."

Maggie took thirty dollars out of her wallet and handed the money to Amira. Maggie had gone back and forth about paying, only because she didn't want to insult Amira. But then she decided that if they would use Syrian bread regularly for communion, Amira should get paid for baking the bread early in the morning. Amira tried to refuse, but Maggie held firm.

The children and the big boys came into the kitchen and went out through the kitchen door. Amira smiled. She pointed at them and put her hand up high to represent Brock and Mason. "Good."

"Yes, they are good," Maggie agreed.

∞

Sunday morning was the usual flurry at Loving the Lord. As Maggie was looking over the bulletin to make sure she had all the pieces of worship in her head, Amira came in with a small basket. *The bread.* Amira lifted a cotton cloth to reveal ten rounds of Syrian bread. Maggie could smell their delicious aroma. They were still warm.

"Thank you," Maggie said and gave Amira a hug.

"You . . . are . . . welcome," Amira said haltingly.

Maggie put the bread on the plate set in the middle of the communion table and covered it with a white cloth napkin.

When it was time for communion, Maggie said, "The bread we will share today was made by Amira and Sabeen."

Both women looked up from their pew when they heard their names. They didn't understand anything else in the service but came every Sunday with the family. Maggie took them to the mosque every week and enjoyed the different surroundings as she prayed.

"This is traditional Syrian bread. It reminds us we are part of a small world with many breads representing our cultures and diversity. Thank you, Amira and Sabeen."

Maggie continued with the service. When it came time to share the elements, the parishioners lined up and came forward. They each received a small piece of Syrian bread and dipped it in one of the chalices of grape juice. There was a deeper sense of connection, not just with their new family, but with another country. Communion felt like communion.

After church, Priscilla pulled Maggie aside and said, "That bread was delicious! Do you think we could buy it from Amira and Sabeen on Sundays? You know, to take home and gobble?"

Maggie laughed at her friend. "That's an idea. If they wouldn't be too tired to bake, I think they could make a nice little 'church business.' Let's talk to them later."

Amira and Sabeen were slightly overwhelmed by the effusive attention they received from their pew-mates. Hugs and loud words—"DE-LICIOUS BREAD!"—made both women smile and look at the ground in embarrassment.

Myra went up to Sabeen and said, "I'd like to learn how to make your bread."

Sabeen didn't understand but smiled at the woman who had first made her feel welcome in America.

"I will come to your house this week," Myra said, "and we will use hand signals until we understand each other." Myra held Sabeen's hand for a moment, then went to find her own brood of grandchildren.

Maggie found Myrna and the twins in the nursery. Myrna's stomach was growing nicely round.

"How are you feeling, Myrna? You look beautiful with your bump."

"Well, thank you very much, Pastor Maggie. I'm feelin' good, but tired, which is not surprisin'."

"I wanted to thank you for inviting the Nasab family out to your farm for Thanksgiving. I was going to change our plans to be in Blissfield, but your hospitality is appreciated. Do you need any help baking or anything? I'd be happy to contribute to your feast."

"That's nice of you, but you don't seem to know when to quit doin' everthin' for everybody. Mama and I have the whole meal planned. And I think the kids will all have fun together. Don't you worry, we'll give them the whole hoopla. They won't know what hit 'em when they see our table! Jasper bought three twenty-five-pound turkeys. Won't that be a sight?!" Myrna laughed heartily.

"Well, thank you, again. They will get the American holiday experience at your house, that's for sure."

26

Maggie, Jack, Mimi, and Dirk drove down to Blissfield on Thanksgiving morning. Maggie carefully packed five pies for the journey. Mimi and Dirk had driven from Zeeland to the farmhouse the night before. Now they were going to Ken and Bonnie's to celebrate the day. Maggie was relieved not to be hosting Thanksgiving dinner at the farm that year. She had worked hard to prepare the Thanksgiving church service the night before and was worn out from the past three months.

"What are you thinking about?" Jack asked his wife as they drove.

"Oh, bits and bobs, odds and ends, this and that. My mind is flitting about."

"It was a lovely service last night," Mimi chimed in. "I think people needed to focus on what is worthy of thanksgiving in our lives given the juxtaposition of our government." She sniffed airily. Mimi was daily annoyed by the bombast of the president-elect.

"Thanks, Mom. I think the childcare center is a happy focus for our whole community." She turned to Jack. "But I'm glad we will be with your family today. Life is a little too busy. I talked with Harold after church last night and found out there is good cause to take action against Martha Babcock. That's both a relief and sad. She hasn't been back in church since the day she walked out during the service. What happened in her life to make her so mean?"

"You're preaching to the choir, madam," Jack said.

Maggie ignored him and continued. "I'm relieved the Nasab family is at the Barnes's farm and the Gutierrez family were invited to Tom and Marla's. Addie could hardly wait to have Gabby and Marcos over to play. Irena is going with Keith Crunch to his family in Lansing. I've worried about her since the first Thanksgiving I was in Cherish, except I wasn't in Cherish. I went home and found out Irena had been all alone. Hopefully, everyone else will be settled happily for the day."

"Maggie," Mimi said from the backseat, "you must put down your shepherdess staff today. And if you can, turn down the volume in your brain. You have permission to enjoy today without responsibilities."

"Well, thank you. I will try. But I will have one piece of work. Andrew, Brynn, and I are going to make the seating plans for the wedding. They will have folding chairs in the large room upstairs. We'll figure out where the musicians will be and some of the other logistics for the ceremony. That doesn't feel like work. It will be fun."

"Allowed," Mimi said.

"So, Queen Mother," Jack said to Mimi, "are you excited to see Bryan next month?"

"Yes," said Dirk. "She doesn't let on in front of you two, but she is very excited."

"I'm always happy to see either one of my children," Mimi said, "and my son-in-law. I like him too."

"He's pretty great," Maggie said. "We're excited to have Christmas at the farm. Do you think Bryan will like it?"

"He will love it. He will love it because Cate will be there."

Mimi hoped, along with Maggie, there might be an engagement announcement this year.

"Jack, how is work going?" Dirk asked. "Is there word on the free clinic?"

"Work is busy. I have four mothers who will deliver in the next two to three weeks. But I look at it as new clients for the childcare center. As far as the free clinic, Sylvester Fejokwu and the board are in the process of purchasing land south of Cherish. They got a good deal on the land. We will begin looking at preliminary designs right after

Christmas. We'll have a better idea of completion once we have the plans and a contractor to give us a time line."

Maggie loved to watch Jack talk about the clinic. His face became animated, and his passion snuck out from behind his calm demeanor. Jack knew he had skills to heal the sick. That's what he went to school to learn. But his heart for the poor was what drove him.

"To be honest," Jack continued, "since the election, I'm concerned about what is going to happen with the healthcare plan in our country. Although the ACA needs to go further to control the insurance companies and big pharmaceuticals, it has extended care to so many people who couldn't afford insurance and protects children and pre-existing conditions. Unless the new president is just spouting rhetoric, there's a chance some people will lose their care in the coming year. It's so backward and damaging."

"There will be much to watch next year," Dirk said solemnly. "When one party runs the government, and that party seems not to care about the poor and disenfranchised, we might see a great deal of suffering."

"We don't know what we don't know." Mimi's practical voice came from the backseat. "So, we might as well think positively and carry on with doing all the good we can. Fortunately, we have different skills to help people in a variety of ways. The free childcare center and the free medical clinic are perfect examples. Hope is not gone, and we will not despair, even though it seems we will have the most unprepared president in history."

Mimi's sharp point at the end made Maggie laugh out loud.

"Mom, I wish *you* were president. It would be a joy to watch you run the country."

When they arrived at Ken and Bonnie's, the house smelled like heaven. Maggie and Jack set the five pies on the counter and agreed there was enough food to feed the five thousand. They greeted Jack's family and Brynn's too. Andrew and Brynn's brothers were playing a video game in the family room. Ken and Richard were looking out the living room window, talking of crops and prices and retirement.

Bonnie pulled casserole dishes out of the oven and put other casserole dishes in. She had the dinner perfectly timed. Mimi put on an apron, and she and Nicolette grabbed stacks of plates, bowls, and silverware. The large farmhouse kitchen table would be filled to capacity.

Brynn came up behind Maggie and gave her a hug.

"Only three weeks from Saturday!"

"What?" Maggie asked, then gave Brynn's beautiful brown hair a tug. "You seem excited."

"I just want to get married *today*. We are so ready!"

"If you have your license, we can do it," Maggie said, knowing they hadn't applied for their marriage license yet. "But I do think three weeks will go by quickly."

Leigh walked in and wrapped an arm around Brynn. "Your problem is, you don't have enough to do. I'm swamped at Kanga and Roo. Come and work for me until the wedding."

"You wouldn't want me to work for you." Brynn laughed. "I'm so distracted these days. Sorry, all I can think of is marrying your brother. I'd probably forget to charge your customers and just put cute baby things in bags and give them away."

The Thanksgiving feast was long and merry. When Maggie's pies were sliced and set down the middle of the table, everyone groaned and said they were too full. And yet, not a single piece of pie remained after all the complaining of "stuffedness."

Maggie's phone rang as she put the last bit of cherry chocolate ganache pie in her mouth. She left the table and went to the living room.

"Hello, Maggie speaking."

"Hi there, Pastor Maggie. It's me, Myrna."

Maggie felt a chill. "Hi, Myrna. Happy Thanksgiving."

"Well, it was until those kids of mine took the Nasab kids out to the barn between turkey and dessert, and Samir fell off a hay bale and broke his arm."

"What? No! How is he? How are Mahdi and Amira? Oh, good grief."

"Well now, he broke his arm, as I said. The bone stuck right out of the skin. I have to say, I thought I might throw up, being pregnant and all. But I held it down. He's goin' to have some surgery tomorrow and hopefully go home within a week or so. Mahdi and Amira are confused, but figurin' it out. Jasper took them to the ER. Samir screamed until he passed out, poor little guy. But I'm here at the hospital with Amira, and little Samir is all drugged up and sleepin' like a kitten. Jasper took Mahdi, Sabeen, and the other kids home. So, we're about as under control as we can be. I'll stay with Amira tonight."

"Jack and I will be home soon. I'll come to the hospital with Jack. I'm sure he'll want to see what's happening. Then you can get home to your family."

"Well, we'll see what we see. You be careful comin' home."

They hung up, and Maggie told the tale of Samir's broken arm to the gathering around the table. All necessary shock and sadness were shared liberally.

"I think it might be a good idea for us to head home," Jack said, standing.

Dirk and Mimi stood as well. Everyone agreed as the four of them put on coats and gloves and retrieved the empty pie plates.

Jack dropped Dirk and Mimi at the farm, where they transferred themselves to their own car and headed west. Before they left, Mimi hugged Maggie.

"I guess you will have to pick up your shepherdess staff after all. They are lucky to have you here. You too, Jack."

When Jack and Maggie arrived at Heal Thyself Community Hospital, they found Samir still asleep. Amira sat limply in a chair, and Myrna was talking a mile a minute about Juliet's latest adventure in the kitchen trash can.

"That little pig is a real little pig!" Myrna laughed heartily.

"Hi, Myrna. Hi, Amira." Maggie went to Amira and gave her a hug. She wondered if Myrna had been chattering the entire time. "Myrna, we can take it from here if you would like to get home. Jack is going to talk with the surgeon, and I'd be happy to sit with Amira."

"Well, if you're sure. I have to say that my back is killin' me in this chair. Dr. Jack, can't you do somethin' about this hospital furniture? It seems to be designed to make sure anyone who sits in it will be admitted."

"I'll work on it, Myrna. Thank you for everything you and Jasper did today. You have gone the extra mile."

"It's just somethin' Jesus would do. We like the Nasab family real well, and the kids just laugh and chatter nonstop. Except when Samir fell. That bone stickin' straight out, whew! Everyone got real quiet, that's for sure. I'll just take my belly and get on home. I haven't had any pie yet, and this baby wants some real bad. Bye-bye, Amira. We'll be checkin' in on all of you."

Amira looked up when she heard her name and smiled wanly as Myrna left the room. Maggie took her hand and held it quietly. Amira began to cry.

"Amira, it's okay. It's okay, I promise." Maggie spoke softly and patted the distressed woman's shoulder. They sat together with no more words, but Amira seemed comforted.

Jack returned with the same report Myrna had given them. Surgery in the morning, home within a week. He smiled at Amira.

"It will be good for Samir," he said.

Amira nodded wearily.

There was a knock on the door. "Hi, all." It was Shrina from Refugee Support Services.

Maggie was so relieved she almost laughed out loud. "Shrina! Thank goodness. It's good to see you. How did you know Amira and Samir were here?"

"Apparently, Jasper Barnes called Darcy Keller, and Darcy called me. I know medical issues can be hard to navigate, but I have the necessary paperwork, and I can talk Amira through the process."

"That is good news. At a time like this, the language barrier is tough. I can't imagine how Amira is feeling. She can't understand anyone, and Samir has been sleeping all afternoon. Thank you for coming in tonight, even though it's Thanksgiving."

"It's my job, and I'm glad to be here and help them through this."

Jack gave Shrina the details she needed, and then Shrina knelt down and began to speak to Amira. Maggie listened as Shrina explained the situation and watched Amira's face change from fear and sadness to relief.

"You two can go home if you wish," Shrina said as she stood back up. "I'll spend the night here."

Thanksgiving Day was over. Jack and Maggie dragged themselves to bed after giving the neglected felines their Thanksgiving treats.

Just as Jack drifted off to sleep, his phone rang. He sat up quickly and turned on his light. Maggie groaned.

"Hello, Dr. Elliot speaking." Jack listened. "I'll be right there."

He quickly got out of bed and changed into his clothes.

"There's a baby on the way."

He kissed Maggie and was gone. When he returned at five a.m., he kissed her again.

"Who's arrived in the world?" she asked sleepily.

"A handsome young man named Jonathan. Nine pounds even."

"Oh, that's nice," Maggie mumbled.

"And Samir is going into surgery in about an hour and a half. Amira is tired but doing okay."

Sunday morning, Maggie stood after Irena finished her prelude with a flourish. Irena had died her hair purple for Advent.

"We have two special parts of our worship service today. First, as we celebrate the first Sunday of Advent, we begin with our Advent wreath candle lighting. I had asked the Nasab family two weeks ago if they would be willing to be our first lighters. They said yes. We had no idea Samir would be healing from a broken arm in the hospital. I am thankful the rest of the family is here this morning. We will hopefully see Samir next Sunday.

"Our other treat is more of Sabeen and Amira's Syrian bread. They not only baked it for communion today, but they baked extra to sell at coffee time. I don't know how Amira did this when her son was in surgery and in the hospital, but they have produced thirty round breads for sale. They will do this each Sunday. The rounds are three dollars apiece."

Applause.

"Now, let us prepare to worship. This is the day the Lord has made, let us rejoice and be glad in it. We can be glad because our help is in the name of the Lord who made heaven and earth."

27

Jack looked at the time on his ringing phone. Two forty-seven a.m. Maggie murmured as the phone rang again. "Is it another baby?"

It had been a late night. Jack, Maggie, Andrew, Brynn, Ellen, and Harold had enjoyed a family dinner as Andrew and Brynn faced their final week of singledom. The winter weather had begun in earnest, and Maggie wondered what plans might need to be changed for the wedding if things stayed so snowy and icy.

"We don't want to steal your thunder," Harold said to Andrew, "but my lovely fiancée and I have chosen a wedding date of our own."

Maggie and Brynn looked at Ellen, who glowed.

"We aren't going to tell anyone until after your wedding," Ellen said. "We want to celebrate you! We're going to wait until Christmas to announce the date."

"But you're going to tell *us*, right?" Brynn was adamant.

"Yes."

Harold put his arm around Ellen and looked at her.

"June third, 2017," they said together.

The other four applauded wildly. Harold took the opportunity to kiss Ellen until Jack told him to stop.

"Okay, okay," Jack said. "Save it for later. We're trying to eat here."

"I have a feeling 2017 is going to be one of the best years ever," Andrew said.

"I know we don't have to say this, but we do. Maggie, will you marry us?" Ellen asked.

"I would love to. As soon as I get these two off my calendar, we can begin to plan your wedding."

"I wonder how many other weddings you will have next year? Keith and Irena? Lacey and Lydia? Sky and Sly?"

They ate and talked and dreamed until the evening was gone. At eleven thirty, Jack and Maggie waved the two happy couples—all bundled up against the frigid weather—out of the driveway. Then they cleaned their kitchen, treated the cats, and crawled into bed. Sleep came quickly.

But then Jack's phone pulled them from slumber.

"No, it's not a baby. Hello?" He heard someone shriek. Then his father's voice.

"Jack? This is Dad." Another wild scream could be heard in the background.

"Dad? What's the matter? Is that Mom?" Jack sat straight up.

Maggie, wide awake now, sat up and slipped her arm through Jack's. She could hear the screams coming through the phone but couldn't understand what was being said.

"Yes. It's your mother. Jack, I have to tell you . . . " His father let out a moan.

"Dad?" Jack switched on the lamp and sat on the edge of the bed.

"Jack, two state troopers are here. They have just come from an accident." Ken's sob and Bonnie's wail were simultaneous. "It's . . . bad . . . Andrew and . . . and Brynn. The ice. They slid and . . . "

Jack's brain raced. He knew the end of his father's sentence. His mother wouldn't be wailing unless there was an end to the sentence.

There was something final Jack had to hear.

Instead, there was another higher-pitched, pitiful cry. It was Leigh. His little sister's cry was more than he could take. Jack brought his hand to his eyes.

Ken caught his breath. "They slid on the ice coming home and a semitruck hit their car."

Bonnie was inconsolable in the background. Jack heard other voices. The police. They were trying to soothe his mother.

"Dad, are they at the hospital?"

Maggie drew even closer to her husband. She could hear everything now, and tears silently streamed down her cheeks.

"No." Ken choked.

Jack knew they were dead. The state police don't come to your house to say your loved one is in the hospital. They come to say, "Someone, someone you love dearly, is gone."

Jack grabbed the side of the bed. Maggie could feel the muscles in his arm tense.

"Dad, Maggie and I will come down. We'll be there in an hour." Jack did not hear his own words or grasp the gravity of what he was saying.

"No!" Ken lost control. "Don't you leave your house! The roads are pure ice. It's been too cold for too long. Andrew and Brynn are dead."

Jack slid to the floor and put his head on the edge of the bed. It wasn't his father's words that finally broke him. It was his mother's wail in the background as she took in the reality one more time.

"Okay, Dad. I'm sorry. We will stay here." Jack was openly crying now. "Can we do anything?"

It was a useless question, but he asked it anyway. Politeness and professionalism, that was Dr. Jack Elliot.

But tonight, he was *son* Jack. He was *brother* Jack.

"No, we will call Anne now. Wait . . ." Ken was a little calmer. "Can you call Nathan in Ghana? Can Maggie get to him through Bryan?"

Relieved to have a task, Jack said quickly, "Yes. We'll call Nathan. We'll take care of it."

Maggie grabbed her phone from her nightstand and paused. She used the edge of her pillowcase to wipe her eyes.

"Dad, we'll call you back after we talk to Nathan. We . . . we love you." Jack inhaled to stifle another sob.

"We love you too."

Maggie watched as Jack clicked off his phone. He was still kneeling on the floor, as if he were a small child saying his nightly prayers.

Now I lay me down to sleep, I pray the Lord my soul to keep. If I should die before I wake . . . I pray the Lord my soul . . . to take.

Maggie slid down next to him. She held her husband until his sobbing stopped. Her tears were silent, for now, but she knew the pain of this night would leave an open wound in their family for years to come. Healing would be elusive.

After the first wave of grief passed, Jack and Maggie numbly wandered down to the kitchen. Jack sat and stared at the wall. Maggie brewed two cups of coffee and brought them to the table.

"Shall I call Bryan? Or do you need more time?" she asked.

"We should call. I need to talk to Nathan."

Maggie called Bryan. He was already up and eating breakfast at the volunteer house in Bawjiase. Maggie could here Fifi singing in the background. Nathan was with Bryan at the table. Jack took the phone Maggie handed him, and he carefully told Nathan their brother and Brynn were dead. Both Jack and Maggie tried to imagine how this news would hit Nathan, being so far away.

"We don't know any plans yet." Jack winced. *Plans. Arrangements. FUNERALS.* "But it will be good to have you home. Wednesday, right?"

"I'll be back on Wednesday, yes. For the wedding." Nathan was reeling. His ticket home was for the coming Tuesday so he would arrive on Wednesday. It was booked so he would be back for Andrew and Brynn's wedding. "No, no, not the wedding. Oh no. I'll call Mom and Dad. Should I call Mom and Dad?"

"That would be good. Just so they can hear your voice. It's . . . it's rough, you know. Mom is . . ." Jack cleared his throat. "We'll call when we know more. Love you."

"Love you too."

Jack dialed Ellen's number. He figured his parents would call Ellen's parents. Bonnie and Ellen's mother were sisters. The news would be quickly and tragically disseminated through the family, but he wanted to call Ellen himself. He told her the news and heard her intake of breath, and then her cry.

"Oh, no, no, no, no! No! We just had dinner. They are fine. They are getting married in one week! We are going to their wedding, and it's going to be beautiful, and they are going to be happy." Ellen dissolved into tears.

Jack wiped his own eyes and let her cry.

When she caught her breath, she said, "I'm so sorry, Jack. I'm so, so sorry. I'll do anything to help. Please . . . please tell Aunt Bonnie I'll do anything." The tears began again.

"I'll tell her. Thanks, Ellen. We'll call later."

They hung up, and Jack looked at Maggie. He watched as she picked up her phone.

Maggie hit the speed dial for her father.

Dirk answered sleepily. "Yes, hello?"

"Dad, it's me."

Jack stood and staggered upstairs. He couldn't listen to the news again.

"Maggie?"

"Yes, I'm sorry to wake you. It's important. Can you put your phone on speaker?"

She heard light switches from the lamps on her parents' nightstands.

"Hello, Maggie. It's Mom."

"I've called to tell you . . . *gasp* . . . some bad news. Some horrific news."

"Bryan?" Mimi whispered.

"No. No, it is not Bryan. Bryan is fine. I'm sorry." Maggie felt guilty. Her brother was fine. It was Jack's brother who was dead. "It's . . . Andrew . . . and Brynn." She took a deep breath. "They were killed tonight in a car crash. They were driving home from our house. We had dinner together. Harold and Ellen and Andrew and Brynn. We talked about the wedding." That was it. Maggie felt the pain and another wave of guilt like a punch to her gut. *If they hadn't been at our house, they would still be alive.*

"Oh, no." Both Dirk and Mimi took in the horror of Maggie's words.

"They're both *dead*?" Mimi asked.

"Yes. It was icy, and there was a . . . truck." Maggie inhaled. There didn't seem to be enough air in the room.

"Where's Jack?"

Maggie heard the shower upstairs. "He's in the shower. We are trying to figure out when to go down to Blissfield. His parents don't want us on the road, but Jack wants to get there as soon as possible."

"Maggie, we are so sorry. This is difficult. No! *Impossible* to comprehend. It's too much." Mimi's emotion flowed through the phone.

"I know. I feel sick, like this is a mistake. Someone reported something wrong. They were just here. We had such a fun evening and Brynn . . . Brynn told me in the kitchen that she'd had Andrew's wedding ring inscribed with their wedding date and the reference to their chosen verse. She was so excited to show him next Saturday."

"Does Bryan know?"

"Yes. I called him, so Jack could tell Nathan."

"Oh, Nathan. He's so far away."

Mimi tried to imagine what Bonnie was feeling. She would want him home. But then Mimi did not want to imagine anymore. No mother did.

"Nathan will be home on Wednesday. He had that planned, you know, to be home for the wedding. He's one of the groomsmen."

Silence.

"I mean, he'll be home Wednesday." Maggie was lost in the two realities of a wedding and now two funerals.

"Good. That's good."

"How is Jack?" Dirk asked.

"He's in shock. I've . . . I've never . . . *gasp* . . . seen him cry before. He and Andrew were close. I don't know what to do for him."

"He needs you." Mimi spoke calmly and firmly. Only Dirk could see how white her face was and feel her fingernails in his hand. "And you need him. Try to eat. Rest when you're tired. Give yourselves permission to step out of conversations with people who want more from you than you can give. Protect each other."

"Thank you. I will call you later when I know more."

"We will do anything we can to help," Dirk said. "We love you and Jack very much."

Maggie said softly, "We love you too. Goodbye."

Jack came down a few minutes later. He was dressed for the day ahead. His eyes were red, and Maggie could see tears hovering. She stood up and hugged him. He clung to her. She could smell his soap. One bit of normalcy.

Jack called his parents to tell them Nathan knew what had happened. The crying and wailing had ceased on the other end of the phone for the time being, but grief was not gone. It would rise up again in waves, surprising its victims as it slammed down on them at unexpected moments and inconvenient times. There was no escape.

Cold cups of coffee sat on the kitchen table. Jack and Maggie silently watched the sun rise over their snowy fields, as if it had no idea how painful its brightness was in the midst of their darkness.

How dare it shine!

They waited for a decent time in the morning to call others, but they didn't want to call. This news was too unbelievable. Shock kept them quiet, each with their own thoughts swirling.

Maggie thought of how good Brynn's hair had smelled as she gave her a hug goodbye.

Andrew had hugged her and said, "You're not going to cry during our ceremony, are you? If you do, I'll make a face at you."

"I might sob all the way through so that no one can hear a word. Who knows?" she'd teased back.

She thought of the laughter at dinner as the final wedding plans were completed. Then she thought of her wedding notebook, sitting on the desk in her study. She had put each piece of the service together. She had written the wedding sermon full of stories, anecdotes, and happy, holy promises that would be made that day. She had also written a very special prayer for Andrew and Brynn. She and Jack had asked Arly Spink to use her calligraphy skills and print that very prayer over a painting of the Blissfield farmhouse. Arly produced a masterpiece. The painting was wrapped in gold and silver wedding paper, waiting for the special day. It would wait, unopened.

At nine a.m., Maggie called the church office. Hank answered. Maggie gave him the news.

"I don't have any further information, but Jack and I are driving down to Blissfield now. When I know more, I will let you know."

"Pastor Maggie, if it's okay with you, I'll make arrangements to have the church service covered tomorrow. You will need to be with Jack's family, I'm sure." Hank's voice was shaky.

"I hadn't thought of that, Hank. Thank you. I'll call you later today."

Then the first day of hell opened up and swallowed the Elliot and Thomas families. The double loss of Andrew and Brynn was more than anyone could bear as both families, along with some extended family members, gathered and mourned and wept in Blissfield.

Ellen and Harold drove down at noon. Ken and Bonnie's neighbors did the only thing they could do. They brought food. Casseroles, salads, cakes, and snacks filled the farmhouse table by dinnertime. Maggie set out plates and silverware so anyone who was hungry could help themselves. She found extra boxes of Kleenex in one of the bathrooms and set them around the house. She washed dishes, picked up trash, and listened to endless stories about her brother-in-law and almost sister-in-law. She cried and laughed and cried some more.

After dinnertime, many family members left. Soon it was only the two nuclear families. Bonnie and Nicolette sat with swollen eyes. Ken and Richard looked hollowed out.

"We've got to make some decisions," Bonnie said. "We are expected at the funeral home tomorrow at ten a.m."

"What decisions?" Richard asked with a cracked voice.

"About the service. When, where, we have to look at . . . coffins. We will have to decide where they will be buried. How do you feel about the funerals being together?"

Nicolette let out a small groan. "Of course. They can't be separated." Then she burst into tears.

Bonnie was out of emotion for the moment. "I agree. I think they should be together. Ken and I have two plots at Pleasant View Cemetery. If you like, they can be buried there."

Nicolette looked at Richard, who nodded mutely.

"Yes. They will be close to all of us that way," Nicolette said.

"Yes." Bonnie looked at Ken. "To be perfectly honest, I don't want Pastor Tim to do the service. I've attended too many of his funerals. He uses a boilerplate service and never does anything personal about the one who died. I won't have Andrew leave this world without his spirit being remembered and celebrated." Bonnie's voice was flaming with anger.

"Our pastor is an interim," Nicolette said. "I think he's about ninety, and I'm sure he puts himself to sleep with his own sermons. Goodness knows, the rest of us are fast asleep." Nicolette was either catching Bonnie's organizational attitude, or her anger.

Maggie winced. Ken and Richard both looked pained as their wives spoke so cavalierly about burying their children. Maggie knew that grief showed up in many disguises.

"Maggie!" Bonnie said her name so sharply, Maggie jumped.

"Yes, Bonnie?"

"You have to do it."

Bonnie opened her mouth and let out a soundless scream. Ken put his arms around her. She looked at Nicolette but couldn't speak.

"Yes," Nicolette said as the tears flooded once again. "Maggie . . . You were going to marry them . . . you have to . . . you have to bury them. You loved them as your family, and you knew them." She leaned into Richard's chest as the torrent of grief assaulted her again.

Maggie stared dumbly. "I can't. I'm so sorry, but I can't bury them. I can only mourn them." She looked at Jack.

Bonnie looked at Jack and then Maggie. "Please."

28

The next morning at Loving the Lord Community Church, a bereft congregation filled the pews. Whispered conversations were everywhere. Irena, with a box of tissues on her organ bench, played "O Come, O Come, Emmanuel" but stopped every few seconds to blow her nose. The used tissues were discarded on the floor like a skirt around the organ.

Finally, Harold stood up and spoke to the congregation.

"I received a call from Pastor Maggie this morning. She sends her love to all of us and is thankful for the prayers that I assured her we were sending up and around for the families. This is what is known for certain. There will be a double funeral for Andrew Elliot and Brynn Thomas this coming Saturday, December seventeenth. It will be at Blissfield Community Church at eleven a.m. They will be interred at Pleasant View Cemetery. There will be a lunch at the Elliot farmhouse following the service. Instead of flowers, both families ask that we make donations to Refugee Support Services in Ann Arbor. Nathan Elliot is in Bawjiase, Ghana, now and will fly home this week."

Harold looked at Ellen, who wiped away more tears.

"Oh . . ." he said. "And the service will be officiated by Pastor Maggie."

∞

The week passed in the relentless flurry of decision-making and plans for the double funeral. Ken, Bonnie, Richard, and Nicolette huddled together each day. Death forged an unexpected bond between the two couples. They made each decision together.

Jack and Maggie spent most of the week in Blissfield. They ran errands, went to Ken and Bonnie's church to work out logistics with the local funeral home, and took down the chairs that had already been set up on the third floor of the farmhouse for the wedding. The catered food ordered for the wedding dinner was now on order for the funeral lunch.

"What about the photographer and the florist?" Maggie asked Bonnie and Nicolette. "Would you like us to cancel them?"

"Yes, and the DJ."

Bonnie gave them the notebook she had kept information in. Nicolette had the receipts of deposits and payments for each. Maggie looked at the notebook.

"There's also the wedding cake."

Both mothers stared blankly. Brynn's favorite cake was lemon with cream cheese filling, and Andrew's was marble cake with chocolate icing. Their wedding cake was planned with each cake every other layer.

"I don't know who would order such a cake," Bonnie said slowly, "and I'm sure it's been baked already and frozen. Shall we have it sent for the funeral?"

Nicolette nodded, then looked at Maggie. "Please ask them not to put the cake topper on. Just leave it plain."

Andrew and Brynn had chosen a bride and groom made of white and dark chocolate, nestled in a silver candied heart. Their names were written, one on each side of the heart.

On Wednesday morning, Jack and Maggie drove to Detroit to pick up Nathan.

Maggie's phone rang as they waited in the cell phone lot for an arrival text from Nathan. It was Harold.

"Hi, Harold."

"Hi, Maggie. How are you doing today?"

"We're busy, and that helps. We're picking up Nathan now."

"I just wanted you to know that things are under control here. I'm with Hank, and we've put a bulletin together for Sunday. We know you and Jack won't be here, and we've planned a hymn sing with Irena. That was a trip. Anyway, several people have offered to either read verses from the Bible or lead us in prayer. Hank has received a stack of cards here at the office for you and Jack. I would expect you have more at your house. Would you like me to collect them?"

"No, I'm going to drive up tonight, take care of the cats, and spend some time putting the funeral service together. Jack will stay with his family, especially now that Nathan will be here. But thanks, Harold, and thank Hank too. How's Ellen?"

"She's working, which helps. She and I will be in Blissfield on Friday night and stay for the funerals on Saturday. This whole situation defies understanding. Both Ellen and I can't get over the fact that we all had dinner at your house on Friday." He was quiet for a moment. "And now they are gone. It doesn't make sense."

"I know. We feel it too. It's the injustice of it all. Everyone feels it. But we're at the airport now, Harold. Call again if Hank or anyone needs anything."

They hung up.

Nathan sent a text of where he would be after picking up his luggage, and Jack pulled up to the McNamara Terminal. Jack and Maggie waited and hoped the police wouldn't chase them from their spot.

When the large glass doors opened, Nathan walked out. But he wasn't alone.

He was followed by Bryan and Cate Carlson.

Maggie leapt from the car, hugged Nathan, then went to her brother as Jack and Nathan embraced each other.

Maggie grabbed Bryan. "You are home," she whispered. "You weren't supposed to be here until next week for Christmas." She searched his eyes, the eyes that matched her own.

"We had to come back." He pulled Cate next to him. There were no squeals or laughter or any of the joy that this surprise would have brought on any other day.

"Hi, Maggie," Cate said as she hugged her pastor and friend. "Bryan and I didn't want Nathan to make this long trip home alone. And it's only a few days early. We also didn't want to miss the . . . funeral . . . funerals."

Maggie looked at Nathan. Jack had his arms around his little brother. Maggie waited, then went to Nathan and hugged him again.

"I'm so sorry, Nathan."

Jack put suitcases in the back of his car. Bryan and Cate brought their bags over and loaded them in. Jack drove to Cherish. With Bryan and Cate as comforting surprises, they decided that Maggie, Bryan, and Cate would go straight home. Cate would stay with her parents and Bryan with Maggie. Jack and Nathan would go back to Blissfield.

Maggie and Bryan spent the day together, and after calling Mimi and Dirk to fill them in on Bryan and Cate's arrival, Maggie spilled out the whole terrible story to her brother. Cate came to the farmhouse after dinner. The three talked through what the weekend would be like.

"It's so good to have you home," Maggie said.

"This is too important. We're all one family," Bryan said. "Jack is my brother-in-law, but Nathan feels like my brother."

Bryan took Cate home late. Then he returned to the farmhouse, went up to the spare room, and fell into an exhausted sleep.

Maggie spent the wee hours of the night writing the funeral service for Andrew and Brynn. She loaded up her car in the morning with everything she needed for the weekend. Dirk and Mimi arrived before noon. They would stay at the farmhouse with Bryan until Saturday morning, when they would drive down to Blissfield.

"I'll see you Saturday. Thanks for taking care of the cats."

Maggie drove away, leaving one family for another.

∞

Maggie was at the Blissfield church early on Saturday morning. She arranged her Bible and notebook in the pulpit. She found the church kitchen and got a glass of water to also put in the pulpit. She walked down the center aisle, placed her hand on each pew, and whispered a prayer.

"Whoever sits in this pew today, comfort them, O Lord."

She repeated the prayer until she had touched every pew. Then she sat in a small library next to the sanctuary and prayed some more.

She heard the florist van drive up to the church and saw them bring in bouquets of flowers. *Why do people do that when the family asks for no flowers?* Once the flowers were placed on the altar table, Maggie looked up and saw two hearses.

Andrew and Brynn had arrived.

Jack and his family pulled in behind the hearses, and Maggie saw Bonnie crumple into Ken's arms as she got out of the car. The night before had been visitation at the funeral home. Everyone was exhausted after greeting wave after wave of guests. Maggie was disappointed that only Howard and Verna Baker and Winston Chatsworth had driven down from Cherish. She thought more people would have come to comfort Jack.

She should have known better.

After the family arrived, Maggie watched in silence as car after car pulled into the church parking lot. She watched her congregation— riding together in cars and the vans from the Barnes family and the Nasabs—solemnly walk into the church with the other guests and friends from Blissfield.

Each pew Maggie had prayed over was filled to capacity. Jack's family was swarmed with love from the Cherish people who grieved with them as they stood in front of the two coffins. Even though they did not know Brynn well, the Thomas family was also blanketed in love.

Before the service, Maggie stood with both grieving families in the small library and prayed. She felt as if she were floating above the little gathering. She seemed to be looking down on the whole situation. She watched herself pray. She heard herself give the directions for the families to follow the coffins down the center aisle of the church. They would sit in the first few rows of pews, which were reserved. She would come down last.

Maggie felt nothing. The music began.

Andrew and Brynn were escorted down the aisle by their families.

Maggie walked between the two coffins and up to the pulpit. The floral arrangements spilled their heavy perfume into the air. Maggie hated the smell. It was a smell of death. She looked out at the church, where people were standing along the back wall and down the side aisles. She saw strangers, and she saw the blessed people of her own dear church. But she could not focus on that now. She must honor Andrew and Brynn without tears of her own. She would cry later. She had learned from Ed that if nerves overtook her when preaching, she should look over the tops of people's heads, not at their faces.

Maggie's eyes skimmed the tops of heads.

She cleared her throat.

"Our help is in the name of the Lord who made heaven and earth. We have gathered here today to remember and celebrate the lives of Andrew Kenneth Elliot and Brynn Eileen Thomas. Hear the words of the prophet Isaiah: 'As a mother comforts her child, so will I comfort you.' And from the Gospel of Matthew: 'Come to me, all you who are weary and burdened, and I will give you rest.'

"Let us pray.

"Holy God, we have gathered here today under protest. For how else can we gather when we have lost two young people whom we love? How can we celebrate life when all we see is death? No, we protest today because parents shouldn't have to bury their children. We protest because today would have been their wedding day, and instead, we will put them in the ground."

Maggie's voice was strong and clear. Her anger gave release to those seated in the pews and standing in the aisles, those who felt anger and despair over this injustice.

"We are supposed to bless you when you give, and bless you when you take away. Today, blessings are not on our lips. Our words are choked down and our hearts are torn in two. So, Lord God, if there is comfort here today, show us. Send your Holy Spirit and mend our souls. Amen."

It was as if the congregation communally released a breath they'd held for the past seven days.

Maggie continued with the service. She read Scripture and gave a eulogy that represented Andrew and Brynn, from their sweetness to their goofiness to their deep love and generosity. She wove the stories of their childhoods into the love story they had grown into. She shared their faith and hope.

"Because of their deep faith in God and their desire to live as followers of God, the faith and lives of others became stronger and better for knowing them. Today would have been their wedding day. They had planned to make vows to one another and give and receive rings. They were ready to live a life together. We are left with all the good they inspired. We are challenged to live our lives with their joy, thoughtfulness, and kindness. Everything we do that honors them, keeps them alive in this world. We are their legacy."

After Maggie finished her eulogy, she directed everyone to stand and sing, "Amazing Grace, How Sweet the Sound."

Following the emotional hymn, she invited Jack to come forward.

Jack stood in the pulpit as Maggie stepped back. She looked at Bonnie's stricken face. Then she turned her gaze to her husband's back and listened.

"I am Jack Elliot, Andrew's older brother. I speak today for our families. We have endured an unimaginable loss. Not only my brother, but the woman who would have become part of our family this afternoon. We share grief with the Thomas family. Each of our families has been broken and depleted by the deaths of these two vibrant people. To our parents: Ken and Bonnie Elliot and Richard and Nicolette Thomas . . ."

Jack stopped. Maggie took a step forward and put her hand on his back. Jack coughed and spoke again.

"We can't imagine your grief. Parents are not supposed to bury their children."

Maggie could see Bonnie in the front pew. She listened to her oldest son while tears streamed silently down her face. Ken, with his own red-rimmed eyes, had his arm around his wife, and Anne held Bonnie's hand. Nathan and Leigh were both openly crying as they watched Jack.

The Thomas family was huddled together in the front pew of the "bride's side" of the sanctuary. The incongruity of the two coffins in place of a happy bride and groom dancing on the third floor of the Elliot farmhouse hit Maggie again.

She felt dizzy and closed her eyes, waiting for the jarring reality to pass and give her respite for a few more minutes. She opened her eyes and looked at her mother. Bryan was sitting next to her and Cate next to him. Mimi looked directly at Maggie and gave an almost imperceptible nod. Maggie took a breath. She turned her attention back to Jack.

"We would like to thank all of you who drove here today to be present at this unbelievably tragic time," he said. "We treasure your friendship and support. We will need you in the weeks and months to come as we process what has happened and pick up the pieces of our lives. We ask for God's mercy and trust . . . we will . . . receive . . . that mercy."

Jack's strength was gone. He wiped his eyes, turned and hugged his wife, and sat down with his parents and siblings.

Maggie stepped forward. "I began this service in protest. I protested because I know God can take it. I will end this service remembering this: Death isn't final. Death isn't the end. Death doesn't win. We live in the sure and certain hope that Jesus Christ came to this earth, died, and rose again so that we would not have to face death without hope. For a place is prepared for us. And a promise has been made that we will not be separated from those we love, but on one great and glorious day, we will be reunited with those who have gone before. We will be with Andrew and Brynn for eternity.

"Let us sing, 'Great is Thy Faithfulness.'" While the congregation sang, Maggie drank the entire glass of water she had set on the shelf of the pulpit. She was almost done with the service.

She prayed. She looked over the tops of people's heads and gave the needed instructions to the people.

"We will have the committal service at Pleasant View Cemetery immediately following this service. After that brief service, you are invited to the Elliot farmhouse for lunch. The address is listed on your funeral bulletin."

Maggie slowly followed the two coffins down the aisle, led by the funeral directors. Once at the doors of the church, Jack, Nathan, and four male cousins were the pallbearers for Andrew's coffin. Randy and Michael Thomas, along with four of their relatives, carried Brynn.

The cold wind blew at the graveside. It chilled the guests, and the gray skies infiltrated their grieving souls. Maggie completed the brief committal service. The family waited for the coffins to be lowered, side by side, into the ground. The only sound was the howling wind as the families and guests silently watched their loved ones disappear. Then they got into their cars and drove to the Elliot's home.

Jack and Maggie arrived home the evening of the funerals. They were overwhelmed with exhaustion but could not sleep. Jack held Maggie in the darkness of their room and whispered in her ear.

"I don't know how you did it today, but thank you for carrying all of us through this. I'm so thankful to be your husband."

The tears finally came. Maggie and Jack held each other and wept.

29

One week after the funerals, Maggie walked into church. It was Christmas Eve. As she headed to her office, she stopped when she saw Hank's desk, ready for the evening service. His blue tarpaulin was draped over his desk and chair and held down with hymnals on the floor. A welcomed bit of normalcy.

She heard the large oak doors open and looked to see who was there. Irena, who was dressed as what could only be described as a slutty angel, saw Maggie and went straight for her.

"Pastorr Maggie, how arre you on dis night?"

Maggie realized Irena had never asked her how she was doing. Ever. Irena's gold sparkly eyes blinked at her.

"We are feeling everything, Irena. We cry, we laugh, we feel guilty, and we feel thankful. We just accept it as it comes. It sucks."

Irena nodded. "Eet ees de vorst."

"Yes, the worst."

"Eet vill get better, but eet ees stupid to tell people dat. Eet neverr helps. Eet is de path, and eet must be traverrsed. Traverrse ees de vord, rright?"

"Yes, traversed. Passed through, negotiated, crossed. We will traverse this unwanted journey."

Maggie remembered when her beloved professor and mentor, Ed James, died of a heart attack. She had refused to traverse the path, and she had lived in her grief, ready to let go of everything and everyone she held dear. Grief had a way of dragging its victims down the wretched path anyway.

Maggie thought of the previous night. She'd woken up when she felt the bed shaking. At first, she didn't know what was happening. Then she felt Jack's back. Silent sobs racked his body. She'd put her arms around him and felt him turn toward her. His warm tears slid slowly down her neck. They lay silently in the darkness until the latest serving of grief had passed. Jack was broken, and Maggie didn't know how to put the pieces back in place. She must wait.

Irena spoke and brought Maggie out of her thoughts. "Ve arre vith you. Ve vill alvays be vith you."

She turned and toddled to the organ on her slutty angel stilettos. Then she crawled up on her bench, turned on the organ, and began to practice.

> Silent night, holy night
> All is calm, all is bright . . .

That night, Maggie methodically led the service. Lessons and carols were intertwined. The story of the Christ child was told and sung. Maggie prayed. The sanctuary lights were dimmed as each parishioner lit their small white candles from one another.

Irena began "Silent Night" while the candles were being lit. Everyone sang about the young mother and holy child. The final verse was a cappella—just the voices of the congregation. Maggie couldn't sing the last verse. She looked at the people, her people, with candlelight glowing around each face. Each one singing with the hope that light would overcome the darkness.

After the service, as everyone gathered to eat their "Happy Birthday, Jesus!" cupcakes, Maggie and Jack slipped from the crowd and walked through the snow and moonlight to their farmhouse. They had the evening to themselves. Dirk, Mimi, and Bryan, who had all been at the service, were now at Cate Carlson's house getting to know Cate's family better with a Christmas Eve meal. Jack and Maggie opted out of this celebratory evening. The next day after church, there would be another family gathering in Blissfield. A joyless Christmas this year.

"I hope you like this," Maggie said, handing Jack a wrapped box as they sat in their cozy living room.

"I hope I like it too, or I will have to give it back to you." Jack tried to smile.

Maggie had asked Bonnie if she could make duplicates of some of the childhood pictures of Jack and Andrew. Bonnie, of course, said yes. Maggie made the copies and returned the originals. Then Maggie made a small photo album of Jack and Andrew. She'd copied the dates found on the backs of the originals under each picture.

"I love this," Jack said, looking at each photograph carefully. Some of the pictures had Nathan in them. They looked like three little stair-steps, Jack always the tallest. "There's nothing I could have wanted more than this. Thank you for putting it together."

He handed her a large box.

"What's this?" she asked, tearing off the paper.

She lifted the lid and pulled aside layers of tissue paper. In the box lay a clergy robe. It was white with two gold crosses, one on each side, that would rest under her collar bones. She pulled the robe out and saw four stoles underneath, one for each season of the church year: purple for Advent and Lent; white for Christmas and Easter; red for Pentecost; and green for the very long season after Pentecost—Ordinary Time.

"I thought you should have this. You are a pastor, and you are a reverend. This robe fits the title and the holy work you do. I bought it before Andrew and Brynn died. But after the funeral last week, I knew you had to wear this to lead us in worship. It is a sign of who you are as God's servant. And the pastor of our flock. I can't wait to see you wear it tomorrow. Christmas Day."

"I love this," Maggie said, fingering the velvet around the collar. "Thank you for the reverence of this robe. It is a holy gift." Maggie tried it on. It fit her perfectly. "I think Ed would have loved to see this. He always wore a robe when preaching or officiating services."

"He would have loved it because he loved you. I love you too, Maggie."

It seemed Maggie's heart broke over and over again, not just with the loss of Andrew and Brynn, but from the quieted voice and tear-filled eyes of her husband. He was an open wound. She knew it would take a long time for any healing to come.

They sat by the fire in their new living room, sipping spiced apple cider and eating pigs-in-the-blankets and gingerbread cookies. Marmalade, Cheerio, and Fruit Loop were curled up on the Christmas tree skirt.

"I think I needed this," Jack said. "Just one quiet night. No noise, and no expectation to take care of everyone else. We buried them one week ago. It seems like only a day, and it seems like years ago. Christmas will never be the same. I know I will count every year. I will imagine how he looks as he ages. I will wonder about the family he and Brynn might have had. I will always remember that he hid her engagement ring in a bale of hay covered in roses."

Maggie held her husband as his pain poured out again. She had never felt so helpless as she did on this first Christmas Eve without Andrew and Brynn.

After a beautiful church service full of promise and light, all the hope in a manger where the Christ child lay was elusive to the young couple crying together in the fading light of a fireplace and the sparkling illuminations of a Christmas tree.

The next morning, Maggie put on her new robe and the white stole. As she came through the secret door into the sanctuary, the congregation looked at their pastor, who looked quite pastoral. Irena finished her prelude. She looked at Maggie and gave a solemn nod of reverence. Maggie stood behind the pulpit. The weight of the robe felt comforting.

"Merry Christmas." She forced a smile for her congregation.

"Merry Christmas!" the voices shouted.

"This is the day the Lord has made. Let us rejoice and be glad in it! We can rejoice because our help is in the name of the Lord who made heaven and earth!"

Epilogue—April 2017

Jack looked at his phone. It was two thirty a.m. "Hello, Dr. Elliot speaking . . . . Yes . . . Okay . . . That sounds good. I'll be right there."

Maggie murmured, "Is it a baby?"

"Yes. I need to get to the hospital."

He kissed her, pulled on his clothes, and left.

When Maggie heard his car leave, she woke up all the way. Unable to fall back to sleep, she went downstairs, fed the yawning kitties, and made a cup of herbal tea.

It was Wednesday of Holy Week. She was prepared for the Maundy Thursday service the following night. The Good Friday service would leave the sanctuary draped in black. Then, Sunday morning, an Easter celebration would bring assurance of resurrection, new life, and the end of death. Maggie had poured herself into the preparations for these services. It was almost a mad frenzy for her to get through the funeral of Jesus on Friday and then step into all the hope and confidence of everlasting life on Sunday.

Maggie knew that Andrew and Brynn colored much of how she prepared for each Sunday now. She was more careful and detailed than she had been before. She studied the Scripture passages and looked them up in the Greek and the Hebrew texts she had learned to translate in seminary. She used to dismiss these ancient languages, but now she found new truths that English couldn't always translate easily or well.

So much had happened in the past few months. She thought back over the time that would always be remembered with darkness. Jack's grief came in softer and less frequent waves, but it still came. Ken and Bonnie had remained on their farm, unable to move forward with retirement. Everyone gave them the space and love to just *be*. Leigh had moved back home for the time being.

The national political situation was in turmoil. The new president and administration were like salt in any and every wound. Maggie wouldn't think about that now.

Happily, the childcare center had opened in January, and Marla was running it like clockwork. Maria Gutierrez worked there, and she and Juan had settled thankfully into the condo. They and Jack and Maggie made a deal for a sale. It would take some time, but they would know the joy of owning their own home and be able to raise Gabby and Marcos in love and safety.

Sylvia took it upon herself to right the injustice of Martha Babcock, "wicked slumlord." She called the health department to check on the property the Gutierrez family had previously rented. The house was in such disrepair, it was condemned and shuttered. The health inspector said it was completely uninhabitable. Martha would have to pay for many a repair if she wanted to rent it again.

Martha, seething with anger, had gone straight home after the hearing about the property and given G. Gordon Liddy Kitty an earful.

He ignored her.

The free clinic was scheduled to open by the first of November. Jack was hopeful to see one of his dreams come true. The focus on the clinic helped heal a tiny bit of his grief. Maggie noticed, whenever Jack talked about the clinic, some of his old animation shone through his eyes and voice. He was a true doctor, a man who healed ills and administered precision care. His greatest gift was the compassion he lavished on his patients. Dr. Jack was beloved.

Maggie smiled as she thought of the wedding dates marked on her calendar. Harold and Ellen on June third. Irena and her Captain Crunch on August twelfth. Sylvester had proposed to Skylar on her birthday in March. They were going to be married on October fourteenth. Darcy and Jennifer were still making their wedding arrangements, and the biggest surprise was when Max Solomon, down on one rickety knee, asked Beth Becker to marry him right during coffee time in front of the whole congregation. Both Becker sisters would be married sometime in 2018.

But the wedding Maggie was most excited about was Lacey and Lydia's.

After the Nasab family had settled into life in Cherish, Lydia and Lacey had made a special point of inviting the family into their salon every month for haircuts and pedicures for Sabeen, Amira, Iman, and Jamal. At first, Sabeen refused to let them touch her feet, but Lydia had gently coaxed her to put them in the warm, bubbly water. It only took one time for Sabeen to realize that her old, tired feet had never felt so pain free. She loved her pedicures from that day forward.

The residual effect of Lacey and Lydia's salon care was Lydia joining Lacey in church each Sunday. Lydia had read the Scripture lesson once during Lent. She told Charlene Kessler that she would be happy to teach Sunday school if needed. And one Sunday, she took Lacey's hand and held it through the entire service.

People around them noticed, but the third "Big Fight" Maggie thought the church would endure fizzled out. The congregation of Loving the Lord Church had seen the worst of hate and cruelty in the past year. They didn't like it much. They had decided to listen to their better angels and let love be love. The people who didn't agree with this slowly disappeared from attendance. (There were only a couple of them.)

Lacey and Lydia would be married on November fourth in the sanctuary of Loving the Lord Community Church.

When Jack finally arrived home from the hospital that day in April, he had a tired smile on his face.

"How's the new family, whoever they are?" Maggie asked, brewing him a cup of coffee.

"Very well. Maggie Barnes is healthy and hearty."

"What? Myrna had her baby?"

"Yes."

"And she and Jasper named her *Maggie*?"

"Yes. Another 'M' child. They will call her Meg to avoid confusion with their pastor."

"Well, I guess that leaves one less name for us."

"We will find the perfect name for our little one," Jack said.

He put his arms around his wife, gently touched her small baby bump, then kissed her on top of her head.

-The End-

BUT WAIT! THERE'S MORE. . .

To Have and To Hold
~ Book Two in the Pastor Maggie Series ~

Welcome back, Pastor Maggie!

Pastor Maggie, of Loving the Lord Community Church, has settled into her new position and finally gained the trust and respect of her congregation, but they will all be tested when the church comes under attack through a series of malicious break-ins and vandalism. Maggie tries to hold everyone together and determine if the threat is from an outsider or someone actually sitting in the pews of her church each Sunday. Can she keep her beautiful church safe? Will she still be able to accomplish the planned mission trip to Ghana if the money from a fundraiser is stolen?

While Maggie desperately waits for a whisper from God, she also fears that a major event will be ruined by the well-meaning, very loving members of the church. How will she maintain her own blossoming romance with tall, dark, and scrumptious Dr. Jack Elliot and support the daily needs of her congregation through life-and-death matters when it all feels one step away from collapsing?

Will they catch the villain before he ruins everything?

Get your print or ebook copy today!
www.Pen-L.com/ToHaveAndToHold

FOR RICHER, FOR POORER
~ Book Three in the Pastor Maggie Series ~

What's Pastor Maggie up to now?

Life at Loving the Lord Community Church in Cherish, Michigan, isn't always easy. Learning how to adjust to a new marriage while caring for her many parishioners keeps Pastor Maggie on her toes. And things get more complicated as she prepares a group of church folks for the coming holidays—AND a two-week mission trip to Ghana, Africa.

While in Ghana, the expectations of good-hearted people clash with the real needs of the villagers. Maggie's frustration boils over and her plans begin to crumble. All her beliefs about rich and poor, success and failure, poverty and wealth, opened hearts and closed minds get turned upside down. The lessons learned in Bawjiase are life changing for all.

As her spiritual beliefs are threatened, Maggie knows her ministry will be transformed once she returns from her time in Ghana. But will she be the richer or the poorer for it?

∽∾

Get your print or ebook copy today!
www.Pen-L.com/ForRicherForPoorer

Discussion Questions

1. Maggie is going full speed ahead. What parts of her ministry caught your attention the most?

2. What did you anticipate in the face-to-face meeting between Maggie and Redford?

3. Do you believe there are some people who cannot be redeemed, or don't want to be? How does forgiveness work in these situations?

4. Maggie has her hands full, both at church and at home. What are the pros and cons of pastors living next door to their churches? How do personal boundaries get set?

5. The backdrop of the 2016 election causes friction and factions within the church and the community. How does a congregation care for one another when views are so starkly opposite?

6. Darcy Keller decides to go ahead with his own plans without the church community. How does this help or hinder others?

7. Did the year of the election cause issues within your own family or church? How did you handle the differences?

8. What did you expect with the Syrian family's arrival in Cherish? Would you be interested in being part of a resettlement project similar to the Nasab family's?

9. What in this story surprised you the most? What were the "for betters" and the "for worses" for you?

10. Which characters surprised you the most? Who did you learn something new about?

11. What did you find brought the congregation back together (for the most part)?

12. Who made you laugh the most? Why?

13. Did anyone make you cry? Why?

Recipes

MAGGIE'S STIR FRY

2 tablespoons of extra virgin olive oil
1 medium onion, diced
2 cloves of garlic, chopped
10 cups of chopped veggies, such as broccoli, zucchini, squash, cabbage, bell peppers, cauliflower, or fresh corn. Or whatever Sylvia left on your desk this morning!
¼ cup low sodium soy sauce
1 tablespoon brown sugar
1 8 oz. package of brown rice noodles, cooked according to package instructions
(You can add meat or tofu for protein—about 2 cups cooked, chopped, or shredded)

Heat a large wok or frying pan. Add oil. When hot, add onion and garlic. Stir for 2 minutes (don't let the garlic burn as Maggie did).
Add veggies and stir for 5-7 minutes until the desired crispness or softness.
Add soy sauce and sprinkle with brown sugar. Combine well.
Put veggies over noodles and get ready for the doorbell to ring. You'll have plenty for drop-in guests.

GRILLED CORN

6-10 ears of fresh-picked corn on the cob (still in husks)
1 tall beverage pitcher, tall enough for entire corn cob to submerge
1 stick butter (not margarine)

Soak husked corn in water for 2 hours (you can use your sink or a cooler full of water). Put soaked corn on preheated grill in a single layer. Grill for 15-20 minutes, turning every few minutes. You can pull back one of the husks to see if it's cooked the way you like it. Fill tall beverage pitcher with hot tap water. Melt butter and pour on top of hot water. Take corn off the grill and let cool slightly. Pull husks back from cob, but not all the way off. Hold husks (as a handle) and dip corn in the pitcher. Remove your perfectly buttered corn and enjoy! One of Jack's favorites.

MAGGIE'S CHERRY CHOCOLATE GANACHE PIE

Ingredients for crust:
1 ¼ cup finally crushed chocolate wafers or chocolate graham crackers
1 ½ tablespoons sugar
4 tablespoons melted butter

Mix all ingredients and press into 9-inch pie plate.

Ingredients for filling:
2 15 oz. cans of tart, pitted cherries in water, drained, reserving 1 cup of liquid
1 ½ cups sugar, divided
1/3 cup cornstarch

Dash salt
1 tablespoon butter (not margarine)
4 drops of almond extract

Preheat oven to 425 degrees.

In a medium sauce pan, mix ¾ cup sugar, salt, and cornstarch. Slowly whisk in 1 cup of reserved cherry can water. Cook and whisk over medium heat until thick and bubbly, then cook and whisk an additional minute. Take off heat and add remaining ¾ cup of sugar, cherries, butter, and almond extract.

Pour filling into chocolate crust and bake in preheated oven for 30 minutes. Remove from oven and let cool while you make the ganache.

Ingredients for chocolate ganache:
1 cup of heavy cream
1 cup semi-sweet chocolate chips
1 tablespoon butter

Put chocolate chips in medium bowl and set aside. In small saucepan, heat heavy cream until simmering (not boiling, but just about to boil). Pour hot cream on chocolate chips. Stir slowly as chocolate begins to melt. Add butter. Continue to stir until chocolate and butter are completely melted. Pour over top of cherry pie. Spread to the edges.

Pop completed pie into the refrigerator and let it set. Once Jack (or your family) finds it, you probably won't get a piece. Sorry about that.

MAGGIE'S MONSTER COOKIES

Ingredients:
1 cup softened butter (not margarine)
3 cups creamy peanut butter (28 oz.)
2 cups white sugar
2 ¼ cups brown sugar
1 tablespoon light corn syrup
1 tablespoon vanilla
6 eggs
1 tablespoon baking soda
9 cups of quick oats
2 cups milk chocolate chips
2 cups plain M&M candies

Preheat oven to 350 degrees.

Cream the first four ingredients well. Add corn syrup, vanilla, and eggs and cream until light and fluffy. Sprinkle baking soda over creamed mixture and beat through. Add oats, chocolate chips, and M&M candies and mix by hand to combine.

Scoop batter with a large cookie scoop or small ice cream scoop onto ungreased cookie sheets. Bake for 12-15 minutes, just until lightly brown. Let cool one minute, then transfer cookie to cooling rack.

You will have millions of these (more or less). You must have some neighbors who would enjoy a plate! Perfect for church meetings.

Acknowledgments

God whispers and shouts. I am thankful.

The First Congregational Church UCC of Grand Ledge, Michigan. It was a joy to spend the past seven months with you as your Bridge Pastor. Thank you for your grace and kindness. God bless you all.

Duke and Kimberly Pennell, my publishers. Thank you for valuing the written word.

Editor Susan Matheson. You are the first to see the roughest of rough drafts of each Maggie book. Your feedback and encouragement with storylines is invaluable. Thank you.

First readers, Dr. Mimi Elzinga Keller, Judy Elzinga, Joan Isenberg, Leanne Harker, Marsha Rinke, and Dr. Doug Edema. You all helped make this a better book.

Editor Meg Welch Dendler. You always take my final effort and clean it up beautifully for public consumption. Thank you.

Dr. William Marx, mentor and friend. Your lovely and understated idea for the cover of this book was perfect. I can't thank you enough.

Kelsey Rice, graphic designer extraordinaire, you brought the cover to life. I love the work you do. Thank you for making the Maggie books so beautiful.

Author G.M. Malliet. Always.

Dr. Charlene Kushler, for your constant encouragement.

Ethan Ellenberg.

Police Chief Bruce Ferguson of DeWitt, Michigan. You helped me once again with law and order in Cherish. Thank you.

Jessica Flintoft. Your knowledge of the prison system was invaluable. You educated and saddened me with your wisdom and stories.

Thank you for what you do to make things better in this broken system.

Shrina Eadeh and Anya Abramzon of Jewish Family Services in Ann Arbor, Michigan. Thank you for taking the time to be interviewed and answering my follow-up questions. The work you do with refugees is important and powerful. Thank you for caring for the most vulnerable people seeking a safe life here in the United States.

Sylvester Fejokwu, thank you for the use of your name, your intelligence, your class, and your charm.

Thank you to Ryleigh and Zoey Teater (actually your parents, Charlie and Kali) for allowing me to use your names. I'll meet you in the next book.

Judy Teater. Friend, supporter, excellent baker. Thank you for the monster cookie recipe from a mission trip a long, long time ago.

With love to Charley, Kathy, and Allison Budd. I'll remember your stories of Andrew.

To Doug. You read, you listen, you know all things medical. Thank you for coming to Cherish with me whenever I ask. I love you the most.

About Barbara Edema

 The Rev. Dr. Barbara Edema has been a pastor over twenty-five years. That sounds astonishingly boring. However, she is a great deal of fun with a colorful vocabulary used regularly in and out of the pulpit. Barb has spent decades with people during holy and unholy times. She has been at her best and her worst in the lives of the people she has cared for. Now she's writing about a fictional church based on her days serving delightful and frustrating parishioners. Pastor Maggie is young, impetuous, emotional, clumsy, and not to mention a crazy cat lady, who steps into ministry full of Greek and Hebrew but not much life experience. She learns quickly.

Barb lives in DeWitt, Michigan, with her husband, Dr. Douglas Edema. She is the mother of Elise, Lauren, Alana, and Wesley. Like Maggie, Barb is an avid feline female. Hence, she has collected an assortment of rescue kitties. Barb enjoys date nights with her husband, watching her children do great things in the world, a glass of good red wine, and making up stories about the fun and fulfilling life in the church.

Enjoy visiting Cherish, Michigan, and Loving the Lord Community Church. Pastor Maggie will delight you!

Visit Barb at:
www.Barbara-Edema.com
Blog: www.BarbaraEdema.Blogspot.com
Facebook: The Pastor Maggie Series
Twitter: @BarbaraEdema1